Deputy Vail knew why the man was here, for McCraw did not hide his intent to break the law, nor did he care about a houseful of witnesses. Both men seemed rigid with anticipation.

McCraw was the first to speak. "Vail. Here, now. Or wherever you want. Don't matter to me, but you might want to spare your wife and family the sight of your dying."

The deputy said nothing. McCraw did not seem to need an answer. There was no question of what he would do now. The man stepped back and to the side, then circled with his left hand to invite Vail to move outside. A direct invitation to be killed.

TEXAS SPRINGS

Belinda Perry

BALLANTINE BOOKS • NEW YORK

Sale of this book without a front cover may be unauthorized. If this book is coverless, it may have been reported to the publisher as "unsold or destroyed" and neither the author nor the publisher may have received payment for it.

Copyright © 1993 by Belinda Perry

All rights reserved under International and Pan-American Copyright Conventions. Published in the United States of America by Ballantine Books, a division of Random House, Inc., New York, and simultaneously in Canada by Random House of Canada Limited, Toronto.

Library of Congress Catalog Card Number: 93-90518

ISBN 0-345-37428-2

Manufactured in the United States of America

First Edition: December 1993

For Kate Osgood, Karen Nord, and Don West;
thanks for listening.

PART ONE

CHAPTER ONE

Something flashed in the browned scrub. The man looked up quickly, hazel eyes searching a pattern, hands tight on the length of rope. The yearling colt lay still, pressed to the ground by the man's weight hard on his neck and shoulders. The flash came again; the man rose stiffly, one hand touching the butt of the pistol strapped to his side, one foot planted firmly on the bay colt's neck.

The outline of a horse and rider emerged clearly from the brush, and the man let out a deep breath and looked away, immediately indifferent. He went back to the chore of doctoring the red-lipped wound trenched in the yearling's neck. Heat from a bucket of tar rose in shimmering lines, and the tall man inhaled the smell as he worked. Tar sealed out flies, prevented infection. With the treatment of the wound, the bay colt might live through the winter. A big, strong colt, a good addition to the slowly growing herd of horses.

Finished with his work, the man stood up and yanked the rope. The colt was still for a moment, stretched out on the ground. Then he found his legs and came to his feet, shook against the stickiness of the cooled tar. The man slapped the rope on his leg, and the colt started, sliding backwards. He kicked out, then raced with gathering speed toward the bunched safety of his friends. James McCraw paused to watch, and to wipe the accumulation of sweat from under his hat. It might be coming on to fall, but in the rough desert south of Fort Davis, the sun took a daily bite without mercy. McCraw waited until the colt was safe, then signaled for the next injured animal to be pulled over.

He gave little thought to the passing rider. There had been five this week alone, more than he used to see in a good two months. The whole land was infested, crowded with settlers and drifters, worn teams pulling dried wagons, fancy rigs with suited passengers. McCraw shrugged at the anger ready built in him; he needed to get the work done. He watched Miguel haul in a lamed mare.

The vaquero, perched on his bright sorrel, grinned down at McCraw and offered words to slow the work: "She's got a maguey tooth in the ankle, señor. She was of the band who drifted up to the Chisos Basin. It is infected, of course, but . . ."

Miguel knew he was telling the señor what was already known, but it was good to hear the sound of his own voice once in a great while. The air was still, the wind did not blow, the trees and brush did not rattle, and the señor did not talk. Silvestre sat on his big horse, on the far side of the pen, to hold the restless horses. There would be no thoughts worth speaking in that great empty mind, so Miguel Lujan held the head of the injured mare close to his knee and played with her long ears while the señor did his work.

The thin little mare did not take kindly to the pain of her treatment, and the señor cursed her roundly in fluent Spanish as he moved from the reach of her front hoof. He fashioned a small loop in a rope, and when he closed in on the mare again, she pawed and he caught up the hoof, laced the rope over her neck, and tied it securely. Hobbled on three legs, the mare could no longer strike, so the señor cut carefully at the spine imbedded in her fetlock and knew that Miguel would keep the snapping teeth from tearing his back. Miguel was proud of the señor's easy way with the mare and proud to be trusted with his portion of the job.

James McCraw paid no attention to the flow of insulting, soothing words from the vaquero. The sorrel gelding, rock still, steadied the mare; the tip of the heated knife sliced through swollen flesh and a yellowed fluid ran free. McCraw heard the curses strengthen, felt the whisper of cloth as the mare's teeth brushed his back, and still he did not stop the cutting. The spine came free in his fingers, the blood flowed a bright course, and then McCraw dabbed the wound with more of the thickening tar.

"She is a most wicked lady, señor. She would bite me even though I am not the one who hurts her. I have tried to explain, but she will not listen."

McCraw did not answer; he pulled the neck rope loose, slipped the loop from the raised hoof, and stepped back. Miguel shoved the bony head from his thigh and dropped the reata from the bowed neck. The mare turned to her tormentor; McCraw slapped the rope on his leg and the sound broke the mare's intent. She spun around fast, hit the soreness of her front leg, and limped to the small herd.

Miguel opened his maw to speak again, but the señor lifted a hand and waved away the words. Instead, Miguel guided the good sorrel toward Silvestre, a distant rider on a patient bay. He knew it would be some time before the señor returned to the work. That was fine with Miguel; he was hot now, and thirsty. He did not at all mind the long breaks in the day's work, it was the long silences he found wearing.

The tall man tipped back his hat to let the hot sun find his face. The hazel eyes blinked in the heat, the damp graying hair stuck to the bone of the long face. Behind McCraw a rough adobe hut stood some distance from the pens, a two-room structure barely big enough to hold three men, a table and stools, a crude rope bed for the señor. The two vaqueros slept outside when it was warm, and in the harshness of the Texas winters, they slept inside the low-roofed barn, warmed by several ranch horses and an ancient paint mare.

The small spread, set close to the Rio Grande, was a remnant of the collection of huts and low adobes, the village known as Spencer's Rancho, a reflection of John Spencer's power more than twenty years ago, before the division of the war. McCraw wiped at his face again, felt the grit of fine sand stuck to his skin. He'd grown up working this land, fighting it for a meager living under John Spencer's name. Ten years now he'd paid a debt owed to Spencer. The man gave him title to a piece of the land and demanded small payment in hard coin. Two vaqueros rode for the McCraw brand, two old men past their prime, hard-pressed to find and keep a good riding job. McCraw used them, fed them, and offered them a place to sleep; in return they accepted his word instead of hard coin. Owing the vaqueros, paying off his debt to Spencer, these were burdens unfamiliar to James McCraw.

Suddenly restless, he jammed the hat back on to protect his burned eyes and found himself thinking of the rider that had come through earlier. Too many strange riders had come through these summer months. They were caught up in finding a new Eden, a different promised land. The rest of Texas was burned again by the sun, yet the *Despoblado* had drawn in unusual rains, until the grasses grew tall and ungrazed. Word went out—and the strangers crossed the land. They believed it would take hard work, and some luck, and then the land would give back to them.

McCraw knew better. The two years of rain had the newcomers fooled into believing the big tanks of surface water, the wet summer streams, would never fail. He knew; they would be gone with the usual long summer and dry fall. The sun never failed above the *Despoblado*.

There were two kinds of water in the basin along the east edge of the Rio Grande: the flat banks of the river and its streams, and the hidden springs. Not many of the newcomers knew about the springs, or bothered to ask on them; they were pleased to file claims on the muddy pools and laugh at the worry of old men. But the springs were the land's one gift, and McCraw valued his portion of the riverbanks, his hard-won knowledge of the bubbling ground waters.

He took in a gulp of the hot air, held it until the sound inside his ears was like the rush of water over flat stones. His lungs expelled the air; he drew in another gulp. There was a fist bunched in his gut, pushing up toward his heart and lungs until he would burst. One thought stayed close in his thinking, a deep, hidden certainty that no one or nothing would move him from his land. His pa had staked out a life here; the son would stay and make it work.

There were remains of McCraw's family blown in the dust along the river: a mother and father, a barely remembered younger brother. Their bones had long dried and powdered since their death thirty years past, but they were all James McCraw could claim. He didn't look around, there was nothing left to see. But he knew where the ruins of the house lay, scratched and sanded by the wind until not even a low mound remained as a tombstone.

McCraw stretched his arms along the railing of the fence. The wood dug into his back, the dried bark scraped his worn shirt. The vaqueros had allowed their horses to drift near a shade tree and uncorked a canteen; he was aware of them, of their waiting on him. But right at the moment, he didn't care. His shoulder ached badly where it touched the fence, the pain of his leg nearly crippled him when he walked. Daily reminders of his age—and part of his struggle to get past the accident that killed the old woman and came close to killing him more than a year ago.

There was a bitter humor to the days that McCraw appreciated. It all came to survival. Since the Apache had been gelded by Victorio's death late in '80, the railroad had come to the *Despoblado*, and had brought with it the settlers. Before that time, only a few men had taken a place along the river, only a few like old John Spencer, or Ben Leaton, or Milton Faver. Men like these had fought hard to live. Now there were travelers coming through, staring out the smoky windows of the trains and coveting the miles of grass.

It was a strange business for James McCraw. Ranches came to life, new breeds of cattle arrived almost daily, walking in on stubby legs or freighted by the puffing trains. Good business for him, if he could do the work. The ranches needed horses, and McCraw had been breeding tough stock for all his years. The money waited for him, palmed by eager hands, asking for his brand on a broke pony. But a shadow dogged him, one he had not yet roped down and cut from his mind.

The shadow came in the dark night, when he could not rise to his own defense, and showed him it was too late for him, that he was to be passed by with the black smoke of the train, the fast words of the newcomers.

He could no longer start the young horses—his bones did not take the stiffened legs and hard pounding as the half-wild colts fought for their lost freedom. McCraw knew it now; he'd left his youth in the pay of another man, and he hated himself for the knowledge. The stampede a year ago took what was left of his old ability.

The cursing ran through him again, the pain of it bit deeper than the mended leg and the muscles torn from his shoulder. He hugged his arms across his chest and cursed over and over, the words spilling from his mouth full and bitter in the hot day.

The beginning and the end of it was to say that this land was a damned place, meant only for fools. Anyone who rode along the banks of the river knew without being told it was no fit place to find a living. Up in the Chisos Basin, where the band of mares liked to drift, or up by Fort Davis, or near the new settlement of Marfa, there the land was fertile and clean, there the grass blew fresh, the cattle fattened and gave birth.

But not down here, not slammed against the river's cut sides, drawn up to hard rock and brittle cactus; here a man could not take enough to do more than keep his soul alive. Even John Spencer learned that early and had turned to supplying beef to the army when it built the fort in '54. Spencer tried raising horses; the Indians burned and looted and stole until John Spencer had to retreat.

Here, with his back to the river, his eyes sharp to whatever moved, a man could fight off the Indians and keep his body barely fed. And here stood James McCraw, long after the Indians were gone, leaned down and scarred by the years of fighting, bent and stiffened from losing the wars.

A fool by himself, a poor man raging, alone, at the wind and dust.

A cow bellowed for her calf, a foal nickered. A man coughed and spat. McCraw saw movement and shielded his eyes with his hand to stare. Another rider, leading a horse, crossing the gully close to the yard. McCraw watched, saw that both vaqueros had wheeled their horses and were readied to meet the new enemy. They sat like statues, hands to their saddle guns, heads lifted under the shadows of their wide-brimmed hats. To one who did not know, they would be a threat. To James McCraw, they were two old men, almost useless men, named Silvestre and Miguel.

McCraw yanked at his hat and cursed one more time. Then he walked quickly across the yard, conscious of the sun's height, the time already lost, the morning's chores still needing to be done. Whatever was asked for this time, it would be given quickly and the man sent on his way.

McCraw came near the vaqueros and smelled the heat of the horses, the stench of the riders. Miguel shifted the sorrel to allow McCraw room. Silvestre did not stop watching the approaching horse and rider. McCraw spoke too loudly, out of his private anger; the bright sorrel flinched as if spanked by a quirt.

"Get that one gone. Fast. We don't take in drifters. Too many of them on our range. Silvestre, you set this one going right quick."

The fat vaquero had already started his bay toward the intruder, keeping his horse to a measured walk. McCraw grinned up at Miguel, who knew he would not wish that smile on his own multitude of enemies. Silvestre's good bay stepped out proudly, neck arched to the bit, legs lifted from the hot ground, tail flagged in anticipation. It was a sight to tempt pride in a man's most private heart.

Miguel watched—and for a moment forgot what was about to happen. Then the oncoming rider stopped his own horse, a bony and lamed nag of no consequence, and Miguel remembered the reason for the march. No one passed Silvestre without seeing him; the rider was coming to certain trouble. Miguel straightened in his saddle, the sorrel shifted, immediately ready. Beside Miguel, the señor took in a deep breath, and the sound held a strange sadness to it. It would be done soon.

The small horse stopped, the rider hidden on the off side. The man knelt and lifted a front hoof, held it carefully in both hands. The little horse touched its muzzle to the man's back. Silvestre reached them and stopped the bay, leaned over to mouth the words sent out by the señor. Miguel held his breath.

The kneeling man was careful as he let the hoof touch ground. Then he rose slowly, head cocked as if to listen to the fat vaquero speak.

But the man on foot turned his back to Silvestre, as if he did not choose to hear. Miguel could guess it all; Silvestre was passable with a horse, a genius with the rawhide reata, but he could not talk to a man without speaking an insult. He would stab any man's pride, scour the ends of all souls with his careless tongue. Miguel wiped an appreciating hand over the white scar tracing his jaw. A token of an earlier stranger's knife, brought out of hiding by Silvestre's words.

It did not matter; it was a hot and boring day, the sun was still high, the wind blew fine sand. The horses were lazy, the cattle unwilling to run for sport. Something would come from the spoken words—and it would take away the August dullness.

The man quartered from Silvestre, presenting his back as if such an exposure were of no consequence. Miguel could imagine his *compadre's* growing puzzlement. Then the man turned back, and the sun found him, outlined him for Miguel to study. There was little of merit to this one, ill clothed in patched leather trousers and high moccasins, a faded shirt to cover his bony chest, a vest stripped of all buttons, a frayed rag tied around a dirty neck. There was the necessary wide hat to cover and shade a man's face from the high sun and the judgment of another's eye, so Miguel knew he was of the country. Little of the face could

TEXAS SPRINGS

be guessed, but there was no sign of fear in the man's stance, no gesture of humility to appease Silvestre's ill temper.

There was a moment when Miguel wondered if Silvestre had spoken at all, for the man picked up the reins to his nag and walked the small horse past the nose of the bay. As if it, and its rider, and the broad hand touching the butt of a shiny pistol, did not exist. As if the big bay was but a rock to be passed by on a continued journey. Miguel looked to the señor for a cue, as he could not sort out what he saw with his own eyes.

But the señor was already several steps past Miguel, limping slightly on the broken leg, hands loose and held free of his own pistol. Miguel did not know what to do, so he settled the sorrel and let the uneasy horse drift closer.

The señor was almost to the trespasser, and Silvestre had crowded his bay next to the lamed pony. Miguel saw the leanness of the two figures on the ground blend into each other from the bright lines of the sun, the haze covering his eyes. He opened his mouth to call to the señor, for he suddenly did not like what it was he felt in his heart. But the unwanted man dropped the reins, cupped both hands under Silvestre's booted foot, and heaved up and backward, lifting Silvestre from his saddle.

For a moment the other foot was held in the scarred *tapadero*, then the faceless man shoved again, and Silvestre was thrown from his horse. Dust covered him as he fell, and the patient bay gelding leaped sideways and kicked out. A hoof caught the top of Silvestre's shoulder as he struggled to rise. The crack of breaking bone was clear and sharp. Miguel shuddered from the sound, touched his horse, and the sorrel reared. Miguel looked to the señor for what he must now do.

It was the strange man who spoke first, and Miguel had to strain to hear the words. The man nodded his head toward Silvestre, then looked at the señor.

"That one told me I couldn't come talking to you. Told me to take my horse and ride on." The man gestured to the ground-tied animal, a pale strawberry roan, then half raised his head to McCraw: "That hoof's got a spine shoved through the sole. I keep walking him, I ruin a good mount. No need to treat a horse such. I won't be listening to that one on the ground, I want to hear from the boss man himself. No man worth his salt'll turn out a horse to die sure enough."

The voice was that of a young man, with a fluid lilt of Spanish to the clear English words. Spoken to the señor as if, of course, the boss would be the Anglo, as if the vaqueros would always be nothing but hired men. An insult to Miguel, a dig to stir buried feelings. There was already much to this young one that Miguel did not like.

Then the boy turned his face to the señor again and raised his arms as if to remove the wide-brimmed hat in slow deference. Miguel did not speak then, as the wide hat was slipped from the face, but then he could not stop the small sound caught in his throat, and he imagined the same noise came from the belly of the señor.

The young one stood there proudly, head lifted, hat removed, motionless in his ragged clothes, indifferent to the stirrings of Silvestre in the dirt behind him and to the hard stares of those he faced.

Then the boy whistled as Miguel had heard the señor whistle, and the sound disturbed him. The señor raised a hand to his hat; Silvestre tried to lift his head and groaned mightily. The lamed horse stepped forward to the call, limping to the side of his master and touching a white muzzle to the waiting hand.

Dust puffed from the halting steps, the wind blew the sand to wash Miguel's face and dried the sweat trickling across his cheeks. The same sun touched the exposed face of the rider, and its unbending light marked each angle and plane. Miguel could not keep the cry in his throat, even though he covered his mouth with a big hand. The young one would hear, and there would be revenge for the insult. Miguel was afraid of what faced him.

CHAPTER TWO

He always had to fight down the urge to duck his head and let the flow of black hair cover that side of his face. He never had accepted the stares, but he knew the game well, knew he could show no weakness in front of these men, or any of those he came up against. The wound was made fresh and raw inside him each time, but he would not let it scratch away his pride. The one behind him was stilled finally. But soon enough, that one would also rise and see him. For now, he had to hold his own against the stares and earn a grudging acceptance, or he would be afoot in this miserable land.

So he raised his head and let the wind blow the lank hair aside to expose the marking on his face. A badge of honor, his mother called it; the mark of the devil, others said behind his back. He stood completely still, other than to work open his right eye as far as the damaged tissue would allow. He steadied his gaze on the tall Anglo, ignoring the old man on the sorrel. In different times, he would kill for a horse like that sorrel. But it was the Anglo who mattered now, the Anglo who would give the orders to accept or reject him.

He began in rapid Spanish, words directed to the tall man who carried his years in the gray streaks of his hair, the lines dug around his eyes and mouth. There was power still in the wide hands, with their scarred knuckles that spoke of hard work, the loose shoulders with a layering of muscle. But there had been a hesitation to the man's walk, a lameness he would attempt to hide, to keep it from softening the harsh message of his eyes.

"Señor, I wish only to rest my horse, earn his care for the few days he will need after I pull out the spine and put a poultice to the heat. I ask this for the sake of the horse. He does not look like much of an animal, but he has the heart of a lion. I will need a small pen, water, and some of your dried grass. It is not much that I ask, and to deny me these things is to send me to certain death. It is little that I ask, señor. But it is my life."

He allowed no defeat in his words or the tone of his voice. He had been well taught; his mama and his *abuelo*, they had coached him in the use of sound, the gift to understand and give value to each note. To put insult carefully in its place, to dig deep to a man's worth and give him the chance to appear most gracious in his defeat. It must work this time, for the roan was badly lamed, the sole of the hoof heated to the lightest touch. If ridden more than another mile, or even led by hand, the little horse would go down, and he, Mateo Iberra, would be left in a bitter, dirty land to die on foot.

Matt would curse whatever drove him to ride here, but he held the cursing inside and showed only his proud and ugly face to the rude Anglo and the idiot vaquero. The one behind Matt groaned once again, as if to remind the three men standing of his existence. Matt did not bother to hear; that one was of no importance, sprawled helpless in his great bulk. It was the tall one who had his attention. Matt must show this one no weakness. The tall one was a horseman, with a keen eye. Matt would speak his piece about the roan and let the conscience, and the arrogance, of the Anglos do the rest for him.

"Señor, if I must walk the roan from your yard, on your orders, then he will fall and I will shoot him to end the suffering. It is now your choice. Señor."

Miguel felt the intentional insulting as if it were his, and the sorrel gelding under him twisted from the tension in his big hands. But with the hard edge of his palm the señor made a slashing gesture across Miguel's blurred line of vision. It was a demand, an order, that he remain still. That he yield only to the señor's orders and not to the demands of his honor. There was nothing in the stare of the drifter, or in the weakness of his thin body, that could threaten a man such as Miguel. He would be as nothing to Miguel's fury.

It was only the señor who kept Miguel from riding the young one down. And it was with great difficulty that Miguel eased up on the sorrel, crossed his big hands on the flat horn of his fine saddle, and sat back, willing himself to wait. He was content that the señor would deal properly, and quickly, with the insolence of the ugly child. But *mi Dios*, such a face. It was not possible that one could be so proud and so ugly.

The kid was different. Not just in the marking of his face. McCraw held his judgment and thinned his mouth to a scowl. There was no hurry, there was time to watch and see.

But the kid was queered enough to start his own war. Silvestre already taken out, useless as usual; Miguel huffed and puffed but eager for the signal not to come from his *patrón*. Counting on McCraw's good sense to keep him from the first blow.

McCraw waited. The big sorrel gelding quieted under Miguel; Silvestre lay back, moaning, eyes shut, hands unclasped. The handle of his knife was loose between his fingers. McCraw watched, knowing that the kid would break first.

The little roan made a move; the big head lifted and dropped the kid's arm. The kid did not respond, so the horse lowered his head, cocked a hind leg and extended the lamed forehoof, and half slept in the hot sun.

The silence stretched; McCraw kept waiting. The kid took the hard stares and did not flinch. Head high, eyes cleared of the sheltering hair, face exposed to the stares.

McCraw was impressed. He scratched the edge of his own brow, wiped at the sweat. The kid was quiet, hands to his side, hat held in tight fingers. As if nothing had happened in the few minutes passed, as if nothing were wrong with the face he showed. As if he hadn't walked past a mounted guard and right to the boss of the outfit—and laid out his shame and his need with no thought of refusal.

McCraw had seen destruction before, but not walking and talking like this kid. A brutal gouge ruined his face, from the middle of the hairline over the right brow, to skip the eye socket but pull the lid wide open. The exposed white of the eye was bloody from grit and blown dust.

The trench ran across the high cheek, carved in deeply, to lift at the ear and become a light tracery that disappeared in the dark stubble of the heavy beard. The whole face was a mockery, but the kid stood to it and did not stop his own appraisal of McCraw and his vaqueros, evaluating the men as he himself was judged.

It became a standoff. McCraw got past the terrible scarring and saw the kid would have been handsome. Tanned skin, black hair falling well below the collar, a wide mouth, a nose still unbroken.

Surprisingly there was a kindness in the untamed hazel eyes that gave lie to the hard set of the face. The body was thin now, but the lines of promise were there; strong shoulders, lean waist and hips, a length of leg. A born horseman.

The shudder came before McCraw could stop it. The ruined face was what was seen, not the promise. Disgust showed quickly in the hard young face, disgust for what was flowing in McCraw. It was close to another insult, but McCraw would not accept the challenge.

Behind him, Miguel was muttering in Spanish. McCraw felt the motions of Miguel's hand and saw more anger sweep the terrible face in front of him. He sighed, let out his mounting confusion. Miguel would be making the sign of the cross, to ward off the devil of the ruined face with mindless prayers and ancient signs.

It would be easy to send the kid on his way. Then McCraw looked at the three-legged roan and had to shake his head. The shudder went through him quickly, and he was helpless with unexpected pity. The kid moved slightly, half raised a hand as if to wipe out what had not been said.

The hazel eyes flickered, the torn one burned a brighter red. And the kid looked away, as if McCraw had failed a crucial testing. McCraw's shame turned quickly to anger. There was something here he did not like, something he could not understand, and yet the sounds of his words caught in his throat and he had to spit twice before he finally spoke them, brutally. "There's no staying here for you, kid. You're already too much trouble, you and that miserable cayuse."

He'd spoke in range English, to leave the kid some pride. But the arrogant son gave him no room. "Mister, you heard me out, and you know the truth of it. You send me out there with this bronc and we're both dead. I ain't much of a loss, but the roan'll come to rest on your conscience. If you got one.

" 'Sides, you got a man down back there, a sorry son lying on his backside and calling out. Someone's got to fill his boots while he finds his courage again. Might as well be me, seeing as you blame me for his poor showing."

McCraw shook his head again, impressed by the kid's gall. A smart kid, and a tough one. McCraw waited, wanting to clear his head. The strawberry roan pushed at the kid, impatient with all the standing. Without looking, the kid cupped the roan's muzzle in his hand and pulled at the whiskered lips.

McCraw watched the pair, then he looked at his pen of half-wild stock and back to the weight of Silvestre laid out on the ground. Behind him, Miguel continued to mutter his curses.

"Kid, all right. Take that sorry bronc back of the stable, put it in with the paint mare. She won't bother him none, and that roan's too poor to pick on her.

"Then you toss your gear on Silvestre's bay. You cost me a man, so you do his work. Only fair, like you said."

That was settled, and now he and Miguel could pick up the fat Silvestre and haul him to the house, treat the shoulder, and get back to the impatient chores. But the black-haired son didn't give McCraw a chance.

"And from all this work, señor, what do I receive in return?"

As if he were due something. The quick Spanish was flawless, and smiling with insult. McCraw almost smiled in return, but thought better of it, and barely looked at the kid. This one would see into him if their eyes locked, if McCraw had to look at that red orb, or the depth of the brutal scarring.

"You get room for the lamed bronc, hay and water, with you mucking out the pen. You sleep in the stable, long as you don't light a smoke. You can take your feed with Miguel and me, and Silvestre. That's what you get for your working, and that's enough."

He half turned his back, but the kid would not let go, and again McCraw heard the fluid, lilting Spanish.

"Ah, señor. You are too generous. But I am worth more than this one still lying wounded on the ground, castrated by his terrible pain." The voice switched to English and a Texas drawl: "I am a top hand with the horses, mister. You watch me, you'll know what I am worth. Only be here the time it takes for the roan to heal, might be you'll get more than your money's worth in feed. Might be I'll take that sorry son of mine in hand and walk away and you'll lose more than me. Señor."

The bragging was unbearable. McCraw walked past the kid to the shaggy roan. The force of his temper rode with him, gutting him with each careful step. It was a time to hold on, but he truly wanted to lay out the kid with a hard fist deep in his taunting face.

Instead, he raised his hand to the roan's face, to touch the damp neck. The horse didn't flinch. McCraw stroked the roan and checked the kid's outfit. The bridle was hand-plaited rawhide, the bit a simple ring snaffle, the reins of woven hair. The saddle was an old Spanish rig, much patched and reworked, the stirrups were worn through and padded with rawhide. The blankets that covered the roan were thickly woven and new, and tied behind the high cantle was a tangled canvas roll and a stained leather pouch. Not much for show, but it told McCraw what he needed. The horse had been given no cause for fear, and the working gear showed good care despite its age and hard use.

But he couldn't let it go yet, there was too much inside his head. "Tell me again, boy. Tell me what makes you special, what makes it right I take you in, feed you and this mange-ridden horse? You a Mex, boy? Or a 'breed? Some Indian hiding in you? Tell me again why I got to let you stay?"

He was near enough to see the scalloped bone on the high cheek flush red, then blanch almost white as his words dug in. He came close then to regretting the harsh questioning, but there was an ugliness to this child that went past the torn face and clever mouth. McCraw held the right to ask the questions, and he was owed a straight answer, and one that made sense. There was suddenly too much happening to wait on range courtesy.

He hadn't thought on it, but even when the kid's words had a humor to them, there'd been no smile on the ugly face. There was a carved set to the almost pretty features. But now he smiled under the questions, and McCraw understood the extent of the kid's pride and the damage to his face. For that smile carried the torn muscle across the wide cheek, to open the spoiled eye and expose its bloody white, pull the right side of the face into a strained grimace, a mockery of a grin.

The child was truly frightening then, and beneath his own skin McCraw felt the depth of the hurt. Behind McCraw, Miguel choked loudly and would be making the sign of his cross again. There was a long silence until the words came, and McCraw again envied the nerve of the kid.

"I am whatever you wish, señor. My mother was of pure Spanish. But my father, señor ... My father was a *Tejano*, one of you. One who ran back to his miserable home when the blue soldiers destroyed the *Tejanos* in the canyon near

Glorieta, many years ago. Twenty-two years, señor. You know of that battle, you know of the *Tejano* shame?

"Does this answer what it is you must know? My blessed mother did not speak to me the name of the man, for there were so many who would take a woman against her will, for their pleasure."

The ugly face paled, the smile died away, the scar softened. But the bitter picture remained. McCraw felt shame at his own words; whatever he said drew blood from the damaged rider. McCraw himself had been in that campaign twenty-two years ago. He had come back beaten and lost, but he had not taken a woman who did not want him. His woman had come willingly. The act of hatred that created this angry boy was not his, yet he felt the weight of responsibility.

He opened his mouth, but the boy spoke for him: "To answer what you cannot ask, señor. My name is Mateo Iberra. The Anglos say Matt, as they cannot fit their clumsy tongues around the right sounds. I am a bastard come from a war. A half-breed, but half Spanish and half *Tejano*. A fine mixture, don't you think, señor? Part of me came from this terrible land of yours, part of me is *Tejano*, but my heart comes from my family up north. And my face, señor, my face belongs to the devil."

Those final words were aimed to spook Miguel. The sorrel he rode spun in a tight circle, with Miguel's grim face barely visible above the dust cloud. Then the unnerved vaquero drove in his spurs; the sorrel bolted, reined straight for the unhorsed kid and his terrible face. Before the collision, the sorrel broke right and the roan swung his quarters to kick. The weight of his efforts on the lamed hoof dropped the horse to his knees. McCraw jumped wide, grabbed for Miguel, and missed. He fell hard and caught himself on outstretched hands.

The dust settled back, and McCraw stood and wiped his eyes clear, quieted his pounding heart. He took hold of his temper, found it possible to let his hands hang by his sides, ease his back straight, and let the hot desert air come in and

TEXAS SPRINGS   21

out of his lungs; to soothe himself as he would calm a frightened horse. Then he checked for the damage.

The sorrel was nose-to-tail with the roan, and Silvestre's bay had wandered close to the awkward pair. Miguel knelt at his *compadre's* head, holding his friend securely in his big hands.

The kid was there, by Miguel's side, a torn bandanna in one hand. He looked down at Miguel and the fat vaquero and spoke soft words to the two. The black hair swung around his terrible face as he spoke. Miguel seemed to listen; Silvestre had closed his eyes. Then the kid gathered the reins of the three horses and walked close to where McCraw stood.

Iberra spoke first, before McCraw's uncertain temper settled on what to throw at him: "Señor, I will put this roan where you have told me, and resaddle the good bay. So we may return to your work. This is enough, señor?"

"What did you say to those two? What miracle came out of your clever mouth to settle them in like babies? You added black magic to your tricks, you got more I need to know?"

Iberra straightened slightly, shook his head, so the damp black hair again covered the scar. He switched to English, so there would be no misunderstanding in the words between himself and the señor. And, too, the vaqueros would not be so eager to hear if the words were spoken in the foreign tongue.

"I told them the truth, that the devil did own my face, but that I had made a pact to keep my soul for myself. And my family. I told them their God rode with such as me, and that they had no reason to be fearful.

"I have told them the truth, señor. That I have been blessed by their priests and sealed free of infection. It was enough to convince them, and they will not bother me for a while—they will remember and leave me alone, until the next time. But you, señor, need to fear me, as I must guard myself from you."

He chirped to the horses and took the bay and the sorrel

with his left hand. Then, with his right hand near the roan's bit, he gently urged his horse to step forward. McCraw watched the parade and was puzzled by the warning. Here was a strangeness he had not met before. The kid had stood to face ridicule and attack and had drawn no weapon, shown no knife or pistol, and yet had won the fight.

There was no logical reason to fear him, but McCraw felt the twist in his belly again as he watched the string of horses turn into the stable. He would take Iberra's words and listen to them again, then he would put the rider to breaking the stock and pay him a few pesos, send him on his way when it was time. There could be no harm in such a simple, necessary transaction.

They did not stop at noon. Iberra worked easily, giving Miguel and James McCraw little chance to find fault with him. He rode the fine-headed bay with a sweet hand and knew what was to be done before McCraw directed him. It was simple to forget Iberra was new to the ranch, as the rhythm of hard work reached inside all of them and soothed the morning's anger. Now there was nothing but the heat of the late sun, the smell of scorched hair and flesh, the bloody pile of testicles dropped in a wooden bucket; nothing but freshly spilled manure, squalling calves, the sweep and reach of the long reatas, the stretched bodies of tied animals.

The horses sweated; the men eased them for a time, allowed them a sip of water, and took their own drink from the soiled water in their canteens. The sorrel gelding lifted his muzzle from the muddied tank, lipped the drops of water from his bit. The bay shook heavily, loosening his new rider and drawing laughter from men too tired and relaxed to remember their earlier confrontation.

They went back to the work, Miguel on the kid's left. It was unplanned, but it was easier for Miguel if he did not have to look into the damaged face. Used to that reaction, Matt accepted the need. When it was necessary for him to ride on Miguel's left, he dipped his head and let the flow of lank hair cover the scar. It was a practiced gesture.

McCraw finally raised his hand to signal the end of the work. It was cooler now, the sun long hidden by the distant hills. McCraw expected his two men to ride to him, put up their horses, and begin to look for a meal. But Miguel raised his fist in a half salute, the kid circled the bay and brought the horse up into the bit. Then he spun the bay quickly; the sorrel half reared and followed.

A horse race. McCraw was amazed. A child's folly at the end of a long day. He could do nothing but watch, but the horses would be specially tended and cooled before their riders ate. The kid leaned over the bay's neck, Miguel rode straight up and deep in his saddle, rocking with the horse. The bay and the sorrel raced beside the streambed, stride for stride, heads bobbing in seesaw unison, until the bay pulled ahead, flicked his long tail, and passed the laboring sorrel.

It was a wonder to McCraw. He knew both horses, had bred and raised them, and the sorrel was the faster, the younger, from better stock. Yet the fine-headed bay was running free and alone.

He watched the uneven race, enjoyed the speed, the flash of the legs, and he did not hear Silvestre until the man was at his side, wooden stick jammed into the packed ground for support. Silvestre spoke softly; McCraw had to lean toward him to understand the words.

"He is not a bad one, that boy who rides with the devil. He will not harm Miguel, or me, again. But you, señor. You must watch out for that one. There is something of him that will not let go in you. Be most careful, señor. Please."

McCraw looked up. Both Silvestre and Miguel spoke English, but they were lazy and rarely chose to make the effort. Thinking was not for Silvestre, yet he had listened and understood the kid's warning; McCraw knew he should pay attention. But the vaquero limped away, and McCraw focused on the two horses walking toward him; Miguel's head was bent to hear the kid as he talked. The kid was alive, hands gesturing, hat pushed back from that terrible face—it was tough remembering Silvestre's warning right then.

Silvestre did not know from what place in his soul the words had come for the señor. They had been out into the dry air before he knew what had been spoken. And he did not care to wonder. Silvestre had what little he needed: a bed on which to rest, a bottle of tequila to ease the pain of his poor shoulder, and the company of Miguel and the señor when they were done with their work.

There was the new one now. Silvestre crossed himself, then looked to be certain no one had seen his actions. There was only the señor, stooping down to pick up the cold iron, and the sounds of the horses walking to the pens. Sounds and pictures Silvestre understood, that let him know everything was as it had been, always would be. He grinned in pleasure, imagining the taste of the waiting bottle. The stories he would tell.

CHAPTER THREE

Robert Vail knew it was up to the law to inform the owners of the returned cattle. He'd taken down the names of the three silent sheepmen who'd driven the missing strays to the pens outside of town and had even offered them thanks for their effort. The sheepmen had been abrupt, as if dealing with a deputy sheriff wasn't good enough for them. They were nothing much themselves, only more of the black-haired, dark-eyed border Mexes doing a little easy work and looking for a big reward.

Gregorio Diaz, Abateo Flores, Secundino Peña: sheepherders pushing their small flocks on open graze. Vail stood in front of the low doorway of the jail and watched the trio drift downstreet, mounted on slab-sided mules, wide hats tilted to shield them from the sun, bodies swaying to the motion of the slow walk. A girl joined them, mounted on an old brown mare. Vail saw the sweet form of the woman and knew immediately it was old Flores's daughter. He watched them, and sighed when they finally disappeared.

There wasn't much to his town yet. But there was more than there'd been a year ago. And, of course, still more than in two years past, when he'd first been sworn in as Inspector of Hides and Brands for the county of Presidio. His wife made him take a small adobe house in Marfa rather than stay in Fort Davis after the accident. And in this summer of '84, Marfa had already doubled its population to a hundred. Vail had begun to think his wife had been right in her choice. Sheriff Nevill still had the office in Fort Davis but, eager to spend more time with his own ranching, he was glad to have a deputy in Marfa, to spread around the office's power.

He shook his head at the thought; he, too, had tried ranching. And had lasted less than a year. He'd come in just after the soldiers brought down the crafty Victorio, and he'd tied up two sections in the name of Robert Vail, with lots of free graze to spread out his cattle.

The defeat of that enterprise had taken less time than he'd spent building his rough stone house and buying a few horses, getting his herd scattered out on the graze. His beef wandered off and fell in the sudden washes, they stumbled on broken legs, starved with cactus spines imbedded in their greedy mouths. His pond dried up, while his neighbor's stayed clear and full. His wife complained. His oldest daughter, Elizabeth, ran off with a so-called preacher.

And his youngest crippled by drunks. Galloping their runty ponies through the Fort Davis street, shooting out glass newly installed in the Headquarters Saloon. His youngest, his sweetest. A bright-haired child with long legs and a coltish figure, with eyes that glowed in the sun's light, a smile made only for her father's pleasure. Then she had run across the street to her mother and had been knocked down and trampled by the uncaring hooligans who pulled at a bottle of tequila and drove roweled spurs into their half-wild mounts. Unwashed, ignorant border scum, who left an innocent girl bleeding and broken in the street. Men so worthless and low that their features disappeared in the nameless, faceless herd of black-haired Mexes running wild along the border. Men lost in the crowd that quickly surrounded Orianna and her father, men he stared at longingly in his anger and could not come to identify.

Vail felt the palms of his hands stinging. It was hard even now to see Orianna, not to shudder when she limped toward him, twisted, maimed by that accident. His fists loosened, he looked down at the marked flesh of his hands, imprinted with the bloodless track of his nails. It was not a rancher's hand, not a callused palm grimed and soiled by work in a field or barn. His were the hands of a man not suited for much of anything, the hands of a man elected hides and brand inspector and then deputy sheriff of Presidio County. The hands of a man who could not rescue his own child.

He raised his head; a wagon moved slowly down the bare street. A team of four pulled the heavy vehicle toward Humphris's new store. Now there was a man who had faith in the future of Marfa; he and his company had already bought out Wiles Mercantile, and Vail had seen their six-mule hitch crossing one of the creeks, hauling hay into town for the winter.

A three-legged dog ducked under a sleeping horse's belly. A hoof stirred up some dust; Vail heard the dog howl as it was bowled out past the tie rail. The dog struggled to stand, then hurried toward the safety of a side street. The horse shook its head, stamped the accurate hind foot twice, shifted its weight, and closed its eyes again.

Robert Vail was tall and broad shouldered, with only the beginnings of a belly to exhibit his settled life. He was alone now, with his thoughts; but it better pleased him to stand in conference with the unofficial town fathers. He towered over them. There was short and slender William Bogel, with his fancy education and fine words, his small hands and dainty feet; there was John Humphris of the new store, broad in the gut and stoop backed, with a bald head and drawn mouth. They gave him much pleasure in their contrast to his fine form. Chester Woodson was sometimes included in the group, fresh from the state of Tennessee, pockets empty of cash, as he'd paid full for his cattle. And Thomas Kersey, small and bowlegged, mouth full of mush, eyes refusing to stay with a man, wisps of hair straggling from under an old bent-rimmed hat.

Vail enjoyed his measuring against other just men—they might hold power in words, but he was the law, he was the man folks looked to, he was the one for action. There were few men in the big land east of the Rio Grande who could match him for the cut and measure of their form. The old ones, like Don Milton Faver and John Spencer, there was nothing left to them but a myth and a bunch of wild cattle. Faver couldn't even round up his herds, and Spencer had let go of his wealth to get into the impossible scheme of mining. There were few to stand with Robert Vail—Den Knight, Bob Ellison, Royal Channing—none could match his height and breadth, and his charm. Even the odd one, McCraw. Though he came close in height, the man was unfriendly and sullen.

The surveying he'd done in his mind reassured him, as it always did; there was no one to touch Robert Vail.

The sting was gone from his hands now. Vail let himself lean against the upright holding the shaky roof. There was talk through the county of moving everything down to Marfa. There was talk of a courthouse and a new jail. Vail preferred to think on these matters; it was too painful to keep seeing the pictures of that afternoon in Fort Davis. The fragility of his beautiful child, the shocking red and white of her leg. Those thoughts blasted at him with great fury. He had done nothing then; there was nothing he could do now, to change what happened.

A door slammed down the street, loud voices broke the quiet. Three men walked toward Robert Vail with a purpose. He watched their progress: John Humphris, William Bogel, and Chester Woodson. They walked in military precision. In one smooth motion, Vail pushed away from the post and let his hand fall easily to hook on to the carved buckle at his waist. Whatever was on their minds, he was ready.

Bogel began to speak before the trio reached Vail: "Deputy, there's trouble at the store and we want you to come right now." There was no room for question. Vail tugged at the heavy buckle, lifted and released the well-oiled pistol, and nestled it in the holster before he spoke up.

"Mr. Bogel, you tell me what's going on and I'll do what needs to be done. I'll—"

"There is a man at Mr. Humphris's store, and he is bothering the customers and making a nuisance of himself. We want him gone, right now. It is your duty to remove him, and we are here to see that you carry out your duty."

Woodson nodded his agreement to Bogel's demand, and John Humphris didn't bother to speak; he spun on his boot heel and walked back toward the store, clearly expecting the deputy to follow as ordered. Vail slipped the pistol from its holster, sighted down the slick barrel, cocked the hammer, and spun the cylinder.

"Now Mr. Bogel, you know I do my job. But I got to see both sides, do the law fair. I'll be coming along, Mr. Bogel, and I'll be certain to do what the law says. That's my sworn office."

Vail jammed home the pistol and tugged the brim of his hat. Bogel turned back, but Vail was quicker, slipping his shoulder in front of the smaller man and forcing Bogel out into the street. Chester Woodson was a length ahead, and the deputy saw him check back over his shoulder. Vail saw the dark eyes, the black hair under the stained hat, and wondered again about the mix of Woodson's blood. Then

TEXAS SPRINGS 29

Bogel was behind him, Humphris disappeared into his store, and Vail hurried to catch up.

Inside the crowded building, the voices were loud, the words a jumble of English and Spanish, but the angry tone was clear. Vail put out his hand to block any interference, then hurried into the center of the crowd. This was Vail's job.

He knew the Mex, the sheepherder Abateo Flores. Vail grinned. The girl would be here also. And there she was, waiting in a corner, head lifted, eyes flashing a private amusement, face stained a gentle red. This Mex girl caused more trouble in Marfa than any group of yahooing Texas cowhands.

So it was old Abateo Flores and his whelp causing the ruckus. Vail steadied his legs and touched the belt buckle, lifted the weight of his gun from the holster. He watched the girl first, gauged the width of her waist, the swell of her hips, the hand span of brown flesh spilled from the front of her blouse. Vail hitched at his pants again, then counted heads and checked faces before he made a move.

The two men closed in on Flores were well known to Vail. Pomp Wooten and Charley Hocker, two men often out of work. But Vail knew they did day work for W. T. Bogel. Questionable characters, both of them, but not enough to be driven out of the county. Hocker was a wide-backed son, thick through the neck, dull faced and lank haired. And the looks were deceiving, Vail also knew that. Behind the pin eyes and loose mouth was a brain quick enough to keep Hocker always with jingle money. And free of the law.

Wooten was what he seemed: a small man made big only by the size of his gun. Thin faced, blue eyes sharp and sullen, long hair curled past his collar. Where one of these two was seen, the other would be hidden close by. Vail watched as Hocker raised a hand to slap at old Flores, and Flores stepped back. The old man was caught by the store counter. A knife slipped into his hand, and Hocker stepped back, licked his lips, even looked to the deputy before lowering his head and trying for a laugh.

It was enough for Vail; time to settle the issue. "Old man, you put down that knife and ease up. Charley here was funning you, no reason to prick him with that toothpick you carry."

Flores's head snapped around as if Vail had slapped him. The black eyes stared at Vail; the deputy shifted his feet, touched his belt buckle, checked on Hocker and the motionless Wooten. Vail heard the teasing laugh and saw the girl as she came in closer, close enough so he could smell the heat of her body.

"The lawman is brave, no?" The words were spoken in English, the inflection cruel and taunting. Vail flinched as if she had touched him, then heard a whisper as the old man returned the knife to its case. Hocker planted himself close to the old man, and Flores did not look at his tormentor.

Vail had to assert himself and his office: "Hocker, you back off some and forget this. The old man is leaving, and the girl. You and Wooten got better things to do."

Vail figured it was settled then. But old Flores picked up a package from the counter and spoke to the owner: "Señor Humphris, I will pay for this now. And the flour I order. But the coffee on the floor, that I will not pay for, as it is Mr. Hocker who thought it a joke to knock the purchase from my hand and scatter it on the ground. He will pay for that coffee; it is fit only for such as he to drink."

The stubborn, dumb Mex. Vail touched the old man on the shoulder, pushing hard with his big hand, feeling the bones of the old frame give under his power. "You leave now, Flores. You caused enough trouble here, and I don't want that kind of trouble. Marfa is a quiet town, and it's going to stay that way. You best get used to watching your manners here."

Abateo Flores, the sheepherder, looked into Vail's eyes; the deputy had a rough moment holding the stare. The seamed and faded black eyes scoured his face, the mouth worked silently on an unknown Mex curse. Vail had cause now to haul the old man in, but the dark eyes kept him from his duty.

Then it was the girl who crowded in behind him, brushed up against his arm, touched his hip and thigh with a close warmth. Vail drew in his breath and told the old man again: "You leave now, Flores, or I'll lock you and the girl in the storeroom we got us for a jail. I remember you got two other babies at camp. You best think on them before you cross me more."

He saw the change in the old man's face and knew he had won. The girl moved past Vail, the old man dropped his gaze. Vail looked around; there was a smirk on Hocker's face, and Wooten stood behind the bigger man. Something passed between Humphris and Bogel, and Vail suddenly didn't know if he'd done the right thing. Chester Woodson, who had stayed by the door, quietly went outside. Hocker and Wooten followed.

The girl swung her hips as she moved between Bogel and Humphris. The old man was careful to put down the package and follow his daughter. Bogel spoke softly to Humphris, and both men laughed loudly. As Vail left the store, he felt the crunch of something underfoot and saw the waxed brown of coffee beans in the dirt. The old Mex got what he deserved, Vail had no doubts in his mind.

His hair was well streaked with gray. Miguel took his long knife and cut at the base of a clump. He held the strands on his palm. The underside of his hand was tan, the hair a mix of white and gray, and some black. He admired the colors for a while, then lifted his hand and blew hard, and watched as the strands lifted off and fell to the ground.

It came to him he was being foolish, and he looked out, hopeful that no one was watching. Silvestre was in sight, spread under a cottonwood, snoring loud enough to raise his own white mustache. There was no sign of the señor. And Miguel didn't care where the kid had gone. He was alone, with no one to witness his childish act.

He was worried about the señor. There was a change in him the past days, and Miguel knew it was from the ugly one. Miguel was worried about the ranch, and his job. True, it was not much of a ranch, but the horses were good, the food plentiful, the work not past Miguel's strength. And most important of all, the señor had hired him, and Silvestre, where others of the Chisos Basin—and all the way to Fort Davis—were not as generous. Miguel chose not to think closely on this fact, for it hurt his great pride. There was much untruth to the rumors that he, Miguel Lujan, and the big ox named Silvestre had, at times, placed their reatas around the necks of horses and cattle that did not belong to them or to their employer. And there was another ugly rumor, that he, Miguel, had a gift in redrawing brands so that owners would not recognize their own sign.

Miguel had hoped the groundless rumors would die their death in the long years, so that he and his friend would have little to worry them but the closeness of remaining time. Miguel could count, and he knew at least fifty years of his life, and even more belonging to Silvestre. They were no longer so swift after an escaping mother cow, nor could they ride the stampeding broncos to a finish. They could rope and ride with great skill, but it wore them hard to ride to the end of the day. They needed rest where a young man would go forward.

Miguel slapped his palms together. There was a worry for him and Silvestre in the spirit of the young one. The ugly one, who could ride all the day, who could take one sip from the canteen and hold the water in his mouth, swallow and smile with the instant renewal of his strength. Miguel could come to hate the young one, if only for the fewness of his years.

He stepped from the coolness of the barn, to once again find the señor leaning on the fence. There was no sign of the ugly one, and Silvestre still slept noisily under the shaded tree. Miguel watched the señor intently, wondering what would have to be done this day.

There were many stories about Señor Jaime McCraw. Stories Miguel listened to over and over, stories he himself had laced with his own wit to draw out the night. Of the señor coming to the land then called the *Despoblado* as a child, stories about the massacre of his family by the Indians. His coming to manhood under the guidance of the old one named Limm Tyler and the approval of John Spencer.

Jaime McCraw had left the *Despoblado* only once, to go north along the Rio Grande with General Sibley and the Texas Brigade, to conquor the territory of New Mexico in the name of the new government of the divided country. Many of the Brigade did not return. Those that did, came back defeated and worn down.

This is what Miguel had learned: that the señor came back alone, much later, half starved and leading only a small paint mare of little consequence. The old mare lived still, long and yellow in the tooth, bad tempered and lamed. The señor spoke little of his journey, so there were only rumors and idle talk of his adventure, gossip shared generously by the ladies who once dwelled outside the confines of Spencer's great rancho. The ladies would share their favors, and their talk, for the exchange of a few pesos and a drink of new wine.

The señor had stayed on the land since that time, first to work for Señor Spencer, then to become his own boss. The land on which Miguel stood had been a gift from Señor Spencer. There had been no house on the land, only a mound of rubbled brick and stone. Miguel came to work for Señor Jaime then, with the fat and lazy Silvestre, and together they had built the sturdy two-room hut.

There had been an old woman who lived with the señor. A witch named Rosa Ignacio, who died the year past in the accident that lamed the señor. The she-witch was buried in consecrated ground, even though she had been nothing more than an ancient *puta*, living from the pennies of men who came to visit her beside the river.

The old woman haunted Miguel, and there were others to frighten him: rumors of ghosts; of the family buried in the discarded rubble; voices in the night; figures walking the river's course. And even the ghost of the old man, Limm Tyler. It was almost enough to move Miguel from the ranch and on to safer places.

Miguel sighed to himself; it was a dream, for him to ride from his work. No one else would take him, no one else would pay him. He sighed again, enjoying the sadness of his thoughts.

Then the señor moved from the fence, and Miguel grinned. There was no reason for him to bother now with the old times. There would be work for him today, and then there would be a meal and a drink, a time to savor the tortilla wrapped around spiced beans, with perhaps some shredded goat. The young one could cook, for all that he was ugly. Then it would be time to sleep again in the shade of the adobe hut. There was no need to think beyond such pleasure, no reason to bother himself with worrying about the past, or questioning what would come. Today was enough for Miguel.

CHAPTER FOUR

"Coffee, señor?"

James McCraw stretched and rubbed both fists into his eyes. It wasn't dawn yet, but the smell of the coffee woke him easily. He would have a quick cup, then get to the early chores. Have a running start on work before the real heat came in, then sit and enjoy a good breakfast that would hold through the day, until the blessings of the evening cool.

He pushed his long legs off the bed, felt the pull of stiff muscle over ribs as he reached his arms to the wall. There was no hurry this morning, no quick worry to bother his mind.

"And biscuits, if you wish."

TEXAS SPRINGS 35

The voice brought him up quickly. He remembered finally and almost laughed. It was Mateo, called Matt. The kid who rode in three days past and was already a sweet addition to the small work force. Coffee that didn't taste hard boiled, biscuits light as air, even tamales that had a flavor beside beans and hots. Stewed meat, different spices; Matt something. A good trade.

McCraw walked out into the false dawn, headed toward the backhouse, shivering from the cold of false dawn. Around him horses nickered in low, hungry sounds, a rooster found enough voice to crow.

As McCraw returned to the small adobe, chores done, he stopped suddenly, raised his hand to wipe it across his face. There was a new smell this morning, a different taste. There had been little rain through the long summer months, but now there was a clean scent to the wind, almost a taste of water. McCraw smiled; it would rain soon enough.

He'd best ride to Spencer's Rancho and pay the old man his due work, before the trail turned to solid mud and the horse under him slipped and went down. Now he didn't have to worry about Miguel and Silvestre going off on a drunk. The kid'd keep them in line; McCraw'd left him as boss, made sure the vaqueros knew. Told them in Spanish and then English, giving them no chance to say they didn't understand. He could trust to Matt that the work would be done, the horses started, the cattle moved. It was a new pleasure.

He drifted inside and there was a steaming cup set in the middle of the table. He took it for his own, raised the welcome heat to his mouth, let the bitter aroma flood inside his head before he took the first swallow.

"We need more beans, Mr. McCraw. If you ride near a storehouse today. And flour, real short on flour. And anything else you think you can get. Three of us, and you, to feed now. And we is close to out of coffee."

It was the kid, of course. Miguel would never speak so, and Silvestre could never think to find those words. Both would use their own language, not this rough, hard-coated

English. Sometime McCraw thought he would ask the kid where he learned to talk, how he got clever at placing insults sharp in two tongues. McCraw nodded to Matt's shadow, lifted a cup in mock salute, and took a big swallow before he answered.

"It's going to rain. I'll be gone two, maybe three days. The old man will be needing help. I owe him, owe him too much. You keep working those horses, don't let . . ."

As he listened to his own talk, he wondered why he explained anything to this kid. Loyalty was expected on the range, and the kid had no need to understand more than that. Yet McCraw was telling the boy more, and wanting to fill in the story. How old Spencer took him in when his family was killed, how he paid him a man's wage when he did a man's work. There were years of his life, and none of them the kid's business. McCraw glared at the new cook, angry at the memories the boy's presence called up.

There'd been no change at all in the kid since he'd rode that first afternoon with Miguel. He worked hard, gave nothing but what had been dickered for and agreed. Cooking had fallen to him as Silvestre's replacement, and that had been a relief. Since Rosa Ignacio'd died, Miguel and Silvestre had fought for the right not to cook. Silvestre usually lost, and they all suffered. But McCraw had no sense in a kitchen, and it was agreed that the *patrón* did not do such work, that Silvestre, with his clumsy hands and slow mind could feed them daily on grease-soaked tortillas and beans, stewed goat, an occasional deer. Crude fare, but no one starved.

The kid could cook. But when Silvestre crossed the line and asked how and where he learned such a skill, there had been a short silence before the kid put down a steaming pan, leaving it to burn through on the hot fire, and left the adobe hut. He returned an hour later, through the front of the house, to find Miguel and Silvestre staring at the blackened mess of beans and spices, and, saying nothing, he picked up the ruined pan and threw it out the back door. There was another old pan high on a shelf, and the kid went back to his cooking. Miguel opened his mouth once to phrase a question, but showed some sense when the kid put the new pan down hard on the fire. There would be no answers, and no more questions.

That night there had been pie, with dried fruit and honeyed filling. Almost a peace offering. Miguel had kicked Silvestre hard on the shinbone when the clumsy man, proving he had not learned, almost got out the words to another question. There was a long silence, then four heads bent to the pie, four knives worked to catch the last of the cooked fruit. The rest of their agreement had come then, with little discussion: Miguel fed and cared for the horses brought in for work, Matt cooked, and Silvestre, even hampered as he was by the binding on his shoulder, scrubbed the tin plates and long knives, the wooden bowls and crude spoons at the end of each meal.

All in all, it hadn't been a bad bargain the past few days, to have the kid as part of the working crew.

McCraw still directed the day's orders to Miguel. He didn't feel easy looking at the ruined face—and he knew that curiosity would drive the kid permanently out the door—so he kept his talk to Miguel; no one thought of Silvestre. The kid seemed to accept he would be ignored, at least for now.

"Catch up the blond sorrel, Miguel. And I need a day's pack of food, the extra rifle, and shells. And a slicker. By God, it's going to rain on me this time. I'll be gone two, three days at the most."

The thoughts that traveled Miguel's face in quick succession were close to funny. He'd be here alone with the kid, Silvestre didn't count; the *patrón* would be gone, and there was much to settle. McCraw didn't let too much time for Miguel's thinking; he went on to the rest of the orders.

"Get the cattle to good graze, turn them back if they wander much. Put them near Bitter Springs, that'll keep them in close. And turn back any stuff not ours that's eating what don't belong to them. It's a waste of grass and water, letting too many graze near a spring. We know better, but some of these new folks, they think the water will last forever.

"When that's done, you help Matt here with the horses. Go easy with this bunch, Miguel. Let the kid do the deciding. They're good-blooded horses, but their education got left behind a year. It'll be criminal to break them, but it's got to be done. My fault . . . Work these colts right, they'll be a money crop."

He was conscious of speaking directly to Miguel, even though he wanted the kid to listen and understand. It was the kid's touch that would start the colts. McCraw's own cowardice galled him, and he finally made himself look straight into the kid's eyes.

It had to be the sun; its rays slanted through the crude high window and crossed on the tough face. It turned in McCraw's belly, and he knew the kid saw him flinch. A quick hell showed in the golden hazel eyes, the chin raised an inch; the black hair was tossed back in that practiced move, and the scar was outlined in bright yellow.

Damned 'breed. McCraw wanted to strike the ugly features, destroy the calmed eyes, wipe out the ancient knowing in them. Instead, he raised up the cooled cup of coffee and took the last sip, apologized in his mind to the motionless kid. Then he rose without further orders and went out the back, ducking to avoid the lintel. He knew Miguel would follow, to catch up the blond sorrel and saddle while McCraw packed.

He didn't like what he carried with him, the knowing the kid was inside holding to a last look of pity. But damn his mulish hide; he'd carried that scar long enough that he didn't need to make a fuss.

Then McCraw realized his error. Matt hadn't mentioned the scar once, except to own its belonging to the devil. It was the smallness inside James McCraw's heart, and Miguel's, and Silvestre's, that raised the scar each time. It didn't come from Matt at all. McCraw almost went back into the kitchen to speak out something to ease his conscience. But he knew he wouldn't have the words, that what he said would be all wrong. It was best left alone.

Miguel brought up the sorrel, and the kid came out with a bulky pouch. McCraw filled a canteen and tied the slicker in place. It was a relief for him to mount the eager sorrel and spin the horse around, let it leap into a run before they'd made it halfway across the yard. He would outrun the confusion of thinking left in the adobe house, the old barn, the pens holding a half-dozen unbroken, blooded money horses.

He never did pay much attention to time. He'd come back to the *Despoblado* and gone to work for John Spencer. Until the need to have his own place bit him and he talked with the old man, shook on the deeding of his land. Then, it was all that he needed: Spencer's word, Spencer's signature put to a piece of paper. More than enough to claim his rights.

Now he had questions about the ownership. McCraw slowed the sorrel to a jog and wiped the wetness on his forehead, looked around as if for the first time. Dust rose from each step of the sorrel. The belly-high grasses were cropped to the roots; plates of leathered cow manure and hard pellets from sheep told him the culprits. McCraw sighed. He thought of the early summer, when he could reach down from horseback and pick the grass stems, roll the seeds between his fingers, and let the wind take them. Now there was nothing left but bared roots.

The big sorrel wove easily through the thick sotol clumps and cropped chino grass. McCraw barely thought to guide the horse, confident of the gelding's stride. He looked up and straight ahead, saw a rise of dust, heard the sounds of distant cattle. Not distant enough. More numbers being driven across the land, more mouths to tear and destroy what had taken years to grow. He shifted in the saddle, restless with the gathering worry. An abrupt cut in the land stopped the sorrel, and McCraw guided the horse down the side, headed him straight across the bottom, and then angled him up the other side.

He let the horse rest to catch his wind and leaned his arms on the wide plate of the horn. There were laws now in the *Despoblado*, to both take and protect. And he would use them, take the land belonging to him and protect it. Spencer's paper, signed two years ago, gave him rights to the land. That paper lay with a few old letters and important notes heaped inside a rusted metal box. McCraw wondered now on the worth of that paper. Someone could already have filed on Spencer's grant, even though McCraw had lived his life on the parcel. And he also knew the small section was not enough to hold all the cattle and raise his horses. He would have to take as much as he could and fight for the rest.

McCraw shook his head. He had lived with the world flowing around him, washing past him, softening and splitting new ideas against his stubborn will. Now the world was folding over to trap him with its laws and words. Maybe it already had him, caught as bad as a coyote snapped into metal jaws. The restlessness grew inside him; his belly knotted, his mouth soured. He shook as if something walked on his early grave.

He went to the familiar for his peace; he spoke to the sorrel, and the horse picked up a long lope. But the pace could not outdistance McCraw's thinking. He had always played the game alone, without even knowing the rules. Now the rules had changed, and he had to ride headlong into the new world around him. It wasn't a choice, it was a force taking him full gallop.

The sorrel beneath him flinched and sidestepped; McCraw swayed with the violent move. A small herd of cattle, a mix of Mex longhorns and a new stump-legged stock. Red-coated mother cows, suckling neat red calves. McCraw laughed and patted the sorrel, until the horse finally relaxed. Another man's cattle grazing on land McCraw thought belonged to him, another man's herd frightening his seasoned cow horse.

He lifted the sorrel into a lope; they traveled smoothly around the litter of cactus and rock that led to Spencer's Rancho gates. The wide adobe walls were the first sight of the old forted house, walls now cracked and left unpatched, crumbling along the top, with big chunks broken through the sides. McCraw rode between the opened gates and let the sorrel drift to the water trough.

The wooden bowl was dry, its sides cracked and splintered with great holes. McCraw dismounted slowly. There were two horses in a pen; old ones with their heads down, their lips loose and flapping. The tails barely lifted to slap at flies, a hoof stamped, a head swung in meager protest. The trough in that pen was half full and green with slime, a puddle shining under the connection of an old pipe. McCraw let the sorrel in, stripped its gear, and hung up the saddle, overturned the wet blanket to the sun. The sorrel drank greedily while the two old horses thought to threaten him; bony heads lifted, long ears flattened. The ribby buckskin waved a front hoof, then stretched out the leg and shifted balance to take away the strain. The wide back sagged, the big head dropped. The two horses had made their stand.

"That you, Jim Henry?"

It was the old man himself, leaning on a cane. He was a surprise to McCraw; John Spencer was always a surprise. The fine head was bent and silver, the walk pained and slow. McCraw went to him and held out his hand, nodded to the greeting, and waited while the cane balanced the old man and McCraw could walk him back to the house.

He went right back outside to do the chores. He cleaned out the stinking water trough and filled it with clean water. The two old horses stood and watched, then came over to drink eagerly. He let the sorrel in with the pensioners, and the big young horse played gleefully in the fresh water. Then he repaired a broken section of corral fence, rehung a door that had slipped from its hinges. Old chores done with a familiar rhythm; he'd grown up here, he'd lived and grown on John Spencer's sufferance.

* * *

His chores were done before dark. When McCraw came to the wide door of the old house, there was no servant to meet him, no smiling border woman ready to show him to the señor's office and then return to the evening meal's preparation.

He walked through the dark, empty shell, hearing the echo of his hard-soled boots on the wood floor. An old woman shuffled through the kitchen, a fat one whose face disappeared in folds, whose streaked hair was bound up in greasy cloth. She did not look up as McCraw stood in the doorway, but he heard the old man's voice calling from another room and he followed the sound, glad to be away from the woman and her work.

It was the room that had once been the center of the ranch's activities. McCraw remembered it, the high windows set into the long sides, the great desk lost in the middle, the pattern of the now worn carpet that covered most of the floor.

Papers were still piled on the top of the desk, and more papers were tied in bundles; but the room had changed its function. In a cleared space at the far end of the desk, a tin plate sat alone on a colored square of cloth. A high-backed and carved chair was drawn close to the desk, and an ancient, hide-covered stool sat beside it.

John Spencer sat in the large chair, his head rested on the back, his hands splayed across the shiny arm. James McCraw hesitated, for he remembered entering this door as a child, not quite a man, but come to ask for a man's wage. The same awe came back, even though the old man facing him showed the years of change. And the old man's mind was sharp, for he answered the question McCraw had not yet asked.

"You been working your land for ten years now to pay a debt. Jim Henry, the land is yours, according to my rights. Me, I quit ranching, quit selling cattle to the army. Got all my interest in the mine now, all my money chasing silver over to Shafter. That land's yours, son. More than yours."

The old eyes flickered, the worn face came into itself, and for a moment the old John Spencer relived his power and his glory. Then memories flooded the seamed face and the visage of an old man returned.

"My oldest, he never took to the land. Never came much of a son to me. Never worked like you. But he's mine, I guess. Jim Henry, you ride to Fort Davis and you do what the new law says. Make it legal in their eyes, boy. No one'll take my land. They'll set and wait till I die, then tear out what they want. My sons won't stand to them, so it'll come legal and all.

"You, you take the paper got my name fixed to it. That name got weight now, but when I die, you watch for the wolves."

The light faded, the shadows changed inside the empty room, and the old man sat wrinkled and toothless, older than his years from the harsh realities of his life. Then the old woman came in, bearing two plates. The sour smell turned inside McCraw, but he owed it to the old man to sit and eat with him, listen to his stories, and live with the past for one more meal.

He felt the fool, a raw kid loose in a new world. He, James McCraw, who'd lived most of his forty-some years in the *Despoblado*, didn't know squat about business. File a claim, the old man said. Stake out the land and hold it legal. And he didn't know the beginnings—how to describe and file the marks of the land he'd bled into, the land that clawed and drew him back the one time he rode away. He was a fool.

He saddled the sorrel in early morning to head back. Spencer took his leave standing at the doorway and lifted his cane in mock salute. In McCraw's pocket was another of Spencer's notes. It had little authority behind its flowery writing, but it would be something.

As he let the sorrel drift north, McCraw saw the land with a new eye. The section where he'd lived all these years wasn't suitable for a full-time ranch. With no need to keep a neighbor at his side, a rock wall at his back, he could pick a better place. He could go to a spring, he could choose good grass and open space.

He had no illusion of owning the land, only controlling it. No one held the *Despoblado*; it would give its lush grass and sweet water, its high pine shade and bright sun. And it would take these gifts back with no mercy whenever the strong snows came, or the rains flooded the riverbanks, or the clouds refused to release their promise. It was from men he must protect himself with titles and surveys and records and money. There was no protection from bitter winds and dried ground.

It was always water. The river had a supply; it could fatten a number of cattle, it could raise a small herd of horses. But there was a limit to the surrounding land. And the springs, hidden deep in the uncharted canyons, were truly the gift of the land.

Bitter Springs. The name he would give to his new ranch. The name he'd first spoken more than twenty years past, for a spring hard on the high side of a narrow wall. Bitter Springs. Known to the Indians, and to John Spencer, and the old man, Limm Tyler, and the boy, Jim Henry McCraw. He would file on the springs and the surrounding grass. They would become his new home.

He let the big sorrel run the last mile, glorying in the long stride and the power. Excitement paced inside him; he'd find and lay out the markers, count off the land he wanted, ride to Fort Davis, and make a claim. Then the knot in his belly would untie, the pain inside his head would break . . . and he could become his own man.

CHAPTER FIVE

Most of his time here, he was working at what he did best. But inside the hut, the slow words and sly glances passed about his cooking made him fight a temper, hold it long enough to tell the boss, and the two idiots working for him, that cooking wasn't what he did. And that if they liked the food so well, they by God better sit on their smart talk. That silenced them, that and the burned beans, the sweetened fruit pie. But the words passed back and forth in front of him anyway, never directly put but always there, clear and too loud in the small adobe hut.

The questions about his face were the same, but Matt had learned that lesson over ten years' time. He knew he couldn't control a man's thinking, so he settled for the peace of curious silence. It all didn't matter a shit pile; he'd be gone soon. After the roan's hoof had no more heat, when the little horse could walk with an even stride.

When the boss had pulled out to see the man named Spencer, Matt went to the unbroken stock churning in the pen. He hung over the top rail and waited until the excited geldings quit their spook and tired of racing the small circle. When they settled, he made a choice. Pulled out three of them into a separate pen.

Miguel came along as figured, mouth flapping, wide maw drawing in wind and exploding curses and foul smells. Matt let it go, knowing he couldn't change the man. He spoke McCraw's name and repeated the orders that left him, Matt, in charge. Finally Miguel had to admit he remembered. It was enough, for a while.

He had his own way of working horses, hard learned from the Indians who drifted through where he had lived. He'd been little more than a half-wild kid, wire-tough and eager, almost twelve that spring, and badly frightened when he came to the Indian camp and stood to their inspection. It was the mark on his face that insured his safety. But he had to stand quiet and let their chief run blunt fingers deep in the crease. The scar was fresh then, barely half healed, and painful to the touch.

He had to stand and allow the inspection; even as a child he knew that much. The old Indian muttered strange sounds as he peeled back the raw skin and dug to the core of the wound. Matt remembered still, in undiminished shame, the tears that had streamed down his face. The pain disappeared, healed by a numbness of fear and the words of the old man.

Others came to poke and pry, until all curiosity had been satisfied. He would tell them nothing, and they could ask little in their curious tongue. But he could show them by the signs from his hands, the gleam in his eye, what he wanted from them in exchange. To watch their work with the wild horses, to see them tame a range stallion until it became a favored war pony.

He wanted those secrets, he needed that knowledge. And his price had been to let them tear out his scarred soul, turn it around in their gentle hands, then return it to him—stronger, tougher, sealed again deep inside him.

He learned well enough; to sit in a pen, to watch each horse, it was all the same to Matt, blooded race stock or range scrub. Sit and listen, watch carefully, sing to them softly, wait until each horse belonged to him in its mind and wild heart. Then he would haul out the ropes and the saddle, put a line to the snubbing post, display the blanket. The work was easy for Matt. The horses fought less, the way he came to them, and were left with a spark of their own soul intact.

Miguel, he was like all the others. He would not listen, even after Señor McCraw gave word that it was for Matt to

TEXAS SPRINGS 47

start the horses. Miguel was to tend the cattle. Stay away from Matt. Said in those words, said loud and clear enough that Matt could hear his name across the dusty yard.

And yet it came fast and hard, like he knew it would. McCraw's dust had barely settled when Matt felt the heavy steps behind him. Matt sat inside the corral, back resting on a post, hands quiet, eyes watching the restless track of a buckskin gelding. Off to one side, another noise turned his head; the fat one, come to gloat, was following Miguel's walk. Matt cautioned himself to remember, to watch out for the old fat one and his cane.

Miguel leaned on the gate, the fat one stayed his distance. Before the big mouth opened, Matt slid his back along the post and stood to his full height. The buckskin whirled and snorted, head lifted, eyes wild with the anticipation that was fear. Matt wanted to tell the young horse that he, too, felt the same dread, but he was not allowed the time. The grating voice began on him:

"Why you do something like that? Why you sit and do nothing when the señor, he tell you to get to work? Sitting will not break the horse to ride, yet you call yourself a horse tamer. Hah."

Matt could not stop his grin. Anything would do to start this fight. He was slow, deliberate, as he picked up a dropped rope, coiled it carefully, watched it slide through his hands, felt its texture, smelled the sweat and fear attached. He hung the rope on a post, then walked quickly to the vaquero, eyes hard on the dark face. The ceaseless wind blew the cover of black hair from his face but he didn't care. He wouldn't give Miguel a chance.

"Bad enough you losing your job to a 'breed, huh? But it's got to be an ugly one like me. One who's a hell of a better horseman than you ever got to be, in all your years. Tough, ain't it? But you can stay to watch, maybe learn something. Then you can clean the shit piles out of the corral when I got these broncs ready and going."

The move was there for Matt to see, and yet he only half-stepped back. The big fist caught him on the jaw; he staggered but kept his footing. The fat one stiffened and broke wind from excitement; Matt heard him struggle with the cane. Miguel's eyes widened as Matt withstood the blow. The vaquero's arm raised, his shoulder bunched; Matt let that blow begin, then stepped into the swing and buried his fist in the hanging belly. The burst of air sickened him as he hammered into soft flesh. Miguel Lujan suddenly sat down, eyes rounded and teary, hands crossed over the center of his new pain.

Matt swerved on instinct but wasn't fast enough. The cane sent him reeling. He didn't go down, but came around and saw the stance of the fat one, the cane raised for another blow. Matt ducked close to the man and grabbed the tip of the cane. The fat one was stronger than Matt guessed, and he was yanked off his feet and spilled near the boots of the barely moving Miguel.

Then, Miguel was moving, and Matt saw heavy boots fly close to his face, a spinning spur rowel grazed him as the boot skidded past. He grabbed blindly; the vaquero bellowed and came down on one knee. Matt rolled frantically as the cane lashed out from nowhere and bruised his shoulder, raked his throat. The tip dug into his scarred face and he cried out. Then he doubled his legs and shoved hard, slammed into Miguel's gut. They both went down this time, Miguel on his back, Matt riding him.

Crouched over Miguel, Matt pummelled him until Silvestre's cane beat on his back and ribs and he had to escape. Out of reach, he spun around, hands raised, back and face throbbing. Miguel was curled in the dirt, pale arms again wrapped around his belly. Fat old Silvestre stood on wobbly legs, face pale and beaded with sweat. The hand gripped to the throat of the cane was trembling, the wide mouth had spittle at the corners.

No one moved; all were conscious of the silence, the sudden unshaded sun, the clatter of panicked horses in the corrals. The cane was jabbed into the ground, and the fat man leaned on it for support. Matt almost felt pity for the two, until he wiped an arm across his face and saw blood on his shirtsleeve. Miguel rolled over then, very slowly, and came to his knees, climbed to his feet.

Matt backed up—and wished for the old knife packed beside his saddle and blankets. Used last to cut out the spine from the roan's hoof. He watched the fat one; he would not be beaten by that cane again. Miguel's face was swollen, his mouth puffy, one eye almost shut. The fat one stayed hanging on his cane; Miguel did not speak. Neither man reached for Matt, yet they did not leave.

It was Matt who walked away, taking careful steps to avoid the pull of muscles across his back. Blood still ran from a cut on his face, the old scar burned. He said nothing as he opened the gate and went back inside the pen. The buckskin colt raised his head and snorted, blowing hard at Matt's presence. Matt found the same post, touched it gently, squatted on the corral floor, and forgot about the two old men and their stubborn pride. He went back to his taming of McCraw's broncs.

He didn't go in for a noon meal. And no one came out to inquire if, indeed, he was to do the cooking. It was as if Miguel and Silvestre had retreated into a different world.

Matt was in his own private place, where he sat inside the big pen and watched the horses. At first they circled and ran from his shadow, bucking playfully, kicking at one another, laying back long ears and taking bloodless bites out of supposed enemies. Then the running became serious when he did not leave, until finally the exhausted horses slowed to a ragged trot, then walked with heads lowered, sweat lathered between their legs, ribs bellowing in and out for more air.

He sat through the performance patiently, waiting for them to accept him as a fact. It was as he thought; the buckskin colt stopped first, came around to stare at the threat of Matt inside the pen. Matt stayed hunched over, eyes down, hands loose between his knees. The big youngster stepped forward, snorted again, took another step . . . and was spooked by his own bravery. A bay near the fence whinnied; the buckskin sidestepped and ran back to the herd. Matt continued to wait patiently.

As he knew it had to happen, the buckskin returned, this time even closer, almost willing to reach out and touch Matt's torn sleeve. This would be the horse he would start tomorrow. This would be the best one of the group.

CHAPTER SIX

When he thought on it, late that night, Matt wondered why McCraw ever trusted him. The man knew nothing of him beyond the lamed roan and Matt's quick mouth. Yet he rode off on the blond sorrel and seemed willing to let a wild-eyed rider use his judgment in working the stock. The more he thought on it, the less Matt understood. And he had a lot of time to think; the bruises and cuts would not let him sleep. He would doze, then move, and something would groan; he would wake himself with his own noise. Matt snorted in disgust and went back to the thinking. There was little else to do.

He knew enough of himself to see he was prickly and miserable in company. He started out at this ranch by wading into Silvestre and breaking the man's shoulder. Now Miguel carried his marks. Why had McCraw given Matt Iberra the right to do his work?

The word that came to him was *trust*. He lay on the hard pallet and rolled his head on the folded dirty shirt that served as a pillow. It made little sense to him, yet the word stayed in his mind. He blinked his eyes, felt the blackness inside his lids, then opened them to the closeness of the

Texas sky. He shut his eyes again, angry at himself for liking McCraw.

None of it mattered in the morning. Matt was slow to rise; the side of his head ached, his back burned, and there was a knot on his jaw that made eating rough. Still, it was a pleasure to sip hot coffee and wait for Miguel. The man was unable to look straight at Matt through his swollen eyes. Matt lowered his head into the steam of the coffee and smiled to himself. He had made soft eggs for breakfast, and new biscuits. Silvestre did not show for the meal.

It didn't matter. Now he would be left alone, to work the horses the way he wanted, the only way he could.

He went quietly into the pen. The buckskin colt saw him first and walked forward, ears pricked in curiosity. Matt was pleased; the colt was deep chested, with good quarters, not a stout roping horse but a long-legged, sixteen-hand runner. There was no sign of fear in the dark eyes, no worry in the quick walk.

Matt began murmuring, softly at first, then louder as he found the song. The chant returned to him; he forgot where he was. The buckskin edged closer, arched his neck and extended his head to almost touch Matt's hair. Matt kept to the singing, careful not to look in the horse's eyes, careful not to become a threat.

His left hand rose of its own will; the fingers wiggled slightly, and the buckskin hesitated, shook his head, then lowered the black muzzle to touch the hand. The song continued, its sound rising and softening as the horse puzzled out what it could not understand.

Coarse whiskers teased Matt's fingers, rough lips opened, and short teeth gripped the flesh. There was no pressure in the hold, only a gentle testing. Matt raised the hand slowly; the teeth tightened their grip. Matt leaned forward, took in a deep breath, and released it close to the muzzle. The buckskin blew out a breath in return; Matt smelled the dried grass, the sand. The buckskin dropped the tasteless hand and briefly laid the weight of the big head on Matt's shoulder. Then the searching teeth found the junction of neck and body and took hold enough to prick the skin.

Matt let the words take shape and speak through his hands alone. *No way to make friends. No way to be friends. You bite, I got to bite you harder. Leave it. Get back. Enough, buckskin. Enough.* As he followed his thinking, he pulled himself away from the buckskin, put his hand to the wide chest, and pushed gently. The buckskin took a half step back and let go.

The colt lowered his head; Matt laid the rope against the gold neck, and the watchful eye rolled back. He stroked the warm skin, felt the hard muscle slide under his palm. The rope passed over the dropped head, a black ear tipped in question, and Matt sang his mindless song.

When the rope was tightened on the golden neck, the buckskin reared and struck out at nothing, came back down to stand on trembling legs. Matt was there to touch and reassure him. The gelding blew through a foamy mouth and was still. Matt tugged on the rope; the buckskin went up and came back down, front legs landing hard on the corral floor, dust cupping out from the concussion.

Matt let his hand go forward and shake the line free of tension. The dark gold head lifted, but no white showed around the eye. Matt walked two steps, pulled on the rope. The buckskin refused; Matt sang to him, and still the horse hesitated. The rope tightened again, the horse reared and came down, and Matt was there, to sing the song and stroke the now wet neck.

Then he walked away, the line slowly tightening until the buckskin had to feel the pull. The head went up, the ears flattened, but the eyes were glued to Matt. The song could be heard, soft and easy, and the buckskin decided to follow its familiar sound.

Miguel opened the gate without being asked, and Matt led the trembling horse into a larger pen with a worn snubbing post in its center. Close at hand were a matted and stained wool blanket and the old patched saddle. Matt

TEXAS SPRINGS 53

wrapped the line around the post. With the slack he put a loop in the rope and slipped it on the black muzzle. The horse pulled back tentatively, felt the pressure on the softness of the nose, behind his ears, and remembered his lesson. He dropped his head and was willing to stand.

The blanket came next; Matt rubbed it on the buckskin's neck and let the colt sniff its scent. He placed the blanket over the gold back, and the horse shivered but did not move. When the weight of the saddle touched the horse, the gelding raised a hind foot in warning, but stood to the sounds of Matt's voice. Matt leaned under to catch the *cincha*, dragged it through the near ring, and folded a loose knot.

The buckskin blew out a deep breath. Matt held the end of the *látigo* and waited; then he tugged a notch tighter. The buckskin squealed. Matt tucked the leather through the ring and walked away, to leave the horse alone with the puzzle of what sat on his back.

It didn't take long for the horse to decide he didn't like the new burden. He kicked at his own belly, slammed himself into the post, rubbed his side on the splintered wood. The stirrup caught up and then swung free, slapped the buckskin's ribs. The spooked colt backed up, felt the pressure of the rope halter, reared, felt the new pain on his nose and poll, then came back down to stand, braced and blowing, tail lifted across the gold back, head high, but with the rope to the halter loosened.

Matt leaned on the railing to watch. Miguel sat on the top rail, with Silvestre near the gate. No one spoke for the five minutes it took the buckskin to figure out the halter and saddle. The horse walked cautiously around the post to discover the halter tightened too quickly. He kicked out in anger; the rope pinched his raw nose. Then the horse squealed again, half bucked, unwound himself from the post. The colt sighed and looked over at Matt, lowered his head, cocked a hind foot, and relaxed.

There was water near the pen, in a leather bag hanging from a tree. In easy reach. But Matt knew he needed a gesture, his version of a truce. So he spoke up quietly, watching the buckskin gelding rather than either of the two men. If the horse was startled, Matt wanted to know.

"You got water out here. Don't want to leave the colt, and I got more work to be doing. Be real thankful for a drink of water."

The buckskin barely raised his head at the words. Silvestre moved first, to take down the half-filled bag and hand it to Matt. Water beaded along the sides; the leather became slippery as the moisture turned the dust on Matt's hands to mud. He pulled the stopper and drank greedily of the foul water, letting it overflow his mouth and run down his neck, soak into his shirt. He handed the bag to Silvestre, nodded a thank-you.

Miguel said nothing, but there was a shine in the one open eye that spoke of some understanding. Matt nodded to him, wiped his forearm across his face, and smeared the mud into his mouth. He spat in the dust, tugged at his hat, as he walked back to the horse. He had more work ahead of him, the best part of the work.

The buckskin was wet; steam rose from the soaked hair and filled the air with its salty smell. Matt touched the wetness under the *cincha*, and the colt kicked at him. He untied the horse, and they walked the circle of the pen twice. In a smaller side pen, one horse nickered, and the buckskin flapped dried lips in a silent answer.

Matt stopped and wound the length of rope around his hand, stood at the buckskin's shoulder. The horse turned in curiosity; Matt shortened the line, patted the black muzzle. When his weight tugged on the stirrup, the buckskin reached for his head and felt the pinch of the halter line.

Then Matt was on the colt's back, feet jammed in the stirrups, one hand gripped on the line, the other rubbing circles in the wet hair in front of the saddle. His lips formed the tuneless song, and the horse listened. The buckskin crouched slightly, wagged his head in distress. Matt touched the line, sang his song, and felt the body under him relax. Perhaps this would be the one that did not have to fight.

He was wrong. The buckskin immediately struck out with a front hoof, reared and spun sideways, ducked his head, and came down on rigid legs. Matt swayed in the rig, grabbed the shortened line, leaned forward with the rear, fell back as the colt came down.

Someone yelled coarse words in Spanish. Matt felt the colt plunge forward and took a short wrap on the line. He yanked hard, and the horse squealed; skidding along the rail. Matt was too slow, and his leg was dragged and skinned by the fence. He dug in a spur, felt the big muscle over the ribs give, and the horse screamed. The colt ran from the new pain, leaping across the pen. He hit the snubbing post shoulder high and dropped to his knees. Matt grabbed at the big head and pulled it to rest on his leg. The long mouth opened, the teeth touched his thigh. Matt yelled and slapped the muzzle; the horse came up under him, slid on the churned ground as Matt fed out the wet rope. The buckskin circled once, came to a ragged trot. Matt's legs squeezed the heaving barrel and asked the colt to move.

When he tugged on the line this time, the buckskin came obediently to a stop. It took Matt a long time to shift weight and lift himself from the horse. An inquisitive breath touched his neck; he trembled and reached out to the buckskin's face. The horse pulled away, then relaxed and allowed Matt to pat him on the jowl.

He rubbed the lathered spots under the rope, and the horse leaned into the new pleasure. Finally Matt tugged the *cincha* loose and stripped the colt. He took a blanket and wadded it, rubbed at the steaming back. It wasn't until he slipped the rope off that the horse realized he was done. The big head poked Matt in the belly to get another rubbing, then the buckskin walked away.

Matt looked down and saw the torn leg of his pants. He aimed toward the corral fence, blinded by the high sun and a pounding inside his head. Miguel and Silvestre were still there, watching him closely. He must not stumble and give them an excuse. He looked again, and the boss was there. Sitting between the vaqueros. Judging Matt, watching the duel with the buckskin and comparing its easy ending to others' battles. To bloodied horses and broken riders. Matt raised his head against any unheard mocking and straightened out his walk. This was how he rode a horse, this was how he tamed the instinct to fight, without breaking the spirit. He would take no complaints from the old rancher, even though he owed the man a few days' work. He would change his way for no one.

McCraw had ridden to the corral, and no one saw him. It wasn't until he tied up the sorrel and climbed beside Miguel that the man knew the señor had returned.

Miguel had been quick to speak, and there was a new tone in his voice McCraw did not figure.

"He is a mad one. He will not let us tie up that devil, or blindfold or hobble him while he flaps that foolish blanket around. He will talk to the horse, and sing to him. As if the beast would understand. I thought I could understand him, señor. But he is truly mad."

McCraw was impressed by the short battle, but not surprised. He'd already felt the stubbornness of the kid and seen the skill in his hands. There were obvious bruises on Miguel and comparable marks on the kid. And Silvestre again carried a badge of a fight. McCraw wanted to know what happened in the one day he was absent, but he knew it was foolish to ask.

When the kid was on the ground, McCraw spoke to him, slowly, as he wasn't certain the kid's head was right. The kid moved slow, and the gold eyes did not look focused or sure.

"Matt." He waited until the head lifted and the eyes sought his. "Matt, that was a good ride. And a tough horse you picked for yourself. I'm betting tomorrow he'll give more of a fight. Then maybe, after two or three more rides, he'll settle enough to work. But you sure put a good start on him today."

The ugly face looked right at him; McCraw knew the movement had to hurt. But the kid opened that scarred eye until the white turned crimson and its rawness became a reprimand to McCraw. The kid said nothing, but went back to the center of the corral and held to the splintered snub post. McCraw stayed on the top railing and wished he'd had enough sense to be quiet.

The dumb son picked up the coiled rope and walked to the buckskin gelding. He fashioned a halter on the dark head. There was a sound beside McCraw; he looked around, saw Miguel with his mouth wide open, his jaw hanging. McCraw shook his head. No one knew what in hell was going on. He surely didn't understand.

The buckskin accepted the saddle quietly, even stood still while the kid climbed back on. McCraw waited for the explosion, but the horse did nothing but walk from the pressure of the kid's legs. It was a straight line to McCraw, and the colt was guided by the light rope on his neck, the touch of the hands and legs. The colt stopped, and the kid finally had his say. Even Miguel was silent, to hear what the wild one would speak.

"Señor, any bronc I ride won't fight again. I don't break a horse, I told you that. He ain't broke inside, he ain't hurting like most rough string. You watch. You get down and ride him, ask him to do for you. This is a good one. He'll give you what you ask for."

The kid had been challenged before. And McCraw knew there had been more than what he'd seen to the colt's taming. As if the saddling and the mounting, the riding and the stop and start, had been afterthoughts, exercises in understanding.

He had to take the invitation. He slid down the fence, and, when he reached the colt and took the rope, the horse shivered. McCraw remembered from his past and put his fingers near the buckskin's nose and wiggled them. The horse blew out quickly, touched the new hand with stiff whiskers, then swiped at the upturned palm with clenched teeth and whickered softly. McCraw held his ground, and the colt quickly lost interest.

He wanted to give the colt back to the kid, but the dark face refused him, the red eye flared. So McCraw found the stirrup and climbed gracelessly into the saddle. The horse shook under him; the kid said something and touched the rigid neck. McCraw felt the great barrel lift and relax and knew to ask for a slow walk, an easy jog. The colt was awkward, still new to the balance of a rider. But the kid had truly worked a miracle and filled his boast. McCraw was more than pleased when he dismounted and gave the buckskin back to Matt's hand.

"That's good work. You earned your meal here today."

He tried to make it light; Matt's was a good hand on a good horse. But he couldn't easily forget the truth—a few years past it would have been his horse, his choice, his hand on the rope. McCraw felt the old pain of the busted leg and torn shoulder. His legacy from the stampede, his new need for the wild kid with the strong body and strange mind.

It came out wrong, he knew that as soon as he spoke. But the kid turned from him as if he didn't exist. He needed to explain, to praise Matt for the work. But the kid went to his chores, and stayed with them longer than was necessary. McCraw knew it was on his account, that he'd spooked the kid worse than a gun-shy bronc.

He looked to the sun, saw the low rays across the ridge to the west. They had been at the corral longer than he thought. Too late for him to start for Fort Davis now. The paperwork would keep until tomorrow; tonight he'd eat the kid's good cooking, get some sleep, and ride out first thing. Maybe he'd even get his chance to speak out his mind.

There was a difference at the ranch now. Maybe it was his thinking of filing a claim, maybe it was seeing the young stock put to work. But there was a change in the place, and McCraw approved.

Then again, maybe it was connected to the rider limping across the yard, gimpy now that he thought no one was watching. Maybe it was nothing more than a scrub kid. But there was a change, and McCraw wanted to settle it out.

He waited inside for the kid. The words were in him that needed to be said, the praise about the colt, the thanks for the cooking. But the kid got past him too quick, mouthing about getting to supper, cutting up a steak, kneading fresh biscuits. More work tomorrow, no time tonight.

The chance went by, and McCraw wasn't certain how it happened.

CHAPTER SEVEN

It came as a shock when she finally realized it: they had not told her the truth. They had spoken only a version they believed would please her. They had lied to her, with intent, and, in his case, with malice, and now there was little she could do to change that lie.

She had made the long journey on the strength of their words, and she had been greatly disappointed. Texas was not as they had allowed her to believe, especially this particular section of the state.

Margaret attempted to assume the blame, but she would not hear of such foolishness. Mr. Dutchover was guilty in the fabrication of the lies. The mistruths, as Margaret gently called them. Beautiful, they had said in the carefully written letter. Lovely, with tall green grass, vast shade trees, clear water bubbling through ranch property. Acres of wonderful land waiting to be settled. There was room for her with them, they said. In their new home—built out of local brick and stone, constructed for comfort, and for safety.

That was her mistake. If she had attended closely, she

would have come to question the implicit acknowledgment of the need to build for safety. But most of the words enchanted with their romantic flow. And she had a great need to believe them, to believe that something, someone, waited for her.

At first she had been puzzled as to why her brother-in-law, Edward Randall Dutchover, would encourage her dear sister to engage in such subterfuge. Why would he be willing to accept another soul for whom he must be responsible in this rough and poorly ordered land? There were few laws here, and fewer constables to enforce what laws were passed, and an indifference in most of the citizens to the matter of personal safety.

She had not fully comprehended what passed for Mr. Dutchover's Christian morals, until he mentioned quite casually that perhaps she would allow him to invest what remained of Emerson's estate in the enlargement of his own holdings. Dear Margaret sat and listened to the preposterous idea, as if she did not understand what her husband was admitting. Harriet quickly understood, and would have laughed if it all were not unbearably sad.

There was no estate; there had been no trust put aside for her; there were no funds carefully invested in a city bank. She was completely without the barest means of sustaining life. And Mr. Dutchover wished to use up what he assumed was available.

Harriet Gliddings put down the shell comb and worked carefully to unplait her generous hair. Her glory, her late husband called it. Her crown. He would stand behind her in the late evening as she sat by the low mahogany vanity; he would rest his hands on the back of her neck, touch her warmed skin gently as he drew fine strands of her hair through his fingers. Taffy colored, Emerson called it, luxurious hair that had an electric life of its own; it caught in the corners of her mouth, shaded her eyes, and wound itself into long, hanging curls.

Emerson sometimes asked her to leave the hair free, and she would comply with her husband's request. Then he would seek her eyes in the beveled mirror, and she would blush, suffused with the most pleasant warmth, which seemed to emanate from the stroking of his fingers on her neck to her throat, across her uncovered bosom. With his eyes locked with hers in the mirror, with his body pressed against her back.

Harriet shook the fine hair and felt its slight stinging on her dry skin. Emerson was dead; she must concentrate on that fact. Emerson was dead . . . and she was in this terrible land. He had died suddenly, killed by a single pistol shot. "Assailant unknown," according to the authorities. She had been left with nothing to her name, no funds to keep the fine apartment along the avenue, no experience to comprehend what the law told her of the death, no friendly lawyer to read the contents of Emerson's neglected will and find in her favor.

She brought up her head with great difficulty and forced her eyes to see past the wavy imperfections of the small looking glass, to examine what was shown to her. A thin face drawn much finer by traveling, wrinkled in the month of living in her new home. The fine taffy hair floated in a static cloud that formed a halo around her face.

The eyes held her chief claim to beauty: wide, green-flecked orbs lined in dark lashes. The nose was long, the forehead broad. Harriet frowned, then swiftly reached up to soothe the new lines; she must be more careful. This face—the eyes and nose, the mouth faintly pink and full lipped, the thick hair piled and plaited around her skull—this was all she had now for her fortune.

Margaret had been clever in her writing, talking of the quality of their new life in Texas. Describing carefully the great number of men populating the new land; fine, hard-working men who were expected to succeed. Lonely men looking for a wife, a companion, a mother. In places the letter had been vague, and Harriet had been eager to take Margaret's lead. Dear sister spoke brightly of working alongside her Edward, of fashioning her own sunbonnet because the skin burned quickly out in the dry, clear air.

There was little said of distance, of loneliness, of daily hardship, and Harriet chose not to read between the lines.

It was the immediate size of the land that shocked her. Riding behind the dogged engine that pulled the cars, they traveled for days across an unendingly yellow landscape. Mountains seen tantalizing in the distance became mounds of bare rock as the train brought them closer and passed them by.

And the heat ... The terrible choice of opening a window to allow in some cooler air and, as quickly, the inevitable cloud of soot, sweeping through and covering everything. Harriet learned quickly to fold a handkerchief and cover her nose and mouth. Almost as if she were passing through the worst parts of an Eastern city slum.

She had not cared at all about the lines in her dear Margaret's face, or the roughness of the hands that held hers. But the ranch, about which Mr. Dutchover boasted incessantly and which he had overblown in his description, the ranch had forced her to open her eyes and truly see what she must now accept. The "bricks" were a clay mud mixed with straw and offal, the rock nothing but crude shale, the water a muddied stream some distance from the hovel. And one could not walk outdoors for pleasure without the aid of a parasol and a stick with which to beat at the sharp bushes for venomous reptiles. Even the few plants that were attractive had thorns and spikes in them and were definitely to be avoided.

She could not seem to stem the bitter turn of her thinking. Yes, there were men here, too many men. Harsh, lean men, with broken hands and worn faces, lacking in the meanest sort of grace and refinement. Men who might speak of the finer things in life, yet kept their families imprisoned in dirt houses, forced their suffering wives to cook outdoors on nothing but the semblance of a fire tamped between smoothed river stones.

There had been a man who came to a gathering complete with the finest references, a man who most definitely did not live up to Harriet's standards. He was reputed to have claimed a great number of these Texas acres; he was said to be a hard worker, a fine gentleman, one of the founders of the town of Marfa. A man to whom success would most assuredly belong. Margaret had said little of the man physically, being too delicate to discuss such matters with her older sister. She did repeat that he was well mannered and respectful, and looking for a helpmate. That was of the greatest importance in the proposed meeting.

Harriet had dressed herself carefully to meet this paragon of manly virtue. She had taken much time and thought to clothing her body, washing her hair with the last of her scented soap, touching her throat and bared arms with a dab of the scent, artfully placing such flowers as were available in this wilderness in the golden waves of her hair. She was ready, she was willing to meet this fine-tempered man.

The gentleman's name was Thomas E. Kersey, and his place of residence was described as a short distance down the creek from Mr. Dutchover's ranch. Five miles, a small trip to be taken in a good buggy, pulled by a sturdy horse. Only five miles, so if there were a liaison, the sisters would not again be cruelly separated. Harriet was encouraged by that bit of information.

But her younger sister had not told her about the severity of those miles, the lack of any sort of road, the brutality of the intervening ground. The proliferation of huge rocks, the growth of large cacti, the deep-cut banks across which no buggy could traverse. Where wild cattle grazed with ease, where the small native ponies galloped with no concern, a lady mounted even on a sturdy cob could not be expected to make the journey in less than a day's time. A journey of five miles, indeed. And for her travels she would need an escort, a strong man who would reclaim the narrow trail each time, cut back the foliage, so the lady would not be injured.

There were few roads in this wilderness, and they went mainly to the fort and surrounding villages. There was a rough trail to Presidio, as it had once been an important place in the area's history, and they were building a new road to Marfa. That village was becoming the core of what was called civilization out here, and Harriet was careful not to laugh at the appellation. The local paper had a share of advertising that she found amusing: the Marfa Hotel proclaimed "meals at all hours." Such an excuse for eating in this establishment Harriet did not wish to contemplate. There was a store that offered general merchandise and ranch supplies; and Labatt and Ruoff, Receiving, Forwarding & Commission Merchants, Hides & Wool, handled the enormous numbers of sheep populating the surrounding lands.

The meeting with Mr. Kersey was a memory she wished to bury. Harriet straightened the silver-handled brush and its matching tortoiseshell comb laid out on the crude table. They were all she had left of her years with Emerson. And they were plated silver. Perhaps she could look to their imperfections as a blessing, for had they been of more value she would have been forced to sell them and would have nothing of Emerson's love, except those few memories not clouded by grief or fear.

She must approach her life now on a logical plane; she must consider always her doubtful position. Thomas Kersey's arrival at the gathering had been much heralded. Harriet had even allowed herself to become intrigued by the glowing reports of the man's high character and determined energies. She would not take notice of the lack of physical description; she would be willing to attribute the oversight to a delicacy of concern for her emotions. Such mention of the physical placings of the paragon's features and form would intrude on the most private aspect of the relationship between a man and a woman. She proceeded with renewed enthusiasm for the upcoming celebration and the shared meal that would accompany it.

There had been strain evident in Margaret's sweet face as she came across the flat grassland that served as the gathering place. But even then Harriet denied the apparent. A man walked with Margaret: Thomas Kersey. A shortened, stubby-legged man a decade and more past her thirty-plus years. The browned and lined face was set in a grim mold. What hair he kept was barely visible under a stained hat, which he removed in a courtly gesture as he bowed to her announced presence. The gesture allowed Harriet to take sight of a circlet of naked pink scalp and its border of dirty, matted curls that hung from each side of the tanned head.

She would give him marks for proper behavior, evidence of some schooling in his ancient past. He took her proffered hand so gently and held it with obvious reverence—and spoke kind words as to the gracing of her beauty and manner on the poor and unknowing souls of Marfa. She was gracious, and allowed sweet approval for his recognition of quality.

But it was beyond her to accept his leather hands, nor could she bear the faint sweetish odor of animals that clung to his scrubbed face and form. And most of all, she could not condone his scrawny back and sloping shoulders, his bandied legs and awkward walk, his words drawled from crude sounds, the bareness of his patched muslin shirt.

The full edge of that memory ran through Harriet as she stared unseeing into the mirror, and she shivered involuntarily. Thomas Kersey had asked permission of Mr. Dutchover to call on his sister-in-law, the Widow Gliddings. Mr. Kersey could not be faulted for his formal address. He could not be faulted for his choosing. But she trembled to think of how the man must live, the coldness of the cabin in which he resided, deep in his vast canyon holdings. The shudder went through her in repeated tracings, drying her mouth, fluttering her heart, quickening her breath until Harriet knew she was in the throes of an attack.

To consider the womanly duties attached to this man's suit ... To consider the work required of her, the demeaning chores and incessant labors ... To consider his hands on her at night, his body close to her in the narrow bed, his right to her spiritual and physical emotions ... It was much more of a price than she was willing to pay.

There were other men in this vast expanse of land; Margaret had listed the names. But the remaining lands were not of the best, and the overflow of water was disappearing in the heat. Mr. Dutchover daily stated that he believed those now coming to Marfa, now seeing the vision of what could be done, would find themselves quickly outside the true adventurers, the true pioneers, those who had already laid their claims and chosen their sites. And, according to Mr. Dutchover, Thomas Kersey was one of those quick to see the future, quick to file on good land, quick to seek out the most valuable location and plot it for his own. The future belonged to those such as Mr. Kersey, even though the present demanded much of these men in time and energy.

Mr. Dutchover was so bold as to tell Harriet outright, one evening after a delicious supper, that he believed Mr. Kersey was her best chance. That he would make a fine husband to her, that the man had expressed interest to Mr. Dutchover in her form and manner, her ability and character. As if Harriet were a brood cow waiting for the proper bloodlines of her mating.

Mr. Dutchover was quite deliberate, although softspoken about it, as he pointed out the harsh facts she did not wish to hear. She was no longer a child; this was said carefully, as Mr. Dutchover was more than her age. She was without an education that could provide her with an existence. And she could not live with her dear sister forever. Unless she became more directly involved with the labor necessary to insure the success of the Dutchover endeavor.

Harriet finished her hair, knotted its bulk at the end of the long braid, wound the length slowly across the bone of her head, and pinned it in place. She would wear the faded calico dress provided by her sister, and she would undertake to weed out the summer misery of their supposed garden. She had seen a pair of the crude yellow gloves worn by most of the women in this land, and she would don them to protect her white skin. There was a bonnet Margaret had left, and a scarf to hide the back of her neck from the sun.

The garden would be weeded and saved; perhaps she would carry a bucket or two of water from the stream to bring some of the plants back to life. She would prove to Mr. Dutchover and herself that she could help sustain them on the ranch. She would earn some of her keep—and prevent herself from having to accept Mr. Kersey's unspoken offer.

He'd forgotten about the new claim along the east branch of Alamito Creek. A family had been here less than a year, settled into a rock and 'dobe cabin under a clump of small trees. McCraw couldn't help but look at the position of the house and recollect the years of defense against the Indians. Anyone foolish enough to build in such a spot would have been killed immediately.

When Chief Alsarte and the Chisos Apache were forced into the Mexican interior, it was the end of the Indians on the border. A lot had changed then, for the white man; it took the Texas Rangers, the Mexican government, and the U.S. Army a whole lot of years to bring the Indians down, but now it was done.

And now these folks were trying for a real home. There was a small garden, half dried and weedy but still alive, a round pen to work saddle stock, a small barn. Even had colored curtains in the windows and a chimney leaned due west from the flat-roofed cook wing. He couldn't remember the name, but they were making a try. He wondered why they settled close to the stream and didn't have a pipe to the house. But it weren't his place, his stake, so he'd keep his mind out of their business and ride on by.

The sorrel whinnied, asking for company, and a horse greeted him from the pen. McCraw held his legs on the lonesome gelding to remind him of his manners. It wouldn't do to gallop into a stranger's yard, so he kept to a cautious walk. It was the second ranch they'd passed on the trail to Fort Davis, and both reminded McCraw of the pressing need to file on his own land and stake his overdue legal claim. He hadn't thought of neighbors as enemies before.

A flash of color, a strange sound, sent the sorrel dancing.

McCraw settled the horse, then raised his arm and waved at the figure moving in the garden. McCraw shook his head, wondering at the ignorance of folks. Planting vegetables and flowers in a desert took too much water, too much time to be of certain value. But some folks didn't learn easy; it seemed to him people always were wanting what they'd left behind.

He waved again, but the figure still did not respond. It looked to be a woman working inside the picket fence, a tall woman from what he could judge. He steadied the horse, stood up in his stirrups, and called out to let the lady know she had company. But she did not see him or hear his calling. McCraw frowned and let the sorrel drift closer.

The horse almost jumped out from under him when the woman screamed. McCraw spun the horse and heard the cry again. She jumped backward, put hands to her face, and screamed again. The bonnet slipped from her head; he saw enough to memorize the color of her hair, the whiteness of her skin, as he leapt from the sorrel, drew the saddle gun from the scabbard, and jumped the low fence.

The woman was pinned to the picket slabs, hands fluttering at her face, mouth wide, eyes frightened. McCraw guessed quickly—a poisonous snake or lizard. He scanned the immediate ground, the rifle resting easy on his hip. The woman saw him then and screamed again, covered her mouth with one hand and waved the other in a vague gesture. The lady was unharmed, to judge from the strength of her cries, but something bobbed and wove through the scrub and out through the fence in erratic flight.

McCraw raised the rifle as he closed in on the woman. She gasped; he could see the paleness of her fright, smell the dark fear. Her eyes came to his. He nodded to an unspoken question, waved a small circle with the rifle as a comforting gesture.

"Ma'am, you tell me what you saw. Where it got to. Nothing much come to this garden be dangerous for you, 'cepting a rank coyote or a snake. You got the yard pretty well clipped; snakes don't like having no cover. Ma'am, you tell me what got you spooked."

He meant to be reassuring, but the words came out flat and hard—and the woman showed only scorn for the intended gallantry. He sounded like a country fool, and she still had not answered. So he tried again.

"Lady, whatever it be, it ain't still here. You're safe, ma'am. Ain't nothing going to harm you."

He was the fool, his tongue thick with poor words running in his mind. She could feel nothing but contempt for him, for the childish sentiments he tried to give her. A fine lady, city bred, isolated in a strange wilderness. Dealing with the rough mouthings of a stranger. He felt for the brim of his hat, knowing the gesture came too late for any good.

She continued to glare at him, cross with the rudeness. Finally she tugged the dangling bonnet back into place—and he was sorry she had covered the bright hair and hidden her face. For she was beautiful, the most beautiful woman McCraw had ever seen. And he knew she already despised him. He was truly the fool to become tongue-tied by the sight of another man's wife working in a garden. He let the butt of the saddle gun rest on the ground and now tried to pretend to be concerned with her well-being, when all he wanted was to get back on the sorrel and get the hell out of this damning place.

He must think her a silly female, to be surprised and panicked by a rabbit jumping out of the weeds and hopping past her face as she bent down to tug out a spiky plant. Which stuck a needle in her palm and stung her badly. A silly, foolish woman.

He showed little concern, said nothing disapproving to her, and yet she had not answered his repeated questions as to her condition. Harriet wished only to hide as she gazed at the face of her savior. How could she tell this man why she had been frightened? True, it was a big rabbit, bigger than any she had seen before, but still it was only a rabbit.

She tried desperately to compose herself, relying on the

old habits of fixing her hair and repinning her bonnet, tying the bow carefully, pulling the ends to be even and neat. Then she lifted her shoulders, drew a comforting deep breath, and tried to look at the man with all the strength and dignity left at her command. Her skin still burned from her shame, but she would not let him know that.

Be calm, rational, answer the questions, ask him if he would care for a drink of something cool before he resumed his journey. Possibly the stalling techniques would allow her to recover enough to explain and even make a small joke at her own expense, to apologize for the inconvenience.

She took a long look at the man, and she was surprised; he was handsome, tall and lean, with brown hair grayed at the temples, a good face bronzed by the sun. The clear eyes looked steadily at her, and she flushed again. It became difficult for her to hold her gaze; as if he could see into her and know all her deficiencies.

True, he was not at all well dressed, but ragged and travel stained. Perhaps he was little more than one of the many drifters Mr. Dutchover warned her about. But there was a substance to him in the strong shoulders and long legs, the shirt carefully patched, the pants lined with greasy leather, that led her to suspect he was a local rancher. Whoever he was, she had never seen his like in her life before.

He held his weapon casually. Harriet found she could not take her eyes from the small circle of the barrel. Steeled and perfectly round, the black hole glared at her. She was suddenly glad the man had not seen the offending rabbit and shot it. She was unused to weapons; Emerson had carried a small pistol, a derringer he called it, snugged inside his tailored coat. For protection against the rough elements, he would say. And he rarely distressed her by putting the pistol in the open. She had appreciated his concern for her nature.

But this man was different; he stood motionless, one hand loosely curled around the weapon, the other hand at his side. She had seen his belated attempt to remove his hat, but he made no attempt to introduce himself. He was at quiet attention, waiting for something from her. Harriet felt the blushing begin at her throat, and she let her gaze fall more properly to the ground in front of her.

"Sir, I thank you for your kind rescue. But I am ashamed to say it was nothing more than a large rabbit that so frightened me. It must be as frightened as I am, for it left here quite rapidly. I do apologize for my interruption of your errand, and thank you for your attention to my distress."

The inane explanation would not stop coming. The man was a local ranch hand, a cowboy. A man more used to the comfort of a rifle than the company of a lady. She did not understand the distress she felt. She did not understand it at all.

She thought him a complete fool. Standing close to him, mocking him with her words. He was uneasy hearing the clear voice, watching the sun's colors cross her face. He thought he'd met the folks living here; he thought he remembered a skinny man. Named Hanover. And a younger wife. Younger than this woman, and pretty. But not like this woman was beautiful. If he had seen her before, he would have remembered. She could not be Hanover's wife. McCraw wanted to wipe at the sweat on his face and scratch the itch under his belt. Instead, he risked another look at the woman.

The sweet delivery of her words made him conscious of his ignorance. She had the stand and the sound and the taste of something much finer than life on the plains. He read her eyes and flinched from what he saw. A beautiful face, pleasing to a man's gaze, and more else than he would ever know.

The heat rose in him; she was a lady, someone else's lady, not a woman for a man's base thoughts, but a woman to grace his house, strengthen his courage. She would give him a good family, the pride of strong children. His face turned bright red; he half raised the rifle, then dropped his head in the semblance of courtesy. Once again he tried politeness in his speech:

"Ma'am, most things are scary if they jump when you ain't ready. Me, I've gone sideways from a falling leaf, and that sorrel of mine, he's dumped me plain in the road for speaking up after a quiet hour's ride. We all got things going in our heads. We all jump sometime when it ain't needed."

It was awkward and stupid to his own ears. But at least he was freed from standing awestruck in the middle of their garden. McCraw looked at his feet and blushed again; he had both boots planted firmly on a wilting vine that carried bright-colored flowers. He picked up a foot to release the vine, and the woman let out a small cry of alarm. McCraw balanced for an impossible moment, one foot dug into the dry soil, one foot hung in midair, like a half-stuffed scarecrow in a dried August field.

The man was a bumpkin, yet he meant well, for he again tried to soothe her fears, and he had come to her rescue without hesitation. Even though she jumped from him, as if he and not the poor rabbit had been the one to frighten her. Harriet put a hand over her heart and felt its wild thumpings, then realized the direction of her hand. How could she ever explain to the poor man that he had acted correctly, and—

"Ma'am, my name's McCraw—"

"Sir, I am Harriet—"

He laughed gently and held out his hand in a gesture of kindness. He was offering a graceful way in which to end an uncomfortable situation. The hand waited between them, the long fingers uncurled, the broad palm scarred with old lines. Harriet Gliddings accepted the offer and touched his dry skin, then tried again to explain.

"Sir. I am Harriet Gliddings, Mrs. Emerson Gliddings." As soon as she spoke Emerson's name she saw the strange man flinch. "I am sister to Mrs. Dutchover, whom perhaps you have already met. You are a neighbor of theirs, sir, or perhaps a traveler through this hot land. In either case, I thank you again for your gallant assistance. I will know the next time not to scream at the approach of a rabbit. Even if it is a Texas rabbit of large proportions."

She was wife to another; McCraw felt the wound. Dutchover was the rancher's name, related to her by marriage. Her words had stopped, and she was waiting for a reply.

"Name's McCraw. James McCraw ... ma'am. I live downriver, near Spencer's Rancho. Didn't know there was more living here past Dutchover and his wife. You and your ... husband must be new come to here. Ain't been by in six months or more. Headed up to Fort Davis—"

He stopped abruptly, conscious of the meager quality of his words. And the woman had little more to add, which left them both in embarrassed silence. Until the sorrel gelding whinnied and was answered by a distant horse. McCraw turned and saw movement through the bushes, along the stream on the opposite side. He scanned the sparse trees, the rifle held to his hip, and quickly picked out the shaded silhouette of a wagon coming along the dusty road.

The vehicle was pulled by a mismatched team of a paint and a lazy gray. The driver was Dutchover, and a lady sat beside him who was his wife. Mrs. Gliddings waved, the woman waved back. Dutchover guided the team past the stream crossing and into the yard. McCraw stepped back and offered Mrs. Gliddings the path to the wagon.

Margaret was smiling at her from the wagon seat; Mr. Dutchover was scowling, no doubt on Mr. McCraw's account. Harriet hoped that her sister would think to invite Mr. McCraw to stay for a meal, or the night. It was close to evening now, and the land around them could be dangerous. Then she smiled at the silly thought. Mr. McCraw obviously knew well enough to care for himself in this dramatic landscape—and still had the generosity of spirit to care for others who fancied themselves in dire need of rescue.

As she walked ahead of the man, she became too aware of the loose construction of the calico dress she wore. A soft cotton garment that had too few petticoats under it for decency's sake. There was little to hide her from a man's imagination. But then, she had seen little but disapproval in Mr. McCraw's eyes, and that would not change. Except perhaps to derision as she stumbled now on the path.

Margaret Dutchover loved her sister with the devotion of an adoring child. She idolized Harriet's beauty and education, her fine temper and delicate ways. And she had accepted Emerson carefully, too aware of Harriet's love for her husband to ever voice her own concerns about him. Despite the dark circumstances of his passing, it was a pleasure to have Harriet's company now, although Mr. Dutchover did state occasionally that Harriet was too refined to survive as a rancher's wife. Margaret was much divided on the subject. If Sophie Bogel could not only survive cooking on her outside fire and living in an adobe hut, but could even create a literary atmosphere at her place, then certainly Harriet would do as well, once she understood more completely the demands of a wife in this wilderness called Texas.

As the wagon stopped in the yard, Margaret was able to make out the features of the tough-looking man who walked behind Harriet. She had met Mr. McCraw only once, more than six months ago, and remembered little of the meeting, as the man barely spoke to her or to her husband. It was said that Mr. McCraw had lived here most of his life and knew everything about the land. Mr. Dutchover had asked his advice, but Margaret realized her husband would not follow it, that he did not like the man or trust his knowledge.

Margaret looked again at her sister. There was a change in Harriet, a softening of her mouth, an altering of her rigid walk. The pale cheeks glowed, locks of hair had escaped the bonnet and curled about her face, framing it most lovingly. Harriet's beauty put Margaret's wan prettiness to shame at that moment. Then Mr. Dutchover gripped Margaret above the elbow, and his thin voice broke in ahead of her gentle question.

"McCraw, good day to you. Is there something we can do to help you, or is there a problem of sorts? We will be of assistance, of course, if you will be so kind as to explain the circumstance."

McCraw placed the man now, had seen him in Marfa a few times, Fort Davis, too. Hadn't taken much to the man—and found no improvement in him this time. There was little sympathy or humor in Dutchover, and no good sense with his animals. The team was sweated and gaunt even though water ran in the streams they'd had to cross. The man's wife was flushed and hot, her face drawn and tired. She'd been that way when he'd met her and her husband in Fort Davis, at Shield's Dry Goods. Man ought to take better care of what was his.

Mrs. Gliddings stood near him now; he could feel the tension in her caused by the abrupt questioning. McCraw shifted and put his shoulder ahead of the lady's arm, holding her silent by his rudeness. It was easy enough; she already knew he had no manners.

"Dutchover, ain't nothing wrong. No trouble. Came in to water my sorrel, been a long day with miles ahead of me. Got to talking with Mrs. Gliddings here, even though we ain't been properly introduced. She was taking on her neighborly duties, offering me a drink and a bite, if I wished." He turned to the beautiful woman and bowed, conscious of his stiff posture. "Thank you for your kindness, ma'am. But I got some riding still to do. Mrs. Gliddings." He touched the brim of his hat and smiled at her, then looked to Dutchover and his wife. "Ma'am. 'Preciate the kindness. Mr. Dutchover."

He was gone then, but not before Mrs. Dutchover thanked him profusely for keeping her widowed sister company while she and Mr. Dutchover were unavoidably away for the day. The bright sorrel danced a jig under McCraw, and McCraw shared his mood. He felt a lightness in his final salute. Out of sight, he let the sorrel run full-out.

The "Widow Mrs. Gliddings." Sweet words to ride with him to Fort Davis.

CHAPTER EIGHT

McCraw finally reined in the sorrel and forced himself to think sensibly. Then he felt the pulled muscles in his face and knew the stupid grin was back in place. She was a widow. He laughed wildly, head thrown back. She was a widow.

He would work hard and add to the ranch, build up a bigger herd of cattle, even add on a room, or think of moving, building a new house with details just for her. It wouldn't be much work for him; then he could ride to Dutchover's and make his offer.

He slapped the sorrel on the neck; the stout horse squealed and jerked sideways, and McCraw was loosened in the saddle. His right leg twisted under him, and he felt the hard strain, felt the bone creak as pressure jammed it in the stirrup. It was a reminder he needed. He wasn't a youngster, a kid first time in love.

But he could see the woman's face clear and plain, he could smell the sweet honey of her skin, touch the texture of her hair. That vision was enough.

There had been other women, and one way past in time. When he had been a boy, a soldier lost from his company, riding to Texas along the banks of the great river. A woman whose safe passage had been entrusted to him, whose child called him shyly by name. The journey stayed with him, long after the nights of paid women. A bitter and sad picture. He had failed the woman, had lain senseless in the dirt while her son, Tomás, had killed for the life of his mother.

McCraw grunted with the strength of that memory; he had never come to deal with the pictures. A child had saved him. And the woman had taken him, held him, given him life and love in the warmth of an old barn. An act of faith and hope that kept them both in peace while the injured child slept and finally recovered.

The mother and son rode with him, the conscience of that time was with him, always. He had failed, badly. It would not happen again; he would not fail Harriet Gliddings. She would come to him and he would protect her, console her, love her, and keep her with him. She was a second chance for him, the center of the new life he wanted to build. He was brightened by her vision, made whole by the texture of her words. He could not fail this time.

Then the doubt flooded him; it couldn't work, too foolish, childish. All wrong for an old man like himself to want such a woman. A woman who would share with her man, perhaps come to love him. It wasn't for a man living a life in this hellhole, not a life of loving.

Too many differences; she was beautiful, educated. Probably laughing even now at the oddness of her cowboy rescuer, talking to the sister, dismissing his unmentioned interest. She could have no interest in him.

But a lightness in his mind, the heavy throbbing in his groin, told him differently. He was confused, lost, bewildered. And it didn't matter. It couldn't work. But he would try. This one more time.

It took the best part of two days for McCraw to reach Fort Davis. He stuck to the old trail, one he'd ridden many times. He remembered clearly the first time he rode into the new town; he could still see the stark outlines of the slab huts, crude tents, hastily built corrals. There had been a dusty military parade ground bordered by old trees and a strange assortment of people who came with the new settlement, eager to make their mark, take their profit.

He'd ridden here with Limm Tyler, fell in love with his first girl. He couldn't remember her name now, but he never lost the pleasure of the turmoil of feelings and urges that held him as he watched her from a distance.

He was caught wide open, flooded with the past. Limm Tyler—found drunk outside in a storm, taken with fever and chills and gone in less than a month. Buried six years, mourned by Rosa Ignacio while McCraw came to understand her love.

Rosa Ignacio—died more than a year past, victim as McCraw had been to another violent storm. A herd of panicked steers stampeded through a fence to overrun the yard and carry Rosa beneath their hooves as she ran to stop them. Their power cracked her like a melon torn too late from the garden. McCraw saw her disappear and ran into the herd, was bowled over and trampled and broken.

A week later a neighbor rode into the yard and found McCraw, wrapped in a stinking blanket, sleeping close to water. Despite the July heat McCraw was cold, shivering from a high fever, the result of festering wounds. Even hurt, he'd been able to stack a few stones over Rosa Ignacio's body before he was too weakened by his injuries, and he'd had the presence to find himself a warm blanket and get close to the water before he passed out. The neighbor was awed by McCraw's tough instinct and spread word of the story to the newcomers who might still believe the land was easy for the taking.

He was shaking now, hands barely wrapped on the reins. It was the impatience of the sorrel gelding that brought him back; the horse snorted and bucked sideways, ears pricked at the thick brush. He had to pay attention. McCraw cursed the horse and touched a hand to the saddle gun at his knee.

It was nothing more than a horse and rider proceeding quietly along the side of the new road. Almost to Fort Davis. The unknown traveler disappeared, leaving McCraw to laugh at himself as he pushed the sorrel through the brush and out to the packed earth of the track. Making more work for himself, keeping blindly to an old way when the new worked quicker, simpler. It was time, now, for him to remember this day and this year. To remember Harriet Gliddings and let her temptation draw him even with the rest of the world.

Fort Davis was quiet, too peaceful. Even the figures seen from a distance moved slowly, as if something more than the summer had taken the heart of the place. What McCraw had heard in Marfa a month back made sense now, a statement from one of the newcomers, a slender little man named William Bogel. The words puzzled McCraw then, but fell into place from the lessons of the past three days.

"Fort Davis is dead, sure enough. A town that doesn't want the railroad coming through, that town will waste away and die. The future is in the trains, the railroad's the mark of the new day. And if Fort Davis doesn't want the railroad's business, then another town will take the work and the money. The railroad is our future out here."

McCraw wondered briefly if Fort Davis still had the county records. Or should he have ridden to Marfa, where Bogel made his proclamation? The town had a hotel now, and a new owner for the mercantile. But he'd always ridden to Fort Davis on business, like listing old Tyler's death, and then Rosa's, when he could travel in a wagon. Though no one seemed to care much about the death of an ancient Mexican woman.

The force of an old anger came back; McCraw had to steady his trembling hands on the sorrel's neck. Old thoughts and habits were giving him hell. It was no good for a man to ride with nothing but buried memories and lost desires for company. It made him full strange, allowed him to talk in foul words unfit for others' ears.

He rode into Fort Davis slowly, guiding the sorrel along the familiar streets. The sounds came in around him, wagons drawn by laboring horses, groups of people busy talking. Sights and smells flowed over him: wooden houses set back from the street; garbage rotting in the closed alleys; buildings boarded up over empty windows. Fort Davis was founded an Anglo town, yet the streets were lined with wooden walkways, covered by the deep, slanting roof called a *ramada* farther south. Even though Anglos ran the post town, they appreciated the necessity for shade in the fierce Texas sun.

Then he realized he didn't know where he was going and saw a man stooped over by a hitching rail. He leaned down to greet the man and ask his questions.

"Mister, where does a man file on land here? The county records still kept here, or I got to ride somewhere else?"

The man looked up at McCraw, teeth clamped around a chewed pipe, eyes shaded by a wide-brimmed hat. The man removed the pipe deliberately, spat to the side and wiped his mouth, then ran his fingers down his pants leg. McCraw wanted to hurry the answer, to reach down and prod the man with his finger. But he held in his temper, conscious he was the outsider, the stranger asking his question.

The man opened his mouth to speak, then appeared to change his mind and stuck the pipe back in place, shook his head fiercely, and waved an arm under the sorrel's nose. The horse stepped back in alarm; McCraw clamped his legs to the horse and almost dismounted, then shook his head over the whole incident. He put spurs to the sorrel, and the horse sidestepped close enough that now the wordless man himself had to step back. The man tripped on the closeness of a wooden walkway and grabbed for the hitch rail. When McCraw looked back, he saw the man sitting on the boards, pipe stuck in his mouth, hat jerked down to cover his face. It was almost enough to soothe McCraw's touchy temper.

"I saw you trying to speak to Wister. And I would bet you got a poor answer. If I were a betting man that is. Wister's dumb, hasn't said a word in the four years he has been sitting right in that spot. I don't know what the problem is, he can't tell us. Doesn't write, can't speak. It is a hellish way to go through this life."

The friendly voice came from deep in the *ramada*

shadow. McCraw climbed down off the sorrel and tied up the horse, loosened the *cincha*, and slapped the animal's damp neck. He thumbed back his hat, then jerked it down on his forehead. He could not see the face of the man who spoke to him, so he would not be easily visible, either. He stepped up on the shaky walkway and looked into the shade.

"I did ask him a question, looking for directions to the land office. If there is still an office here. Want to file on some land. That son, he made to speak, then said nothing. I purely didn't know."

The voice opened up friendly again, and McCraw relaxed.

"Sometimes Wister does that. Kind of a strange way to pass the time; seems a poor joke. But it must please him somehow, for he is apt to behave as if he could answer the question, then he puts that infernal pipe back in his mouth and waits. I have seen him beaten and dragged for that behavior. Yet he persists. Very strange."

It was a townsman, suited and wearing a light collar and loose tie; he could see that much, but the man's face remained in shadow. McCraw judged the man was tall and thin, but his face and eyes remained hidden. He drifted to the railing and looked out to the street, then glanced sideways at the man who had tried to set him straight.

"I thank you for the explanation, mister. But I am still needing to know where I record a title. Can't spend the day standing with a stranger; got my chores to do here, then more work waiting at home. Thanks for the information on your town fool, but I need to get to my own business."

He put a finger to his hat and made as if to leave, then heard a slight chuckle. It did not set well with him. McCraw put his hand to his pistol, planted his feet, and drew a deep breath.

"I do apologize. Mr. . . . ?"

McCraw didn't answer. He would not yet accept apology. He didn't like being in town, didn't like the conversation, the waste of time. Then the odd man spoke again, and finally McCraw relaxed.

"I do indeed apologize, sir. I am the man whom you seek this fine day. I am a lawyer practicing in this town, and can help you file your claim, fill out the forms. My fees are mild, and my conversation good once I stop playing and get to work. I am truly repentant for my mischief; please step inside. I can see you are too busy a man to afford patience with such fools as I am. My hand on this, sir."

McCraw saw the white hand flash toward him, saw the white line of teeth in the man's smile. He went over the words and felt the raw edge of his temper. Too jumpy, too quick to take offense. He had to remember he was with people now. He took the offered hand, pumped it twice vigorously, and let it drop.

"Name's McCraw. James Henry McCraw. I live down near Spencer's Rancho. Let's get to business. What's the fee, how long does this take?"

"Ah, yes, Mr. McCraw. I have long wondered about you. Wondered when you would feel the weight of the world and find it necessary to make legal your long tenancy on the land. We have had old-timers such as you lose their land to the greedy eye of a new rancher. It is sad but legal. No one yet has filed on what it is known you claim, but I would not trust chance much longer. There are too many people hurrying to our piece of heaven, Mr. McCraw. Too many, and among them will be some with lesser scruples than the rest of us. Come inside. We will get right to work."

The strange man opened a door hidden behind his long frame and pointed for McCraw to go in ahead of him. As the man came in behind McCraw and closed the door, he continued to talk.

"Of course I jest, sir; Fort Davis has made its dying decision and this town is no longer leader in the county. A terrible mistake, to reject the railroad's passage through the land. A terrible mistake. But for now at least, you must still come to Fort Davis to record land transactions, and I am always ready to serve. How much longer this will be the case, I do not know."

As he walked into the dusty office, McCraw wondered where all these folks with their fancy word-stringing had come from. Where did they learn to talk such, and why would they bother to puff up their thought to twenty words where two would do better? To confuse a man, throw him off his straight line, befuddle him with dancing ideas until he was dazed and quieted, hog-tied and ready to be branded.

He'd been doing the same, shuffling and mumbling and working his own trick, using cowboy ways instead of dime store words. He'd been no different than Dutchover and now this man, making quick judgments, using his old-fashioned manners and habits to get what he wanted.

McCraw laughed then; he'd been more than a fool these past days. The lawyer laughed with him and stepped into the light near the desk. Direct light came through a window; McCraw could see the man's face and relaxed.

McCraw stuck out his hand again, and said, "Name's McCraw, like I said out there. Your name?"

"Ah, yes, excuse my lapse. I am Wilson Voeckes. Your lawyer, here to serve you. Pleased to meet you, Mr. James McCraw."

Voeckes was not his age, but maybe ten years younger. Tall, past McCraw's own height, and thin, with a white face and long jaw. Big ears stuck out at either side of the skull and big teeth showed under the sandy mustache. The eyes were bright, and glowed a fiery blue as the man looked straight at him now and gestured McCraw into the chair on the near side of his desk. Voeckes kept moving: hands touching something on the desk; smoothing his thinning hair; feet slipping on the wooden floor; eyes swiveling to see everything in sight.

McCraw liked the set of the man, the energy and confidence in his bright blue eyes. It seemed Voeckes agreed, without needing to say it, that the two men could trust each other.

They got to the business as promised: Voeckes sat behind his desk and spread out the maps. The paper cracked easily in his hands, and McCraw could make no sense of the crossings of red- and black- and green-colored lines. But he was patient this time, certain that Voeckes knew his job.

"You will be claiming land to the south and west of Mr. Spencer's, so I would assume. His land is not claimed, but I have marked it on the map and try to dissuade new people from attempting to file. Mr. Spencer may be more involved now with the mines, but he has a claim few courts in the land would dispute. Spencer's power is diminishing, as is Faver's and most of the old guard, but they have the name yet, and it is still potent."

McCraw almost objected to the callous dismissal of John Spencer, and Voeckes must have read the dismay he felt, for his face softened and he hastened to relieve his new client of unnecessary worry.

"The land is his in the time-honored manner, and there are few who would take the quarrel to him. But his son's whereabouts are unknown and his family is gone. Sometime soon the old man will die, and a hardy soul will stake a claim that I will be forced to record. I am sorry for that, James, but it is the way. Which is why I am glad you are here now, to prevent this happening to you. Show me what you wish to have."

With Voeckes's assistance, McCraw read through the map and found his boundaries. He could claim one section, or two, of land with water on it. And he could have as many as seven sections of dry land, provided he could stock it and hold it from the other ranchers. Or he could claim the water and lease the remaining land. Few would quarrel, as without access to water the dry sections were valueless. McCraw began to understand the map and its laws, and he finally saw a pattern.

The government surveyors had not known everything about the land. Some of the springs were not marked and those sections were considered "dry." Bitter Springs was not shown on its section of the map, and McCraw saw that.

TEXAS SPRINGS

Voeckes didn't notice a change in McCraw, but went on marking and explaining for his client's benefit, making everything clear.

"The government is adamant about filing, James. I am assuming you wish to have that section along the Rio Grande that Spencer gave you. Ah, yes, don't be so surprised. Everyone knows about John Spencer and you. You are both almost legends. So it is a given that you will keep that section, but you must take more land. That isn't enough to survive."

A legend. McCraw snorted to himself and listened as Voeckes talked on. He suffered only a short battle with his conscience before he decided what he would do. Some of what Voeckes was saying began to filter through, and McCraw began to listen again.

"The State Land Act, passed in eighty-three, doesn't allow a rancher to take more than one section, which is ridiculous here. So most are picking their main section, then leasing the rest from the railroad or running their cattle where they choose and periodically rounding them up for counting. It is possible to take two sections, but only one of them may have water. You already have the river section, James, so you might as well try for a dry section and keep things as legal as possible. You can run your cattle out there at will, and no man will contest your claim to the river."

It was quickly settled; he would take Bitter Springs as if it were dry. And he would claim the land between there and the river by word of mouth. Without water on it, the land toward the Santiago Mountains, west toward the Bofecillos, would have no value. He would be safe. The Chisos banded him on the right, the river was at his back, the edge of Spencer's claim was to the left. No one knew about Bitter Springs. It was his by right, by years of association. He would not pay the government price for what was already earned.

He clamped down on the anger inside, for Wilson Voeckes was looking at him strangely, and his hand pained where he clenched the arm of the chair. It was a poor collection of thoughts that were with him as he signed his name and claimed his land. Voeckes had Spencer's bit of paper unfolded and smoothed out on the desk.

"I will have to keep this for some time. It must be recorded in the books, and copied several times. But it will come back to you, James. All proper and legal. Is there something wrong?"

He had to be normal, relaxed, even pleased with the business at hand. It wasn't for Voeckes or anyone else to understand what he felt as the signature and seal, the mound of legal papers, ended his freedom in the *Despoblado*. He looked at his signature on the forms: shaky, unused, barely readable.

Voeckes finished his share of the signing and handed the dry pen to McCraw. "One more time and I'd say you've done a good day's work. And I would also say we take ourselves to a fine establishment of your choice and celebrate your emergence into the world around you. For you are no longer of the past, my new friend. You are a signed and thriving, industrious member of our county, and as such deserve the best poor Fort Davis has to offer. Will you join me, James?"

The outstretched hand. The pen held between two fingers. The words suggesting friendship. McCraw fought a short battle of conscience: what he was doing was no different than what others had done. And what he knew came from the hard years when no one else fought or cared. He would take Bitter Springs, he would become successful. And he would take his suit to Mrs. Harriet Gliddings—and there would be no ammunition to hold him back.

He coughed, and Voeckes flinched. Then McCraw grinned across the width of the desk. It wasn't easy to figure Voeckes's way of talking, but that, too, was part of his new world. McCraw felt different, ready for his new start. He dipped the pen in the inkwell and began to write one more time.

"Mr. Voeckes, you got yourself a taken invite."

CHAPTER NINE

The dark buckskin colt was turning out even better than Matt hoped. And he had to keep reminding himself the horse didn't belong to him, never would. He had claim to the strawberry roan and nothing more. Matt let out a breath and forced himself to see the truth. The roan was healed and getting fat on grass and water. The little horse was spoiled now. There would be fireworks when Matt saddled to ride out, like he'd said he would two months past when he'd pushed his way into the ranch out of desperation.

No one cared that he stayed. McCraw gave him work every day, and the two vaqueros, they did nothing to set off his temper. He'd bet they had grown use to his cooking, spoiled like the little roan with too much good food. It didn't make sense no other way; the fat one's shoulder was well healed, the broncs well started.

Matt wasn't certain how or why, but in the rough men he worked with, and the desolate land of the ranch, he'd found himself a place.

It weren't a place you could point to on a map or call out by name. No sir, the boss took care of that. When he'd come back more'n a month ago, he'd come in waving a piece of paper and rattling a collection of bottles in his war bags. Drinking liquor with a sweet taste to it, not like border mescal or gut tequila. Smooth wine from El Paso, he said, with an easy taste going down.

The next day was pure hell but no one complained. McCraw said they were celebrating, and that they did. Drank all the wine, ate the whole carcass of a sheep spitted over a slow fire, tore through two pans of Matt's biscuits, and finished off three pies, down to licking their fingers and running them inside the pans. The tastes seemed to go with the flavor of the wine.

Another night came, and Matt didn't remember a whole lot of it. It was lost in the heady feeling of bubbles trapped in his skull, it disappeared in the brightness of the stars, the cool air, the company of sometime friends.

The company of friends. Matt shied from much thinking, but he kept these pieces intact. McCraw's hand on his shoulder when he made a toast. Miguel accepting the bottle and drinking from the unwiped neck. Silvestre grinning with all those white teeth and patting Matt's shoulder, thanking Matt for the last piece of pie. A maverick group, but a company of friends.

First thing McCraw promised, they moved the house. Not just moving it, they took out everything could be used again—the doors, the window frames, the long poles for the roof. And dragged all that a long distance to a new place. Matt didn't see the why, but he followed the orders, head ringing from the wine, belly swollen and ready to explode.

He blamed the wine for his taking the chance, but Matt knew better. He did it; he tried out the buckskin colt that day, dragging poles wrapped with rawhide. If he'd been sober, he never would have tried, but he roped the poles and took a loose dally around the horn. He talked the buckskin into the first step; the colt felt the pull from his back—half kicked at the rope on his side and stood still, trembling under Matt's hand but quiet. A few words, a hand on the tense neck, and the big colt stepped into the rope and snaked the poles forward.

A lot changed after that day, but Matt kept his worry about it to the back of his thinking. He didn't have time to do otherwise; McCraw was obsessed. Miguel complained and Silvestre moved slow, but they stayed and they did their work. McCraw ordered Matt around as if he were hired on, wanting him out working the colts, wanting them used hard, tempered with miles of travel. So Matt went out to check the cattle, rode the lonely miles across the grass to show the young geldings what was expected of them.

The new place was big, with a good kitchen, a room McCraw called his office, and rooms off the back. Bedrooms Miguel and Silvestre thought were theirs, until McCraw showed them the rest of the plans. A new barn, and a longhouse where the hands would sleep. Matt listened to it all and guessed McCraw was serious.

Water bothered Matt. He'd lived most of his life near the Rio Grande, more to the north but still where water was the first importance. And when McCraw moved away from the river against all common sense, Matt was worried. Until he was set to digging a ditch, putting down half logs hollowed out, to pipe water into the house. McCraw showed him the spring, and Matt smiled at the boss's face when he dug his fingers in the dirt and brought up mud, then freed the sweet-tasting water. Matt quit worrying about McCraw at that point and began to think on the stock.

He spent a lot of miles circling the cattle, watching for lamed mamas, sored calves, yearlings bogged down in sand, clusters of flies on a bull's hide. Anything that threatened the herd. McCraw was strong on the work, and it was a lot of riding for Matt. But it was better than shoveling mud and straw for bricks or raising walls and dragging out dried cactus and stumps for fencing. He'd work half dead on horseback before he'd do much on foot, and McCraw knew that. Silvestre and Miguel didn't have the same pride. And the riding taught Matt the lay of the land, the rise and fall of the arroyos and cuts, the bogs and wet springs.

He had the buckskin colt under him now, and they were headed toward the big Chisos Basin. The other three broncs were easy to break and ride, smooth-gaited and even-tempered like most of McCraw's brand, but it was the big colt that took Matt's fancy.

He was worried. Somewhere out ahead there should be a small band of mares, the stallion, and most of last summer's yearlings. McCraw told him some of the mares bred late and he wanted those foals checked before winter got to them. Matt'd seen signs, the passage of unshod hooves with a good number of babies. But it was as if the stallion knew Matt was looking for him and was set in his horse mind to keep the band hidden. Matt didn't blame the old horse, but it was his job to check on them.

And he was worried some about the yearlings. Shoved out this summer by their new nursing mamas, ready to join in with the two- and three-year olds. They were all branded, so no one would think they were wild stock and free for grabbing. Matt laughed at himself; no decent *mesteñero* would mistake one of McCraw's band for a wild bronc. No one could put a rope over a good horse like any one of those and believe he was hauling in a range pony. The man would be outright lying to himself, thieving another man's money.

Matt figured he knew. He'd roped and wrangled the wild ones and worked the good-blooded stuff. Never had any doubt which was which, though once or twice, or more, his rope had settled on the wrong neck. It was lying and pure theft, he knew that.

He'd ridden a wide circle in the morning and crossed the tracks of the main herd coming out from watering. But close water didn't always bring in the young stuff, at least not in the last two days. Matt couldn't figure where they were drinking, and it bothered him. Fall heat shimmered in the distant mountains, and the notch of the Chisos Basin was easy to see. There was even color in the high trees, a light-shaded yellow and some red. The band of misfits and babies could be drinking up there. Matt was pure concerned.

He divided his time in watching the ground and glancing at his direction. He needed to check for tracks, and he had to keep knowing where he was headed. He glanced at the sun, wiped at his eyes. It would be time soon enough to find shade and give the buckskin a rest. A boulder would do, or the off side of a wash bank. A horse sweated out his heart in this country. A poor rider could take the life out of a good mount and milk his own self dry without much thought. It was time to rest the buckskin and give them both a sip of water.

Where he was now seemed familiar to Matt; he recognized the downhill slope into a dry wash. One with a steep banking on the south that offered shade for horse and rider. Time for water. Time to loosen the buckskin's *cincha*, punch the crown of his hat, and offer a sip, then pour water on his kerchief to wipe his own face, rinse out his mouth, and set back, think some. Time to try to outguess the lost broncs.

Matt slipped the colt's bit and hung the bridle off his neck. The lazy bronc showed no interest in wandering, so Matt gave him a hatful of water, had his own swallow, and then sat back against the cool wall to puzzle out the disappearance. He looked out across the wash, eyes burned by the shining sand. Hot enough now to wash out most of the sky's color, hot enough to soak his shirt with sweat only setting quiet, thinking, dozing in the slow midday quiet.

Voices startled him. The bronc must have heard the noise, for he lifted his big head and drew back his lips to call out. Matt rolled on his knees and wrapped his hands on the black muzzle. The sound was choked in his fists; the buckskin skidded back, and Matt almost lost him.

The bright sun surprised both horse and rider, and Matt had time to draw the big head down by pinching the nostrils below the soft bone. He bridled the colt and shoved him back in the underhang, stroking the skin of the muzzle until the colt quit fighting and was still.

Voices in rapid-fire talk. The words were brittle and clear—and almost overhead. Matt tried to listen. The words were shoved back and forth in border Spanish and broken English. How many were talking? How many riders were above him? Two that he could separate, one more butting in, cursing. There were many horses shuffling and milling around, hooves stomping, raising a dust cloud that drifted into Matt's eyes, got into his throat, and tickled his innards, set him up to cough.

The buckskin pulled again; the voices came louder. Matt choked in his hand and spat out phlegmy dust. The words were harsh and brutal as the unseen riders argued.

He began to make sense of the fuss: they had McCraw's young stock. And they were split on what to do. One wanted off McCraw's land today, one wanted to hang on in the small canyon and brand before they packed up and moved out.

One, who sounded old and tired to Matt, wanted to drive the stock out by the base of the window, across Tornillo Creek, and up to Fort Stockton. Had to sell the stock out of the area, McCraw's brand was too well known, too tough to hide. A man laughed, another cursed. A hand slapped against wet skin. A heavy Spanish voice argued to take the herd across at Boquillas, deep into Mexico. He had a cousin, there was good money waiting there.

Mack drew in quick breaths and let them escape in small gasps. The buckskin leaned on him, rubbed his wet head on Matt's belly. Matt caught the flesh of the tender nose and his fingers squeezed gently, keeping him silent; the colt was motionless in the caress. The argument continued overhead.

Take a few days to change the brand. Who the hell would be out looking for the horses now? Get the job done in the canyon, drive the herd north.

Get going now, before McCraw came looking.

No one took charge of the mindless bickering. A horse whinnied, a man spoke up as if the decision were his alone:

"We move them out today. Now. Ain't got time to wait on any of you making up your minds. We get going now."

The other voices simmered and died out, extra words lost in the hot air of movement. Horses moving, saddles creaking, bit chains rattling, spur rowels singing. The group moved from Matt's hearing, picked up speed, and rode along the lip of the banking.

He had to follow them. If he went to the ranch for help, time would be lost. By the time the herd would be trailed, the outlaws would be watchful and ready.

Matt tightened the *cincha* on the buckskin, buried his

head in the colt's wet hide, and tried to think. He would have to ride careful, hold back, swallow his pride and wait, grow unfamiliar patience. The number of men would give him a wide trail, their own dust would hide his.

If his luck didn't run well, they would leave a man behind to check for strays. Or have one waiting at the mouth of their canyon. Another gamble he would take. It was McCraw's horses they were stealing.

Time didn't have much meaning in his life, but he'd learned somewhere to watch the sky and track the sun, live by the guesswork of the shadows. He forced himself to wait by leaning up to the sandy bank and pushing his hat over his eyes. But when he checked the sun next, only fifteen minutes had passed. This time, he could wait no longer. The buckskin was eager under him, sensing the rider's need to hurry. Matt kept his eyes to the ground, lifting them in concern when the tracks of one horse broke off and disappeared right.

He bit at his lip, held his temper, and thought some. Decided to stay with the main bunch. He was relieved when the same tracks rejoined the other riders. Private business, nothing to do with the ugliness ahead. Too many beans perhaps, a bit of spoiled meat. Enough to send a man off in need of a friendly rock and a handful of dried grass.

These men he tracked knew the land. They crossed the ridges surely, slid down the easy slopes. Matt kept a watch on his back trail, conscious he was headed away from what little he knew. He could be trapped. The dust cloud was heavy, the bunch traveled a good pace. The horses' strides were long, spread out, then the dust boiled and collected in one place.

Matt reined in the colt, half stood in the saddle to watch. They might well place out a rear guard soon, and he faced a decision he did not want to make. He waited patiently, stroked the buckskin on the neck.

The dust moved again. Matt let the buckskin head straight to the last point. As he thought, tracks separated there, into three trails. One man alone, one small group, one larger. Matt followed the single set of tracks and wished for a bandolier of ammunition, an extra handgun, a better rifle than the old Spencer in its patched scabbard.

The single tracks angled right, then back, as if knowing where to go. Matt followed carefully, building an anger in himself, stoking the need to fight. He was alone against an army, he would soon face a sentry. He needed whatever he could find in himself.

Chino grass stopped him; a solitary bird flew up fast, out of place, afraid. He watched the long blades of the grass move back and forth in the windless air. He drew a deep breath, unsheathed the old knife. A flock of the small birds flew up; Matt slipped off the buckskin and tied the colt. He looked past the grass, tried to hear the man, guess where he was hiding. A shape moved, a shape not part of the rocks. A man's arm appeared, then the outline of a head.

Matt folded, wiped his hands dry, picked up his knife, and steadied it. The head had no features; the man was turned from Matt, watching the back trail, unaware of being watched.

Matt leaned on his forearms, pulled himself over rock, across cactus. He felt a sharp point dig his belly. He slid cautiously; the man ahead of him stared into nothing. A long spur caught his old scar. Matt bit down, held back the groan. The head turned; Matt froze. He swallowed puffs of air, let his eyes unfocus. The head swiveled back; Matt pulled himself ahead.

The shadow moved; Matt watched. An arm reach up, a glint of a pistol in its grasp. The choice was there for Matt. He swallowed hard, tasted copper bile. The end of the pistol stared briefly at him, then was rubbed on the man's unseen neck. The sentry was a poor thief. But he was there, waiting for Matt, keeping Matt from McCraw's horses.

It was easy. The long blade slipped in between hard ribs, and the man turned quickly, coughed, spewed blood, blinked rapidly, and looked hard to see Matt, finally, with widened eyes. The pistol was slow to rise, then it fell away. There was no sound but a bubbling from the mouth, a slow gasp, first pink froth and then a spewing of thick red blood as the man choked on his own insides.

Matt retreated from the dying. He moved fast, no longer bound by the need for silence. There was blood on his hand, new stains on the cuff of his shirt, and a foul taste in his mouth. He took time to jab the knife blade repeatedly into loose sand. Then he raised the blade and saw a few grains stuck to the hard metal of the knife, red flecks highlighted by the sun. Nothing would clean the blood from his clothes.

He rode past the body with eyes cast down, scanning for tracks. There were few marks on the hard soil, but he was careful. A broken twig, a clump of turned ground, white lines on a gray rock. The buckskin stopped and lifted his head. Matt slipped down and clamped his hand over the fluttering nostrils.

The answer came: a high-pitched sound, the dead man's lonesome horse. Matt let the buckskin choose the course, and they quickly came to the ribby bronc. Matt pulled the rigging off the bay and fashioned crude hobbles from the reins. He knew the scrub would follow him and the buckskin, but it would be slowed enough by the hobbles to keep them all safe. Matt would be done and out long before the sorry bronc could catch up.

He loped the buckskin along the wide swath of tracks. The land rose steadily and split itself into narrow draws and small gullies. The tracks had a hurried shape to them. Matt looked back, trying to fix where he was. The Chisos window was to his right, McCraw's place would be straight in back of him. The dark lines far below him were deeper gullies and dead-end washes. He needed to remember; he would bet a good month's wages he'd come back this way in a real hurry.

Again he stopped the buckskin and tied the colt, fixed a rawhide thong around the black muzzle. He knelt and ran his fingers through the dark remains of a big fire. Several fires, as if they camped here and made no attempt to conceal their marking. If they believed they were safe, they must be near home ground. He snugged the buckskin to a heavy mesquite and gave the *cincha* an extra tug. The ground sloped quickly down, and from here he could almost hear voices.

Matt lay down, eyes inches from the fresh tracks. He began crawling, lifting himself over the rocks on his forearms . . . careful, slow, ready for everything. Over the quickness of the breath that came much too loud in his ears, the rasp of his leather vest, Matt finally heard the definite sounds. Horses, a lot of them. Racing, squalling, slamming into one another. Panicked by something Matt couldn't see.

He cautiously lifted his head; by his reckoning he'd crawled two hundred yards. Almost on top of him was a mass of mesquite poles and ocotillo ribs that blocked the mouth of a small cut in the mountain. Dust boiled through the fence and poured over the six-foot top. Matt squinted and saw the hard legs flash through the fence. McCraw's herd of young stock. And the same voices arguing.

Matt took inventory: the old knife; the pistol jammed into his belt at the small of his back, its holster left tied to the saddle. Wiggling on his belly through the brush could work the gun loose, and he couldn't risk that. Granpap's reata was coiled across his shoulder and down one side. He was ready. He let his head fall to the ground, closed his eyes, and tried to think it through.

They hadn't stopped talking yet, still arguing, still confident no one knew they were here. So he had surprise going for him, with the guard dead a mile in back of him.

He raised his head and checked: none of the men were mounted. They were in a circle, faces almost touching, hands waving in sometimes violent disagreement. One of the men turned toward Matt; he flinched, convinced the man saw him. A big man, wide through the chest, with no neck at all, pale brown hair sticking out from a shapeless hat. Even in the heart of arguing, there was no expression on the wide face.

They were armed: the man had a .45 stuck in his waist and a Henry was clenched in his fist. He seemed to be the one the others listened to most. Except for a black-haired Mex with a belly as big as the other man's. He, too, seemed to stare right at Matt, but returned to the yelling, with his face inches from the big man's, his hand holding a long knife, his burned face wide open in anger. The man had two teeth that glowed in the dark skin of his face, and Matt watched the loose mouth flap as the words went back and forth.

The thieves circled around themselves; small groups backed the two shouting men, the argument continued. Matt saw that no one would be paying much attention to the outside while those two came to a decision. Once it was made, there would be no time for him to act.

He pulled close to the fence and yanked on a rail. The whole fence wobbled badly, the uneasy horses scattered, whirled, and stared at him. He peered through, saw the young stock huddled together, watched the big two- and three-year olds bite and kick at one another. And then the cluster of men broke apart. He suddenly didn't have much time.

He slid along the fence line, pulling free the bottom rails, loosening the whole fence. He came to the end, where the poles were buried in the wall. He was far away from the angry men; here he could move quickly and have less chance of being seen.

It was easy to slide Granpap's reata under the bottom pole. He dug the buried end of the poles out of the wall. They'd woven a barrier of dried mesquite and ocotillo and thorn, and Matt cursed each touch. He half rose, took a deep breath, and shoved his arm through the fence. Reaching down blindly, fingers hunting for the reata, he slowly moved the rope with his other hand to guide his touch.

He finally hooked the end with his finger and leaned against the fence until it gave enough with his weight. Then he pulled the reata tip up to feed it through the fence. He pulled slowly, and didn't think of the men at all. If they saw him, he was dead.

The reata snagged, and Matt had to lie flat in the dirt to

wiggle his hand through and gently, carefully, work the line until it freed. His back itched, sweat burned his eyes, he tasted salt in his mouth. But he made a loop, tied strong knots, and pulled to test their strength. It would have to hold. He slid on his belly, knelt and doubled back, headed toward the buckskin colt. He wouldn't get close, but near enough to see the outline of the horse and have himself a running start.

Matt came quickly to his feet, let the reata slide through until the end caught his fingers. He took a wrap, started running, and let the weight of his run jerk hard. The snap brought him up short. He took a turn around his palm, looked back, jerked hard, and ran again.

A shot rang out, dust leaped in front of him. The fence collapsed; the horses inside spun madly. A horse screamed; the herd panicked, scalded by their own terror. Matt ran backward, hauling on the fence until he stumbled and sat down.

Another shot followed him, then more in a rapid fire. He dropped the reata and ran. The buckskin lifted his head, and Matt saw the movement, changed his direction. He jerked the reins free, slid the rawhide strand from the dark muzzle, and swung into the old saddle. The buckskin bunched under him, and Matt brought up his head, lined the colt away from the canyon. With the big colt more than willing, Matt leaned forward and touched his spurs to the gold sides as he let the reins go.

The buckskin almost leapt out from under him. Matt clamped down, wove his hands into the wire mane. Behind him there were curses and shouts, more shooting mixed with the flight of the escaping herd. Horses were scattered across the plain, ears back, eyes white, teeth drawn. Flying from their prison. The buckskin swerved and fought him; Matt jerked on the tender mouth and drove in his right spur, hauled the colt's head until they were headed away from the thieves.

They dived into a shallow wash; the buckskin stumbled and went to his knees, came up bucking. Matt clung to one side, no stirrups, hat gone, scrambling to find the saddle. For a moment the shooting was blocked by the wash, and Matt's head cleared without the noise. He slowed the buckskin, sat in the middle again, and reached his stirrup. They eased along the base of the wash; Matt asked for a quick turn upslope, and the buckskin leapt high. Then they hit the plains again and ran.

There were no more shots. Matt risked a glance behind him—the thieves had settled in to ride him down. He counted four riders coming fast, others headed toward the scattered herd. He cursed them, and turned around barely in time to see the hobbled bronc. Motionless, head high, tail flung over its back, and dead ahead.

Matt hauled on the right rein. The buckskin fought back until he slapped the left side of the colt's neck. They veered quickly and passed behind the hobbled pony. The bronc kicked out and fell; Matt spurred the buckskin and slapped him hard. In two strides they were running wild. Matt bent over the black mane and hung on.

He heard one shot and nothing more. He risked a glance behind him: the riders had not gained and he couldn't see the hobbled horse. He eased up on the buckskin and began to pay attention to where they were headed.

The dark line of a gully showed up. He tried to remember it, tried to guess its depth and the slant of the walls. Lined with mesquite and Spanish dagger, dotted with maguey plants, he had to choose fast and right. A wide gully, a path dug down its side. Matt checked the buckskin and looked back. The riders had already broken off and were headed for the cut. They knew the land. He didn't.

The gully was straight ahead; time to gamble. The buckskin showed no signs of tiring, so Matt aimed where he saw the gully was narrowest. He tried to rate the colt, to gather the animal and ready him for the jump. But the buckskin dived into the twisted brush at full speed, with Matt jerking on the reins for control.

Then the gelding saw the dark hole and spooked. Matt yelled; the buckskin came under him. He felt the big barrel rise under him and gave the colt his head. The buckskin rose in a leap; Matt closed his eyes and buried his face in the black mane. They landed hard, covered in brush, and the colt squealed when a branch jabbed into his neck. Matt reached out as something drove into his right arm. It burned quickly and turned numb. The colt dropped his head and bucked twice.

Matt drove the horse out of the brush and into the open. There were shots then, coming from the left, raising puffs of dirt wide of their mark. Matt saw the outlaws rise too late out of the gully, watched their horses labor in the deep sand. The buckskin ran at top speed, the other horses fell back with each stride. A booming shot came from the bunched riders. A small mesquite near him exploded. Matt huddled against the buckskin's neck and prayed that the owner of the rifle was a poor shot.

His arm ached; Matt craned his head and saw red streaks down the torn sleeve, saw the clean end of an imbedded mesquite stub. There was little pain and nothing he could do. The arm hung loose, useless, but the buckskin ran, and Matt rode him easily.

He felt the colt's stride falter, he heard the starved lungs work for air. No horse could keep up this pace for long. Matt leaned back, guided the buckskin with his balance until the frantic run was slowed. The outlaws' horses were also tired.

A shadow came on his right. Matt risked a look. Riders coming fast, closing the gap. He could see their rifles. The rest of the outlaws, but no sign of the scattered herd.

The buckskin skipped a stride, took a gulping breath. Matt touched the reins, and the colt slowed, unwilling but obedient. Matt eased up more, watched the riders on the right. The great rifle boomed again from the left, a Spanish dagger was shattered. Matt cursed hard, let his hand stroke the soaked neck. Then he sensed a shift in the colt, a renewed eagerness.

A pulse beat in Matt's head, his lungs called for air, his heart pounded. He lost track, felt tangled between the sweat of the lathered colt, the clatter of black hooves on hard rock. No one was shooting at him; he let the colt find his own pace. His arm was numb, his fingers barely able to feel the wet string of blood that drenched his sleeve and streamed out across his hand. The horse in stride, the wind screaming past his ears, the taste of copper. There was nothing but the buckskin colt racing flat-out.

Then, unexpectedly, the colt broke stride. Matt sat up and back, used his weight to steady the colt, softened his hands, and let the horse come to a lope, then an awkward trot. There was no energy in either of them. And when he did lift his head and look back, Matt saw there were no horses chasing them, no riders waving smoking rifles, yelling curses in two fouled tongues.

Far behind him there was a dust cloud, ahead was a familiar embankment. He knew where he was. A mile or less from McCraw's place. The air went out of his lungs, his eyes blinked against moisture. He brought the gelding to a walk, listened to the great ragged breaths drawn through strained lungs and trembled at the sound. He forced the colt to walk a hundred feet or more; when the ribs under him slowed their rise and fall, he could finally ask the buckskin to stand.

He grabbed the horn to dismount, but his hand would not take hold; he fell hard, still holding the reins. The buckskin shied from him and stepped back. The bit pulled on his mouth, and the horse was too tired to resist anymore. Matt felt the yank on the reins and tried to sit up. It was too much work; he closed his eyes, rested the weight of his head on the comfort of soft sand, and slept for almost ten minutes.

He came to full consciousness quickly. His arm throbbed, his head ached, his mouth was full of sand. He saw the bulk of the buckskin gelding above him and sat up. The reins pulled away from him—there was no feeling in his right arm at all.

He couldn't figure why he was tired and sore, couldn't understand what brought him down until he saw the horse standing close to him. The big head hung to the ground, white lather dried in clumps along the belly and neck and in a thick paste between the hind legs. Matt flinched at the sight and groaned with the effort of moving. He remembered now.

No horse should stand still after such a race. Matt made the effort to stand and staggered a small circle until he fell down. He sat a moment, let his working hand find the stick jammed in the muscle. The arm throbbed and new blood ran down the soaked sleeve.

He tried again to stand, this time pushing himself up with his left hand and using a bush to grab. When he could stand free, he waited until the white spots stopped circling his eyes and went to the colt. He would water him first, lightly, and then walk him. It would be cruel, but it had to be done.

The colt raised his head and whickered at Matt. The black muzzle was streaked white with salt, the lips covered in mud and dried dirt. The dark eyes were half closed. Matt was slow in opening the canteen; the colt heard the water and the black ears pricked, the eyes focused. Matt spilled water over a bandanna until the cloth was soaked. Then he held the wet cotton to the colt's mouth and wiped the white gums. The eyes opened completely, the teeth caught the cloth. The colt sucked and then chewed. Matt laughed, a cracked sound that spooked the colt. He took the dried bandanna out of the eager lips and resoaked it, offered it again. When the colt was done, Matt tilted the canteen and tasted a mouthful of the stale water.

There was one more thing he had to do before moving. Matt closed his eyes and leaned on the colt, made his left hand cross his chest and touch the numbed right arm. Only a stick, jammed in the muscle, well away from the shoulder joint. A stick. His fingers felt out the story. Not bleeding now, but there was blood crusted around the hole and the flesh was hot and dry. Touching the stick made a pulse throb in Matt's scar. He coughed and spat; only a mesquite stick.

He wrapped his fingers around the stick and pulled quickly, almost fainted from the flare of pain. Just a stick, had to remember that. He opened his eyes to bright sun, rolled his head on the colt's shoulder, and tasted the dried salt of the rough hair. Only a stick.

It came out easily this time, greased by new blood. Matt went to his knees; the buckskin didn't bother to do more than snort. Matt looked at the bit of wood that weakened him. Not more than six inches long, not much of anything. He could feel the drain of new blood down his arm. The dried bandanna made a bandage, tied tight enough to stop the flow.

Then he caught up the stiff reins. The gelding didn't move on command. His muscles were frozen, his legs swollen and sore. The colt shook his head against the pull of the bit but did not move.

Matt leaned on the shoulder and pushed; the colt went off-balance and had to take a step. The colt groaned; a human sound echoed in Matt. The colt took another step; Matt chirped encouragement through dry lips and flapped the reins to make the colt walk. It wasn't far, but it would become a long walk for both.

His face burned; Matt realized he'd lost his hat. He hauled the colt behind him, conscious of the effort of each step. There was no reason for him to be tired, he hadn't done the running. Yet he had to concentrate on the placement of his feet, the energy needed to pick up a foot and put it down.

He had to think of what he would tell McCraw. The thieves, the horse herd. The description of the fat-necked man, the potbellied Mex. Where he thought the herd had gone. But for now, he needed to think on walking. Every bone and muscle told him to lie down and sleep. And the colt agreed, resisting each step, pulling Matt off-balance. But the right arm spoke out the loudest.

A stick, nothing but a goddamn stick.

CHAPTER TEN

A horse and rider walked near the spring, black shadows caught in the bright sun. McCraw knew Miguel and Silvestre were in back of the new house, piling slab rock to start the kitchen wall. He let his hand reach for the rifle nearby and was glad for the feel of the wood stock cradled in his arm.

He could not figure what was wrong with the horse and rider coming toward him. He could see the horse vaguely, shimmering in the hot sand, its form lost sometimes between the brush and rocks. Then the man's head and shoulders would appear, sometimes hidden behind the horse, sometimes silhouetted on the blue sky. The pair made a straight line toward the springs, as if they knew where it was located. McCraw guessed there weren't more than five men in the territory knew where that spring was. He stared at the stiff-legged walk of the horse, judged the stumbling gait of the man, and decided he could afford to stand and wait on what would happen.

It wasn't until horse and rider passed him, still at some distance, and until the sun was no longer in his eyes, it wasn't until he could see the set of the man's back and catch the coloring of the horse's quarters and the flash of the long black tail that McCraw knew for certain who it was. He yelled once, but the man did not look up, the horse did not shy. So McCraw began to run, cradling the rifle across his chest; cursing the bum leg that slowed him.

What had the kid done to the buckskin? Damned kid, if

he'd ruined the colt, been careless and foundered him, McCraw would nail his hide to the side of the new barn.

He didn't reach the pair until the horse had stopped near the spring and the kid leaned over to fish out the wooden bucket left there. McCraw slowed and waited, watched the labored movements of the kid, saw the white rime covering the horse. The kid offered a sip from the bucket, allowed one gulp and took the bucket away, had himself a drink, and then poured the water over his head and shoulders. The dust layer turned quickly to muddy stripes down his face and scored the ruined side. The buckskin whinnied softly as the kid filled the bucket again and offered it to the colt. Another sip, then the kid poured the bucket over the colt's head.

McCraw relaxed; so far the kid hadn't done anything foolish. The pair paid him no attention; both were intent on the splashing water. The kid moved slowly, turned stiffly, refilled the bucket with odd movements. He went through the ritual of offering a sip of water, then pouring the rest over the colt's head. The buckskin enjoyed the washing, and McCraw shook his head in wonder.

McCraw could see the exhaustion; rust stains on the kid's arm, red rivulets on his shirt and side. The kid watched the big colt's head. Even though McCraw approached the pair from the colt's rump, the kid was too intent on the tired horse, did not see McCraw at all. McCraw saw the kid's face, the eyes only dark circles, the face much too white. All movements were too slow, too stiff and wooden.

McCraw got close to the buckskin, put his hand reassuringly on the colt's flank, and the long black tail dropped tight between the quarters, a hind leg was lifted to kick out. McCraw waited, held his hand on the flank, and the exhausted colt quieted down.

The kid had stiffened at the colt's alert. Now his head came away from the buckskin and he looked into McCraw's face, yet there was no recognition or reaction.

McCraw was patient, but Matt went back to his doctoring, and McCraw finally had to break the silence.

"Matt? What the hell did you do to this horse? You run him to ground, or been chasing ghosts? What the hell happened?"

The kid saw him then, worked his mouth to try for words, but nothing came out. He quit suddenly, dropped the bucket and sagged against the horse. The buckskin arched his neck and lowered his head across the kid's back, pulling Matt to his chest. McCraw went to grab the kid but saw him struggle, waited while the kid uprighted himself and pushed away from the horse. The dry mouth worked, and finally the words came out:

"Found a buncha riders after your stock. Young stuff, good money. Tracked them, turned the broncs loose. Last I saw ... scattered to hell. Tried to stop me ... Couldn't catch the colt."

A hard pride in the words, a shine in the half-closed eyes. McCraw felt some of the pride himself; he'd signed on quite a maverick. It might do to make the kid an offer.

"Colt's got heart, McCraw ... Outran them others. Pure outraced them, and they had them a start. Can jump, this old colt. Deep gully ... Sailed over. Shoulda seen it ..."

The bloodred eyes looked hard at McCraw, the ruined face pulled itself into a mockery of a grin. Then the sun-darkened skin paled; the kid staggered backward, sat down on the wet ground. McCraw went for the kid this time— pushed the waving hands aside and hauled the kid back to his feet. He was close enough to feel the ragged breath weave in and out of the kid, smell the acrid, dried sweat, the sweetish odor of fresh blood.

A blackened bandanna wrapped around the kid's right arm was the culprit. Fresh blood blotted out the blue pattern. McCraw tugged at the bandanna; the kid gulped hard and slapped at McCraw's hand.

"It ain't much. Some goddamn branch stuck in me. Came through the brush like a wildfire, jumped that gully ... Ain't ridden the likes before. I'll wash this out, put some tar on it. Be nothing."

McCraw sat back on his heels and had to listen to the kid. That arm looked more than a cut, but the kid wouldn't let him near the mess. He waved McCraw away again and grabbed the stirrup of the saddle to pull himself erect. There was a new steadiness in the kid's voice.

"The colt's plumb wore out, Mr. McCraw. Needs to be walked some, needs more water, and hay. A couple days' rest and he'll be fine. I walked him in, didn't want to ruin him. Too young for that kind of run, but by God he has the heart."

McCraw let the kid go then. If he wanted to see to the horse, let him. It was only a dumb range kid with a scratch on his arm. Nothing more than that. And he was responsible for the condition of the buckskin colt. Admitted it, took full responsibility, didn't ask for favors.

McCraw settled back on a stump and watched the kid walk the buckskin in a large circle, bring him back to the spring, and offer another sip from the bucket. The colt slobbered in the water, and the kid pulled him away, kept him walking. The white salt clumps slapped between the buckskin's legs and thick foam showed under the loosened saddle. The horse stopped abruptly, lowered his head, and shook violently. Clouds of dust and salt filled the air.

"Mr. McCraw, the buckskin . . . He needs a good grooming now, maybe some water on his legs. Let me finish him, then I'll get to the others. This one, he needs some care."

There was a pleading in the kid's voice, as if he doubted McCraw could understand. It was almost an insult, but McCraw remembered the smell of the kid's rank sweat and the tiredness in the strange face, the loss in the dark hazel eyes. It must have been quite a race. McCraw almost wished he could have seen the big colt run.

"You take your time, Matt. Do what's best for the colt, then see to your arm. Medicine's in the house. You come in when you're done. Don't worry none about the others. I rode the bay and the rest can wait. You take care of yourself, and the colt. Come up when you're done."

It sounded callous even to his own ears, but the kid didn't seem to know the difference, so McCraw bit in on what he really wanted to say and watched the kid walk away.

An hour later, or so he guessed by the low sun, and still the kid hadn't come up to the house. McCraw got curious, so he went outside, close to the corrals and the new barn.

The buckskin was flat-out and asleep by his lonesome in a small pen. The colt lay in a loose pile of hay, and there wasn't a speck of dried sweat on the huge gold body. The long black tail came up lazily and slapped at a pesky fly, a black ear twitched. McCraw smiled; there was nothing to worry about.

He heard the kid inside the barn shell before his eyes adjusted enough to see. A light snoring, a cough, a missed beat. Sleeping, too. Laid out on his back in a mound of hay, head rested on a wadded blanket.

McCraw stood at the kid's feet and thought on waking him. The soles of the upended moccasins were wore through and patched twice. McCraw snorted. A man needed a good pair of hard-soled boots to work out here. Moccasins were for the 'breeds. The old leatherpants were shiny along the inside seam, patched badly, in places worn through to bare skin. The leather vest was spotted and badly stained, the muslin shirt colorless except for the new red spots. The matted hair was fanned out on the blanket, the mouth open and slack. Bubbles formed with each gulp of air, burst and dribbled down the dark chin. Not much of a picture, and made uglier by the revelation of the terrible scar.

He had to admit he was fascinated; McCraw stood close to the kid's face and stared hard at the indecent skull. The scar went to bone, as if from a heavy weapon swung down in great rage, or hatred. A blow meant to kill.

The scar now was sun cured and healed, but McCraw

marveled that the kid had survived the attack and wondered how, and why. He knew this one would never volunteer to tell—and asking would only earn more silence and the kid's moving on. McCraw didn't want that; the scar would have to stay a mystery.

He looked at the right arm. The kid must have done his own doctoring, for there was a lump under the torn shirt, a bandage of some kind. It was the kid's choice to do his own work. McCraw wasn't going to worry on it.

To hell with him! McCraw jabbed his boot toe into the soft moccasin and stepped back quickly as the kid groaned and immediately reached for the long knife at his side. The blade glinted in the air, and McCraw thought he read the same flash in the kid's eyes.

"You had enough sleep yet? The colt, he's sleeping, too. Must have been quite a ride. Come to the house, get a good meal in you. Then you can sleep all night, be feeling better. Come on, kid. Get going."

McCraw didn't like what he was saying, but he couldn't come up with better words. Talking as if the kid's race had been nothing, as if finding the young stuff were unimportant. He wanted to thank the kid, let him know the loyalty and risk were accepted and important. But McCraw looked into that face again, saw the quick temper of the hazel eyes and felt his own temper rise in response. Damned kid, always made him feel on-guard, ready to fight over any misplaced sound. Damned kid.

He tried again at the meal. The shredded goat was charred, the biscuits half raw, the beans gummed and tough. He hadn't meant to have the kid cook, but no one else volunteered, and the kid went right to work. McCraw watched him, saw the use of his left hand, counted the times the kid stopped to take a deep breath and wipe his sweaty face. Damned kid! If he hurt, let him say so, let him sit down and tell them it was too much.

As if the kid could read his thinking, the gold eyes lifted and met McCraw's stare, and the older men flinched from the contact. He almost opened his mouth to tell the kid to sit down when Matt slammed a pan on the stove and spilled the stewed meat and sweet sauce. McCraw expected him to start complaining, but the words weren't what he expected.

"McCraw, I reckon the horse herd'll come in tomorrow with the stallion and mares. They'll be spooked for certain. Good idea, put out some hay, a treat. Remind them where it's safe. Might be good."

Calm, thinking all the time. The son stood there with burned sauce on his arm, clumps of something smoking on the stove, and he made suggestions about a herd of motherless horses. Ideas it was McCraw's business to have. He decided it then, that the kid didn't operate like other men. Maybe he was the child of the devil, marked for the rest of the world to see.

When the kid backed away and left the kitchen, McCraw knew that what he had been thinking had come to his face. And he was shamed. That one had rode hard for the brand and got nothing back but dumb words and harsh thoughts. McCraw bit the side of his mouth ... To hell with it. He stuck something on his fork and shoved it in, chewed slowly, spat out a lump of burn. He didn't know what or how to talk to the kid, didn't know about the raw temper in the quick eyes. To hell with it.

It got no better in the morning. The kid was slow, breakfast was late, the coffee boiled to thick mud. McCraw kept quiet and swallowed hard, but Silvestre didn't have sense and spat out the grounds, started to speak up when he saw the crusted mush on his plate. Then Miguel got into the act, did something McCraw didn't see, for Silvestre grunted hard and stared at his friend, but the big oaf did not finish what he started to say. Finally the crude meal was swallowed in silence.

McCraw found the kid in the small pen, brushing the buckskin's neck and talking to the big colt. He tried again, searched for the words, but the kid reached down for an old reata, picked up a headstall, and left. Headed toward the other horses, leaving McCraw with more questions. He

TEXAS SPRINGS   111

called to the kid and got no answer. He tried again, louder this time, anger full in the reach of his voice. The kid roped out a rugged brown, slipped the bridle on, and never looked back.

McCraw finally let it go, said to hell with the kid, again, and got to the doing of his own work.

Two nights later, McCraw heard a noise in the yard. He came up fast and was in his boots and had his hand on the rifle before his eyes adjusted. Outside, a shadow moved near the well. McCraw raised the rifle and sighted. Then he heard the sound again, a deep groan of distress.

It was Matt. McCraw knew the tilt of the shoulders, the slow moving, saw the long hair dip over the sagging head. Falling to his knees hauling up a bucket of water. Drunk, by God.

McCraw reached the kid as he fell again. Grabbed for whatever he could catch, and the kid cried out. McCraw felt him pull away, felt the stickiness on his hands. The kid sat down. McCraw didn't speak. He put down the rifle, felt the bare skin of the kid's chest, and was shocked by the heat of it.

The right arm, swollen and hot, sticky with fluid. Blood boiled from the wound. McCraw touched his hand to the kid's face and felt the heat burn through his palm. The kid sat quiet, swaying gently but making no sound. McCraw half lifted him, spoke to him, urged him to try to stand, walk to the house. For once the kid didn't argue, but leaned toward McCraw and let the boss carry him.

It had to be the light Miguel held up to them, or the sight of Silvestre looming in the half shadows, face stupid with sleep, mouth stuttering. Suddenly the kid was gone, fighting with unexpected strength. One blow caught McCraw high on the cheek and staggered him. Miguel lowered the candle and raised his fist in defense, ready to strike.

McCraw yelled then, and Miguel turned to him. The kid's blow missed its target and landed on Miguel's shoulder.

"No. Don't. He don't know what he's doing. Son of a bitch, he took sick from that arm."

The kid swung toward McCraw's voice, and for a moment the rancher was awed by the fury in the terrible face. The devil's face all right, the devil's sign there to read. Then the kid came in at him, hands raised, eyes blazing, and McCraw sighed deep inside himself, bunched his hand, and hit the offered jaw hard enough to drop the kid.

McCraw caught him, ordered Miguel to lead inside to McCraw's bed. Silvestre stayed outside, bewildered by what he could not comprehend. McCraw sent them back to their sleep and sat for the rest of the night with the kid, leaning his chair back to the wall and catching some sleep near dawn.

Miguel rode out at daylight for the help of a *curandero*. A *curandero* did not come to the ill or injured, but this one was a cousin of Miguel's and had treated McCraw after his accident. The uncle of Miguel's mother's brother. He would come here.

The kid looked serious, pale, restless, with red streaks fanning out from the slow-bleeding hole in his arm. A yellow fluid leaked with the blood and fever burned the thin body. All this McCraw explained carefully to Miguel, so the *curandero* would understand the immediacy of the trouble and bring the right herbs and potions.

McCraw washed down the kid, soaking a cloth in clean water and swabbing across the face and chest. He was gentle in wiping the old scabs of blood from the arm. There was even dried blood buried in the scar on his face and fresh blood that would have come from the midnight battle. McCraw's belly knotted as he touched the scar, and Silvestre muttered a broken prayer from the doorway.

The kid moved, and Silvestre prayed louder. McCraw sat back and looked at the kid's arm, then raised his eyes to the ruined face and saw that Matt was half-awake. The eyes drew him in, flecked with gold and brown. Brighter now, filled with the fever's power.

"Mister, ain't you seen a body before? You looking at me . . . something new. Ain't more than a hole . . . a stick."

The eyes closed and the mouth rambled, often speaking sounds McCraw did not understand. Gradually the words were mixed with groans and cries; the dark head rolled on the blanket, the eyes fluttered open and shut, sometimes staring at McCraw with no seeing in them.

The kid fought to get up; McCraw leaned on him to hold him down. At his touch, the kid screamed and hit out, rolled away and screamed again as his own weight pressured the infected flesh of his arm. McCraw tried spooning tequila in the kid's mouth. He accepted a swallow and spewed it back up.

McCraw ended up feeding the kid wine diluted with water. He didn't see the difference between the wine and tequila, but the kid accepted the soothing drink and it stayed down. The wine started the kid talking again, nonsense words mostly. The only words that made sense were talking about the ride on the buckskin colt. Over and over the kid rode his race across the plains, over and over he leapt the gully, outran his pursuers. Then the kid quieted some, before new words started. McCraw watched, saw the kid worn down and sweating from a new fight McCraw did not understand.

The hazel eyes flashed open and there was clarity in them, the voice called McCraw's name, over and over, like the retelling of the ride. McCraw moved closer. The kid was anxious, fighting again. McCraw strained to hear the whispered tale:

"Good horse, good bronc . . . I ever . . . a racer." The voice faded, and McCraw figured the kid was finally wore out. But the eyes opened again and the mouth worked. McCraw leaned close enough to feel the heat of the kid's shallow breathing: "You know . . . thought to ride . . . Good horse . . . 'most took . . . done it 'fore. Way to live . . . stealing. Almost . . ."

That was all. McCraw sat up. A horse thief, self-confessed, by God. Disappointment went through him; he'd come close to trusting the kid. Who was nothing more than a horse thief.

Again, as if the kid knew what was running in his mind, the left hand reached out and caught McCraw's wrist. There was no strength in the gesture, but it drew McCraw from his blind thinking. The rancher leaned over the white face to listen. "Almost stole . . . couldn't. Wrong. Too good . . ."

Then the eyes closed, the heat rose from the kid in a stinking cloud. McCraw tried to sort out what he had heard. A confession of some sort, things the kid did not have to say. No one would have known until the horse, and the kid, were missing. Almost enough, but the bare truth came out that the kid was a confessed thief. McCraw shook his head, disappointed in them both, the kid for the confession, himself for believing too quickly in the odd, quirky rider. A horse thief wasn't right, not ever, not in a land where a horse meant its rider's life.

He closed his eyes then; he knew the judgment was too harsh—it put distance between himself and Matt. Maybe this was what he meant, when he first walked into the ranch and outright told McCraw to watch out for him. Maybe this was the fact of the warning. It was very easy to hate a horse thief. But there was more to the kid, always more.

Then an aching tiredness swept over James McCraw, from the long night behind him, the long days still ahead. He rocked back in the chair, stretched his arms over his head. Too much, too fast. Coming at him in waves.

He let the legs of the chair slam to the floor. The kid moaned and rolled his head; McCraw stood up. He walked the room twice, three times. Pushed hard, restless, uneasy. Then he sat back down by the bed and waited.

CHAPTER ELEVEN

There wasn't a doctor for miles. The custom and dictates of the land were at times difficult for Harriet to accept. She had learned it was necessary to make do most of the time, to use her imagination and hard work to smooth or disguise the reality of the life she now lived. But to not have a doctor within driving distance was unforgivable.

Yesterday morning, Margaret had awakened with a bad cough and a slight fever. Harriet had treated her sister with their mother's home remedies, but this morning, Margaret was no better—her fever was higher, her cough slightly worse. So Harriet had demanded of Mr. Dutchover that he send a man for the doctor.

There was no doctor, at least not in Marfa or its surrounding villages. And the one in Fort Davis was a good two days' drive and not likely to be there when he was needed.

Mr. Dutchover was quite heartless about the illness. He explained that there was no point in sending a rider to Fort Davis; there was too much work to be done on the ranch, and there was a local healer who could be asked for medicines. He was considered effective, and all the local ranchers used him in an emergency.

A *curandero*, Mr. Dutchover called him. Harriet recognized the root of the title, but she truly doubted anyone indigenous to this backward area could cure anything with only the strange native plants and a witch's brew of knowledge. To rely on a dirty little man with no formal training, no instruments or accepted treatments or current information, was a horrifying concept, but there was no other choice left.

Even though it was well into the month of September, the sun was far too strong for a lady to be out driving. But Mr. Dutchover was adamant: if she chose to seek out the *curandero* rather than use her home remedies, then it must be she who would drive to the *curandero*'s hut to ask for his help. No men were available, so the journey was hers alone.

Mr. Dutchover drew a map and told Harriet to pay close attention. And he scoffed at her ladylike concerns. The indians were gone, driven out by the superior forces of the white man. And there were no robbers or thieves who would bother a white woman. He explained, carefully, that this was not the East, where such things were commonplace.

Much to her surprise, Harriet enjoyed the drive. The early morning air was clear, the sky a brilliant, sweeping blue. There was a fall sweetness in the breeze, a tantalizing reminder of the edge of winter. The gentle wind brushed her face, the clopping of the horse's hooves soothed her nerves. The path she took followed a dry creek bed, crossing and recrossing it. Birds flew up as the mare and buggy passed by, and their flight cheered Harriet.

It *could* be considered beautiful here. Not like the mountains in the East, or Europe, or the grandeur of the ocean. And there were no miles of pleasant green fields to soften the eye and ease the mind. But there was a beauty hidden in the stringent lines. The mountains were a secretive blue, opening to expose wild blocks of fallen hillside; scattered streaks of hot-colored earth painted in their own pictures. The vistas of decayed plains were not a vivid green, but there were pockets of colors, daubed sparely; speared cacti topped with fuschia, stringy plants rowed with yellow top hats.

Overall, the landscape often appeared muddied and strange, and it frightened her at times. She felt she had no business in this forsaken land. And yet there were sights and smells that were important to her now. She certainly had had little time lately to mourn her beloved Emerson. She rarely thought of him during the days, too occupied with the need for her labor and her support.

The fat gray mare whickered, a lonesome call with no answer. Harriet flicked the whip over the wide back with no expectation of response. Her mind jumped to her rescuer in the garden, as it had done of late. She had not yet separated his face from the embarrassment it caused in her. The man was not part of her life, yet he came to her in odd moments, as if trying to establish a claim.

Mr. Kersey had begun to call on her. Twice in the past weeks he had ridden to Mr. Dutchover's, twice he had sat and talked business with his host, taken the meal with them, and spent a few minutes with Harriet before resuming his long journey.

There was little he had to say that was of interest to her. But he was willing to sit and watch her, as if taking notes for future private musings. Harriet did little to encourage him, but she had to sit and listen to Mr. Dutchover's listing of the man's prospects.

There was no mention of the knight-errant in range garb who had come in answer to her distress. A light showed in Margaret's eyes when she questioned Harriet about the incident, but Margaret was still a child in many ways—and still maintained notions of romance and sweet pleasure. How she managed such a fiction while living with Mr. Dutchover was past Harriet's worldly comprehension.

There was no future in such ramblings. Harriet shook the reins over the mare's back again. According to the map and Mr. Dutchover's directions, the *curandero*'s hut would be around and to the left of the broken boulder ahead on the path. She encouraged the fat mare to a slow trot and was pleased with her increasing skill with the lines.

The hut was there, lost in brush near a steep hill. A horse was tied to the railing and smoke came from in back of the hut. Small children hurried in and out and paid no attention to Harriet.

She was afraid to step down from the buggy, so she called to the house, aware of the weakness in her voice and the vast open space around her. No one could hear her. No one came to the door. No one was curious. Even the horse tied to the gnawed rail did not pick up its head and look.

So the voices from behind her gave her quite a start; she put her hand to her mouth to cover her cry. The voices were loud, speaking in a language she did not understand at all. Spanish was familiar to her now, but this was different entirely.

They were two men, one walking beside a burro, hands busy tucking and pulling at different bundles packed on a high wooden saddle. The other man saw Harriet first and stopped suddenly, and as quickly removed his hat in the time-honored gesture of deference. That one nodded to her with eyes cast down, then continued to argue with the smaller man standing near the burro.

Then, as if a word cut through the argument, both men came straight at Harriet and her buggy; she unthinkingly picked the whip out of its socket, and the fat mare shifted in the traces. Harriet waved the whip in no particular direction, and the men stood still.

The bigger man started talking; his English was labored but comprehensible.

"*Buenas días*, señora. We are having a favor to ask you. This old man, surely you know of his powers, for you have come to search for him. He is the *curandero*, señora. The best, even though he is my— Ah, señora. The favor, yes."

It was obvious they wanted something from her. The man speaking was most definitely a peasant, of the sort Mr. Dutchover said were plentiful here. Wide shouldered and strong, with long arms and thick, clumsy-looking hands. A gray mustache covered his mouth, and his long shiny hair was tied back. She could not guess his age from his face, but the skin was seamed and rough and the mouth had only scattered teeth, which showed when he grinned. A frightening person, but for the dark eyes, which held a natural deference Harriet Gliddings took as her right.

"Señora, please. It is true you have come for this one's help. But he must come first to me, to treat vaquero works for Señor Jaime. We must to hurry, señora. And this stubborn— He will not ride on my horse but must bring his medicines on the back of the burrow."

Once she could translate what was being slowly asked the fear subsided. And a name was familiar: Señor Jaime. She must listen more closely and try to understand. Harriet waved her hand and, magically, the man started in again.

"Señora." The grin widened, the big hands flailed the air. "Señora, we must to get to Señor Jaime's for his rider. There is a sickness in the boy only this foolish *curandero* may heal. It is please, señora."

The big hands waved in the direction of the buggy and the resting mare. Of course, to carry the healer and his arts to the sick man. She remembered Dutchover's contemptuous explanation—McCraw allowed his hired men to be too familiar; they called him Jaime.

"Of course you may use the wagon, if it will be of help."

The señora's voice shook badly and her words were soft, but Miguel was able to find agreement in the lady's face; he wasted no more time in picking up his ancient cousin and setting him on the seat next to the lady. He undid the bundles from the burrow and placed them carefully in the wagon bed. The cousin knew better than to object, but sat and muttered to himself.

Miguel mounted the tired sorrel and rode beside the wagon. "Señora, please to follow me."

Occasionally the kid's eyes opened when McCraw came close enough to check, but he said nothing. Mostly he slept, a restless, hot sleep that bathed him in rank sweat. McCraw left a tin cup of the watered wine by the bed and had to refill it twice. But he never saw the kid take a drink.

He was thinking impatiently of Miguel and the *curandero*. He walked outside and across the yard, then turned and went back into the house. Midmorning already. He recrossed the dark room, conscious of the smell, hearing his boots hard on the packed flooring. He stood over the kid, seeing the swollen arm again. McCraw knew enough to be worried.

It didn't take much to bring a man down. A small hole like this one, a damned stick from a mesquite bush. Not much, yet enough to kill if the *curandero* didn't get here soon. McCraw knew the signs, from twenty years ago, from the narrow canyon north of Santa Fe. When the great General Sibley caved in to the Colorado troops and fled south, leaving his injured men behind to die.

McCraw had stayed. Injured only slightly, wanting to be with a wounded friend. He had seen it, the wounded dying in the long days after the battle. Dying from the smallest cut. Or taken in makeshift ambulances to Santa Fe, to die in the hospital beds, washed and bathed and fed on meager supplies, watched by helpless doctors as they faded and disappeared.

It was hell, a useless way to die. Death by a shot full in the chest, to go under a stampeding herd, to roll from a falling horse, drown in a flooded river, those were deaths a man full expected. But this, to waste and rot from nothing. To swell up and stink and stop breathing from a twig shoved into him.

He listened to his rambling thoughts, spoken out loud to the indifferent walls and the restless invalid, and wondered about his sanity. Then he looked down to see that his angry words had awakened the kid from his half-sleep.

"Just a fool, kid. An old one at that. Thinking too much, been alone too long. You'll be fine. Fine. Miguel's coming with the *curandero*. You know what—?"

McCraw quit talking abruptly. The kid knew what a *curandero* was. The kid spoke Mex and English and that other tongue. McCraw felt the fool, talking before he thought.

It was Silvestre, hollering from the yard, that kept him from making the fool bigger this time; hollering to wake the dying. McCraw was at the door, saw the wagon clouded in dust, a rider coming in ahead of it. Miguel's wide frame slumped in the saddle. McCraw hurried to greet the wagon.

A lady drove the buggy, with a fat mare harnessed to it. Mrs. Gliddings, miles from the Dutchover place. McCraw's belly turned on him and he had to wait. But there wasn't time to ask questions; he waved for Miguel to pick up the bundles as he helped the old man down. Mrs. Gliddings climbed out by herself, and McCraw made his manners to her, felt the slow thickness of his tongue, the flush in his face and neck. Why was she here? It didn't matter. He went to hurry the old man to the house.

The *curandero* would not be rushed to his new patient; he asked McCraw incessant questions. How was the señor's leg? Did the shoulder pain him much? If so, there were more herbs that could be of help. McCraw replied in the border speech, telling of the days of recovery, the stiffness that sometimes plagued him. And the miracle of the old man's cure. The small face of the *curandero* smiled, and McCraw offered a polite bow.

Then he began to talk on the kid, but the *curandero* held up his hand, the palm a startling white against his brown arm. Miguel had told him the story, there was little left to know. He had brought with him the necessary herbs and potions, the seeds and fresh leaves. But, he would be needing items from the señor. A bit of sugar, a bar of yellow soap, the fat from a deer or goat. He had brought deer fat with him; it was rancid but would do if the señor did not have the fresh item at his disposal. A goat would be the best, but a goat was of much value, and if the injured were not of importance, perhaps the señor would prefer . . . ?

The old man went inside alone, and Miguel was told to kill and bring to him the kidney of a goat. It was done quickly. McCraw saw the Gliddings woman seated near the spring. He watched her but made no move to visit with her. Miguel brought the kidney, and McCraw went inside, where he found the old man with the boy, talking in his thin voice, asking questions that were answered in a mixture of tongues while the old man nodded thoughtfully.

A pouch was opened, a series of small leather bags were placed carefully on the table. The contents of each were inspected and tasted, then emptied into a coarse wooden bowl. The smells mixed and rose in the dim air, a yellow dust scattered through the hut. McCraw started to cough; the old man looked at him until he choked down the need. The kidney of the goat was cut and pounded and herbs mixed with it. Blood and dust covered the old man's arms.

There was a shape in the doorway. McCraw did not immediately identify it. He waved impatiently, to not interrupt the old man's work. Soft footsteps entered the room; he knew it was Mrs. Gliddings. She was next to him . . . He could look sideways and see her lovely face. He had forgotten about her, left her in the hot sun. He offered a chair, she smiled and sat down; he put a finger across his mouth to remind her of silence.

A bottle was in the *curandero*'s hand, a dark shape stoppered with carved wood. The old man pulled it free, and the released odor filled the room with its pungency.

"To cleanse the wound, señor. To destroy the thing eating this child's flesh. I must cleanse the wound and I will have your help. To hold the child still, as this will hurt much. He understands. I have told him."

The old man looked at Matt and smiled, a toothless and leering grin. The kid widened his eyes and returned the smile, and McCraw saw the recognition between the two. A recognition that excluded him.

He went to the head of the cot and held the kid's shoulders. He guessed there would be little fight, out of great pride and the knowledge there was a woman present. The *curandero* did not wait; he poured out a green solution, undiluted and odorous, over the inflamed wound, and a sickening stench bubbled from the arm. The boy's face froze in its grin, but he made no sound. The lips drew back, the teeth bit down hard, and blood stained them along the gums. McCraw's hands held the bony shoulders, and there was no movement in the kid at all.

The Gliddings woman gasped, and McCraw knew she

would faint, in keeping with the manner of well-bred, Eastern females. He was wrong: a slender white hand touched the boy's wet forehead, to offer its gentle sympathy. The old man was bent over the wound, mumbling strange words and scooping the liquid into the hole, until the bottle was empty. Then he wiped at the thickened mess covering the kid's chest and arms, staining the torn blanket laid under him. McCraw let go of the kid; the woman stepped back with her hands crossed, her fingers wavering. The kid let out a long, sighing breath.

The *curandero*'s hands went over the kid, touching a shoulder, the knob of a wrist, the pale exposed underarm below the elbow. Then the hands went to the upper arm, to the muscle stained green around the inflamed hole. The hands circled that flesh, pressed gently on the length of the red streaks. The old man mumbled; the kid was quiet. Only his eyes betrayed him—shining, leaking tears, burned by exquisite pain. There was no sound in the room but the old man's undecipherable words and the shallow breathing from the kid.

The brown bottle was shoved aside; empty, it rolled on the floor and did not break. Another bottle came out of a new pouch. With it came a muslin sack with a musty scent. McCraw's nose itched; he saw Mrs. Glidding rub her face. The *curandero* worked on the kid, letting his fingers press and squeeze around the arm and shoulder. McCraw sighed deeply; the kid looked up at him. Already the glaze of fever was less in the strange eyes.

The old man spoke, and Mrs. Gliddings jumped closer to McCraw.

"There is much infection and it will now pain but not kill. Child, I will put more herbs on your small wound and the señor will put fresh ones there tomorrow. And the day after that.

"You must sleep now, and tomorrow. To let the herbs do their work. But, then you must get up even if you do not wish to. For if you do not begin to move around, the poison will command you and you will suffer from it the rest of your days. You must be up and moving in two days' time."

A small bottle appeared, and its contents poured in the wooden bowl. The herbs mixed to a paste with the blood from the kidney and were applied over the hole. Something from a clear bottle was offered to the patient; he drank quickly, until the bottle was taken from him. Then the eyes closed, the tension was gone from the face, and the kid was asleep.

The *curandero* looked to McCraw and the woman standing near him, and he smiled his toothless smile.

"He will be fine, Señor Jaime. He will work again for you. But do not ask much of him in the beginning, for he has come too close and it will take time. He must have time. It is a small thing, time. But it will respect his life."

He spread the fingers of his dark hand over the sleeping boy and touched the deep track of the scar very gently. Matt stirred at the stroking but did not awake from his drugged sleep. The fingers followed the path of the wound, from the high forehead to the brow over the eye, the deep indentation across the cheek, to where the scar thinned and disappeared above the ear. The old man shook his head regretfully.

"There is nothing I am able to do for this. It is of a great age, especially for one so young. But he can see from the eye. That is good. The mark is a great burden for him to bear. He has learned to live within its ugliness, no señor?"

The tired voice asked another question McCraw could not answer.

"He is of a mixture, señor? Of your Anglo and good Spanish stock. Yet how did this come to him? He is young; the scar is half his years. I do not know of this one, señor. He is not of our land. But he is not of the new ones come here. Who is he, señor, and why would he come to you?"

McCraw spoke in the same formal pattern, choosing carefully, speaking slowly, working the inflections in his Spanish that mattered a great deal.

"He is Mateo Iberra. He has said little, but I guess he

comes from the place above El Paso. Alongside the Rio Grande. He will not speak of his marking, but he has ridden my horses and they do any man's bidding. More than this I do not know, except that he is a fine cook. Which is unusual for such a young one."

The *curandero* appeared to listen, and smiled upon hearing some of McCraw's words. Then he touched the scar again, laid his fingers deep into the torn flesh until Matt's head rolled from the pressure and the eyes fluttered open.

"He is a good one, señor. He will grow here and you will be proud. He has much strength for one so young. You may believe what this one will tell you. He will speak only the truth. To others, I do not know. But to you he will keep his word. Remember that, señor. For it is of great importance."

The *curandero* held out a pouch, and McCraw took it. He spoke then of what must be done to heal the injured child. McCraw half listened, having heard the old one speak before. Only this time it was for another, not his own wounds.

The kid groaned once, and Mrs. Gliddings went to him. But the old man was quicker to put out a hand and touch the wet skull. He let the weight of his arm rest heavily until the head stopped its moving. Words were spoken softly and the boy quieted, the clenched fists opened. The eyes held closed and the kid slept.

Mrs. Gliddings watched the old man repack his bags, and her mouth was half open, her eyes wide. McCraw guessed she had never seen a sight like the old man and his bag of tricks.

McCraw waited outside for the old man and pressed a few coins in the dark hand. He offered his hand, but the *curandero* instead put his fist against McCraw's injured shoulder and pushed until McCraw had to step back from the insistent force. The *curandero* grinned, and McCraw accepted the man's power.

"He will be fine, Señor Jaime. And now, so will you.

Señora, for one who has waited so kindly, how may I help?"

CHAPTER TWELVE

The *curandero* listened gravely and gave her a muslin bag of powdered herbs, a bottle of liquid, a gentle pat on her hand. If she had not seen his work with the rider in Mr. McCraw's employ, she would have tossed the herbs to the wind and poured out the smelly concoction. But now, she found herself a believer.

Twice daily she was to brew a tea of the leaves and the dust and be certain that Margaret drank the cup fully. The brown bottle was to help her sleep, but only at night. The herb tea was to clear her lungs. It was that simple.

She thanked the old man and paid him with the silver coin from Mr. Dutchover's purse. There had been a curious light in the old man's eyes as he took the coin, and she had not felt silly when he bowed in a courtly manner and took her hand in his. This was an extraordinary old man, one she would not have accepted or considered six months ago. Or even a day past.

It was just past noon; she could tell by the rise of the sun. It was midday and it was hot. Too hot for her to drive back to the Dutchover place with her tea leaves and her brown bottle and a few words of explanation. Unless it was an emergency, everyone in their right mind ceased moving in this heat. She had considered the custom quaint, a way in which to get out of working, until she had felt for herself the full sweep of a noontime sun and became dizzy. She learned quickly to be thankful for shade and a quiet place in which to rest and wait.

She also knew she did not want to leave McCraw's ranch, with its half-built stone walls and yellow, freshly peeled fence railings, the horses standing motionless in the shade of the sloped *ramada*.

She did not want to leave. The morning had become special to her, and she needed to sort it through, understand its significance.

And she was trying to fool herself, for she knew the reason for her reluctance to leave. Mr. McCraw. His company, his quiet voice, and simple concern. The man barely acknowledged her in the morning's work, and she did not blame him. He had looked directly at her twice, while the old man was making up the poultice and mixing the liquids, touching the sick young man and washing out the terrible, smelly hole in his arm. Beyond that, Mr. McCraw barely knew she was here.

It was foolish of her to think of the strength in Mr. McCraw's face, the manner in which his eyes changed and lightened when he smiled, the easy way in which he found her a shaded place to sit. He offered her a drink of the good water from his spring and stayed awhile to explain.

She had never seen water bubble out of the ground like this, she had never tasted the mineral sweetness of the deep underground, never felt the bite of deep cold against her teeth. Mr. Dutchover had a flat rock positioned in the river that flowed behind his house, where she and Margaret could kneel to draw up the water for the house. Yet he spoke often of the luxury of water piped into the house, a luxury he would someday provide for them. But the women still had to pull up the buckets of water—unless they could chide Mr. Dutchover until he assigned that work to one of the men.

Mr. McCraw stayed to show her the wooden pipe that carried water to the house, to a large barrel by the back door, and to the corral where the horses could drink their fill. He showed her the horses later, the lovely mares with their babies, the stallion whose pride and carriage took her imagination.

Mr. McCraw was careful with his words when he spoke of the stallion and the mares. As if not to offend with any illusion to the mechanics of creation. As if Harriet were herself not a widow, had not held the attention and love of her husband. She smiled at Mr. McCraw for his concern, pleased with his shy attempts at civilized conversation.

There was a difference in her now. Out here, close to threatening death as they had been only this morning, such delicacy no longer mattered. And now, resting comfortably on a rock by the springs, she watched Mr. McCraw walk from the house carrying a flat pan. The sick man had needs that could not be attended to at the backhouse. Did Mr. McCraw find her so delicate and refined that she would not presuppose such necessities?

Emerson would have been shocked at her thoughts. And so would have the Harriet of only a few months past. But she had now been in this wild corner of the West long enough to put aside thinking that had no reasonable place. It was a struggle here, for everyone and everything. And to pretend one's body did not function as nature had arranged was senseless and a waste of time.

The heat increased; Harriet unlaced her bonnet and shook her head, delighted with being free of the unnecessary burden. The bonnet could be used to fan her face and throat. And she wished to undo the high buttons of her shirtwaist and allow some air to circulate inside her clothes, but she also would guess such an action would shock Mr. McCraw. If he were watching. So she would be polite and restrict herself to the fanning, and perhaps would repin her hair to keep the straggling ends from lying on her neck and attracting dirt and perspiration.

Harriet spoke a curse she knew Emerson had used and put the bonnet down, removed the pins that held her hair. It was much too hot; she could feel the immediate stickiness of the strands on her neck. No one was looking, no one truly cared. She unbuttoned the top button, then the next two. The air cooled her heated skin. She looked down, unbuttoned two more of the small pearl fasteners. Her hair glided over her shoulders and came gently to rest on the exposed skin of her breasts. She pulled a few of the strands through her fingers, luxuriating in the texture, the smell of the cold water behind her, the free movement of air on her flesh. It was very hot indeed.

He didn't have to stare at her, but he was quick to watch her every move. He wondered if she knew what she offered by her actions. He glanced around; Silvestre and Miguel were sprawled up against a half-built wall, broad hats down over their faces. The kid would be sleeping, stunned by the *curandero*'s potions.

He walked to her. There was nothing to prepare him for the feelings this woman aroused. The temptation she brewed for him.

But he well knew his manners and his place.

"Ma'am. It's coming cooler now. Be time for you to make the drive back. Mr. Dutchover and your sister, they'll worry 'bout you. And she'll need that pouch the *curandero* gave you."

She didn't blush this time at his words or his presence. She didn't play coyly with the patterned bonnet or twist a ring of hair around her finger. She looked at him directly, slowly, as if for the first time. Licked her lips for the lost moisture and took a deep breath that moved the free hair and exposed her white skin. McCraw remembered the softness of that private place below the pulse of the neck and blushed on his own. He had to step back from her. The woman was too close.

She seemed to take no notice of him, but continued to look out, toward the blued shadows of the Chisos. When she spoke, her voice was cooled, gentle, with no hint of teasing, no touch of disapproval.

"Mr. McCraw, your place is beautiful. I have enjoyed spending this time under your tree. The springs are refreshing to the ear as well as the soul. I have been thinking, Mr.

McCraw, and considering the years waiting ahead of me. Do you consider often the choices and opportunities placed in front of you? Or do you go from one day on blindly, without plan or desire?"

She bewildered him, asking such a question. And his confusion must have shown clearly on his face, for when she looked up to his silence, she smiled. A soft, amused, kindly smile that made him uncomfortable.

"Sir, I ask too much. And I am ashamed of my impudence. Perhaps you are right, that it is time to harness the mare and begin the journey home." She stumbled over the last word and corrected herself. "I shall begin my trip back to my dear sister, and Mr. Dutchover. With many thanks to you for your hospitality."

There was a dreamy look to her that teased McCraw, a slow movement of her womanly form. McCraw thought of what he'd seen the *curandero* do. He reached for her hand, held it in his, and marveled at its slender whiteness against the dark grain of his fist. He turned the hand to lie across his palm and exposed the tender wrist to the sun. Then he thought to bring that hand to his mouth and bowed slightly. He felt her resistance then, and looked up into the lady's eyes.

There was no pleasure in her look; he'd been wrong, played himself the fool. McCraw felt the bitterness again, the sense of doubt, the notion of not fitting where he had always belonged. He mouthed a silent Spanish curse and let the hand fall away.

He didn't look again to see what he had done to her, how badly he had offended her. He spoke over his shoulder, staring at the mountain now as if he had never seen it before.

"I'll harness up and make certain you got a jug of water to get you home. Miguel put the old man's herbs under the seat. Best you get them back to your sister now."

He was gone before she could compose herself and find the needed words. The touch of his hand on hers, the feel of his callused skin. The strength inherent in him. The fire in the dark hazel eyes as he tried to speak to her mind.

Harriet felt a new heat in her skin. All the coolness of the spring no longer soothed her. He had startled her, surprised her, so she was not ready for his gesture. Unexpected, out of character. Charming. She had obviously underestimated the man's background.

There was much she already knew about James McCraw. His life was part of the story of this land, told and retold at the big gatherings and small social circles. Harriet listened in fascination, especially to anything about the tall man with the kind eyes and romantic past.

The heat went down her neck and spread across her chest; she suddenly was aware of her naked bosom. An ache fired below her stomach. Harriet had known that feeling with her husband's occasional touch. This was not proper, was not the way in which to repay Mr. McCraw's aborted gesture. If he could see her now, fingers hurrying to rebutton her nakedness, hairpins jabbed into her flesh, he would know her for a harlot and a shameless woman. And he would not come to call at Mr. Dutchover's, he would not think of her as a suitable wife. She had to smile then, at her own folly. A man would take such a woman to enjoy, and would grab her, pull her against him. But the same man would not find full value in such a woman as a companion and wife.

She pinned herself back together as McCraw rousted Miguel to harness up the mare. Miguel knew the look on his boss's face and was mercifully silent. He watered the mare again and patted the heavy jug under the wagon seat. The lady would not be thirsty on her return trip.

Miguel could not help but look from the grim face of the señor to the flushed skin of the lady. The señor was too slow . . . and the pretty lady, she would go home alone.

He was careful not to touch the lady's hand but to offer the bulk of his arm for her use, to put her up in the seat. The señor held back and watched, his mouth a white line, his eyes hot and darkened. It would be a miserable night, with the kid sick in the house and the woman to leave the señor with no parting words.

Then Silvestre appeared and stood behind Miguel—to watch the gray mare make a slow turn about the yard and leave a trail of dust as the woman touched her with the whip. Miguel heard the beginnings of a question and swung quickly with his warning before the señor listened. The señor was less than ten feet away and would have to hear Silvestre's foolish thoughts. He stared at the sleepy face, showed his teeth in his effort, until Silvestre had to understand. If the big mouth dared to open, there would have to be a fight. As Miguel hoped, Silvestre said nothing—and there was complete silence as the blowing dust settled back to the earth.

He'd again been the fool. She would want nothing of him now. Trying to put on the airs of a gentleman when he was a range-cow nurse, a busted idiot past his prime. She was a lady, a beautiful lady, with lines of successful suitors, and he would not dare to try.

The taste in his mouth was of bitter defeat. He had to forget the day and go back to what he knew, go back to the endless miles of horses and cattle, of dry summers and cold winters. The damned ranch, the sick kid inside the house. There was nothing else.

She drove much too rapidly at first, hurrying the mare without mercy. Hurrying on the broken path and hoping for an accident, that he would see. But when she was past sight of the ranch, good sense allowed her to slow the breathless mare and return to the accustomed slow walk.

The pull of his hand was still on her; she could smell the closeness of him, the peculiar mingling of human and animal sweetness, the scent that was his own. The clear voice sounded in her ear, mocking the silly words she had said.

The man was unique, and now he would ignore her; she would be cast back into the rest of the ladies who had come West looking grimly, relentlessly, for a mate.

Harriet watched the hands holding the harness lines, the fingers rigid, the knuckles white. Even with her eyes shuttered, she could see Mr. McCraw's dark hand encompass hers, could feel the texture of his skin, smell the rise of her fear included with the fresh puff of his breath. She wiped the tears away, replaced her gloves, and slapped the lines over the gray mare's back.

CHAPTER THIRTEEN

Matt slept the afternoon, woke once to eat, and slept the next fourteen hours. It was into the afternoon of the second day before he came fully awake. He lay on the wet bedclothing and thought on what had happened.

He worried first about the buckskin colt, then saw the picture of McCraw's face leaning over him as he told him one more time the colt was fine. Matt smiled briefly, staring up into the ocotillo whips that supported the ceiling. One hell of a colt. He'd sure like to find out what the buckskin could do on a good stretch of road. Maybe McCraw would let him, if he still had his job.

There was a lot of the past days Matt could not pull together, a lot that was confusion. Somewhere in the fevered time there had been a woman, her hand on his forehead. He shook himself, wondering if that were only part of the dreaming.

Finally he pulled his legs free of the blanket and found the cool floor. He shrugged out of the bed, to find himself dressed in ragged underwear that was too big for him. Someone had a sense of modesty. He thought it could be at the woman's insistence. Matt grinned to think of McCraw trying to wrap him in these diapers. That had to be a woman's touch.

It weren't nothing but a little hole in his arm. Matt took the first step carefully, caught the back of a chair to steady himself if he needed it. His head was clear, his heart strong. He needed to get outside, smell the clean air, hear the sounds of the horses. And see if McCraw were angry at the lost time.

The britches were a problem, but he solved it by bunching them at his waist with one hand. He wondered: Had the young stock come in to water? Had McCraw put out the feed?

The noise outside intrigued him. Yells, whoops, the sound of Silvestre's temper. He made it to the door and leaned carefully against the frame, looked outside. The sounds were coming from the corral.

The strawberry roan, snubbed close to the post. And fat Silvestre with a blanket in one hand, a quirt in the other. Trying to lay the blanket on the roan's humped back. At the slightest touch, the little horse kicked out sideways, and the fat man cursed him. Miguel was perched on the top railing, calling out names and suggestions in a thick voice. There was no sign of McCraw.

Matt saw the rise and fall of Silvestre's other hand, saw the braided quirt land on the roan's hide. The bronc squealed and kicked out; the quirt rose and fell again. Miguel said something Matt could not hear. The roan reared and pawed at the rope, swung his head, and Silvestre laughed.

Matt grabbed the loose shorts in both hands and started across the yard. He barely felt the rocks underfoot. Yelling as loudly as he could, he began to choke. Tears streamed down his face. Miguel didn't hear him. Silvestre didn't turn and look. Matt tripped and went down; in his weakened state he could not get his feet under him. He was on hands and knees, gulping for air, and he felt the building fury blind him.

It took all his fight to get up. He tugged at the cotton drawers and wiped the dirt from his eyes. Miguel was still on the top rail, still watching Silvestre maul the roan. A saddle was strapped down; the roan bellowed. Then Silvestre sat on the small horse, the roan slammed into the fence, and the fat man cried out. Matt reached the corral fence and picked up a rock. He threw without aim; the flat edge hit Miguel below his hat, and the man tumbled into the pen.

The roan leaped wildly and kicked out; Silvestre saw his friend lying in the dirt. He lost his balance as the roan spun, reared, struck at the air. The vaquero slid from the saddle and lay flat. Newly shod hind feet sliced the air above him, and he felt the old breaking of his shoulder. Miguel groaned once; Silvestre raised his head. The roan danced above the fat man, kicked again, and missed.

Silvestre stayed down this time, frightened and confused by how quickly the fun with the little roan bronc had turned into a nightmare.

When McCraw returned from feeding out new hay, he did not believe the story Miguel tried on him. That there was a great stained bandage wound around Miguel's head, knotted with a clumsy hand he could not deny. But the story was not the truth. "It was the devil's work, señor. The devil's work." That was all the explanation Miguel could give.

Silvestre was no better. He groaned and rubbed his chest and twisted his face in great misery. He had gone out to ride the little roan, to take out the fire of the weeks of eating the señor's good grass. As a favor to the sick one lying in the bed. As had been done for himself when he, too, suffered the wounds of his work. And then, señor, Miguel had fallen from the corral fence with a great thump and he, Silvestre, had spilled from the wicked little roan. That was all he knew, all he could offer for the señor's inspection. And none of it did he understand.

The kid was nowhere to answer questions. His gear was gone, his patched saddle and ring bridle, the woven blankets and rough saddlebag. They had not seen the kid ride, his great vaqueros, they had been tending to their wounds, spitting out the dust from their mouths, and trying to walk. Miguel had seen the tail of the roan, but he did not watch for the direction. His head ached, and truly neither of them cared to know. It was good the marked one was gone. Now they could return to the quiet times, the peaceful days, the way God had intended them in His great wisdom. Miguel crossed himself at this point; Silvestre kissed the ends of his stained fingers.

McCraw listened and sifted for the truth. He knew Silvestre's rough hand on a horse, he guessed at Miguel's goading words. And if the kid had seen a quirt slapped on his roan, there would literally be hell to pay.

He half thought on tailing the kid, just out of a sickbed, weakened and alone. But Miguel was complaining of his head, and Silvestre fussed at cooking the evening meal. The kid couldn't go far tonight; McCraw would find him in a few days and explain. For the moment, McCraw had the urge to saddle and ride, but he came to his senses and worked the evening chores.

It was three days before he had the time to ride out. Miguel needed to be nursed some. A filly smashed through the corral fence and took ten stitches. Three late calves got caught in deep mud near the spring.

There was too much, too many calves still unbranded, too many half-started broncs in the pen. Too many stray folks riding past the gate to the ranch, coming down the fence to ask for handouts or directions. McCraw asked several of them if they'd seen a kid like Matt. But no one knew anything.

They drank his water and looked at the spring, asked about his cattle and the buckskin colt standing solitary in a pen. Their civilization poked him at every turn with its curiosity and its greed, its fear and loneliness. McCraw was caught in a bind and restless.

So he was turned from his search and grudgingly spent a half day in the saddle, reading old trails from the buckskin's back. He came home that night tired, worn down. He slept badly and exhausted from his battle, thought of the woman. He almost felt the velvet of her skin at the end of his fingers, he almost tasted the heat of her near his mouth. He groaned and rolled over, willing to drown her memory as much as she had killed his hopes.

He began to think rarely of the kid, except when he saddled and rode out a half-broke horse or bit into a raw biscuit. Or watched the sun near the spring and tasted the cold sweetness of its water. As if a part of his life he had never known was taken from him. Lost in the face of the woman and the mark of the half-wild kid.

Thomas Kersey stood on the porch of the rude hut and tipped his hat to the lady inside. She smiled graciously at him, with little warmth in her affection. He didn't much care. He said his good night and stepped off the porch, knowing that Dutchover would come with him. The man put his hand on Kersey's shoulder. Kersey knew the signs—the man had something important he wished to speak in private.

"I understand you are in need of more water. I have been fortunate, Mr. Kersey, in that I was able to file on a good stream that does not seem to be affected by the lack of rain, or this particular cold spell. But some of the streams are dry and the surface pools have begun to dry up. What course of action do you intend to pursue, if I may inquire?"

Dutchover was quiet, giving Kersey all the room he would need. It was simple: He had something he felt Kersey needed, information or gossip that would have influence on Kersey's immediate future. Kersey respected the man for his caution; he, too, would be careful, and would want the other man to know a payment was expected. So Kersey began to pay his debt.

"I had planned to extend to the south, and somewhat to the west. But you are right, Ed. Water is becoming a problem. I need a section close by, most likely with a good spring. I don't trust the surface pools at all, and even the streams are suspect. But the records of the land hereabouts show nothing that isn't already claimed up. Don't know rightly what to do, Ed."

He could wait out the man forever, but Thomas Kersey was proving a man to play the game. Dutchover felt himself a good judge of men, and he was careful to watch the shift of Kersey's eyes, the tightening of the thin mouth. And he did not miss the significance of Kersey's choosing to call him by his first name. A degree of intimacy. His respect for Kersey grew as the man talked on; the man knew his lines. Dutchover cleared his throat.

"My sister-in-law paid an unexpected visit to a neighbor south of here. I believe I told you of the incident. When she had to drive over to get medicines for our Margaret. Well, as it has worked out, I have ridden over several times to talk with the man. You know of him, a James McCraw."

Kersey wished the man would get to the point, but he knew Dutchover was enjoying his moment, and he would not deny the man that pleasure. Finally Dutchover came to his conclusion.

"I know the man, and he has absolutely no money. It will be a struggle for him to pay up on the land he has already claimed. And, I happen to know, he has claimed a full section as dry that in truth has a spring on it. An excellent spring. Bitter Springs, he calls it. It is not on a map anywhere, but the spring is there. Just south of your holdings."

CHAPTER FOURTEEN

He'd come off the ranch in pure fury; when it left him, he was exhausted. The roan responded to the fury and spent several miles wanting to buck. When the horse settled, Matt

TEXAS SPRINGS 139

let him pick the direction while he concentrated on staying in the saddle. It didn't matter where he was headed, as long as it was away from McCraw and his two vaqueros.

There were welts on the roan; Matt's fingers could feel their swelling. Each time he touched one, the anger came back full force and he rode another mile. He thought of Silvestre lying in the corral, Miguel struggling to his knees.

McCraw would know by now that Matt was gone. There was a rush of sorrow in Matt; he had come to almost like the rancher. But no, he knew better now. The roan picked out the bare traces of a trail and settled in a single gait; Matt pulled down his hat and cradled his right arm across his chest and let the feeling of the horse under him go to work.

He stopped the roan once, spun around, ready to go back to Bitter Springs. He couldn't; it was done, all tracks behind him wiped out by anger. Brutality, unexpected, had blindsided him.

The load of anger got to him, drove a burst of fuel through his tired body, and he let the eager roan run out his new energy. The rocking stride, the rush of wind, the sense of flying, they felt good to Matt, and he urged the roan on to greater speed.

Finally Matt reined in the horse; the animal was lathered and blowing. Matt had an odd sound in his ears. His hands shook and he placed them, one on top of the other, hard on the wooden head of the saddle. His whole body throbbed, his ears still rang their own tune.

They drifted for another hour, aimless, lost, following bare game paths and occasionally crossing the sign of sheep herded in the area. Matt didn't care much; he knew the land well enough to find water. There was a thin spring somewhere, in the side of a narrow canyon; he'd headed in there once after a muley steer. He looked down, saw the tracks of sheep beginning to form a trail of their own. As if the flock also knew the presence of water.

He hoped for no one at the spring, but it was too late to change his path. He wanted no smelly shepherd eager to talk, looking for a shared bottle and a quick meal. He wanted no one to ask anything of him. He would be alone tonight, and the next nights. There had been too much in the past months, too many confused paths, too much asked for and granted.

It was late afternoon; he'd finished his canteen earlier, offering water to the roan from cupped hands. He had a craving for water, a heat in his body. Matt rubbed a hand over his eyes, felt the itch of sand under his lids. A beat pounded through his arm muscle and he was sleepy, wanting to lie down and let go. He let the roan walk without direction.

He heard the sheep before he saw them, smelled them even before he recognized the sound. He pulled out his pistol, held it close to his side, and sorted through the signals until he realized it was a sheep camp. A man could get himself killed this way, riding and not thinking. Invading territory not his. An easy death.

The sheep huddled back of a small fire, laid out carefully at the edge of a flat rock. A man, standing with a rifle held to his chest, hat pulled too low to see his face. Another figure, smaller, half hidden behind a mule, holding a gun almost too big to point at the intruder. A voice growled words in rapid Spanish, and Matt waited stone-faced through the questioning, holding his temper, wanting his turn.

"I am no thief, señor. I do not want your sheep, or your camp. I want the water, that is all. And a place to camp, to sleep for a while. I am tired and have no wish to bother you. That is not much to ask, señor?"

He had no more patience, and there was no answer given to him. If the goddamn shepherd wanted him dead, let the man shoot. Matt picked out the green of the spring and headed toward it. The sheep jumbled together and slowed the roan's walk. The bleating annoyed Matt, their rush to cling together angered him. He rode close to the shepherd and still could not see the man's face. The rifle was lifted and followed him, but Matt paid it no attention.

A pooled spring, damp and muddy around the water's edge, bright green brush almost hiding the deep source of the well. Matt let the roan drink as he dismounted, lost the reins somehow, fumbled with the canteen and lost it. Picked it up from the green weeds, rattled the canteen. Bone dry, like his mouth. He went to the water, heard the sucking noise as he sank in ankle-deep mud. The roan lifted his head, water dripping from wet lips. The horse snorted and flung his ugly head; Matt dodged and fell.

No balance, no strength left. Nothing to grab and steady himself. Trying to rise, he fell again, hit the roan's legs with his back, rolled sideways. The hole in his arm flowered; Matt groaned in protest. He quit, lay back in the mud and fought briefly against the wonderful, soothing coolness. Then he gave up.

The roan put his muzzle back in the pool and played with the water, snorted as it overran the sides and dripped on the man lying on his back. It washed the man's dry face and forced open the closed eyes. The man looked up and stared at the roan, then shut his eyes, drifted away.

The other figure struggling with the pistol was a girl child. And there had been a younger child hidden behind her. Matt had already been told their names twice but he still did not remember. The old man was Abateo Flores. That much he could hold to. The little girls were his, and there was a third person, who had ridden to town. A daughter named Adelina.

Nati and Celia. The two little ones. It was important; they were Flores's children. Nati was the youngest, the one who hid behind her sister and cried when Matt fell and did not get up. And cried again when the grandfather and the older girl dragged Matt from the spring and stretched him out on a blanket.

Nati was a baby, small and dark like Tomás's girl. With big dark eyes that easily spilled tears, a soft face and round mouth that wrinkled again when she came close to Matt and saw him and began to cry.

Matt sat up slowly. She was frightened by his face. As Tomás's child had been, as most children were. Tomás's girl hid behind her mother's skirts and peeked out and cried when she first saw her *tío* Matt. The easy bitterness came back to him, something forgotten the past weeks. The dizziness was gone, in a bad trade.

Nighttime, dark and cold. A small fire to warm those near it as it heated the remains of a slaughtered ewe. Beans and a sauce bubbled in a pot, tortillas waited, their round shape white against the rock. Matt was hungry enough, but he would wait for an offer. His mouth filled quickly; it had been awhile since he'd wanted solid food.

He would recite the names again, to own them. And to think not so much about eating. Abateo Flores was the host, and the little girls were Nati and Celia. And the daughter who had ridden to Marfa and was late getting back, she was Adelina. The roasting sheep smelled sweet. Matt ran his tongue over his dry mouth.

A slow mare brought the girl to camp. Matt stood with the grandfather; he knew his manners. His legs were wobbling but holding true. He would unsaddle the horse, water her, rub her wet back, and tether her to supper. Anything to hurry eating. The old man accepted the offer and smiled with broken teeth. There was no fooling this old one, he knew the source of Matt's good manners.

But the old man made Matt pay before the meal; he brought Matt to the older child and had Matt stand to the unexpected introductions:

"I wish you to meet my Adelina. Child, this is Señor Matt, who has come to us for the night." Matt could not yet see the girl's face, but she offered him the reins to the mare, her hand was soft and kind and stayed for a long moment in Matt's grasp. The old man was not yet finished—and what he said was not kind.

"Yes, girl. It is a terrible mark on this one's face. But he will be nothing more than a stray. He will not hurt us. He will stay and break bread with us, and he will be gone in the morning. There is little in him for you to fear."

Damn the old man. He left nothing. No room to hold a pride of his own making. The words lanced Matt, but then he realized the girl had not turned away, did not hide her eyes with her hand and pretend fear. She came closer to him, peered into his face, and then gave him the reins to the old mare.

"Please be careful with her. It has been a long day and she has worked hard, as always. And without enough water. I would care for her, but Papa . . . and the girls, they are waiting. . . ."

The flame of the small cook fire burned high with fat; Matt could see the girl clearly and knew she could see him. He saw a woman, beautiful and strong, with thick black hair pulled to show a strong face, a proud, arched nose, heavy brows above the wide, dark eyes. And the mouth, full lipped and red, parted as if to speak again. Matt would place a finger on those lips to seal out the chance of cruelly spoken words. She did not need to talk; she needed only to stand in the light and allow him to watch her.

He wondered that the old man allowed this daughter to ride the plains alone, wearing only the loosest of cotton blouses, a bright robe wrapped as a coat, a long skirt that whirled around her legs and showed high moccasins shaped to her calves.

He raised his glance to her face again. There was no pity there, or scorn. Only the wonder of her beauty, the kindness in her smile, and the repeated sweet words that soothed him:

"Señor, you are welcome to our camp. You will join us to eat, after you are done with the mare? *Gracias*, señor."

No fear, no cruel teasing. Only the flash of the smile, the pressure of her hand as she pressed the reins to his palm. The young woman looked at him in the firelight, saw his face and did not care. Beautiful, young, meant to be tasted and touched, courted and desired. And she did not show a fear of him.

CHAPTER FIFTEEN

Abateo Flores knew every secret, every cliff that meant danger to his flock, every blade of hidden grass, every spring. He would drive the herd across pure desolation, and Matt would worry about the old man, fearful that this time Abateo had forgotten where he was headed.

And then there would come the miracle: a flourish of cool green half hidden in brown scrub; a few strokes with the long blade Abateo carried and the spring would emerge. The old man would scoop out the hidden water and let it flow to his waiting sheep.

When he began to trust Matt, he allowed him the chore of clearing each spring. Matt learned to follow the old man's words precisely. The mud was smoothed out, a shallow trough was shaped to allow the water to run a course to the depression Abateo, or an earlier shepherd, had created over the years. Abateo Flores left nothing to chance if he could help it, and there was nothing he did not know about his flock and its needs. Watching over his family, hiding from the Indians, and now staying clear of the arrogant Anglos, who would follow him to take away his water and his livelihood. His years of pride.

"They would fence me, my young friend. They would have me stand and say, 'This land is mine, this piece only.' As if a man can own such a special place. I use these mountains, I travel across these wide plains, I allow my few animals to graze and eat the nourishment, and then I move them on. To allow the land to return to its strength, to allow the grasses to grow, the water to refill.

"I do not own this land, I do not order the dried summer sun or the strong winds, I do not have the right to call a blade of grass mine. It is given to me for its use, but it must also be given its own life or it will fail me, as I will have then failed it."

Flores watched the strange young one who had come to the meager camp in righteous anger and had fallen in the mud and had not moved. Much like a wounded and ill-used animal. The young man was with them now almost two months, and Abateo was beginning to understand. The man had in his mind the ability to think, to consider, to contemplate. He was a pleasure to argue with, to talk with when the work of the day was finished and the children were seeing to a meal.

"Do you understand me, Matt? What it is I am trying to explain with the poor words that come from my mouth?"

Matt shrugged, and the heavy wool blanket slipped from his shoulders. The gesture was offered in silence, for the old man to read as he chose. This talking had become an evening ritual, and there were times when Matt was bored with its repetition. There were many times when his thoughts had gone instead to the cook fire and the three girls.

Of course the old man had explained at great length about his three daughters—a curse for some men, a blessing for him. Flores said that many times to Matt, to anyone who would listen. A blessing. Boys grew to men and challenged their papa, girls grew up to love and care for their papa, to marry young men who would in turn give the papa a home in his older years. It was much better, of much more pleasure, to have girl children. Especially when they were as lovely as Abateo Flores's three daughters.

Then he quietly coughed and drew hard on the pipe stuck in his mouth. And told Matt the truth—that indeed Adelina was his daughter, and that Nati and Celia were her children. Not his.

It would be difficult for any man to argue with Flores on the beauty of the girls. The youngest, Nati, had the eyes of a sainted Maria, the skin of a fawn. Her dark hair held the touch of fire, her mouth was of the purest wine. And Celia was near to womanhood; already there were fathers talking to Abateo, speaking to him of the quality of her hands, the sweetness of her nature. Their sons were fine young men; Celia would have her pick.

This was how Abateo described his two young ones. And it took time for Matt to realize the old one did not speak so of his true daughter, Adelina. She had passed the years of marriage, and had scorned and burned the young men who came courting. Abateo could not speak of her to the strange young one; he could not talk of the coldness in her. There were many men who rode to Abateo's camp late at night, and more who sought out Adelina when she was not with her father. There were some who were honest in their admiration, who presented themselves for Abateo's interrogation. Young men with fine flocks of sheep, young men who rode blooded horses and worked for the great ranchos. Young men who saw Adelina's walk, who stood close to her and took in great gulps of air and attempted to touch her—and were slapped for their foolish efforts.

Adelina was too old, Adelina was almost twenty-five. And she would go her own way, care for her life as she had always done. Abateo tried to share this knowledge with the strange young man and knew that he would not listen. Adelina would take from Matt what she wanted, when she wanted, and no one, most especially her own papa, could tell her otherwise.

Matt forced himself to come back to the old man's rambling talk. He looked across the dying fire. It was a bitter night, with a dusting of snow sparkling in the flames. Winter had come early and hard, and those who did not know would soon suffer for their ignorance.

"We will move closer to the river, Matt. To a small cabin I have built for such times. We will be close to the water that will not freeze. There will be a big storm soon. There will be snow to keep our poor flock from traveling. So I will take us to the river, where the grass will not die under the snow's hard burden. You will come with us?"

The question took Matt to the first night by the fire, the first time he met Adelina. There had been polite conversation, with a few questions Matt could answer, or not, as he chose. He spoke briefly of working for Señor Jaime, and Abateo's face lit with pleasure. And when Matt told of Silvestre's abuse of the roan and of his own leaving, the blame he placed on the señor, there was indecision in the old man's face.

"Silvestre, he is not bad, only stupid. It is a shame, but the señor will keep him and Miguel to work on his place. It is not right to blame Señor Jaime. He would have no satisfaction in such handling of your brave little horse. Do not put blame where it does not belong, Señor Matt."

Matt wanted to argue, but it would be rude, and he was tired. And in the morning, there was no mention of his riding out alone. There were chores for him, or he could go with a polite farewell and a good breakfast. Matt watched the girl walk to the spring—and there was no need for him to decide. Until he saw pity in the old man's look and read it wrong, put it to the mark on his face and not the desire new in his loins. He forgot the look and did not listen to what the old man tried to tell him, and spent his days in pleasant misery riding alongside the indifferent Adelina.

Abateo set the rules early; he motioned for Matt to ride the off side of the flock, gesturing when it was necessary for him to swing up or down their flow. Never to come too close and set off panic, but to set a boundary for them and keep them from wandering far from Abateo's command.

That had been the pattern for the two months, and Matt liked his acceptance into this family. Nati no longer cried at his face; she even convinced him to let her ride in front of him on the skittish roan. She would rest her head on his chest and babble on in her childish imagination. The roan's ears swiveled back and forth as if he understood her fancy.

There were a few times when Celia asked to ride, and Nati allowed her to share the throne. But Celia was more than a child, close to a woman, and she was shy about leaning on Matt's chest, quiet about her thoughts. And still curious about the marking of his face. He would not answer those questions, and she asked to ride only a few more times.

Adelina came with the flock, sometimes leading the mule, sometimes riding the old mare. Age showed in the gray muzzle and sunken eyes of the mare, and tiredness in her slow gait and bent back. But the mare would trot out if Adelina whipped her, and Abateo would say nothing. A force pushed his Adelina from inside her heart, so he did not scold her for scattering the sheep, but would ask Matt to help him gently gather the animals until the herd was again traveling to the correct destination.

This morning the cold air hurried the sheep, the smell of a storm alerting buried instinct. Matt let the roan jog to keep up, and today Adelina's old mare did not need a switch on her flanks. Nati rode with Matt, a pretty child wrapped in a bright blanket. Where her head rested on his chest a comfortable warmth spread through his body. His hands gripped the stiff reins, their knuckles blued by the wind. Abateo looked up when Matt had to ride past a strayed ewe. There was concern in the old man's face.

"My friend, I have misjudged badly. This storm is here. And our trip to the winter home, it is too late. I am sorry, my friend, for now you must suffer with us as you have chosen to make our life your own."

The old man owed him nothing; Matt felt the burden of his careless flight, the selfish reasons for his stay with Abateo. The shame of his purpose flooded him along with the old man's apology.

"It is truly my choice. Tell me where were are headed. I know we will get there."

Adelina came to him in his dreams at night; she offered him no encouragement during the day. She was his only in his imagination, although he could walk behind her in the camps and taste the scent of her skin, the softness of her hair. He knew without having to hear it that hard coin was the only way a woman would take him. He thought he knew that truly, until he met Adelina and dreamed about her at night.

He could not leave the Floreses now. It would be against his honor. He closed his eyes to the stinging wind, felt the warmth of Nati huddled in his arms. Her small fingers wrapped with his and her small voice had to fight the growing wind.

"I am frightened, Matt. I am afraid. I want to be home with Papa and Celia and a warm fire. Please, Señor Matt."

He'd ridden colder days, slept out colder nights. But it was the unexpected power that froze his blood this time, the sudden drop in the feel of the air, the chilled wind that cut through leather and put an ache in his back and shoulders. He pulled the child closer to him, kneed the roan gelding in a half turn, and watched in back.

The sheep followed slowly. Fresh snow was white on the yellowed stain of their wool. He came up to Abateo and saw the old man stumble on frozen grass. He angled the roan across the old man's vision, stopped the little horse, and slipped free of the saddle. Nati began to cry.

He lifted the old man onto the roan and looked away from the wet gaze. Cold air touched Matt where the child's body had warmed. Walking would bring new heat in his body, riding would renew the old man's nerve.

The small band traveled a full day, not stopping for a tortilla or a noon sleep; the cold drove them. Only Matt walked. The children rode in front of the adults, hidden by blankets. The sheep went blindly, the horses lowered their heads, half shuttered their eyes against the icy snow.

Matt stumbled and went down on outstretched hands. He whimpered in shock; a thorn was driven through his palm. He stayed on his knees; his mouth was numb, his ears crusted with ice.

He was bumped hard, his feet shoved, his backside bruised. Matt leaned into the force, wiped his raw hand across his mouth, and tasted the unwanted sweetness. The pressure on him increased. He swore out loud, a violent curse that was instantly taken by the wind. He twisted around, arched his back, and put a hand out behind him, to feel the greased hair and hard bone of a horse's leg.

He shoved the leg and half stood. It was the old mare, head lowered, whiskers laced white, ears matted into her brown coat. Matt saw the colors of the blankets on top of her, and the head above them. The contempt was clear to see; she looked at him, dark eyes open, dark lashes flicked with snow. Matt wiped at the crust around his mouth, the ice of his own lashes, the heavy clumps frozen in his hair. The woman watched him before slapping the mare and riding past so close he had to step back before the old mare knocked him down.

He followed those deep tracks, plodding over frozen cactus and churned dirt, putting one foot in front of the other as if it were important. Slowly the bleating of the sheep quieted, the sounds of their travel were muted in the snow. The sheep left their tracks on broken red crust; Matt's high moccasins let in the cold air and held in the wetness.

He bumped into the strawberry roan. The horse humped from the intrusion but didn't kick. Matt caught the long tail, followed the shape of the horse to come near the old man's hanging leg.

The words were muffled and cautious, but he could understand enough of what was said to nod his head.

"There is . . . canyon ahead. Shelter. Almost—" The rest of Flores's words were lost in the howling wind. The old man kicked the roan, Matt slapped the wet rump as it passed him, and the horse plodded down trail.

The sheep swirled around him; the wind stopped, and there was new air to breathe before it was robbed in a cold wind. Matt felt close to comfortable in the moments when no snow blew into his mouth or coated his eyelids. He was frightened by this false warmth, a feeling that came just before freezing.

He walked on; a dark shape became a mountain. Matt

stopped, confused, lost. Abateo's voice came as a point he could focus on and define.

"It is the pen, Matt. An old one used these many years. Please . . . sheep to . . . they have been—"

The ground flowed with sheep. Animals fell on slick rock, others climbed them to find safety. Matt yelled; his voice echoed off the narrow walls and called back to him. The sheep separated and came together in a solid force to roll into the pen. The smell of their steamed wool gagged Matt.

The old mare trotted past, riderless, bridle reins tied to the horn. The obstinate mule followed, finally in a hurry. Then the roan flew by, a weight dropped on Matt, and he shifted under the blow that was Abateo.

"There is a small hut . . . rocks . . . pit for fire."

The bearded mouth touched Matt's ear so that it was certain he could hear. The old man guided his family to the hut, a stone dwelling barely tall enough for a man to stand straight. There were no windows; even Celia had to stoop to enter the doorway. But crowded with the two men and the woman, the crying children, the hut quickly became a sanctuary.

Adelina brought in the packs. Nati and Celia untied them, hungry, tired, but mindful of Abateo's stern face. It would not do to stop when there was need for their work. Matt went back through the low doorway; the wind took him immediately, captured his breath and stunned him until he lowered his chin and drew the icy cold to his lungs through the thin wool scarf and could concentrate on what must be done.

Firewood, for the small oven built in the far wall. Anything that would keep them warm. Matt gathered mesquite and dried ocotillo, even a clump of sotol to start the blaze. He shoved the fuel inside and went for more. He drifted near the stock, peered over the rock wall, and saw the two horses backed to the wind, tails drawn between their legs, manes coated with ice. He could not find the mule—until the number of legs multiplied; Matt bared a grin. Trust a mule for survival.

The sheep were a layer of white, constantly moving, softly bleating from the punishment. There was little he could do; the snow piled around his feet and his legs were numbed. He blessed the animals and found his way back to the hut.

The warmth inside was welcome; there was the smell of food steaming by the fire. Beans, frozen lamb, tortillas chilled into flat plates. The wind howled outside and its cold breeze swirled into the hut. Matt unwound himself from his blanket and pinned it to the doorframe with nails there for that purpose. The wind slowed, the blanket whipped and pulled. But it was warmer inside the hut.

The children looked at Matt with frightened faces, as if it were their first time to see him. The raw hurt of those old stares went deep. He had forgotten for a time what the expression on Nati and Celia now recalled. He had forgotten the rest of the world. He was willing to return to the cold, lonely, outside storm.

Adelina dug her fingers into his hard back and pushed him to the fire. She made him sit, took a shallow pan filled with melting snow, and dipped the hem of her skirt in the cloudy water.

When she brought the material to his face, Matt panicked. She cursed him, looked straight at him—and mouthed a word only a man would speak. It was enough to settle him.

"The ice has opened your scar. No matter. You will sit and let me clean it or you will be uglier in the morning. It is your choice."

The old man gasped at the cruelty of his daughter's words; it was not a woman's place to speak so, but that had never stopped Adelina. The fire she wiped from Matt's face was a familiar one. He bit down, drew warm air into his lungs, thought of all manner of things except the boil of his face, the scent and heat of the woman who cleaned him with unfeeling hands.

Matt closed his eyes; a small hand slipped into his, tiny fingers curled around his thumb. "It is all right to cry, Señor Matt. It is all right." Nati. And Celia beside her.

Finally Adelina emptied the bloody water outside the blanket. A meal was shared in which no words were spoken. Nati sat on one side, Celia on the other. The food in their bellies took some of the day from them, and Nati's eyes closed, the plate loosened in her hand. Matt caught it, put it down quietly on the stone hearth. Celia laid her head on Matt's arm and was quickly asleep.

The old man smiled then, and lifted the sleeping Nati to a pallet of waiting blankets. Matt carried Celia carefully, felt the expulsion of her gentle snoring warm his neck.

Abateo lay down, a child snuggled to his back, a child held tenderly to his belly. Matt covered them with a blanket only just damp, patted Nati's dark head, and went back to stare at the fire. Adelina busied herself with picking up the unfinished meal, scraping the plates with her fingers, placing the frozen tortillas nearer to the flame, where they would thaw by morning. Matt saw the flames rise and fall, felt the easing of his back and thighs, the new pain in his frozen hands. He looked up and smiled at Adelina—and was not hurt when she did not return his gesture.

There was a pallet fixed near the fire. Its emptiness cried out in the small room. Matt tried to have his say, but Adelina acted as if he were not there, had said nothing to her.

"I will stay up with the fire while you and your family sleep. Your father and the children are safe and warm, it is your turn."

She was deliberate in her toilet. She positioned herself so that Matt had to see the flow of her legs under the great swirl of her skirt. Brown skin glowing with the fire's heat, flesh that tapered at the knees and swelled out to the top of the thighs.

She made a half turn, came one step closer. Matt could feel the heat of her, taste the salt of her skin. She did not look at him, but she knew well enough what she was doing.

He was warm and fed, tired and comfortable. And a beautiful woman was near him, showing her legs and skin as if he were invisible. The hardness rose between his legs; he placed his elbows on his thighs and pressed down until he could think of anything other than the woman above him. She knew what she was doing to him. He wanted to cry out at her.

It was a fantasy. The warmth of the woman smell, the strain of his flesh against wet leather pants. The food in his belly, the deep tiredness of his limbs. A tantalizing pleasure.

Until he looked into her eyes. Into the mocking sneer that marred her beauty. The pleasure left him, driven out by the hatred of her teasing. Desire that overwhelmed him became hatred.

He bolted outside, butting his head through the blanketed door. He was there for ten minutes, using the cold to calm him, picking more firewood and bits of grass. The cold ate into him quickly; he shook badly and his hands burned.

The old man was no fool; he knew the temper and spirit of his firstborn child.

The cold drove him inside. He was quiet, and laid the wet fuel down near the dimmed fire. He chose carefully and rebuilt the flame until it would smolder most of the night and keep the hut from freezing. But he knew it would be some time before he would sleep; the vision of the woman would rouse him each time he closed his eyes. So he stared blindly into the fire, saw the hatred again and again—until he let himself drift into a half doze.

The cold tried to wake him, but he drew the worn blanket close around his face and pulled up his legs to his belly. He thought then of climbing out of the warmth to rebuild the fire, and that brought him close to wakening. The children would be cold, the old man would stiffen.

Then a brown arm reached across his vision and laid a stick on the coals, returned with a handful of dried grass, another stick, a pile of twisted and broken twigs. The fire blazed into life. Matt's eyes closed, his mind drifted away from the slender arm that had fed the blaze.

Cold air chilled his back above his belt. Matt shifted and wiggled, tried to fit the blanket to him. Then a softness covered him, a new fire bruised his skin. Heat rose in his face, scalded his neck and arms, went down his spine to the small of his back. The softness came closer, an arm slid over his ribs and draped across his belly and pulled him near.

Adelina. Her breath on his neck, her hand gently rubbing his belly. He instantly became hard; the woman shifted her hips and rubbed his buttocks. The old man coughed and snorted, choked and coughed again. Matt's shame softened him; he caught up the circling hand in his and captured it with his fist. Kept it from betraying his flesh.

She brought her mouth close to his ear and whispered curses in different tongues, called out insults until his desire was replaced with anger. He thought to twist sideways and look into the hateful face and answer the accusations. He had never known a woman with thoughts like this one had. She pumped his body with her hips and thighs. The words and descriptions and curses spilled from her in fury until Matt could no longer bear her ministrations.

She wanted this, to inflame him and arouse him until he was all other men and would take her in blind hate and fury. He might carry the devil's mark on his face, but his mind and body belonged to him. He would not give in to a mindless woman to fuel her sadness. He sighed and was still.

He tucked the hand under his side and patted it. Lay as if he had gone to sleep. She relaxed; the warm body softened, the heavy breasts pressed and smoothed out on his back. Matt fought to keep his mind empty of all but the need for sleep, the chores to be done come morning. Anything. The old man and the two children, less than ten feet from him, were a good reminder.

His eyelids were heavy; he floated in the darkness. There was an odd satisfaction that the woman now breathed in rhythm with him. The bright surge of a new fire glowed in the thin skin of his eyelids. He let the glow sear him.

He slept finally, and the woman kept her place behind him. The thick sheet of black hair shifted when she moved; it flowed over Matt's face, grazed his scar, tickled his open mouth, and lifted as he snored. The fire sputtered, the coals turned gray, and then, toward morning, simmered into old coldness.

Abateo Flores woke early. Adelina was tending the fire. Matt had carried in more wood, and the flame once again heated the small house. The girls were anxious, arguing about nothing, still tired and cold, still hungry. But they were alive.

The tortillas were folded around the few reheated beans. Matt found a small pack that had been dropped in the flight to the cabin, and the wonderful smell of coffee flooded the room. Even the girls sipped a shared cup, wrinkling their faces and wondering out loud why grownups liked such a bitter drink.

The blowing snow and ice had stopped, the clouds lifted, and the sun came through in a pale halo. The entire view from the cabin door, down a narrow canyon and out to the plains, was of bent and brittle white grass, coated and shining cacti, brush and trees changed with a layer of thin ice. Even the air drawn into warm lungs cracked.

Abateo watched the strange young man move about the cabin, doing his few chores, rolling blankets that had dried, poking in a few bundles to hunt more food and clothing. And he watched his Adelina even more closely; he knew her well. He was finally satisfied that the night was innocent.

In the years of Adelina's liberty, Abateo had read many faces, of the innocent and the guilty. There was no guilt in the boy's face, no pleasured exhaustion that a night with Adelina left. The eyes were clear, the gaze steady when it focused on Abateo's command.

"Matt, there is much to be done here. We cannot expect

to move the sheep for a long while. You may leave, in a few days. But we would like . . ." He left the young one the choice, and nodded with delight when he saw it in the smile. "It is not much of a house, but there is room and it is warm. The *Despoblado* can be cold when it chooses, and we will have a winter to freeze a man until he can no longer walk on his legs but must crawl like a dog."

He stopped himself, for the children had heard the severity of their papa's voice and were distressed. Abateo became calm—and asked Nati a simple request to shake her from his harsh words.

Matt heard the old man but saw only Adelina. He watched to see if the father's invitation had a place with her. He could not help his staring; she was beautiful. Her long skirts were damp, her hair unraveled, there was a smudge of charcoal high on her forehead. He would wipe that mark away, if she would allow him.

He knew the night had been a dream, a nightmare. His lust had been a base emotion uninvited by Adelina. He saw into her—there was no feeling there, no hatred, no fury. Nothing. He chose to accept that as a delicacy of feelings that he would respect. The closeness of her body in the night, the wandering of her hands, the evil he had thought was in her eyes. That was from the cold, from the instinct for survival.

Adelina was both proud and mannered. And Matt would not sully her with his desires or his imaginings. They had both needed warmth; he could not think of sleeping with the old man, or the two little girls.

A delicate cough distracted him, a well-placed word helped him to return.

"Señor, you will join us, then? There is food here for the stock, for an emergency. And food also for you. Matt?"

"*Sí, abuelo*. I will stay. *Gracias.*"

A slip of his tongue, as if the old man were of his family. Matt hurried outdoors.

CHAPTER SIXTEEN

The fall was like any other time for McCraw, and yet different. More neighbors came to ask questions and listen to his opinion. He didn't much like it, but he couldn't turn them away.

The sun stayed high, the air cooled, the winds blew. Streambeds dried up, and surface pools disappeared completely. Ranchers came along to ask him more about water—and to tell him the local gossip.

Roads got built even as McCraw worked the brush for his stock. Roads from Presidio to Fort Davis, to Marfa and El Paso. There was much talk of moving the county seat to Marfa; new business wanted to ship on the railroad, record titles, and settle land deals all in one town.

Much of this activity didn't matter to McCraw. The fall was dry and cool much too early, worrying him. He watched the clouds in the morning, tasted the strange pattern of the wind, saw the leaves wrinkle and blow away before it was time. He listened to his new neighbor complain about the dryness—and didn't bother to tell him more than once that it was normal weather for the *Despoblado*. He rode his fall chores, did his worrying, and wondered about the winter yet to come.

Miguel and Silvestre were slow to work the fall roundup; McCraw thought about the kid, wished he was working alongside. Cattle had to be moved and counted, fence around the spring rebuilt, horses doctored before the winter snow.

Civilization came to him; Edward Dutchover visited, to ask McCraw's opinions on this and that, about the weather, the condition of the cattle, the graze. And especially water. He asked polite questions about the possibility of rain. McCraw gave his considered answers, and soon enough Dutchover stopped the visiting. The man's company was not missed.

A frost hit mid-October that should have warned McCraw, and a cold snow came in early November that froze two late weaners. If the kid had stayed, they wouldn't have been lost. Silvestre couldn't get them pulled free of the bog in time.

A good mare came up missing, and Miguel found the remains of the foal, a big, stout colt. Half eaten by coyotes, neck twisted and broke in a long fall. The scattered bones of the mare were a half-mile away, tangled in some fool's rope and a mesquite rail. McCraw cursed the sky; everything got in his way. Miguel and Silvestre disappeared for two days, and the work got more behind. McCraw was ready to quit.

A snow came in before Christmas, one that stayed on. Then a long freeze, the middle of January by McCraw's guess. McCraw rode out wrapped in a doubled blanket, strips of wool binding his hands. The chores had to be done. A new one was chopping through the tank of frozen water; an old one was forking out for the stock what little hay he stored in the fall.

Miguel found three dead yearling heifers; Silvestre brought in a nursing filly orphaned in late January.

The days had no time. Chores were repeated morning and night; the goat fed and watered, taken out to grass unless the snow had blown in at night. It was a real desert winter, bitter cold, snow mixed with sand to scour a man's face, make his eyes burn. Then some days the sun would shine, sucking up the last of the snow and fooling a man to thinking winter had gone.

A welcome break came somewhere midwinter, when the ground thawed and the snow disappeared completely. For more than a week the spring bubbled over. Miguel and Silvestre rode off without McCraw's knowing. They were back four days later, red-eyed and thick-headed from celebrating. McCraw didn't ask them what.

He stayed at the ranch, worked double, cursed their stupid, blundering minds, and cursed their hangovers when they came back. He took them back only because no one else was handy.

The cold returned, the snow blew in as penance for the few good days. McCraw began to lose his temper. He rode the horses too hard, stayed up to quarrel with himself late into the night. Nothing was right; he knew it but didn't try to find the change.

The first day he touched a horse to groom and fists of hair came free, he also received a hand-delivered note from Wilson Voeckes. It took a minute for him to recognize the name. And then he used the note as an excuse to ride out. There was no explanation in the writing, only a request he come to Voeckes's office at his earliest convenience.

McCraw told Miguel to move the mother cows close to new grass, set Silvestre to mending more of the broken gear. He would have put out more orders, but Miguel stopped listening, and Silvestre never knew what to do until Miguel told him twice.

He thought of saddling the buckskin colt, but took his time, standing to watch the youngster from between the rails. Another winter had bodied up the colt, put muscle and strength where there had been only promise. He'd ridden the colt through the winter, used the long legs and new power to push through drifts and chase angry steers. But, somehow, he'd come to think on the colt as not his. He enjoyed the willing response to leg and rein, and the high spirits. But the buckskin wasn't his. He opened the gate and let the youngster go.

So he roped the blond sorrel and spent time resetting the shoes, combing through the tangled mane and tail, currying off some of the winter fuzz. McCraw swore at his efforts, as if there were someone to take note of his good horse and oiled saddle, the patched jumper and new pants. He was a man gone old in his mind, with the company of coyotes and lizards and two crazy men to drive him past redeeming. He'd spent most of his life alone, but this time he'd lost the comfort of solitude.

He headed toward old Fort Davis. And he kept by habit to the old trail, the familiar one. He was comforted on the narrow path. He was eased by the clumps of mesquite, the ancient boulders, and then the open plains, the slow rise of the hills, the lines of dark cottonwoods along the creek bed. He was close to the fort; he knew the landmarks.

He'd come here alone when it wasn't safe for a company of soldiers. He'd come through with old Limm Tyler, and again with Hap Railsford. He cursed, angry for letting in old pictures. He hadn't thought of Hap for fifteen years. Cut by a jealous husband and bled to death in full sight of a drinking crowd. With no one to care.

The same epitaph could be written in stone for him. "No one to care." Hell.

Feeling sorry for himself—like a mooning, wet-eared kid and his first paid whore. Not knowing that it was money and not love. McCraw spanked the sorrel with the reins; the horse threw his head and lurched into a trot.

There were signs of sheep all over the land, large areas close grazed but not destroyed, cloven prints headed toward unmarked springs. There'd always been sheep in the *Despoblado*, ever since the white man tried civilizing it. Sheep were easy, ate what no cow or horse would touch, and the Indians weren't up to bothering them much. These herds had been near old springs, and McCraw was secretly pleased; someone else who knew the secrets.

Fort Davis was just below him. McCraw eased up and watched the town. Anger built quickly in him; it was a sorry sight. And he was a poor excuse, for the deviling in his mind when he needed to tend to business. He let the sorrel slide down a hill and step into the worn track of the new road.

Matt worked each day, chopping the spring clear of ice, feeding the year-old hay. It was enough to insure survival but not to cover the ribs of the old mare and the roan. The mule stayed well covered and eager to kick.

Adelina treated Matt as if he did not exist, like she treated the two girls. A plate was filled with food but never passed to him, the pallets laid on the floor now had a separate mat for him. He washed out his own few clothes, folded and stored his bed. She was not rude; she spoke when there was no escaping it. But mostly she ignored him.

The days of cold, the endless chores, took a toll. Nati and Celia grew thin, listless, and Adelina sometimes snapped at them until they would cry, furious with the company of people she truly could not love. But at night the youngsters sat on Matt's knees and listened to his stories, put their arms around his neck, and were quiet. It was a time like he had never known.

Slowly the lived through the days. It was the length of the sun that told them it was almost over. The horses, too, showed the coming of spring. Great clumps of shed hair covered Matt and Abateo when they touched the mare and the roan. They both laughed and watched the hair lift in the new breeze.

An early spring, but it would not fool Abateo. The expected warmth was unreliable, giving way to violent storms and bold winds. Animals stayed hungry, humans half starved.

But as the days warmed, Adelina changed. She spoke to Matt, made requests. And she began to talk normally with the girls, chiding them when they fought, praising them for simple chores. Easy day-to-day conversation. Soon Matt could think of no place more perfect than the small cabin, no sound nicer than the bleating sheep, no sight more wonderful than the long black hair and flashing legs of Adelina as she walked toward him. Face gentle, eyes glowing with recognition, hips moving with a welcome grace.

He was lost in the vision. He was awkward and new, fingers uncertain, mouth dry. Sounds and thoughts caught in his throat. His dreams were half nightmares, and he woke tense and hard between his legs, deeply shamed by the lust.

He slept outside by choice, even though the nights were winter chilled. It was safer outside.

Abateo watched the change in the scarred young one and watched his oldest daughter. He saw the careful plan, and shook his head when she pushed the blouse lower on her bared arms to expose her fine shoulders and the beginnings of her soft breasts, pinched her lips and cheeks before going outside to talk. It was an old pattern.

He felt a great sorrow for the boy. He was sorry for what lay ahead. He could do nothing but let Matt blunder to destruction. The boy would not listen, he would not heed the advice of an old fool. And it was a shame that Adelina would soon go to him. He was already wounded by the world; he did not need her cruelty to deepen the bleeding. But it would come.

There were three days of true sun. Nati and Celia played outdoors, sitting under a budding mesquite bush, where they moved their cornhusk dolls and laughed until Abateo called them for chores. The horses came alive in the warm air; the old mare nipped at the roan, the little horse put on a show; bogged his head, flagged his tail, squealed, and raced around the stone pen, even jumped the sheep that didn't get out of his way. The old mare watched the antics and waved her tail as if she were a filly, the roan a stallion. When the two horses touched noses, there was much pawing and whickering; they greeted each other as if they had not spent the winter huddled together for protection and warmth.

Matt smelled the air, watched the antics, tasted the spring. Time to ride on, time to search out a ranch and a pen of unbroken broncs to earn his living. The old man and the girls would do the work to keep the sheep herd fed and traveling to new grass.

But he stayed to watch Adelina walk the rocky hillsides of the small canyon. He sat with her as she pounded dried ears of corn into paste. The smell of her, the sight of her bared arms, the tantalizing nearness as she bent over to serve him a meal from the blackened pot. He would stay only for those times.

A few stalks of loose hay were caught under a rock. Matt absently picked them up and wove them, one-handed, into a long strand. The voice came from directly behind him. It was her sweet voice—and it spoke the words he waited to hear.

"It is a beautiful day. Would you come and ride with me? These two horses, they are full of themselves. Even the old mare, the *abuela*, she is snorting and dancing like a girl. Papa Flores, he would not mind if we had some of this day. It would do the horses much good, would it not?"

Roping out the mare and cinching up the worn saddle, shoving the high bit into her mouth, was no easy task, but Matt let the old girl have her small rebellion, then insisted, and she gave in.

The roan was more difficult. Matt roped the little horse and snubbed him to a stout post, flipped the rope, twisted it about the bony muzzle, and pulled hard until the roan took his steps. The white eyes rolled at the touch of wool and leather, the hind feet kicked out. As if the horse had never been ridden and handled by the same man who touched him now, stroked his neck behind the flattened ears, and combed his fingers through the tangled mane.

The old mare nickered, the roan kicked out. Tried to bite when the bit was slipped in his mouth. Matt grinned at the wicked showing and slapped the pony's neck. He couldn't blame the roan; he was feeling the same way himself.

Adelina sat on the mare; Matt felt her stare travel up and down his frame as he worked the roan, checked the rigging one more time, and loosed the ugly head from the post. Abateo came to watch, and the two girls. It was surely spring.

He jammed his hat down, threw his leg over the roan, and sat hard in the saddle, both feet in the stirrups before the roan knew he was free.

The ride was for show. Matt grabbed his hat and waved it, slapped at the roan's shadow, yelled into the sun. The

TEXAS SPRINGS 165

roan flew, his great leaps carrying horse and rider around the corral in easy circles. Hard spins to the right, squeals and grunts from the horse, laughter from the rider. It was an old game, a whirlwind, a release from winter's burden.

Adelina turned the old mare and kicked her out of the canyon at a lope; Matt saw the mare disappear. Abateo pulled open the gate; the roan gathered himself and took a leap outside. Matt yelled again, waved his hat, and in a short race caught up with the laboring mare and the pouting girl.

The horses slowed to a walk, the riders silent, concentrating on everything but each other. Matt could not look full at her; a frown creased her face, and he saw the lines at her eyes, the tightness of her mouth. He did not know why, but she allowed him to ride beside her, and for now that was enough.

There was another spring, hidden in a side canyon. Water spilled over the edge of a flat rock, greening a path to the canyon floor. Mosses covered the spillway, grass was luxurious, new ferns rattled in the fresh wind.

Adelina paid no attention to Matt; she was off her horse and climbing up the spill, fingers dark with new earth as she dug into the ground, pulling herself higher, hair streaming down her back. The climb went quickly; she reached the core of the spring and stood alone, turned a complete circle, and saw the white shape that was Matt, waiting still at the base of the water. She circled again, stopped, held her hands to her breasts, and then was gone.

She didn't think of Matt; he would come after her. He had no choice. It was easy to slide the blouse over her head. She bent forward and felt the soft cotton bunch on the thickness of her hair. The warm air tickled her naked back; she was conscious of her freed breasts, their pink tips hanging close to her face. She remained bent over; the blouse was shaken off her arms and thrown aside. She shook her head and enjoyed the swing of hair. It touched her breasts, swept the skin of her arms.

She didn't think of him, didn't consider what he would

think of her, what he would see when he climbed the spillway. He did not matter—the sensations did. She straightened, drew a deep breath, let her fingers slide along the bank of her skirt until they found the one button that held the waist. She picked at the fastener, tossed her head, let her breath out, and touched her belly, snug in the closed skirt.

The air around her changed, a bitter, acrid smell enveloped her. The male smell. Strange fingers touched hers, covered her hand to move it aside. The skirt was opened; the heavy gather of material slid off her hips and lay around her ankles. A soiled petticoat clung to her. She was impatient; the man's hand did not remove this last barrier fast enough. She tore at the knot, tightened it until she could not find the beginning.

Adelina cursed violently. The roan gelding and the old mare looked up. The roan snorted and blew, the old mare switched her tail. But the man said nothing; instead he put his finger to her lips and at the same time gently tugged the string until it gave and the old petticoat lay piled on the skirt.

She stood naked, the moccasins laced on her ankles, legs and thighs pale from winter's hiding. She was quiet now, motionless, legs apart, head thrown back. The wind took her hair, cleaned her face, hardened her nipples, feathered the inside of her parted thighs.

The man watched her. Adelina let her own hands ride the outside of her hips, to cross each other and touch the dark patch of hair at the joining. She could hear the man swallow, could imagine the immediate rise of hard bone between his legs. It was what she wanted now; the hardness, the uncaring lust.

She saw the scarred face and looked away. But he was a man; she could see the bulge in the leather pants, the light in the eyes. She kept her eyes from his face, put out her hand, and barely touched the front of his shirt. Slowly the buttons worked through the holes, until she could take the tails of the shirt and draw the garment over his head.

She was bold enough to put her hands on the fastenings of his pants, but it was too much for his modesty. He turned from her while he fumbled with his clothes.

It was a beautiful back, hard muscled and lightly browned, as was her own skin. Smooth, velvet, iron. Wide at the shoulders and neck, tapered to the rise of buttocks, the swell of thighs that were unmistakably male.

He came back to her, head down, black hair curtained across the scar. She accepted him that way. He was every man she had been with; she would take him here, on the softness of the moss, and would not look into his face or let him see hers.

She walked from him. He stepped out of the pants at his feet, leaned down to unlace the moccasins, and came to her carefully on the carpet of green, willing to have what she would give. Adelina shook her head, enjoyed the wildness of her hair. He stopped, confused, embarrassed by their nakedness.

This was how she wanted him. Subject only to her, caring for nothing but her pleasure. She held him quiet with the palm of her hand, walked to him, stroked him until he was ready. She looked once at the face and closed her eyes. He made no move beyond what she allowed.

She knelt down on the moss, arched her back, spoke to him blindly.

"Take me now. As a wild horse, as the stallion does with his mares. Now."

She knew how to persuade him. She tossed her head, leaned forward on her hands, flexed and swayed, shifted and dropped her belly close to the cool moss. Raised her buttocks in increased demand. No man could resist what she offered.

And he was in her. At first gentle and slow, a light probing, a careful stroking. He gave sweetness, she wanted rage. She leaned back quickly and impaled herself on him. He cried out; she answered with her own curse. Felt his arms reach to hold her swinging breasts. She braced on her arms, dug her toes into the parted moss. He began to rock them, driving deeply, crying out again and again.

It was not enough; completed, he tried to retreat, but she would not allow him. She rested her face sideways on the moss and reached back with her right hand, caught him and squeezed until she heard his pain. Then she began to stroke, circling him with thumb and forefinger until he no longer tried to pull away.

Then he had the sensations of his body, the pleasure of hers. He rode her like the stallion she named. At the sound of her cry, he stopped abruptly—and she called out foul names, cursed him cruelly, dared him until he rode her to the end.

The sleep was sweet and refreshing. When she awoke, she bathed in the cold spring pool. The man lay sleeping still, curled sideways, his hands protectively between his legs. Adelina stood over him for a long time. It was a pity the face was so scarred; he would be handsome without it. It had not mattered to her how his face looked. It mattered what was curled between his legs. He had serviced her well.

She kicked him hard in the thigh, above the arms folded across his leg. He came up quickly, ready to fight. The rod and balls dangled between his legs, and she laughed at him. Men were pitiful. She walked around him, pushed at his backside with her bare foot, and made him stand straight.

"Papa will be wondering. It is best I go back now. You, it does not matter."

She waited for what he must say. He was predictable, laughable, hiding his nakedness with his hands and spilling out the words she did not care to hear.

"Señorita, you are lovely ... We will ... You are the most ..."

She had heard it many times before, even though this one did not beg or cry. His nakedness was in his face, in the longing she saw there, the loneliness of the long winter—he would be easy to drive off. It was almost a pity, for he was mannered and gentle, and Nati and Celia liked him. But, he was just a man.

"You? You do not come back with me. Papa does not expect to see you again. He knows we are here, he knows what we do. Even my children know, they are used to this. But you, you choose not to accept what you are given. You must have the truth.

"You are ugly, señor. Your face ... you cannot think a woman would choose to look on that every day. You will leave now. There are other men, señor. Men much more handsome than you. Men who take care of me. It was the day, señor. Nothing more than the spring day."

She ceased to think of him then. She picked up her clothing and spent much time sorting through and wiping at the dirt, picking off insects and new plants. Shaking the dust from the long skirt, smoothing out the old petticoat. Then she dressed, setting the skirt carefully on her hips, fitting the blouse until it was modest and unrevealing. Her breasts were tender under the cotton; she thought of the passion he had given her. Then she fastened the skirt, pinned her hair, retied her moccasins.

She looked up once, when the small roan gelding whickered. It was little more than a bothersome fly, she decided. Nothing interesting. She watched the old swayed mare and the useless gelding and pitied them both. As she once pitied the young man.

Then she finished her dressing and paid no attention when the roan was mounted and ridden away. The old mare snorted, the hoofbeats faded, the mare whinnied sadly. Adelina did not bother to look.

CHAPTER SEVENTEEN

What rolled and bucked inside him was a pain he could not bear. The pleasure of her, the touch, the killing of her words. It was more than he had ever known.

The words would not leave—that no woman would hold to a man so marked and branded. He had heard that before, listened to the old ones spit out his name, rub it in the dirt with crossed fingers until the mark disappeared. But he had never felt the curse driven in so straight and true.

He passed the trail leading back to the winter canyon and gave no thought to it. The roan kept a long trot that carried them out to the plains. Matt did not think of his gear stacked inside the cabin: the special blanket woven by his mother, given to him when he first rode out from home as a man, the extra shirt; the brush jumper; the patched sheepskin coat Flores loaned him for the winter cold.

He had water in a canteen, the old knife in his belt, a rifle under his leg. And a burned soul.

When the roan went to a gaited walk, Matt goaded the tired horse to a run. He had to go somewhere, he had to move fast, outdistance the blade stabbed in him. He could not outrun his face, but he could bury the new killing in his fast tracks.

Slowly he let go. The reins lay on the wet neck, the horse walked on an unknown trail. Matt stretched his arms, felt the joints of his back pull and crack. He turned right, then left, and the muscle tugged across his shoulders. The nightmare stabbed him, over and over, until the blade was dulled by time.

He saw where he was. A collection of hovels, thatch-sided huts, baked mud walls, rolled rib ceilings. Goats herded by a child; two dogs that ran snapping behind the roan and dodged the expected kick. The center of an unfamiliar village. A mule, a burro, two slat-ribbed horses tied at a sagging rail. Striped shade hid several men from Matt's stare.

He could see little of their presence past white shirts, the shape of heavy dark hair. Voices traded in rapid Spanish, a word of the Anglo tongue, a few local names. The drifting scent of tequila, the hot smell of new spice, the dull flavor of refried beans. He was suddenly hungry, thirsty, ready for anything inside the low-roofed building.

He tied up the roan and walked across loose boards to stand in the shade. The men said nothing as he passed them. A shoulder was turned to him, a head bent, a voice in loud argument. Matt hesitated, saw the back of the neck, the profile of a ponderous belly. A violent picture flashed in his head and he hesitated. A second passed; he nodded to the men and went through the open door.

At the bar, he took off his hat and wiped the sweat from his face. The memory was clear: a band of horses, dust, the mesquite fence. Loud voices, fear. He ordered a drink.

His hand was close to his mouth with the needed taste when three men drifted inside. He heard their step without seeing them. His hand shook. He gulped the liquor, swallowing without first letting the fire burn his mouth. He put the glass down, held his fist to the wooden plank, and shook his head at the bite, pushed the glass forward, tipping it to the bottle still in the bartender's hand. The man poured, Matt raised the glass to his lips. There was no other sound or movement in the small room. There was no door other than where the three men stood.

They came up to him, stood beside him, feet shod in thick moccasins, legs encased in hard britches, faces shielded by wide-brimmed hats. Matt felt a shudder start in him, tipped the glass and swallowed, licked the rim and set the glass down with careful deliberation. He looked to the left and saw the familiar face. He pushed the empty glass toward the bartender and stepped back.

The bartender held out his hand; Matt fumbled for the coin; paid him. A dark hand picked the coin out of the bartender's fist and returned it to Matt. The fingers touched a moment too long on his flesh, a familiarity that was an insult. Matt let the coin drop, waited out the spinning that rolled it to the bar's edge, dropped it over, onto the dirty floor.

The hand disappeared. The man crowded Matt, pushed him. The words were spoken in a low warning: "You are insulted I would offer to buy a drink, señor? Do you not accept such a gift, or are you too proud to drink with such as me, as my *compañeros*? Señor, you will drink?"

Drops of sweat trickled down his back and soaked into the waist of his pants. Matt's voice was even, pleasant almost, when he spoke to the horse thief. The scar cutting his face burned furiously, and Matt wanted to rub it hard. The thief would recognize the scar if he had seen Matt at all.

He leaned on his elbow, ignored the itch of his back and face, and laughed easily: "Señor, I will drink with those I choose. I am not proud, no more than any man. But I will drink with friends, with those I trust. And you, señor, I do not know."

Tensed, Matt let his right hand touch the knife at his side. The coolness of the old carved handle quieted him. The speaker moved away from Matt. The man behind the bar walked to its end and picked up a dulled shotgun, which he held carefully, never pointing it at his customers but showing it in anticipation. A warning quickly recognized.

A man moved away from Matt to the right. The man who had spoken touched a pistol strapped to his side. Matt drew the knife and slashed in one swing, opened a red line on the wavering hand. The thief yelled, dropped the pistol. Matt spun around and lunged forward, dug the tip of the knife into the nearest soft belly.

An expulsion of foul air washed his face; he pushed

harder on the knife, felt the flesh give way. The man he faced gulped hard, tried to pull in his belly. Matt stared into the closed face and spoke as if only to this one man:

"It is here for you, waiting in my hand. You wish to die, you may make a move, speak a word. The killing will be easy. For each of us."

He smiled then, satisfied. It was everyone twisted on the end of the knife, it was everything the days had brought to him. Death would end for all of them. Matt leaned on the extension of his hand. The man cried, pleaded with Matt through wounded eyes. There was a noise behind Matt but he didn't care. A chair scraped on the rough floor, a man coughed. Matt watched the bartender raise the shotgun chest high, level it. It mattered for nothing. Matt pushed into the red circle at the end of his knife. The man cried openly, tears muddying his skin. He spread his hands, raised his arms, to prove his innocence.

The outlaw spoke, but Matt barely heard over the noise inside his head.

"Señor, you have made your point. And I, I have made a poor joke now at Incencio's expense. I am Sergio, and this is José. We are now your friends, señor. You may choose to drink with us, or not. It is a choice, however, that will allow Incencio to cease his wailing and return us all to peace and quiet. We are simple men, señor. Wishing only to join you now in tasting the sweet fruits of another man's labor and skill."

Matt drew back his arm; the man called Incencio crossed himself twice above the wound. But the spoken words were true. Sergio held a fresh bottle high, clean and stoppered. Four glasses were on the bar. And the man behind it no longer had the shotgun at chest height and cocked.

A sudden rage burned in Matt, blurring his sense until he dug his own nails into the palm of his hand around the handle of the knife. He flipped it quickly, let the point come to his hand, rest there, before he tossed the knife with a flexing of his wrist—tossed it hard enough to drive the point deep into the frame of a saint behind the bar.

The one named Sergio reacted quickly, gripped and half freed his other pistol. Incencio crossed himself again. The third man, José, ducked after the knife had been driven home. The man behind the bar did not move.

Sergio let the gun return to its home. He wiped the wetness off his mustache and widened his mouth in an enormous empty grin. This strange man, who pinned Incencio in his belly, who showed nothing on his ugly face but a pleasure to die, this one would be a good *compadre*. For the while.

"Señor, we take what we want, where we find it. And today it is a drink with a stranger who will become a friend. A man of great courage who will give us honor by raising his glass to our toast."

The scarred man looked closely, as if to understand what was behind Sergio's pretty speech. Which would be impossible, for Sergio used words as a guard, a grave for promises he would not keep. Mischief was in him tonight, and the ugly one would be a good sword with which to prick Incencio and José.

The young one made his choice, stepped to the bar and raised a dirty glass full of the golden liquor to his mouth. He drank quickly and did not flinch from the terrible bite. It was enough for Sergio to take his own drink, raise his own glass with Incencio and José. There would be more tonight, much more. But it did not yet need to be mentioned. Not until the one with the great scar dug across his face was too taken with friendship and tequila to question.

Sergio grinned again in his eager show of friendship and stepped closer to the strange one, nudged him with an elbow to the ribs before he raised his glass. Tonight would be to savor, as one did an unwilling woman or a rank horse. The edge was in him tonight, as it often was, and the company of a stranger would add more spice.

Matt didn't remember climbing on the thirsty roan for the return to the village. His energies were concentrated on keeping his balance to the sway of the gait, the bend and climb of the trail, the noise going off in his head. He had to fight the saddle, and deny to himself what he knew they had done.

The noise stayed with him the longest: the terrorized bleating of the helpless sheep; the scrambling hooves on hard rock; the soft thud of a shod hoof rolling a downed body. New lambs made no noise; their mothers' frantic calls rose above the bleating. The ewes still carrying rolled like broken barrels.

It had been sport at first. To ride with Sergio and the other two, their names forgotten as soon as he heard them. A mindless chase that was ugly, cruel, that stained the base of a high-walled trap with innocent blood. The shepherd had been clubbed down with Sergio's pistol; the herd leapt his body frantically, driven by shouts and by echoes of gunfire.

It had been sport until then. And now Matt was haunted by the white shadow of the fallen man, the smell of the frightened sheep, the panic that piled dead sheep on living bodies, animal and human.

The raw remains of the tequila pounded his skull. He rode in darkness, the horses stumbling, heads low in exhaustion, following nose-to-tail, sweat damp on their necks.

They'd left the nameless village at sunset. Matt had seen the sky; he knew the beauty, yet the colors meant nothing. He was lost then, and now, but the liquor dulled him mercifully, Sergio's loud voice gave motion and direction to the long ride. He didn't hear what the man said, but he saw the teeth shining in the dark, saw the flash of a struck flint. The cigar that burned the night air.

At first Matt had thought they were Flores's sheep, and a wildness rode with him—to punish the girl, to see her again. But he was miles away, killing a crop that would support a family. It wove deep in him, seared through the drunkenness. The murdered carcasses, the half-dead scrambling out of the way, the horses' legs rimmed in blood, the sound of flesh striking wounded flesh. Matt groaned; the roan misstepped and went down. Color again streaked the ridge ahead of them, this time a cold gray that lightened while Matt watched.

Daylight, a trail to join a scratched road. Back to the unnamed collection of huts where the night started. Matt yawned, rolled his head, heard the crack of his spine. Then it came to him. He tasted the night's drinking, smelled the soaked blood, and his belly doubled on him, flooded his mouth. He leaned over the roan's shoulder and heaved into the sand.

Sergio laughed, the others were quiet, numbed. Matt wiped his mouth. Sergio spoke up, and Matt tried not to hear what the man said. This time, Sergio spoke the truth:

"The night was long. And the tequila flowed, perhaps too free for your tender belly. But you rode along with us and chased the stupid sheep. They are easy to run, easy to reach down and kill. Their smell is a sweet taste. It is a night's work . . . But now we will sip more of the blessed tequila, find a shaded place, and sleep. It is our way, señor. And you are welcome to it."

The barn was dark, the smell of it strong and rank. Matt took the horses inside and stripped them. He didn't go back to look for Sergio and the others; they were drinking at the cantina. He wanted only endless sleep that would clear his head, drive out the sound and smell of the night.

Matt shaped a pile of hay, padded it with a blanket for his head. The last he remembered was the salty taste of his mouth, the sourness of the barn floor, the rustle of dried grass as he shifted to find comfort.

The toe of a boot rolled him over; Matt felt his own fists dig in his belly. He slid on his shoulder, brought his knees up under him, and reached out for support. Another boot caught him at the spine, arched him and sent him forward. He fought this time, dipped into the force of the blow and almost made it to his knees. A blow numbed his arm and drove him headfirst into the post.

There was nothing he could see. Voices screamed above him, boots and legs herded him, kept him on hands and knees. Matt tried to stand, knew this time the feel and shape of the barrel end of a rifle that cupped the back of his neck and set him flat into a pile of wet manure. Florid cursing, rapid Spanish, more voices. Then a quick shift to Texas bragging:

"You boys don't care for much. Left a trail wide as that herd of sheep after you. Don't know why you set on making a night's game of slaughter. You dumb sons of bitches didn't even take a single goddamn hide to pay for your tequila. But we care, yessir. And you boys got time ahead of you. 'Less of course, you got the jingle to your pocket can pay the fine, buy up that herd of sheep.

"You're lucky that old man got nothing but a bump to his head, missing patches of skin. But you boys crossed the line, that you did. Them sheep may of had a Mex herding them, colored like you. But they belonged to Mr. W. W. Bogel, did those sheep. And Mr. Bogel wants them woollies replaced. We got us a law coming into the books now—you run up a fine, you work the line till it's paid. You got miles of road to dig, boys. Miles of road. And good spring weather."

CHAPTER EIGHTEEN

Fort Davis slept in the middle of the day. The few animals driven downstreet traveled heads hanging, tails slapping occasional flies. The folks McCraw passed didn't look up in curiosity or friendliness.

He let the sorrel drift while he watched the sorry traffic and wondered what had changed. The sorrel horse stopped on his own, right in front of the lawyer's office. Wilson

Voeckes. McCraw swung down. A good enough place to start, a good enough time to find out why he was here.

It was different, this second time entering the small office in anticipation of hearing a friendly voice, of seeing a welcome face. Voeckes stood up immediately and extended his hand, boomed a welcome in his high-pitched voice.

"Well, James. Mighty good to see you. Been a rough winter here, and I imagine it wasn't easier down where you are. Good to see you, James."

McCraw sat down slowly, stiff from his ride, and began to talk of the winter just past.

"You come through it, like I did. Got Godalmighty cold once or twice, come close to freezing parts of me I forgot I had. Hell of a winter. But we survived. Not much goes on near me, but boredom still don't come to visit often." That got him started. And Voeckes made it easy, offered a big cigar, then sat back and propped his feet up on the desk. There was something to be said for friends, even if they were occasional.

The talking eased an ache inside McCraw. He kept going, and watched Voeckes carefully at first, wondering when the man would tire. But Wilson laughed with him, listened closely, asked the right questions. And his eyes lit when McCraw talked of the buckskin colt and the outlaw race. The drifter who broke and rode him. They talked briefly about the threat of rustlers, the number of unwanted riders scattered through the plains. Enough to worry any decent man.

Voeckes went back to the buckskin, said it sounded like McCraw had himself a racehorse. McCraw agreed. Then they sat quiet for a while, each thinking their own line.

It had to come, finally—what McCraw had ridden his miles north for. Voeckes was real careful, and McCraw made himself listen.

"A problem's come up, James. With the land you claimed in the fall. Now, you still got your time to make improvements and payments. But word came back around that where you filed on dry land, you got yourself a spring." Voeckes held up his hand when McCraw sputtered. "It used to be, a man stood his ground, claimed his place and held it by the simple fact of that declaration. That no longer works, James. Which is why you had to come all the way up here last fall, to file on Spencer's grant. A wise move, my friend. But you made one mistake.

"One of your neighbors rode in and told the land agent you have a spring. They looked it up, and sure enough, that parcel is listed 'dry.' It didn't set well with the agent. Not at all."

Voeckes quit. McCraw opened his mouth to bluster and explain, and had enough sense left to shut himself up. It came down on money, McCraw knew that. And no doubt Voeckes knew the exact sum without having to look at the papers in front of him. McCraw didn't want to know; there was short cash in his pockets and debts to be paid. He didn't much like where he sat. He stared at Voeckes and let the man work his finish.

It was a long time coming, but Voeckes began to shuffle papers, then picked out one and read it silently. He glanced up at McCraw, ran a hand through his thinning hair and sighed.

"I did some arguing, but you didn't win it all. Let me see ... Ah, it was already determined you have paid John Spencer for the one section claimed along the river. No one dares question the validity of that claim. No one. But ... the Land Act of eighty-three—it states the price of two dollars an acre for all watered sections. That's over a thousand dollars, James. A good deal of money."

There wasn't much to say. McCraw planted his boots square on the floor. Then Voeckes got started again.

"I did push. The agent would give you the three years to pay, no fine, no punishment. But you got a big piece of money waiting on you. More than that, James, you got a neighbor down near you willing to take over any way he can. I am truly sorry, but the law works this way, and the righteous often come in ahead of the right. You pay six hundred dollars now, this spring, or the whole thousand plus over the time. That's the decision."

The quiet stretched out, then McCraw heard a soft chuckle. He leaned on the desk, cocked his head at the man opposite him. There was nothing said in this room the last hour he could see would be funny. He checked on Voeckes's face, and sure enough a grin split the homely features. Laughing, by God, at another man's misfortune.

Sure he'd tried to get more; in his small conscience there was a hole from the lie he'd signed his name to, but it didn't make him a fool. He couldn't figure what changed Voeckes. McCraw pushed back his chair and rose up. He had a choice all right, to walk outside and ride away. Or punch the lawyer in the middle of his teeth. His fist doubled, his arm tightened with the effort.

The long features calmed from their private joke, the blue eyes watched McCraw's fist, and Voeckes started talking again. McCraw sat down as he heard the words.

"It came on while I was talking too much, James. Enjoying the pompous sound of my elegant words. My mother warned me about this behavior, and my father told me early on I would be a good lawyer. Like the sound of my voice, that I do.

"Forgive me, I had to do some serious thinking on the idea. The laughing was unkind, and for that, please forgive me. But it is too good, too perfect. And a delight."

McCraw doubted his ears. Asking forgiveness when it was his client who was the one to go contrary to the given law. He didn't know about Voeckes.

"Awhile ago you talked about a horse, and the young man who worked for you. You described a race, the colt's speed and heart. The young man's courage. Believe me, I have been wondering now for days what you could do. And now I know.

"You have another new neighbor, to the east. A gentleman by the name of Francis Dewitt Wilson. He is a true horse fancier, and has brought with him several examples of his racing stock. I have met Mr. Wilson, and have enjoyed his bragging and his passion. Don't misunderstand me, James. Mr. Wilson is a true fancier, and likes nothing more than to see two well-matched animals run for the prize.

"He also comes into our country with money, an unusual occurrence. He has suffered some hardships in settling his claim, but he is established and comfortable now, and beginning to look around.

"Think on it, James. Your buckskin, born and bred to these parts, and Mr. Wilson's blooded stock. Fast, yes, undeniably. But used to a smoothed track and a proper setting. Find a jockey, pick a distance, and you have a race. You can put up the buckskin, since the whole problem is that you have no cash. If he is as good as you say, Mr. Wilson will be intrigued. And you can ask for cash as your side, or sell Mr. Wilson's horse back to him.

"Either way, you can't lose more than you already stand to, and the odds for you are fifty-fifty. And I am sorry, James, for laughing without you. But this is a way out of your predicament. As well as bringing an air of excitement to this sad town. What do you think?"

He liked it; a good range horse against an Eastern racer. There was little for him to lose. A gamble for certain, but a chance he didn't have now.

"I need to find the kid. And we got to hit Wilson now, make him the proposition. But I got to find the kid, get the buckskin out running. Hell of an idea, Voeckes. Hell of an idea."

They sat for a while, two silent men in a darkening room. There was an ease in the quiet, as if something large had been dismissed. Until a different track came to McCraw's mind and it occurred to him to ask the question.

"Voeckes, who was it who spoke up to the agent and got me tangled in the law? I know, I ain't blaming him, mind you. Ain't blaming no one for picking up on Bitter Springs. Did that one myself, but I do rightly need to know the son's name."

"James, I would rather not tell you. But it will come out,

and you are right, you best know now. It was Thomas Kersey."

Voeckes had choices right next to his office, two bars, a fancier saloon, a men's club with crimson draperies and a fancy frosted-glass door. Voeckes said he thought Mr. Wilson would be in the saloon, or perhaps the club. He didn't rightly know which, but he would be willing to bet Mr. Wilson would not be found in either of those two particular bars. McCraw followed the long finger down the street and saw that the first bar had smoky stained windows and a broken door. The second bar was boarded up, planks nailed over shattered windows, an empty bottle left at the door.

Voeckes and McCraw went toward the first saloon. Voeckes began talking, rambling on about town affairs. "I'm all set to move into Marfa, James. When our brilliant town fathers turned down the rails, they killed this town. Marfa's where the money's going, so I'm off and away like the rest of my kind. Make a good living, be at the center of things. Right, James?"

He heard the conversation and found it rough paying much attention. It didn't matter to him where the county seat was; it didn't matter how the politics ran. He needed to find Francis Dewitt Wilson and clamp down on Thomas Kersey's scheme to pick up Bitter Springs. But he did cock his head and make grunting sounds to keep Voeckes happy.

The man stopped short, and McCraw dug in his heels to whoa quick enough. The grin was back, the eyes brighter, the whole long body of the man shaking.

"All we got to do, James, is put out the word you got a horse can outrun anything in the county. Put out some bait, let Mr. Wilson come to us. Keeps him off-balance and begging, gives us better odds. It will be great sport, my friend, and hopefully a legal title to your place."

The last was said with a sly look that could have been an insult. But Voeckes slapped his friend on the back and laughed again, pleased with the mechanics he was to set in motion.

It started as a game that McCraw would enjoy. Walk in the door, order a whiskey, sip it, maybe pick up a beer. Talk loud, brag up the colt, draw in others, ranchers themselves, or bored townfolk coming to a new spring, itching with renewed blood.

McCraw liked that part—talking on the colt, exaggerating the bloodlines, smoothing out the description. He was beginning to believe his stories by the third saloon; he was also conscious of a bend in his legs, a wobble to his gait. Drinking wasn't much of a pastime for McCraw, but he watched Voeckes pick his way down the walk and followed willingly.

They came to the frosted door of the gentlemen's club. McCraw was aware of the smell of his clothes, the grime worn into the seat of his britches, the dried crust on his boots. He touched Voeckes, but the man used that hesitation to spill out a bit of gossip he thought his friend might want to know, as it concerned his backbiting neighbor. It wasn't much, but he thought McCraw should know. It took Voeckes some doing to find the words in the numbness of his mouth, and he came close to giving up.

"Earlier, meant to tell you. Why Kersey come to need more water. Married now, widow living with Edward Dutchover. Wife's sister. Harriet, that's it. She is Mrs. Kersey now. Been a month married. Why Kersey went for the water."

There. He'd gotten out the telling. Voeckes was pleased with himself, until he saw McCraw. The man was white, must be sick. For he'd wrapped his arms about his middle. The browned face, colored even through the long winter, looked the texture of dried summer mud.

"You taken ill, James? Something from the last place mustn't have set right in you. Let's get inside, take a dram for your condition."

Voeckes opened the double glass doors, and McCraw went directly to the bar. His belly must be troubling the man, for he clamped down on his side and ordered whiskey. A double. Downed it and straightened some, and

Voeckes could see the lift of his shoulders. He would be fine.

Then a familiar figure walked up to McCraw, and Voeckes had to grin to himself. Their drinking and bragging were about to pay off. A hand slapped his back. A loud voice boomed. McCraw whirled around. A stranger. But the startled face of Wilson Voeckes, directly behind the man, kept McCraw from striking out. The long face was wide open, the eyes sharp, the mouth loose. McCraw lowered his hands, let his fingers play on the seam of his pants leg. The numbing pain of his gut was masked by the quick drink. He wanted another one.

The man who smacked him was tall and angular, and clothed in a hard wool suit, a boiled collar. A tie was carefully pulled and knotted around a thin neck. McCraw saw a dandy and wondered what the man was doing in the rawness of Fort Davis. What he wanted with a fool the likes of James Henry McCraw.

Voeckes made the introduction: it was Francis Dewitt Wilson. The word had spread, the bait taken. McCraw didn't care. He had his drink, and another. Then remembered his manners and offered one to Wilson and Voeckes. They both declined. McCraw drank quickly, put the glass down.

It was about horses. Voeckes was explaining to the man about the buckskin. The speed, the endurance of the big gelding. Horses. Cash money, a bet, a gamble.

McCraw's mouth dried out; he needed another drink. But Wilson spoke, and McCraw needed to listen.

"Mr. McCraw. I have heard much of you. It is nice to finally meet my neighbor, and a local legend." The voice was as perfect as the collar and tie, but McCraw didn't care. He tried to smile, desperate for the next drink.

"I did truly bring in some of my stable. But this climate, and the footing, is not conducive to racing as I have know it, sir. But I am always interested, if the stakes are right."

He knew a point was being made for him, but he lost

track. It didn't matter. Voeckes was listening, he would hear.

He looked at Voeckes. The long face was puzzled, as if there was something here the man didn't understand. McCraw looked at Francis Dewitt Wilson and saw nothing unusual. He wiped his hand across his mouth, felt a wetness on his fingers.

McCraw waved for another whiskey. The bartender was slow to fill the glass, kept looking at Voeckes. McCraw grabbed for the bottle, upended it over his glass. The liquor flooded the top of the bar. The track surprised McCraw; he ran his finger through the golden line and let go of the bottle. It crashed on the floor, but his eyes were focused on the liquor and his mind played with the patterns and swirls in the dirt.

"McCraw, you must have the head of a boulder. To be alive at all after your consumption of last night. Truly, I am respectful of your capacity and ability."

McCraw wasn't certain where the words came from. Last thing he remembered was the whiskey spilled on the bar. All the rest was lost in air, gone in a broken bottle on the floor, the crowds and questions.

Then the full flavor of the night's work swamped him and he finished rolling from the pallet, crawled to the familiar shape of the bucket by the door. He barely made it before he puked.

He didn't know where Voeckes was when the man began talking again. He didn't care, and he didn't have the strength to ask. The man talked on as if McCraw wanted to hear what the lawyer was spouting. He talked on about the night, a horse race, the gentlemen's club where the wager had been laid. McCraw curled up on the floor and let the coldness of the bare wood soothe his head.

The smell of coffee woke him the second time; bitter coffee boiled too long on a hot stove. He rolled over, put up a hand, and waited until a hot tin cup was pressed into the curled fingers. Even the pain of the burning metal didn't matter. Until he put the cup to his lips for a taste and burned his mouth, scorched his tongue, and spat out a spoonful of grounds.

"I'll tell you again, James. That was quite a performance last night. Francis Wilson thinks you are either a hero or a liar. And I'll tell you, if anyone doubts the wildness of the West, the stubbornness of you old-timers, the Indians and the lack of amenities you live with, last night left us no doubt at all. No doubt at all.

"You carried *me* home last night. And I have never seen a man drink as much rotgut whiskey and still be standing. To quote your Mr. Spencer, whom I have had the pleasure of visiting, 'It were truly something to hang an eye on.' And I would suppose from the look of you, that you have no recollection of the night's proceedings. Most of the night need not be recounted, as it was comprised of drinking, fighting, and a taste of the ladies.

"But there is a matter that must be discussed. You have a deadline, James, that may well be your misfortune."

Voeckes finally ran down. McCraw wondered if all last night the man talked on and on. Words. Damn them. Get to a town, have a drink, and a man's mouth roared ahead of his common sense.

There was a piece missing. McCraw wiped his tongue inside the rim of his mouth, coughed lightly, and decided to try the coffee again. He spat out more grounds and made his first try.

"Voeckes, you going to tell me I set up the race, right down to the date and time? And you couldn't get me to shut up? That what you're going to tell me? That what's spoiling your morning cup of coffee?

"I know all that, Voeckes. Know the date and the time. Ain't putting a blame on you. I did this one all by myself."

Voeckes rose slowly from the old chair and had the nerve to pour himself a cup of the ruined coffee before he came over to McCraw's share of the wall and slid his backside down, to sit on his heels and watch the coffee grounds settle and rise in his cup.

TEXAS SPRINGS 187

Then he looked right into McCraw, the blue eyes shot with red, half shuttered, puffy, and old. There was no mercy in the man, and McCraw knew his drinking companion felt no better than he did. Huddled against the papered wall, safe only with his butt cradled on the wood plank flooring.

"You got yourself the horse race all right, James. It is mid March now, and you and Francis set the date to be the first of May. That doesn't give you much time, from what you said last night. Do you remember any of it at all?"

Remember what? He had the date, the distance for the course. Knew the heart and stamina of the buckskin. What else was there?

He winced as he remembered, only partly from the hangover's pain. The kid, the ruined face and tender hands, the foul mouth. They'd talked of Matt last night, but no one knew where he'd got to. As good with biscuits and steak as a horse's training. It had to be the kid riding if the buckskin was going to win.

"Yeah, Voeckes. I remember."

The sorrel was stabled in a small corral, groomed down and tearing into a big pile of hay. Fresh water filled the trough, the saddle and blankets were hung from a beam, the bridle was tied to the horn.

McCraw spent a lot of time rubbing the broad back clean of chaff and hair, then quickly saddled and rode out. He wanted to be gone from Fort Davis before he met up with any of last night's participants.

The sorrel moved easily, yet the rocking gait pounded his head. Pounded, too, at the notions rolling over and over in his mind. Tumbled the thoughts in place until he had to take notice.

A race in less than two months' time. The buckskin colt turned out. A wager of everything he owned on the outcome. Kersey, the goddamn springs. Bitter Springs.

The woman: married. The beautiful look of her lost under another man's weight. Kersey. The hated Thomas Kersey. A pain like no other.

McCraw would not get past the image: Kersey and the woman. The drinking had not dulled the vision. It came back, bright and clear in the new daylight. No chance to ride past it, no reason to stop and think on it.

The woman and Thomas Kersey.

CHAPTER NINETEEN

McCraw came to the track headed to Kersey's canyon. Whatever he thought of the man, Kersey might have seen the kid. So it was necessary for him to head the sorrel down canyon, hold him steady on the trail. The big horse resisted, but McCraw held him tight, kept his legs on the red flanks, and straightened out the animal when he wavered.

It was a stark cabin, with a new room added out back. Plain, untouched by a woman's hand. McCraw allowed the smallest rise in his hopes. There was no hint of color in the small windows, and on the line strung between two poles there were work shirts and pants, no cotton pretties, no yellow dresses, flowered prints.

It had been his determination not to ask a woman like Harriet Gliddings to share such quarters with him, and it was his slow hesitation that lost her to Kersey's hand.

The sorrel shied badly and reared. McCraw brought the horse down hard; the gelding tossed his head up against the bit and soaked McCraw in white foam. McCraw called to the house, waited for the woman to answer his summons.

It was Kersey himself who appeared in the barn door. There was no sign of her. McCraw rode over. Kersey gave out no invitation to step down and have a drink, or even water the horse. There was no politeness in the man, no range courtesy.

McCraw wet his mouth, tugged at his hat. The words were hard coming.

"Kersey. Good day. I'm looking for a man, a rider. Might have come by your place this winter. Kid, early twenties. Dark-haired, Mex-looking. Riding a runty strawberry roan. Hell of a scar on the kid's face. Can't miss it. I want—"

Kersey didn't allow him to finish. "Haven't seen that one. Wouldn't let him here if I did. Not here, not never. Word come by half hour ago—you got a race going with Francis Wilson, for good money. Need that kid to ride. Not good, betting money you need for the ranch. Not good. I got to get to my work. 'Day to you."

The man disappeared inside his barn with that final judgment. McCraw sat, thinking hard. Word was out, and already folks were taking sides. 'Course, Kersey had the best reason to see him fail.

McCraw headed out of the yard at a slow walk. Kersey wouldn't want him to find the kid; Kersey wanted Bitter Springs. Kersey had the woman, now he wanted the water. Of course the man wouldn't ask him to step down—Kersey wanted McCraw gone from his place, out of his sight. Thieving was all right, but not if you had to do it face-to-face.

He held the sorrel to a slow walk, wanting a glimpse of taffy hair, the sound of a clear voice. He halted near the cabin door, but there was nothing inside. He lifted the horse to a lope, eager now to get past Kersey's sour smell. The sorrel took the bit and pulled, half bucking into the run. McCraw let him go.

Her bright hair caught up in a cotton square, she was at the last curve before the narrow canyon opened to the plain. McCraw slid to a halt and was out of the saddle before the horse stopped. The speckled mare harnessed to the wagon threw her head but didn't try to run.

"Mr. McCraw." Her voice came to him before he could touch her. She said his name again, furthering the needed distance between them. "Mr. McCraw, I saw you ride in but I was too far away. You are looking for that young man, so I heard from my sister. He has not been here to see us, and I have not seen him since that day at your ranch. He recovered well, I hope?"

She stopped talking, but the feelings stirred in McCraw did not stop. He put a hand on her arm, felt the tender skin as he caught her wrist, saw the soft hand newly blistered and reddened. She would not look at him, but removed his hand very carefully and refused him her gaze. His hand burned where she had touched him, his face and neck heated. She shook her head, wisps of hair moving with the effort, sticking to her cheeks, caressing the new sunburn on her slender neck.

The years of loneliness were stronger than he had ever felt them. The woman he wanted was near him, and married to a man she could not love. No ring on her finger, no pleasure in her eyes. Only hard work carved into the new lines of her brow and pads of rough callus etched in her hands. He could not see her used so, and opened his mouth to tell her.

"Mr. McCraw, it was good to see you again, good to visit with a neighbor even for so short a time. But I must be to my chores. Mr. Kersey will be wondering. And I am certain you are eager to be returning to your own home. It was a pleasure, sir."

He searched for Matt for more than a week. Rode out daily, asked questions of everyone he met, visited small villages he barely knew existed. He went to Marfa twice because a man at the livery thought one of the teamsters had seen the kid, but the man was out of town right now, be back Thursday. Then the driver had no idea what McCraw was talking about, and McCraw had to ride home on the buckskin colt. He was getting miles and muscle on the colt and no closer to finding the kid. He was about to decide to run the colt himself.

Two mornings later a rider came in with a note for

McCraw. The man smiled down and took a big drink of water, wiped his face with a soaked bandanna, and said he was sure looking forward to the race. Heard that Mr. Francis Dewitt Wilson had a real good English stud horse, but he'd already slapped down his money on the buckskin. Be a good race, if McCraw found the kid. With that word, the rider jammed his hat back on and left, whistling himself out of the yard.

The note was from Wilson Voeckes:

> James, the boy is in the hands of Deputy Sheriff Vail in Marfa. Sheriff Nevill's law was passed—all convicts who can't pay their fines have to supply work to the county. Your boy is digging dirt to make the new road from Fort Davis to Marfa, in the company of three other men. Something about killing sheep. Are you certain you want this one back?
>
> I checked with Nevill, the fine is now reduced to twenty-eight dollars. Please find that amount enclosed. Vail will try to stop you, but it is legal. You pay the remainder of the fine and the young man is free. Yr. obt. svt. Wilson Voeckes.

In with the note was an IOU and several coins. McCraw smiled to himself, seeing Voeckes's long face and open grin. It meant leaving Miguel and Silvestre to themselves again, but this time McCraw didn't care.

The deputy sheriff made it clear to McCraw he considered paying the fine of a convicted Mex border scum a stroke of insanity. Especially this particular convict. McCraw had to sit on the hard buckboard seat and hold to his temper while Vail rambled on.

"That one's been judged and found guilty of property damage, killing sheep belonging to Mr. Bogel. This won't set well with Mr. Bogel, or any of the ranchers, that you hire on a known hooligan. We got a law-abiding territory, McCraw, and I intend to see it stays that way. You might want to know, your 'boy' has caused a lot of trouble since he became our guest. The guards have had to discipline him often to keep him in line. Don't hold much with that kind of scum. You're taking on trouble, McCraw. Lots of trouble. For you and me. And I plain don't like it."

He had his temper in line, but it still took effort to talk politely. "Sheriff, I know you do your job. And I'm doing mine. I paid the fine, the law says he free. Even W. W. Bogel himself will have to agree. I got the kid, and I got him legally."

He would have liked to reach over and wrap both hands around Vail's thick neck and squeeze until the big-mouthed fool ate his own windy talk. The deputy had the face and manner of a city man, and McCraw suspected a good threat would have unlocked Matt's chains quicker than the paid fine and the papers.

Vail was a newcomer. McCraw had to live with them, and their baggage. Laws, roads, streets, taxes, bills. Nothing he could do to stop them now. He glanced at the lawman and saw the white city skin beaded with sweat, the light eyes half closed to the sun. He nodded to the meaningless words as he sat on the sprung wagon seat and looked over the horse's rump, watching for the line of dust, looking for the kid.

It was easy to pick up Matt in the line of faceless men chained ankle-to-ankle, covered in filth. The bend to the kid's back, the set of his head, the lift and swing of his arms. Thinned down from winter but still the cocky son who'd ridden into McCraw's old place not a year past.

A buckboard halted some distance from the prisoners. Matt slowed down and watched, breathing high above the choking dust. He wondered who would be fool enough to ride out on a scalding day to sit and watch a string of unpaid idiots punch the ground with blunt picks.

Then he was reminded—by the touch of a lash—that he was meant to work. The wet shirt offered no protection, and the stinging focused his attention. He felt the swing of the man beside him, stepped forward to raise his pick in time.

Numbed and always angry, Matt disappeared into the row of chained men, moving in step with those next to him. There was nothing else but the rise and fall of the heavy iron tools, the flex and pull of muscle and bone laid into raising them.

The chains tripped him. Matt stumbled forward, steadied himself, and the detail stopped completely. He scanned the line and saw each man leaning on the end of his own pick. Matt rested with them, too worn to be curious anymore.

Two men climbed down from the buckboard. A guard rode up and held the buggy horse while they walked toward the line of convicts. One of them fumbled in his pocket. Deputy Sheriff Vail. An object showed in his hand. They stopped a guard, words were exchanged, the two men looked where the guard pointed. Then one came at him. Matt watched, let his arms hang loose, dropped the pick handle. The deputy had a purpose. Matt clenched his fist, conscious of the useless act. He was chained to eleven other men. He was close to defenseless.

It was the walk that told him to relax. The rancher, McCraw. Matt flinched and straightened, opened his fists. Thought of all the words he could say, the lecture he would get. Damn. McCraw reached him; Matt saw the burned face tighten, the nose wrinkle, the hazel eyes narrow and darken. He was right, he would have to pay hard.

"Kid, you stink. Worse than sheep. And you're dumb to boot. I guessed better on you. Killing sheep, for God's sake. That's a fool's act."

Matt half raised his hands and saw a glint in the steady eyes. He took the first step, but the ankle chain reminded him. He glared at McCraw as if it were the man's fault, and McCraw grinned back at him.

Then he couldn't help it, the man was right. He met McCraw's gaze but would give no more than that.

"Yessir, Mr. McCraw."

The man studied him as if sizing up a gimpy horse or a

busted rifle. He stepped back, lifted a shoulder in a resigned shrug. Matt panicked, thought McCraw was leaving.

"Yessir, it was a fool's chance. I was wrong."

Matt heard the words inside him as well as out and there was a quick surge of energy. He'd owned the act, taken it as his. Out loud, to the world. That speeching was true: he was a damned and shining fool.

McCraw held up a key, to let Matt see his freedom. Then the rancher knelt at his leg, struggled with the dirt-filled lock. The man's head was tipped forward, wagging in effort. There were muffled curses. Matt saw the pale skin at the back of the neck, the gray hairs rising above the collar. It was uncomfortable to have a man at his feet. Matt wanted to shift and stand back, bend down and offer to do the chore.

The cuff fell away. Matt was shoved hard; the guard followed him closely, the round hollow of a rifle deep in Matt's ribs. McCraw, on his feet again, got in the way, hat jammed back on his head, arms crossed on his chest. Vail was behind McCraw, the key in one hand, a pistol sighted at Matt in the other. Both men were angry; Matt wondered what was said between them earlier. It would be about him, and right now he didn't care.

He enjoyed the walking—changed his direction quick, and the guard came with him. Stopped, picked up each foot, and shook it. His own dance, for his own pleasure.

McCraw laid a hand on his shoulder, and Matt flinched from its power. The rancher grabbed his shirtfront and shook him. Matt raised a fist to fight back, then looked into the face with an edge of clarity. McCraw bought his freedom from Vail. Resisting would put him back in chains. Matt went back to the secluded manner he'd learned in the past weeks. He had his moment; he could begin to wait.

He was set down in the back of the buckboard, legs swinging over the dropped tail, hands gripped to the sides. The road to Marfa wasn't completed yet. Vail and McCraw took the hard seat, wordless, grim, eyes trained ahead. Nothing was explained to Matt, but he already knew.

Word had even reached the prisoners about the bet. Matt had placed his own wager two days past, taking the buckskin over the fancy racer. Then, he'd dreamed about running the colt, now he could sit back and wait for the reality.

No one said a word till the buckboard drew up in front of Vail's deputy office in town. The lawman climbed out and left McCraw with the reins. He came around to the tail and shook Matt hard. It would be easy to slap the man, but Matt had learned something this spring.

"You. Iberra. McCraw paid your fine, got you free. Against my judgment, of that you can be damned sure. He got a lawyer and a judge and folks pulling for him. But you still owe, and you'll pay. Now or later."

Matt wouldn't have guessed this law had a grudge on him. But he didn't care. He never cared. A 'breed rider passing through, not much different from any other Mex whelp drifting on the border.

Vail dug in strong fingers, and Matt's face and neck flushed with effort. Much more of this, and Matt would forget his new learned manners.

"You hear me good. McCraw owns you. I been telling him, picking up inferior stock, horse or man, don't make sense. No white man needs a thief the likes of you. We've got more scum than we need. Marfa's going to stay a peaceful town. You take care, boy. I don't forget."

The man sputtered out the madness, spraying Matt's face. He was readied, intent, then McCraw grabbed him, dragged him off the tail of the buckboard, and spun him close. Matt knew his fists were clenched, felt the need to hit back. McCraw's face close to his broke through a haze.

There was the same anger in McCraw that Matt carried. He shook off McCraw's hold, stared into the rancher's sour face, and had to look away, had to let the man win. McCraw was right. Going for the law's throat in front of the law office, on the main street of a town watching the ruckus, was a dumb thing to do, a kid's choice.

He couldn't hear much of what was said, for Vail was headed to the protection of his jail, and McCraw came real close in behind. But the actions told it all: McCraw spoke, Vail listened. The almighty lawman drew in his soft belly and squared his shoulders, but he didn't look at McCraw. Anger would stir a man that way, and lost pride. It didn't matter; Matt knew he caused the trouble, knew he owned the blame.

It was finished. McCraw came down the three steps, motioned for Matt to climb in. He sat in back again, more comfortable with watching the town slide by than setting near the rancher. Miss a readied lecture, have a bit of peace.

There were folks standing in doorways, a new building half raised, a sign nailed up lopsided. More folks in clumps, making no attempt to hide their curiosity. A pretty girl with a gimpy gait walked down street. Matt wanted to wave out, but showed some common sense and settled for holding on to the wagon sides and grinning.

The livery man was waiting. Matt slid off the back before the wagon stopped. He could see the rump of the buckskin colt inside the door, saddled with Matt's rig. The blond sorrel was there, and a hint of the patched coat of the strawberry roan.

"Put the roan with my sorrel, Matt. I don't know yet if the colt'll take to hauling that miserable son."

Matt saluted. McCraw was done challenging him for now. Back to insulting, simple orders. Back to the familiar. A ride to Bitter Springs, a meal, some easy words. He wondered when McCraw would get to talking work.

"I am gambling on you. And you sure ain't a certain bet, Matt. You cut a path this spring a lot of folks don't like. Made a damned fool of yourself, like I already said. Wanted to get it said again.

"But I guess I got a fool streak in me, too. You give me your word, I'll take it. A sucker's bet to most, but it's one I guess I'll take."

The hard-skinned hand came out and hung between them. Matt heard out the speech, felt the treachery as the value of his life and word was set in plain sight. The hand waited for him, the words hit deep inside. It was his choice. One more time.

He gripped the rancher's hand; the fingers took hold and challenged him. Matt steadied, knew what the gesture meant. Then McCraw started talking as if they hadn't met and fought, separated and changed, over the long months.

"Now, you listen while I tell you what's going on. It weren't for charity I went looking. You got a place at the ranch, I got—"

"No way you can run that buckskin without me. Mr. McCraw, you ain't showed much sense making a bet and not knowing where I was. I coulda been in Kansas by now. Taking a big chance—"

"You smart-mouthed son of— You knew why I come hunting. Word moves out here like it were born with wings out of a man's poor mouth. I could have saved all this talking . . ."

McCraw scowled and went to the corral. Matt heard the low nicker and went to the colt. Right by the barn door, waiting. He saw the sweep of the blond sorrel's tail, the gold highlight of the colt's rump. He backed the sorrel out and tied him to the railing. Then he went in to the buckskin colt.

His hands ran automatically along the muscled neck, his eyes took in the winter weight, the shedding coat, the filled-out hip and forearm. The big youngster dropped his head, lipped at Matt's hand while Matt stroked the gold neck and told the colt about his ruin. Then the short baby teeth closed on Matt's finger, hard enough to draw blood. Matt slapped the colt. The buckskin jerked back but kept his teeth clamped on the finger. The big head shook, the dark eyes rolled white, the ears flattened.

Matt waited. The head came down, a calm eye looked at him. He laughed, and the mouth opened, released the finger. Matt brushed the buckskin's quarters, slipped on the ring bridle, and led the colt out to the sorrel and the runty roan. He saw the rancher, talking as usual, and waved that he was 'most ready.

* * *

McCraw questioned his own sense. He couldn't keep track of Matt, who wandered off to the side and behind him. The strawberry roan bucked and pulled on the line, glad to be moving. Pricing him down to the hostler had been part of hiring Matt. The roan had been most of the paid fine, and now McCraw had claim to the miserable horse.

He didn't like Matt riding behind him; he wanted to see the kid's face while he talked. Too much to question, not enough trust to ask.

There was a lot to talk out—getting the colt ready for the race, how Matt figured to pay back his fines, and owning the roan. Why in hell he killed a bunch of harmless woollies. Slaughter like that turned McCraw, made him squirrely about the kid. It didn't all add up, and McCraw was in pure misery.

He looked back. The kid had his hand planted on the colt's neck, yapping his mouth at the colt's turned ear. No anger in the scarred face now, no fury built up to destruction. A kid, on a good horse, crossing wide-open land and headed home.

McCraw looked ahead, to the notch in Turkey Peak to his left. He misjudged the kid on all counts, each time. Thought he was a useless fence rider first. Then ate his cooking and envied his skill with the broncs. When he got to trusting the kid, he rode out without a word. Ended up murdering sheep and working a convict's pay.

He couldn't get it straight. He had no right to trust the kid, yet he rode with his back exposed and wasn't nervy. Vail had returned the kid's weapons wrapped in an old jacket, and McCraw knew the kid stuck the old knife back in his belt.

Didn't matter now. They had six weeks or less to a horse race, and past that McCraw didn't plan. If he won, Matt had a job at Bitter Springs. If he lost, they all lost.

CHAPTER TWENTY

The contrast between the two horses was enough to make a betting man shuffle and put the money back in his pocket. Francis Dewitt Wilson's handsome bay racer stood proud; head raised, tail lifted against the wind. The dark coat gleamed, the long mane and heavy forelock were braided with colored ribbons. Even the rider was dressed up; a bright thin shirt, white pants, high shiny boots.

The buckskin came out of the corral in three leaps. White foam rubbed the yellow shoulders, darkened the gold flanks. The rider leaned on the horse's neck, held the reins lightly in one hand, and stroked and patted the colt until the horse settled and was willing to walk near the motionless bay. A great cry came out of the crowd; the buckskin reared. The crowd roared again, then quieted as the buckskin kicked at the people pushing too close to him.

McCraw wedged the blond sorrel closer, to put the rugged horse between the frightened buckskin and the growing mob. The colt placed his soaking muzzle on the yellow mane, sighed, and for a moment was still. McCraw tried to catch the rider's eye, but the colt shifted and spun around, and Matt was hard-pressed to keep his seat.

McCraw was concerned with a new problem. Matt swore he hadn't started the fight. That three riders from Bogel's ranch had come at him, laughing and wagering on the race. The laughter turned brutal when they passed Matt on the sidewalk; a fist clubbed him down, a boot caught him in the back as he fell. A blow to his head, a foot raised to kick again, and he'd grabbed out, pulled the man down on top of him. They rolled around some, with a few more kicks, until some ladies from the town walked around the corner and the three men got up and left Matt on the ground.

McCraw didn't know that Matt left some of it out, that he'd seen one of the men before. Where McCraw's herd was penned in the canyon, waiting to be stolen. A thick-necked man with colorless eyes. These men worked for W. W. Bogel; Matt didn't want to start a free-for-all the day before the race.

So that was Matt's version of the brawl. It didn't much matter who started the fight. There was a dark swelling at the kid's right eye and he rode hunched over, as if damaged in his ribs. McCraw cursed freely, first himself and then the sweating horse, the bunged-up rider. It would be no race this day, only a romp for the bay and defeat for the buckskin. And total loss for James H. McCraw.

McCraw edged the sorrel closer to the colt, hoping the sorrel's familiar presence would steady the shaking colt. The buckskin refused to move until Matt dug in his spurs and slapped the colt. The crowd suddenly turned quiet; the small group of men waiting at the drawn starting line hushed their talk and looked up expectantly.

The stretch of road running to Murphyville from Marfa was the chosen course. McCraw wanted the race set south, near his land, where the colt's breeding would be an edge. Dodging cactus, climbing sand hills, jumping arroyos and rocks were skills the bay didn't have. But the law opened its mouth, and with a broad smile the town fathers of Marfa—and Francis Wilson—agreed.

The race was to start at the outskirts of Marfa, where big numbers of spectators would gather, where the law had some control. Two miles on Murphyville Road, a left-hand swing in back of an ancient cottonwood past the stream, then two miles back, to end on the main street of Marfa.

No one expected the numbers of folk that turned up for the race. It was supposed to be a match between McCraw's buckskin and Wilson's bay, a wager between gentlemen.

TEXAS SPRINGS 201

But word went out, and the whole county was involved. Now the wide stretch of road was lined with eager bettors, whole families, ladies clutching their small children, picnics spread out under thin trees and small brush. A holiday, one the entire county planned to enjoy.

The buckskin pushed his big head against McCraw's thigh. He rubbed his fingers on the colt's neck, felt the rock-hard muscle. For a second he caught the kid's eye, saw the pride in the bruised face, and the determination. McCraw shared that pride.

The buckskin shook under his rider; sweat dripped from his belly and foamed between his legs. Then the colt saw Wilson's bay and focused on the challenger, whinnied sharply. As if he knew the enemy had appeared. McCraw slowed the sorrel and rode next to the kid.

"How you feeling, Matt? Ribs sore? How 'bout that eye?"

"Mr. McCraw. Sir. Ain't changed in the past ten minutes. Can't see much from the eye and the ribs are hurting, sure enough. But nothing to kill me. The colt's ready, and so am I."

No pain showed in the hazel eyes, no tension in the loose shoulders, the thin body. The kid swayed with the colt's leaps and half bucks. McCraw relaxed; it would have to be enough.

A man couldn't help but stare at Wilson's racer. His rider sat in a strange saddle with no horn, no fenders, and he wore a pretty shirt and high soft boots and held a whip. The bay danced a circle, whinnied, and spun to stare at the buckskin. McCraw looked at his entry and a sickness crawled through his belly.

Matt wore the thin muslin shirt, the old leather britches tucked into his high moccasins. He was hatless, and the late afternoon sun picked out the ravages of the scar. McCraw had his own bet, that the kid was knotted and raging at sitting on the buckskin colt without anyone's supposing he had a chance to win.

He had worked the colt tirelessly, riding in the hills for

long hours, ponying the buckskin to save the colt's legs. Sometimes the kid dismounted and ran alongside the colt, to build his own endurance. Said he learned it from the Apache, when Miguel told the boss what he'd seen.

The meals were eaten in silence, the kid wolfing down Silvestre's cooking without complaint. No one tried to suggest a different routine. The kid even slept outside by the corral, and McCraw heard him at night, talking to the big youngster, describing things in a tongue McCraw did not understand.

Now the colt wore the roan's snaffle bit, with a fancy braided headstall the kid made from the blond sorrel's tail mixed with black from the colt. The kid rode the stripped hull of his own saddle, with one forward *cincha*, straps for the wood stirrups, and a thin blanket folded twice. The long tail had been carefully picked out, and it flowed in a black wave. The mane fell on both sides of the gold neck and the forelock covered the excited eyes. Long hairs roughed the mustang head and thick feathering protected the iron-hard black legs.

The buckskin approached the line. McCraw was waved off by the officials; Wilson Voeckes, W. W. Bogel himself, and the deputy, Robert Vail. Officials eager to settle any dispute and insure a fair start, a clean finish. Chester Woodson came to fire the starting pistol, and with him stood Thomas Kersey.

Robert Vail liked the numbers of people lining the street. Of his town. The whole county was out, eager to place bets, argue about the speed and strength of the two horses, and incidentally watch the race. It was as if the county needed a celebration. Folks had started coming in three days ago, to lay down their claim to a section of the track and settle there, as serious as if they were mining some of the local silver ore.

Of course there were fights, too many of them to throw the participants in what passed for the town jail. Vail knocked heads and talked manners, and most of the combatants quieted down. There were a few of the battles he paid no attention to; he'd seen Charley Hocker and Pomp Wooten and a third man head toward the black-haired son who was to ride for McCraw. He'd closed his eyes to that one, easily deciding that a missing six-year-old girl was more important than the health of McCraw's 'breed.

He thought about the fight this morning, when he first saw the Mex. And he wasn't too surprised to learn that Wooten had a busted nose and Hocker half an ear torn off. With Bogel, they came to him; he made ready to put out an arrest notice. But then they left it alone. When he saw the kid later, walking to a backhouse near the lawyer's office, Vail was satisfied to see a bad limp, shoulders hunched to sore ribs. Some damage had been done. Not enough, not by his reasoning. But some.

And when the kid knew Vail was watching, he straightened up, walked proud, refused to let the pains slow him. Vail purely hated the kid right then, with a hatred burned through him like a hot running iron. It was this kid, this black-haired rider, who wrapped in one package all that Vail hated and feared—and walked it proud and strong, a tormentor to a wounded man.

Vail shook himself, shuddered with the effort. Knew quickly, in a small part of his working, logical mind, that the kid was nothing more than a range bum working for a local rancher. Then the burning anger flooded back, and Vail was forced to put it somewhere other than himself. McCraw's kid; he was responsible.

The town of Marfa was changing, coming into the world on its own. There were preachers in town, black-coated and smiling. His wife attended a service last week, without suggesting her husband go with her. A step forward, she said, a mark of the civilization come to their part of the land.

He could not easily deny it; his Eleanor was usually correct. She had pushed for the town of Marfa, now she had moved the family into a fine, upstanding new house. Built with wooden floors and two stories and painted a bare white on the wooden front. A fine showy house, for the strong member of the law.

Vail nodded at Helen, who saw her papa with the officials and wanted some of the glory. He had only three daughters left; no one ever spoke the eldest girl's name in his presence. Three daughters left—Helen, Rachel, Orianna. None married yet, but Helen and Rachel were much like their mother, plump and dark and most always pleasing. Except when they questioned his word.

Orianna was different; she was her father's child. Vail choked, felt a bite of something turn in his belly. They were all around him, riding their scrawny nags in and out of the crowds, drinking and waving their big hats and howling. One of these same men rode down Orianna, left her bleeding and broken. An accident, his wife said. An act of God, Elizabeth's preacher called it.

Rimfire and hell burned into Orianna's father. That he could do nothing, find no one man guilty of crippling his child. She was healed and mended, the best doctors could do, yet some of the fire was gone, and with it some of the love and sweetness put there for her father. Vail clenched a fist, swore again on what he would do. The shame swallowed him and he half turned, needing to move. He had done nothing then, he still would do nothing.

A voice called to him, a hand waved a pistol; he was necessary again. Vail looked and saw the swollen crowd and was shocked. The bay racer was less than ten feet from him, the buckskin circled in short steps, blackened with sweat, wild eyed and hot. The rancher, McCraw, didn't have a chance. Kersey had explained it to W. W. Bogel, and the small man had quietly explained to Vail. It was needed that McCraw lose.

But a black-haired devil sat on the gold colt. The demon with the marked and branded face. The rage gathered back in Vail, and he held it deep in his mind. Matt Iberra. The monster would die—to wipe out the endless rage and shame that burned a long path inside Robert Vail.

"Sheriff Vail, are we ready now? I believe it is time."

Francis Dewitt Wilson, owner of the bay, eager for the match to begin. People heard the edge to Wilson's words,

TEXAS SPRINGS 205

for there were whispers in the crowd, a restlessness that moved through the close-packed bodies. Vail realized he stood next to the lawyer recently moved down to Marfa from Fort Davis, name of Voeckes. Mr. Bogel was on his other side, and Chester Woodson stared at him expectantly, the starter pistol in hand. And the sour-faced Thomas Kersey was nearby; Vail had heard rumors about the man and McCraw.

All of the town officials, waiting on Robert Vail.

"Yes, Mr. Wilson. I do believe we are ready."

The colt settled. Matt felt the big heart thump between his legs, felt the trembling muscles. But the colt held still. Listened to what Matt told him. Shut out the frantic pitch of the race course, and waited. Matt sang in the old tongue, and the colt swept back his ears. They waited.

The bay was a wonder to Matt; fine-legged, veins highlighted under the groomed red coat. The rider sat in his old saddle with straight legs, toes pointed down, whip carried like a sword.

The buckskin wanted to run, fairly danced under Matt. He didn't need a whip.

Someone called his name. An arm flashed, a pistol sounded, and a voice exploded. The bay leaped into a run; the buckskin went sideways with Matt, then found his balance and jumped. Matt fell back, clamped his knees to the buckskin sides, and called out to the colt, swore in all the words he knew as the gelding went for his stride.

He rode the plunging horse as the buckskin extended full-out to catch the bay. Matt saw the plaited mane, the flag of the long tail, and felt for the colt's mouth, drew back, and steadied the horse. It was a long race, there was plenty of time.

McCraw thought to speak to the officials about the poor start, then saw Vail and knew him to be the final judge. There would be no second start. McCraw watched the gold hindquarters rise and fall, saw the black head of the rider lean to the straining neck. Wilson's man sat erect, guided the bay with hands and spurs. McCraw thought of the ranch, the horses, the new house, the woman who would never live there.

It came back 'round to her too easily. Whenever he forgot not to think of her, the name came to mind: Harriet Gliddings Kersey. He knew she was in the crowd, the woman he could not have, and could not forget. McCraw pushed the sorrel through the screaming mob and worked out to the road. He would loaf on the side, ride back to the finish. He had to do something.

The road was wide enough that the separate tracks were easy to read. The bay was on the outside, Matt and the buckskin to the left. The prints were widespread, light indentations in the dirt. Two horses running flat-out, eager for the win. The crowd along the road thinned, then the track was empty.

Matt kept the buckskin close to the bay, and the colt ran easily. Flowing. Smooth. No sound but the breathing of the two horses, the gulping of his own breath. As if Matt and the fancy jock were the only inhabitants of a world, on the only horses left. The blooded racer and the range buckskin. The rise of a crooked hill to the right. The signs were there; the bay's rider didn't seem to take notice.

Matt tugged at the bit, gathered the reins, slowed the long stride. The black ears tipped back in response, the colt pulled at the restriction. Matt leaned to the right, helped the colt drift out under him. The bay edged away, flying in his own world.

The corner came fast; Matt shifted the colt left, half slid the horse, and plowed the turn. His leg scraped the post set for the marker. A man on a paint horse stood at the side, the last official, responsible for the judging turn.

The bay struggled with speed; the rider yanked on the harsh bit, and they floundered through the curve. The rider bounced, the bay stumbled and threw his head, strained to find his footing. The horses turned; the man on the excited paint whooped and lifted his hat, let his horse run with the racers a short distance.

A hand raised near him—and Matt felt the whip across his face. He jerked back, the buckskin skidded. The whip cut again. Matt felt blood run off his cheek. He leaned into the black mane and dodged the third blow. He screamed out a curse and called for the buckskin to run.

The bay matched the colt stride for stride. The rider was upright, laying the whip across the bay's flank. Matt spoke every name he could, yelled insults and endearments in Mex and English, harsh Apache, fluid Comanche. The buckskin ran, the bay ran with him.

The crowd was ahead, screaming, hats spinning high in the wind. The colt swerved from the sound; Matt dug in his left heel to keep the buckskin on course. A shape ahead, one man standing at the side, a hand raised high holding a white cloth. The official to mark the race's end, the finish line.

Matt risked it and looked sideways, saw the bay straining, nose stretched, legs lost in the churned street. Side to side with the buckskin. Matt's head and heart pounded. He leaned forward, called to the colt, offered up prayers, lay close to the buckskin's mane, rocked with the long strides, and gave what he could to the colt's gallant courage.

A flash of color and motion, a shadow from the roadside; head, shoulders, a man's arm. A shape thrown, an object in the colt's track. Matt hauled on the left rein, threw his weight, fought to drag the colt from tangling in the length of wood.

The horse broke stride, skidded diagonally to touch his nose to the bay's side. Then the buckskin's legs skipped and lost traction, and the colt's own tremendous power brought horse and rider down.

Orianna Vail saw the thick-necked man shove to the front of the crowd. She was glad not to be in that press of bodies. She wondered why he carried a block of wood in his hand, but forgot her curiosity as the two horses came down the main street. Her seat on a neighbor's porch was safe from the push of the crowd, but not close enough to the excitement. She stood carefully, held to a white-painted pillar, and yelled for the pure joy of yelling.

The horse went down headfirst. The huge body arched in the late sun, circled over the head snubbed to the earth and the neck stretched to its length, folded as the bone and mass collapsed. The buckskin flipped over, then slid sideways. The impact lifted a great cloud, and from the crowd rose a groan that covered the terrible sound of weight hitting flat ground.

The rider was flung high, a loose bundle lost in the cloud. The crowd was immediately, completely silent. The bay racer crossed the finish line alone.

The voice was soft. Matt struggled to hear the words. He liked the pattern of rise and fall, wanted it to come closer. He tried to raise a hand; a force pushed his arm down.

His head ached, his mouth was dry. His body hurt. A band tightened on his chest, his head pounded. Then the words of the speaker came clear, and he tried to listen over the noise.

"Papa, you won't even try. He didn't do anything wrong. He isn't the one who hurt me. Papa, you have to try. He's hurt. You can't make him leave the house. I offered to help care for him, and Mama said it was—Papa!"

The bells made no sense to him at all, but he liked the ringing music. Then a cool rag washed his face, touched gently on his scar. He relaxed under the caress, let himself enjoy the scent of the person washing him, feel the smoothness of her hand as she pushed back his hair. She leaned over him, to inspect his scar, and there was a light pressure on his chest.

His eyes half opened; Matt saw the outlines of her, the curve of her cheek and chin, the light color of the hair. He wanted his eyes to open, so he could see the woman's face and thank her.

And he wanted to know what she was saying to the man

somewhere in the room. But the lids of his eyes were too sore; he let them close, stopped trying to know, and went back to a sleep that took away the nightmare of knowing something terrible had happened, he could not remember what.

Orianna saw the struggle go through the bruised face, was pleased when the eyes shut and the tight muscles around the mouth slackened. Good. The young man was asleep. The doctor said he was not seriously injured, but only needed some attention to his scrapes, and some time for his banged head. He would most likely sleep through the night, although how anyone, even a sick man, could sleep through the noise outside was beyond Orianna.

She refused to look into her papa's face or hear the rest of his complaining. She never listened to him when he became like this. Muttering his madness, fussing about a boy who had nothing to do with her accident, yet in her father's eyes was the villain.

It was unfair that her papa and the other officials had ruled the bay the final winner. She had seen that the buckskin was ahead of the bay, until the block was thrown out. Papa made no attempt to search for the thick-necked man as Orianna described him, and the other officials followed her papa's direction in the matter.

They did not want to hear, just as Papa did not want to know now. The boy lying on the narrow bed was not the monster Papa said. She knew he had been on the road gang, and she didn't like that about him. But he was not the one who harmed her.

He lay there, tucked with a white sheet to his face, helpless in his drugged sleep. Scraped raw down the side of his terrible face, with gravel and bits of stone imbedded under the skin, bruises along the jaw, down his neck, and past the startling exposed whiteness of his chest, only partially covered by one of Papa's nightshirts.

The face and hands were dark, just as Papa complained. And he had black hair. But the eyes, when they were open, were a hazel gold, rimmed with thick, brown lashes. And she had unbuttoned the nightshirt to wipe his chest with cool water, and the skin was white and smooth, where it wasn't marred by some old scars and the new bruises.

She rinsed out the rag again and touched a corner of it to his mouth. Dirt had collected there, forced out through clenched teeth. A fine mouth, wide and full-lipped, the shadow of dark hair above it. A strong mouth made tender and childlike in helplessness.

Even though there was no one else with her in the room now except the sleeping patient, Orianna Vail felt a blush come to her face. She had unbuttoned the nightshirt more than one button, or two. To wash most of his belly, down to the beginning curls of dark hair. She had held his ribs, cupped them in her hand. He was a beautiful young man.

Orianna rinsed out the cloth again, watched the gray specks of dirt, the pale red of diluted blood wash into the basin. It was a miracle he was alive. The fall had been terrifying in its sudden violence. She had wanted the buckskin to win, and had wanted so to meet the rider. Because her papa talked about him at the table. Had complained for two months to her dear mother about the insolence and bad temper of "the Mex," and the foolishness of Mr. McCraw's depending on him.

And now he lay under her care, open to her curiosity. Orianna let the tips of her fingers touch the ugly scar, follow it across his face. It was ugly only because she could see it. If the scar were hidden, then no one would know, no one would blame or curse him. For the boy did not limp— she had seen him with Mr. McCraw at the livery stable. There was no damage to him beyond the visible wound. He could see, he could think, he could walk and run.

She was consigned to a doubtful walk, even though her scar was not to be seen. And that fact kept her less wanted in a land where a man wedded for a woman's abilities as well as for her love. For her daily strength and the children from her womb. A woman here must work with her man, or she lost value, was isolated and left to become an old maid.

Orianna touched the scar again, let the tears run freely. She did not know if she cried for herself or for the wounded victim.

When he was awake and hungry, Matt found he could sit up if he was careful. He climbed out of the bed and found a pair of pants, a too big shirt, and hard boots that wouldn't pull on. He went barefoot into the hall—and was halfway down the hall before the dizziness caught him and he sat down. He squatted on a step, dropped his head between his knees, and waited for his ears to stop ringing.

McCraw found him there. He was two steps down from the lowered head and saw the sand between the strands of dark swinging hair. He'd have to dunk the kid in a water trough to get him clean. He waited, until Matt opened his eyes and saw the high boots near him, looking higher and saw the long hands and knew it was the rancher.

"What happened? The colt all right? God . . . that was a fall. Does Wilson own you? What happened, dammit?"

It was what McCraw expected. He didn't answer immediately, saw the kid's shoulders lift and fall, heard the deep intake, and timed it right to interrupt the kid's temper.

"The colt's fine. I told you that twice yesterday. And, yeah, we lost. He's scraped up some, sort of like you. But he's walking out fine, had one cut needed stitching. Hind leg swole up some but it came down. Not much more than that. He sure didn't sleep as long as you. Wake up, kid."

The temper was there in the dark gold eyes. McCraw knew what to expect and knew he wasn't fair to the kid, but a teasing streak in him kept baiting, until the temper broke loose.

"McCraw, damn you! You done playing? What went on there? We had a clear shot and the colt ain't no park bronc. There were no reason for him spilling that way. What happened?"

So he didn't know. The doc said he might not. McCraw was glad for that. He didn't think this time a trip to a *curandero* would have done the kid much good. Concussion, the doc said. Keep him quiet for a few days and there would be no side effects. Seemed he might be right about that—the temper was intact, and the mouth.

"A couple of people, they said a man threw a block out, caught the colt's legs. We took it to the officials but they weren't much interested." McCraw watched the kid, gauging the depth of the building anger. "Yeah, we lost the race, and a lot of money changed hands, none of it mine. Had some call for a rematch, and the sheriff was busy there for a while knocking heads together and hauling losers off to jail. Made a bundle in fines for disturbing the peace, even though there weren't peace in this town until the next morning.

"Quite a passel of folk wanted a rematch, 'specially when they heard about the 'mystery' man. But the officials called it the way they saw. Even Voeckes lost that money he gave me to bail you out.

"It was a hell of a race, kid. You were right—that colt's got speed and heart. He run well enough that Francis Dewitt Wilson, he gave me five hundred dollars for him. Said he'd be proud to run him long as he came out of the spill unhurt. Can't wait to run the colt against all comers.

"You maybe lost the race, Matt, but you won yourself a purse of money. Mr. Wilson gave an extra fifty dollars for your ride."

Food was waiting for Matt when he finished crawling down the stairs. Eggs and side meat, biscuits good as his, and berry jam, lots of coffee with real sugar in it, and milk if he chose. At the end of the meal, he was ready to ride. Didn't matter he was a hero to some folks, he wanted gone from all the nosy eyes and ears come to the back door to peer in while he cleaned the plate of egg yolk with the last biscuit. He had enough fuel in him now to get back upstairs, find the remains of his clothing, and talk McCraw into bringing the strawberry roan. He wanted out.

It had to be the too big shirt; McCraw showed him his old one, cut to ribbons. But the leather pants had been well

TEXAS SPRINGS 213

patched across the rump and would do, and the moccasins lost a button and a lace he could fix easy. The shirt flapped around him and he double-tucked it in his pants. It covered him, it was decent. He was gone.

The roan was tied to the railing outside; McCraw had disappeared, and Matt wasn't going to waste energy looking for him. Matt said his manners to the lady of the house, and Mrs. Vail smiled at him in return. He didn't like the set of her thin mouth, the lines at her eyes, the sadness in her soft voice. But she'd given him hospitality and he thanked her for it.

The deputy law was absent from his own house. Matt guessed he'd come to like the humor in the situation, when he was well shed of Vail's house and town.

Except for the memory of the girl. Mrs. Vail told him her name, and where she was. Waiting for him, she said. Matt spooked at that, swung his head wildly, hit the wall next to the door. A girl waiting for him. He had to face her; he wanted desperately to run.

He opened the screen door—and the new wood floor shifted under his step. A shape moved to the right; he had to complete a turn to see past his swollen eye.

The girl, swinging in a chair hung from the roof. Matt had never seen its like. The girl saw him and smiled, raised a hand to command him. He was careful to stop some distance from her. In spite of her ministrations, he stank like a used goat with his own sweat.

She was a pretty one; that he had not imagined. Her hands would be as soft as he remembered, and her voice would ring like the town bells. He cautioned himself, set his mind. No time to think on a girl. She was pretty, though. The smile, and fair hair bound and ribboned, a flowered dress. A pretty girl. And when she spoke, he smiled. The voice of the bells.

"It is good you are up, señor. Even though Mama and I do not think it is wise for you to be riding yet. Mr. McCraw said you are restless, and eager to leave. I wish you would reconsider, for one more day at the least. But I expect you will leave us."

He bent his head to listen, to watch her closely, to take in the flowers of her dress, and her sweetness. It would be a luxury, to stay here another day. It would be wrong, but he thought quickly of its pleasure, until the memory of Adelina cut across him. And then the girl kept talking; he listened, and he learned to hate her in a few of her well-chosen words.

"Your poor face, it is badly scraped and needs time to heal. You must be more careful, for it will take days for your wounds to mend."

The bells were beautiful, but the words cracked open loud inside him. She was pitying him, she was handing him sweet contempt masked as concern. As if he were little more than the crater drawn across his face. That wound would never heal.

He didn't offer manners to her; he couldn't hear the voice again. He left her quickly, not even taking time to check the roan's *cincha* but swinging up into the saddle and hauling the eager roan around. She was perfection, she was beauty, she was kin to Adelina. She needed to remind him with her perfect words. He knew what he was, how he looked. He knew the world saw him a cripple. She did not have to be the one to remind him this time.

He wasn't there to see Orianna rise from the chair, hold the railing to pull herself up, to balance carefully before she tried to walk. He did not see, could not know, about the twisted and scarred leg hidden under the full skirt. The walk was labored, impaired by a broken bone mended shorter—offset and awkward—the skin and flesh surrounding the break pink and dark red and badly ridged. Ugly flesh she could not yet touch without crying.

Orianna saw the roan gelding buck and sidestep, headed toward the newly built shipping pens. She understood the young man would not return, she understood he would not accept her concerns. She had seen the hazel eyes turn dark with pity. He did not want a crippled girl's interest. Then she shook her head, angry with herself. Matt had shown only kindness and good manners until she herself spoke of his disfigurement. He had not judged her at all. Fear had sent him away, so she must not be harsh with him. She just wanted to be perfect, needed Matt to see beyond her leg.

She took the stairs slowly, a half step that made the trip possible, and wished again for the comfort of the adobe house where they had first lived in town. Cooler, more comforting, and simpler for her to navigate. But not enough for her mother and father, not enough for their position and their pride.

She sat at the side of his bed, and she remembered him. She had sat here and looked for a long time at the maimed face, and she had hoped he could be the one. He carried his own mark, his own brand that the world judged daily. He could have understood what it was she faced. But he had not stayed to hear what she meant to say.

CHAPTER TWENTY-ONE

Once past the last building, Matt was safe. Until the roan shied, the saddle slipped, and Matt dismounted and redid the rigging. He cursed the girl again and remounted.

A horse and rider quartered toward him, a reluctant pack mule in tow. A wave of an arm, a hat raised in greeting. McCraw, with a bottle in hand.

The rancher sucked on the bottle before Matt got to him. He didn't offer a drink—and Matt wouldn't ask. McCraw rode ahead of Matt, yanking at the miserable mule, sucking on the green bottle. Matt would take a drink, but he'd be damned to ask.

They rode for over an hour. McCraw emptied a bottle, threw it high and wide, and Matt heard it break. He picked at what would do the rancher like this. Not a man to drink, not usually a fool. McCraw took another bottle from his bags and pulled the cork. Whatever ate on the man, he would have to do his own talking.

A pair of fools; Matt with his own fire to put out. The Vail girl, in that swinging basket, her voice that mocked him easily. That alone would drive him into a bottle, if McCraw offered.

But Matt figured as he rode behind McCraw, with his head pounding, his ribs cracked, his eye swollen shut, that a headache tomorrow the size McCraw was working on would be double-barreled death. So he left the bottles to McCraw and enjoyed the silence. Until McCraw began his talking—and Matt had to listen.

McCraw tilted in the saddle, and Matt drew up beside the sorrel. The cranky mule snapped at the roan and the long teeth grazed over Matt's knee. He reached over the mule's stretched neck and pushed McCraw upright, until the man seemed to recognize what was happening and righted himself enough to stay in the saddle.

That gesture opened a crack in the rancher, for suddenly he talked of private matters Matt did not want to know. He backed away; McCraw swiveled his head to see Matt and slipped loose in the saddle. The sorrel stopped, as if knowing what would happen, and Matt kneed the roan in closer, grabbed an arm, and tugged the man back to the middle. McCraw never stopped talking.

"Matt, you been in love? Matt? Hell, no, you're a kid, riding every place you goddamn please. Love, not you, not old Matt with a face torn apart and a soul—Hell to you, kid. Love is special, you hear me? Even for a man been hiding most of twenty-five years. I been loved, but not for twenty-five years. You hear that, you listening?"

Matt had the roan walk beside the big sorrel and pleaded with McCraw to let him be. It was no business of his what went on in the rancher. And he didn't want to hear the cursing about his own flaws. He didn't want to know the truth, he didn't want a confession.

McCraw straightened up some and waved the new bottle, looked hard into Matt's wavering face, locking on to him, holding him without the words. It was new to Matt, the power of one man to draw another. Yet he could not ride away, could not leave the man. Matt let the roan match the sorrel's gait and shut off the aches and bruises, shut down his mind, and let the drunk talk on.

James McCraw knew he was drunk. He knew other things, too. He knew the kid, recognized the ugly face and the hammerheaded roan. He could look down and see his own sorrel horse, and the tug of a line over his leg told him the mule was following.

The rest was disappeared: sense, faith, work. Gone. Lost in the blurred form of a woman. Two women: one from a long time back, fighting to keep her place. And the new one, married to the wrong man, smiling at the wrong face. Wrong man . . . She'd married the wrong man.

The fact of her in bed with the man. Anger rose in McCraw, and lust. As he cursed the man, pleaded with the woman to come to him. His head ached with the ravings, his belly turned on him. He dropped the bottle to grab at the horn and heard more glass break.

He studied the saddle horn. The kid sat the roan, held the pack mule line. Goddamn sun hit a shard of glass and burned McCraw's eye. He shielded the light, lost his grip on the saddle. He looked into the sun, looked away and saw the kid again. Too clearly.

The wide mouth was open, the gold eyes shuttered, the skin pale. As if the kid ate a bitter meal, got the wrong story. Then McCraw began to hear the same noise that made the kid sullen, a loud voice yelling the tunes of a crazy man. Yelling about Thomas Kersey's wife.

McCraw shut his yap and the noise ended. He calmed some, grabbed the horn for safety, and kneed the sorrel over to the kid. The grim face didn't change; McCraw knew then he'd given the kid too much, overstepped the line.

"Kid. Matt. It's only the talk of a potbellied drunk. I won't say no more . . ."

A roaring filled him; he needed a drink. A flood of sound held him, names he didn't want to keep; Josefina, Tomás. Eduardo. Riding the river, not the same river. Josefina, back to the *Despoblado*.

He didn't know where it all came from; he'd forgotten those names, buried them in river mud and sand. A cry, his cry. McCraw slumped over, wounded and dying. He needed the wine. Yesterday and today winning over him, tomorrow would be the victor. He cried hard, betrayed by feelings left to rust.

He was aware enough to know the kid had left him. The rigid shoulders taunted him. He needed the kid, needed to end the pity and get home, back to work. McCraw angled the sorrel across the roan's slow path. It got tough knowing where to begin.

"Matt, I— It ain't fair to you. Listen . . ."

McCraw guessed he was listening, because he came back fast and hard.

"McCraw, I don't want to hear no more. Two bottles broke, that gave you the courage you need. It wasn't you hearing what you said, it was me. And I don't want it. There's another bottle in your bag. I'm riding out now. I plain won't work for a drunk."

It was a slap. McCraw craved to fight the kid right then. But he was still, saw the grim face, puzzled on what passed behind the hidden eyes.

"I 'pologize, Matt. I can't quarrel with you." He lifted the flat bags tied behind the saddle, let them fall against the sorrel sides. "Empty, done. Like me. Let's get home."

Harriet Gliddings Kersey. She hated the names. Now she was Mrs. Thomas Kersey, but not in her heart. She had seen the man she wanted, knew his name.

She often talked to herself in the dark, late at night, after

Mr. Kersey climbed on top of her and poked for a few moments, then sighed and lifted himself off to roll over into immediate sleep. The attention left her wide awake and resentful, and most of those nights she would walk outside, or sit in the crude kitchen and talk to herself until she was bored enough to try again to sleep.

She could not fault Mr. Kersey, he was not a bad man. But she wanted a loving man. He had promised her material for new curtains and had finally given her the money, although a small sum, when they were in Marfa for the race. She had not understood his preoccupation with the race, as he was not a gambling man, but she enjoyed the day and the new liveliness of the town.

Until she had seen James McCraw, waiting with the officials at the starting line. Mr. Kersey had been there, too. She was familiar now with Mr. Kersey's manner, and his lack of attraction to her was to be of little importance. He was a good provider, he did not overwork her. He loved her in his fashion. But when he stood near the stirrup of Mr. McCraw's saddle and even looked up at the man and passed a harmless remark, Harriet could not avoid the comparison in her mind . . . and the ache in her heart.

There was a proud lift to the man's head, a strong set to him, a cleanness to the lines of his back and arms. She would be nearer to him, to see the boldness of his hands, the temper of his mind. It was impossible not to compare him with the strange specimen that was her legal husband.

She felt a high glow of victory when word came through that Mr. Wilson had bought the buckskin. And she wondered what soured Mr. Kersey that he yelled at her to hurry, that they were leaving Marfa now. There was no great event waiting on them at the canyon; they could remain in town at least another day, another hour. But Mr. Kersey had a stubborn temper, and Harriet must do what she was told.

She owed her word to Thomas Kersey. But . . . Mr. McCraw had walked past her once in town, stopped nearby, removed his hat, and spoke her name. "Mrs. Kersey, good day." As if to remind her of the promise that tied her to the small, gray, quick-minded, greedy Thomas Kersey.

She rose from the hard-backed chair, ducked her head, and went outside again. The night was soft, warm. A light breeze washed the cotton gown across her legs and belly, tucked the material between her legs, and chafed her flesh as the thinking chafed her heart. Mindlessly Harriet raised her hands to her breasts, lifted the covered weight of flesh, and imagined their smoothness in another's hands.

That was difficult and unsettling; her hands dropped their burden, pulled the gown free of her thighs. She went back inside the small cabin and into the marriage room, where she lay down next to her husband and tried again for the sleep she knew would not come.

F. D. Wilson drove up in a pin-striped buggy, and even in the early heat the man was clean and dry. McCraw wiped his hands on his pants, conscious of a two-day beard, sweat gummed on his face and chest. But Francis Wilson didn't notice.

He had cash with him, to pay for the gelding as agreed. And as promised, a gold piece for the rider. McCraw let the coin sit in the palm of his hand while Wilson talked. Matt was out on a dun mare, up near the Chisos Basin, moving cattle to new graze. When he came back, he'd get his reward.

Wilson was pleased with his purchase and told McCraw he would be interested in buying more horses from him, if they showed a promise of speed. Cash for payment on the land. McCraw regretted the sale of the buckskin, but he shook Wilson's hand and said yes, he would keep a lookout for a good one. The buggy swung wide in the yard, and Francis Wilson left.

McCraw leaned on a nearby post and waited for the dust to settle. One more time wondered what it was he'd said to the kid, and regretted he'd said it. Couldn't forget the drinking, the day after was pure hell. But the words were lost.

And whatever was lost, unplugged from McCraw's bottle, it changed the kid.

Matt worked even harder, and spoke even less. McCraw could find no fault with the kid; the cooking was good enough, the work well done. But there was a residue holding down, fixing to explode. McCraw knew better than to try and talk; it would salt the open sore. So he handed out the chores, saddled the horses, and hoped against hell the kid would ease up.

Late that afternoon, the kid rode in on the tired mare, both of them covered in filth. To report a screw-wormed cow treated, a yearling doctored. A brief report. He said where he left the herd, told McCraw that the streambeds were drying up, that the springs were muddy but still flowing.

It was a mistake, to give the kid the hard cash. McCraw saw that as soon as the gold flashed in Matt's palm. But the coin was meant for him, and McCraw couldn't hold it back.

The gold sparked a rough time; the kid shook his head to McCraw's words and drifted off, holding to his silence. After a half-cooked meal, McCraw watched outside while the kid saddled up the roan. He didn't need to be told what was doing.

Matt rode out at early dusk, the roan packed with his gear. There were no words exchanged, no explanation. But McCraw knew why.

PART TWO

CHAPTER TWENTY-TWO

McCraw knelt in front of the tired gelding and dug his fingers into the powdery ground. He lifted a handful of the soil, opened his fingers, and watched the grains quickly sift away. He touched a clump of the chino grass. The shortened stems pulled from the ground too easily, and the roots were a wrinkled thin brown.

McCraw wiped his mouth, tasted the dirt imbedded in his hand. He looked up to see the sweat dried on the sorrel's chest, tasted again the salt of his own body. No rain since August, and it was now late November, maybe December. The ground was bare, the grasses dead or dying. The air blew cold, an endless wind that picked up what little water was left.

Heavy streaked-gray clouds covered the sun, but there was no rain. The wind blew through him, slipped past the buttoned vest, and chilled his skin. McCraw didn't like what he felt, didn't trust the shifting direction of the chancy wind, the bared ground, the tracks of too many hungry cattle.

Dried manure covered the tracks. They were flat smears crumbled and well cooked, hard balls roasted in the sun. McCraw poked a ball—the outer skin easily flaked and broke apart, a stale odor reached him. He spread out the contents, studied them. Seeds, undigested roots, sand. The cattle had grazed here too recently and there was nothing left for the horses. Too many cows killed the heart of the plants, shredding the system in hunger. There was not enough water; the manure in his hands, the manure surrounding him, was small and dried out too quickly. The herds were starving on their feet.

He wiped the stained hands on his pants and pushed himself up, slow, cautious, the bad leg threatening to quit. He rocked back and forth, trying to understand. Cattle were in the distance, scattered on the grass. Some heads were dropped to scavenge for graze, some of the animals only stood on tired legs and waited. McCraw kicked at the manure; the sorrel snorted and blew out softly.

Miguel and Silvestre joined their boss. They said nothing, used to the boss's long silences. The heart was gone from him now, and Miguel often tried to puzzle the reason. But there was a roof overhead, enough food on the table, and a few pesos each month. He would not quarrel with such gifts.

It would be a hard winter, any man could read the signs. Miguel told his *compadre* to offer up his penance, for there would be death this time, before spring returned.

Silvestre's bay roan reached over and nipped at Miguel's paint. Both horses squealed and stamped their legs. Bored. Restless. The señor looked up; a rare smile opened his face.

"Boys, we got to move the cattle. Bring them in closer to the springs. And chase off what don't belong on our grass. We got a new neighbor, been running close to six thousand head. By the name of Gano and his clan. Claims him a big chunk of the grass. But he ain't got the water he needs, and his herds been coming to our springs, cropping our grass.

"I hate doing this, but we've got to feed and water our own stock first. No rain at all this summer or fall. And now no sign of rain, maybe not until spring. We've got to protect our own."

Miguel felt insulted; the señor thought he could not read dry ground and blank sky, empty of clouds that could water the land. As if he were too old and stupid to know the most basic facts of the desert. Miguel began to build up an angry response, readying himself to speak. Then he saw the señor's grave face. The fine sorrel horse was gray with

TEXAS SPRINGS 227

dust, the *patrón*'s eyes showed through a gritted mask. There was no disapproval in the sad eyes, no anger in the thinned mouth.

Perhaps the señor had spoken as much to himself as to Miguel. Perhaps he needed to hear the words out loud, to see their truth, to know the grave responsibility of his actions.

The wind came up in a fresh, bitter circle. Silvestre's hat was blown free, hanging only by the braided horsehair thong. Miguel clamped a hand on his own hat as the señor closed his eyes, put a hand to his face. This wind was cold, brutal, sanding skin and roughing flesh until small droplets of blood came through the surface. The horses shifted, to tuck their rumps to the wind, lower their heads, and close their eyes. Willing to patiently wait out the sudden storm.

McCraw would not wait; he mounted the sorrel and kicked the horse several times before the animal would respond. Headed into the force, the horses were slow and stubborn. McCraw ducked his head from the wind's strength. He cursed the cold as it came inside his vest, wished for his old blanket coat.

The sorrel shied; McCraw looked for the danger. A mound half covered with drifted sand. A red pile of meat, a dead steer. Neck stretched, skull blindly staring, horns tilted and dug into the earth. Belly distended to raise the legs with gassy bloat. Raised as if to walk in air.

Not one of his, branded with a new sign. One of Gano's big herd, down and dead. McCraw put the sorrel to a ragged trot. The wind came with him, went ahead and circled back, driving sand into his eyes, down his neck. The sorrel stopped abruptly, shook his head. Miguel's paint and the bay roan flanked McCraw.

"We've got to get the cattle going now. Miguel, you swing back and left, bring in what you can find. Silvestre, get to the ranch. You need an ax, a shovel. We got to give our cows something to eat near the water. Chop up the sotol, open up the heads. Cows'll eat that if nothing else.

"Me, I'm pushing that herd back to Gano's range before it snows. Can't let our stuff die to feed his."

Cold pellets stung his face; McCraw licked his lips. He watched the air, trying to focus on the shapes floating past his eyes. Snow; dry, transparent flakes; hard balls of ice. He held out his hand, watched the flakes land and gently disappear, let the pellets roll up between his fingers.

"Ride hard. We got snow, but it's dry, too dry to do any good. Bring in the cattle best you can, Miguel. Going to be a hell of a storm."

He didn't know what brought him back. It wasn't the land—drier, barren, beautiful only in its scrubbed waste and hard color. Now blowing a storm that covered the trail, deadened all sound. Matt let the roan wander, following buried instinct.

He spotted the outlines of Marfa. He touched his hand to a chest pocket; there was enough coin to buy a room for the night, shelter and feed for the roan. It would be a treat to be warm and dry for a night's sleep.

Gone more than five months, back to the remains of his family up north. Gone from Bitter Springs. Too much said from wine, too much stored and brewing. Names from his own life caught in McCraw's past. He had to ride out, had to think and talk and be sure.

So he came back for curiosity; he didn't bother with the rest of the why. He saddled the roan out of his brother's place and headed south.

The town had grown more in the short months. Two raw buildings on the right, a fancy sign over a new saloon, a road fresh scraped out of brush. Matt saw the livery sign through the pelting snow and headed to its promised comfort.

The hostler didn't look at his customer; for the money from Matt's hand, he was ready to take in the roan. Matt walked the empty street, head ducked to his chest from the icy sting. He rubbed a cold hand on his scar. Grains of the ice were caught there; he wiped them clean.

One drink at Tiny's Palace Bar was enough. The stares came as if it were his first time in Marfa. He put down a coin and left, disgusted with civilization and himself. He needed a meal, a place to sleep. Coming back didn't seem a good idea right now, maybe the morning would cheer him.

The snow drifted around him, blown in whirlwinds by an erratic force. Stepping into the darkness, Matt saw the tips of his new boots appear and retreat as he walked, intent on direction, hunched into the windy snowfall. He heard the cry before he felt her. Put out a hand quickly, grabbed the soft weight of a scratchy woolen sleeve. He caught and pulled, knowing in reflex that the body would fall from him. The cry came again—loud, high, female. He held with both hands, pulled at what he could grasp.

The body twisted from him, losing all balance from the collision. Matt slid on slick heels; a hand reached for him. Slipping, falling, he caught a wooden pillar, held on to the weight of her with his right arm. Again a cry; softer; he widened his legs, steadied on the pillar. Blinking snow from his eyes, he drew his right arm in slowly—and a person came to his chest.

"That was close, ma'am. Too close. I rightly apologize for not seeing you, but this goddamn—" He didn't catch himself in time; the curse hung out in the snow-cold air. Matt stuttered, trying to put a respectable word in its place.

The woman laughed, a gentle, ringing sound, light in the hushed cold. Matt quickly let go. He fumbled for his hat, ready to leave, when she finally spoke. He knew her name before she finished the first word.

"Ah, please. I have heard the word before. You need not apologize. And I do thank you for your kindness. It is fortunate you came along, or I . . ." He didn't listen to what she was saying; it didn't matter at all. The girl of the bells. Her face was clear—the girl who mocked him, gave him pity. He had to leave. But the sound, the sweetness held him for a moment. She could not see his face; she did not know him.

"You are Matt. I know you. Papa wouldn't talk about you, but I know you. I'm Orianna Vail. And thank you again, it is good—"

The wonderful voice stopped. He leaned closer. There was a sudden shyness to the girl, as if she were shamed. She touched his sleeve; he waited for the request, spellbound by her closeness.

"Matt, would you walk me home in this snow? I am sorry for being so forward, but I came out to get some medicine for my sister. She has taken a cough and Mama is worried. We didn't know the storm had gotten so bad. Would you please walk me to the door? Please?"

He could not refuse. Matt offered his arm, let her rest her weight on him. She was taller than he thought, almost as tall as he was. Straight, slender even in the bulk of a woolen wrap. He had not seen her standing before, except to lean over his bed while he was half-awake.

"Ma'am, you best tell me where we're going. I got no idea where to find your house. Don't remember much at all of this town."

Too conscious of his awkward talk, he resolved to keep still. The night surrounded them with cold flakes, the wind blew circles, the town was closed, shuttered in warmth against the rising storm.

He waited, but she did not take her step. He became impatient; he had still to get a meal, find a place to sleep. Then she started, and he sensed a lurch in her walk, a sway in the body next to him. Something was wrong. He stepped with her, counted the time between the steps. She halted with each effort, swung a leg forward deliberately. Her side dipped with the work, her hand pulled on him for quick support.

She was lamed, like a bowed horse. Matt eased up, let her tell him how and when to move. She slipped and reached out; he faced her, took her by the shoulders, and kept her upright.

"Do you see now? I wasn't feeling sorry for you when we last spoke. I know what it is like, to face this daily.

"I am a cripple, Matt. Your scarring shows, but it does not stop you from what you chose to do. My lameness cannot be seen, but it changes each day for me. From what my life could be to what it truly is. Can you understand what that is like?"

The rage grew in him like a sour illness. His hands weakened, lost their grip. But the girl held to him, dependent now for her safety. He had to relax, she had to hold his elbow tightly and balance with him. He could not speak. They began the trip to her house.

She talked easily in her musical voice. This time there were no interruptions, he could not escape. She told him everything. The terror, the pain. The long days of mending. The doubts now, the renewed fear of each lonely day.

Then she spoke of her father, of his intemperate anger at what had befallen her, his inability to find the guilty men. Of the new drinking, late at night, and her mother weeping upstairs, while he banged and howled down below. The magical change each morning, when her father faced his town with kind eyes and a benevolent smile. As if he were two people, divided by day and night.

The fury in Matt dimmed; her story smothered its fire. But he could not bear to hear her talk so about herself. He put a cold finger to her mouth to stop her. As if she understood, she half stepped in front of him, leaned toward him, pressed her mouth to the hand resting on her lips.

A doorway was bright ahead of them, the window with a lantern placed in its center. They were not quite in the yellowed circle cast on the snow. Mack sighed; face-to-face, her head was level with his. He marveled at the tendons of his hand, held to her mouth by desire. Her eyes watched him. Snow graced the loose hair above her face, a flake slid down her nose to dissolve on Matt's thumb.

She smiled under his hand. Her breath warmed him. His mouth opened; she put her hands on his shoulders. At once reluctantly and in anticipation, he removed his hand from her lips ... and she stepped into his embrace. Her breasts rose and fell near his chest, the heat of her body warmed him.

Her mouth was on his; the words were loving, new to Matt, amazing him. A gift such as he had never received.

"I love you. Since you were here and I cared for you. When you left, I cried. Matt, could you love me?"

This was why he came back. He could not speak, but he nodded his head to her question, carefully, so he would not lose the touch of her lips.

Then the light on the snow widened, a door opened, a blast of yellow captured them. Angry shouts, sudden commotion. Orianna flinched and stumbled from Matt, went to her knees. He reached for her—and a blow grazed the side of his head and knocked him into the snow. He cried out, stunned, confused. He found Orianna next to him, struggled to protect her from the next blow.

A gun sight drilled into his back. He froze, and the gun dug in until he knew it would draw blood. He recognized the voice as it spoke above him.

"You miserable, low son of a bitch. Touch my child. Kiss her as if she were a— You have no right to be a mile near her. You black-haired, sorry bastard. Stinking 'breed."

The curses went on, then sputtered and died out, but the pressure of the gun did not change. A shaking finger, a trembling arm could put a bullet in his spine. If he lived, he would never walk. Matt did not move. Did not respond.

The girl ended it; she screamed at her father. Faces began to appear at neighboring windows, lights went on, a woman came out into the street. But Orianna did not hush her accusations, and her father could not move from her fury.

"You would blame Matt for this. You take out your hatred of yourself on a man who has done nothing but be kind enough to bring me home. You would shoot him in the back like a thief, a criminal.

"I wanted to kiss him. I wanted to. Me, your daughter. I wanted this. Did you know Matt is fair-skinned, like you are? Did you ever look past his hair and face and see who he is? Did you bother to know he is kind and brave?

"I am not a child, I am a grown woman—"

She tired suddenly. Her mother stood beside her child, hands twisted helplessly in a piece of forgotten mending. The gun barrel dug deeper into Matt, then moved side to side, ran along his spine. And dropped away. He knew by the sounds that the pistol was in its holster and he was safe, for the moment.

Vail let him know. "You, leave town. Tonight. Or tomorrow you will be found in a gully, robbed and dead. Your choice."

The words hung between Matt and the sheriff. And Matt stayed, bewildered by the stirred emotions, concerned for the girl. She was next to her mother, but her face was wild and shaken, her eyes too bright. He shuddered, tasted her kiss. Panted, trying to catch his breath. He wanted desperately to rub the small of his back, but he did not dare move.

The father stomped up the steps of the house, slammed the door behind him. The mother was with her child, Matt shackled and pinned by the vision of the girl. Mrs. Vail tried to smooth out the incident, but the worry crossed her pleasant talking.

"I remember you, young man. Thank you for bringing Orianna home, thank you ... She is a good child." There was a wait, a choking, then the mother began again. "Thank you for bringing Orianna home safely." The tears came in a flood; Mrs. Vail covered her face with the bit of mending.

She, too, went up the steps, tired, weary past facing what awaited her inside.

The front door closed, the wick trimmed down on the lamp. Matt knew he had to leave now. But Orianna held him.

"Matt, this wasn't you. Please believe me. It was my father. You have done nothing but what was asked. You kissed a crippled girl to please her whim, make her be alive. That's all."

She, too, began to cry. It was a sound he did not want to hear, a picture he could not keep in his mind.

"Miss, I kissed you because I wanted to. It was my pleasure to bring you home, my pleasure to kiss . . . Please."

She smiled despite her tears, and snow caught in the curve of her lips. She licked the wetness as Matt leaned toward her. He swept melting flakes from her forehead, then gently bent to her and kissed her mouth. He felt the lift of a smile under his touch; he smiled with her. She pushed him, slowly, with both hands.

"Matt, we must stop. Papa's inside, and I know Mama is upstairs crying. And I have the medicine for Rachel in my pocket. I must go inside.

"You've come back, haven't you, Matt? To stay? I am glad— Matt?"

By the time she climbed to the top step, Matt was gone. He would be back when she needed him to be with her. It would be soon. She prayed quietly before she opened the door.

"Please, let him be safe, let him want to come back. Let Papa learn to like him. Please."

CHAPTER TWENTY-THREE

Matt found the livery and routed the hostler from a smelly room and a half-empty bottle. When the roan hit the dark street, Matt felt the little horse stiffen, half rear, pull on the tight rein. The roan had no more liking for the town and its comforts than Matt did at the moment.

He lined the roan dead center on the main street and galloped the horse flat-out. A war whoop to wake the dead was his parting shot, and a light came on, a door slammed. Matt goaded the roan with his spurs, and the town was quickly lost in the wisps of snowfall.

An hour later they were both cold; Matt shook badly, hands folded inside his coat. The roan was covered with half-frozen sleet, Matt's eyebrows and the tips of his ears were frosted white. He remembered a dark hole, a banking cut away from the spring floods. It would be shelter tonight. Tomorrow, if he was alive, he would ride to Bitter Springs and talk to the boss. It was a long shot, and all he had.

Miguel fingered the new snow in his mustache and blew on his cold hands. He tried to unknot the reata but his fingers would not bend, the leather was too stiff. It was supposed to be afternoon, but it could not be told by the sun. Clouds of snow drifted across the sky, blocking out what light escaped around the storm. He had foolishly sent Silvestre back to the rancho, to find an ax to cut through the ice on the cattle's water. He could not expect a miracle—he would not see Silvestre again until after the storm ended.

The señor himself was chasing other cows. He had spoken clearly: He would trust Miguel with the safety of the missing cattle whose tracks pointed toward a distant mountain. It might be, because of the cold, the coming night, that Miguel would stay out in the storm, once he had found his cattle.

He rode his horse toward the mountain the Anglos called Hen Egg. It was of little sense to call a pile of rubble and weeds a mountain and then curse it with such a name. But he did not pay the wages or make the rules. If the señor wished him to find the cattle and sleep with them through the storm, then Miguel would do what was expected of him. He took risks for the señor, he accepted with pride the señor's trust.

So he rode to the slopes of Hen Egg and drifted through its brush, where he spooked out at least twenty head of thin cattle. Now he would drive them closer to their home range, straight into the wind and through a blinding white cloud.

The paint spooked; Miguel jammed his boots deeper into the *tapederos*. He had forgotten the paint was useless for much except to mirror a man's pride. A beautiful horse with a black coat stained white along the belly, down the arched neck, the proud face slashed with a wide blaze. A horse who saw cattle as wondrous monsters.

The paint shied again from his own excitement and stumbled over a buried cactus, rearing as its spines dug tender skin. Miguel clamped his legs to the black and white sides, slapped the braided end of the reins to the streaked white neck. Dust rose from the blow to mix with new snow. Miguel coughed heavily; the paint danced more and then settled from boredom.

He could just see the herd of cattle amid the whirling snow. The paint trembled under him; Miguel rubbed his eyes. He was not dreaming—the snow came in a heavy blanket. Each step of the reluctant paint balled snow and dirt in the shallow hooves; the cattle drifted. Miguel hit the paint with bare hands. The horse leapt forward, skidded on the packed feet, and sat down.

Miguel tugged the reata free and swung its loops at the steers, whose forms seemed to dissolve into the heavy, white snow. One animal chose not to run, but lowered its head, stomped a bony front leg, and bellowed. Miguel did not like the threat, so he raked the paint with his spurs and rode off the lowering steer, slapped the reata over the raised pink nose. The steer ran from the blow; horse and rider followed, and soon they could count the backsides of more steers, a few cows with half-grown calves. A line of single file, docile beeves headed to home range.

They rode into the wind. Miguel wiggled his chin until it was buried in the collar of his coat. He was unwilling to face the wind, but it must be done. If the cattle were left to drift, they would fade and be lost. Besides, the señor told him to bring the cattle in; he was only following his orders.

But it was too much to drive cattle in such a storm. Too much. Miguel lost feeling in his hand; the reata uncoiled against his leg. He stopped the paint briefly, to wad the reata over the white hump of the broad horn. In seconds the cattle had disappeared. He could not even hear their sounds, their low calling, their hooves striking rock under snow. Nothing but the blending flakes blown beside his ear, touching the end of his nose, sneaking in the raised collar of his coat. Miguel was cold, and perhaps lost. And afraid.

To be alone was not tolerable. Even cattle were better company than his thoughts, and the addled paint. Miguel cursed to the gods for making so beautiful a creature such a poor companion. He scratched the wicked horse with spurs and stood up in the saddle to yell. The startled paint leapt under his rider; Miguel grabbed the horn and yelled again. He would quickly find the cattle, point them toward the ranch, and come in victorious, ready for the warm fire, food, perhaps a drink from the señor's store of brandy.

He galloped with no direction, confident the herd would appear. But the ground fell away, the paint screamed. There was a moment of flying through nothing but the blackness of the night, the loose cloud of snow. A shod hoof cut his thigh . . . He felt the blood wash from him. But he was suspended, there was no pain.

He landed hard, and the air was driven from him. He could not breathe, he could not see or hear.

Somewhere beside him the gelding struggled. Too close to Miguel, close enough so that he could taste the sweat of the animal as he fought. Miguel wanted to speak out, to ask that the paint not roll on him. To wonder aloud where he was.

But words did not come, only snow that entered his gaping mouth and choked inside him. He had to cough, and the convulsion of his chest burst through him. His ribs were broken, he had felt that pain before. His back—he could not move his legs. His arms would lift, but they were weak and useless.

The horse fought its battle; sand and rock and snow

sprayed Miguel's face and rubbed the coldness of his hand. He could see the splashes of white in the black coat. His knee was hard hit; he heard the crack but did not feel the blow.

It was the cold. He was quickly freezing, numbed by the wind. Once he was warmed, he would be all right. Then he would feel the pain and know he was again alive.

The once floundering horse was quiet. Snow mounded quickly on the black quarters. Snow touched and then buried the thin neck, snow blurred the outlines of the ancient saddle, filled the cup of the *tapedero* laid in the wash. Miguel was colder; he could look down the lines of his body and see the snow piled on his legs, caught in the reaches of his boots and chaps. There was still no pain, except for a throbbing in one leg and a humming in his head that went down his neck.

He knew he was lying in a wash. And he guessed the paint was dead. He thought he would live the night and be warmed by the sun, stand up and twist, move his arms and legs, find again he could walk. Not perhaps to take the gear off the paint but at least to begin the trek to the ranch. The señor would come out looking for him, Silvestre would come looking for him. It was only a matter of waiting through the night to begin his own rescue at dawn.

The drifting cattle woke Matt. They came down the arroyo bunched together and spooked at the strawberry roan. Matt sat up, conscious of the horse's snort, the fire's black coals, the cold that shook him. Then he saw the lead steer which, spooked by Matt's sudden movement, lifted its head and bellowed, swung its thin tail, and trotted for several strides.

He counted fifteen head before they grouped close and he lost track. They were branded with McCraw's sign. And they marched as if driven, yet there was no one at their rear, no outrider on their flank. When the last tail switched and was gone, the roan whinnied loudly. There was no answer.

Matt scattered the dead coals. He was cold clear through, and if he looked east, he could see a dead yellow at the base of the sky. Near to morning, time to move on. He wiped the roan's back free of snow. Icicles hung from the gelding's chin whiskers and down the long hair of his legs. The saddle moaned when Matt placed it on the humped back. The horse refused the iced bit, and Matt held it between his frozen hands, rubbing the metal to put some warmth in it. He finally could ride the horse, holding a short rein to keep the roan from bucking.

It was easy to backtrack the cattle. He had to do it. The tracks were deep holes in the fresh snow; black manure splattered less than an hour ago was hard-frozen plates. Matt rode with the reins pulled to his belly, his hands buried in the front of his coat.

The arroyo bent to the right; the roan stopped and humped, threw up his head, and shifted backward. Matt spurred the horse, but the roan would not move on.

A black mound ahead. The roan snorted and blew loudly, trembling, sweating. Matt forced the horse to walk; the roan whirled and reared against his hand. He gave up and dismounted, tied the horse to a stunted mesquite grown sideways from the banking.

His boots dug up dirt; he caught a toe on an exposed root and fell forward. The black mound became the body of a horse, the head toward Matt, the eyes filmed and staring, the mane streaked with white crystals. Deep ruts were cut at the stilled legs. Matt read the struggle and looked for the rider.

The man was past the horse, half buried in white. Matt slid to his knees and peered into the blue face. Miguel. Matt touched his fingers to the exposed throat, waited, leaned closer to hear. There was a fluttering under his fingertips. He pressed hard into the cold skin—the pulse died away, then came back. Matt wanted to shake the man, wake him from a wrong sleep and see him sit up with a groan and start complaining.

The pulse flickered through a distended vein. Matt put a

hand to each side of the icy face and rubbed the skin, forced blood into the deadened flesh. He tried for the pulse again, to find an improvement. There was life under his hands. He rubbed the face until his own skin was numbed, then he sat back on his heels and stared at the corpse.

He could see no bloodstains, there was no open wound, no signs of battle. The horse was a good distance away; perhaps it had not fallen on the man. He touched the tip of a boot, then raised the foot and rotated it. No cry, no opened eyes screaming at him to stop. Matt lifted the other foot, tugged on the leg. Again there was no response.

On hands and knees he scurried to the other side of the man, held a curled hand in his palm, and waited ... for nothing. He skidded around the head, watched to see if the strange movements raised a warning in the unconscious mind. Then he grabbed the other hand and waited again. The head did not roll, the eyes did not flicker. Matt leaned over the face, put his fingers one more time where there had been a pulse. Beneath his frozen hand he touched the slow and irregular beating of the chilled blood.

He stood, wiped wet snow from his leg, took a handful from inside his jacket. There was a sun out now, and each expulsion of air blew gray cloud from his mouth. He rested before the next chore.

It took five minutes to get the skittish roan past the dead horse. Matt placed a heavy rock on the ends of the reins, then shoved his hands under Miguel's shoulders and clawed away the sand until he could wrap his arms around the man and raise up the body. He balanced Miguel over his back and attempted to stand. He fell backward, smothered by Miguel. He cursed, fought the dead weight, struggled to stand, and made it. He took two deep breaths and was quickly surrounded by a steamed cloud.

He had to knee the roan in the belly, jerk the reins, before the horse stood still. Miguel draped easily over the narrow saddle. His hand hit the off side; the roan spooked, Miguel shifted. A hoof came down on Matt's foot; the horse circled, ground his weight on Matt's boot.

It became a foolish dance that no one saw. He yanked the horse to free his foot—hobbled a step and fell down. Took a bite of the cold, clean snow. The chill gave him energy. He knelt, stood up, jerked on the reins again.

The sun was too bright; the sky, slices of blue between fast-running clouds. Light rays streaked at long angles and heated the snow. Cold air steamed up and melted patches from the sand. Matt finally knew where he was. An hour's hard ride would get him to Bitter Springs. Leading the roan would take the morning. He touched Miguel's face, stroked the icy skin of his cheek, patted the wet forehead. It was the best he could do.

Walking was impossible. The foot hurt where the roan had stomped on it. Snow melted and mixed with the sand, filled the roan's hooves, stuck to the bottom of Matt's boots, and weighted him with each step.

The tracks went out of the arroyo and up to the plains. Matt followed the cattle's instinct. At the lip of the banking he slipped and went down hard, scraping his old scar. He grabbed at a bush and stood up; the roan leapt from the bottom of the wash and hit Matt in the shoulder, dragged him a few feet before giving in to the pull of the reins. Matt settled on hands and knees and gasped the cold air.

He limped on the sore foot, dizzy from the reflected glare. He guessed at direction, let the roan pull him along as if the horse knew where they were headed. Sweat trickled inside his shirt, soaked his pants. He opened his coat, unbuttoned the shirt. The roan stopped and snatched at a clump of grass; Matt had to throw snow at the little horse to get him moving.

Miguel hung loose on the roan's back; Matt checked him once to see if he was still breathing, but could hear nothing over the beat of his own heart, the throbbing of his hard-used lungs. He gave up and walked on.

It was past noon when Matt saw the ranch. Snow blanketed the roof, horses were fetlock deep in mud, cattle ranged around the water tank, and Matt guessed someone had cut sotol heads to keep them close. Long brown stalks were scattered, the cattle were head down and busy.

He yelled McCraw's name. No one answered. He walked, slipping in new mud, holding to the tired roan. Miguel's hair brushed Matt's leather pants, and the whisper of sound unnerved him. Matt grabbed the horn; Miguel's face touched his thigh. He yelled again, calling for McCraw as if the man's name was a curse caught in his throat.

The door opened to a black hole. No one moved except the strawberry roan. Matt yelled, and a figure came out from the doorway. Running toward Matt, shouting something he could not hear. Matt stopped and waited for McCraw to cover the last few yards. He was tired.

"What the hell . . .?" McCraw's mouth opened and shut but no sense came out. McCraw rocked back and shoved the hat almost off his head. Matt started to explain, but then Silvestre arrived, big face frozen white, arms flailing as he recognized the upside-down man on the runty pony.

Between McCraw and the fat vaquero, they were able to free Miguel and carry him inside. Matt was left to put up the roan and come along, still limping, tired, cold, hungry. And unreasonably mad. The house was warm, a fire sputtered in the corner. Miguel lay on the cot strung near the flame.

"What happened? What did you do? He's alive, barely. And you look like hell. What—"

"Señor, I do not know." He used the Spanish to distance himself. "Your cattle, they passed by me early this morning and I found Miguel next to his horse. He was not moving but I could find a pulse, and could believe he would live. So I brought him to you."

Anger, puzzlement, sadness marked McCraw's face. Matt waited patiently. As he knew it would come, McCraw stepped away from the challenge of Matt's words and went to practical matters.

"You, saddle a fresh horse and ride for the *curandero*. I'll tend to Miguel. Go."

McCraw used his own tongue, rolling the English sounds

to bring power. Matt would make the ride, but now McCraw thought to command Silvestre to get the horse ready. "One with plattered hooves, the red mare. So Matt will not sink into the wet sand and snow."

Silvestre brought out the fine-headed bay; Matt glanced at the recently trimmed, small feet, shook his head. The ride would tire out the gelding, but he would not bother to complain. Matt finished the coffee McCraw fed him, and the chunk of hard bread. It had been more than a day since he'd eaten, and he was light-headed from the hunger.

His rigging was on the bay. It was a pleasure to ride a good horse again, to touch the rein lightly and have the horse spin in response. The tiredness lifted, and in four strides he had the bay running.

He returned with the *curandero* in five hours. The man had been in the treatment of an injured vaquero and would not leave, not even for his own cousin. Then he had to ask Matt his questions, send his children to find the leaves and stemmy bushes, the hidden cactus.

Matt wanted nothing more than to sleep in a warm, dry place, but he had followed the slow trot of the *curandero*'s burro and considered poking the animal's thin quarters with a stick. The *curandero* looked over his shoulder as if he knew Matt's thoughts. The man smiled gravely. Matt let his head nod, half dozed with the easy walk of the bay, and gave up on the worrying.

He did not remember stripping the bay of gear, or making a pile in the corner. Nor did he remember dealing with the burro at all, but the small beast had its nose buried in a mound of the cut stool. Matt curled up in the remains of the winter hay, wrapped in sweaty blankets that did not warm him. He shook lightly, drops of sweat tickled the back of his neck, his face was greasy. He pulled the blankets closer, smelled the staleness of his breath caught by damp wool. He shuddered, his eyes ached, he tried once more to sleep.

He must have dozed off, for a hand shook him not too

gently—and he came up ready to fight. The lean face close to him was McCraw's. The hazel eyes were glazed and dry.

"Miguel died. The *curandero* worked on him, did everything he could. But Miguel saw us and he died.

"Now the old man wants you. Says you are ill, that you have taken a chill and you must drink his damned brews. I don't know, Matt. We've been here before. But you better come inside, do what the old man says."

The body was little more than a drab length laid out on the cot. The face was covered, the hands mounded in a fold over the chest. Only the toes of the boots showed it had been a man who now lay there. Silvestre sat in a chair, face toward the corpse, head bowed.

Matt sat for inspection. The *curandero* touched Matt's chest over the heart—nodded to him and spoke a prayer for Miguel in a liquid voice. Matt almost hated the *curandero* then, but it was not his place to care.

He let the *curandero* peer into his mouth, open his damp shirt, and put an ear to his chest. It meant nothing, the old one's herbs and powders. It pleased McCraw, but it meant less than nothing to Matt.

There were liquids he must drink, salves he would rub on his chest. He must sleep, eat boiled greens, the meat of a fresh-killed goat. And drink good water until he was cured.

If sleep was the cure-all, Matt would agree. He was no longer hungry, and the taste of goat did not agree with him. But he drank the bitter liquor and did not spit it out. The paste on his chest burned him, and the smell gagged in his throat. He slept fitfully, awoke soaking wet, drank more of the liquor and a gallon of water, and went back to sleep.

He left McCraw and Silvestre to mourn Miguel. They cleaned and washed him, dressed him and wrapped him in a roll of cloth. When spring came, they would bury him under a fine tree. Until then, he would rest, guarded, in a shed behind the barn.

CHAPTER TWENTY-FOUR

The woman was tired. Any fool could see that much. Every move was made slowly, deliberately. She never complained, but he could see. Her chores were completed, but each successive day took more and more from her—and she did not recover through the nights.

Thomas Kersey rose from the table and carried the bare dishes to the tin sink. She looked up him then, with eyes wide, her face drawn and unaccountably plain. "You do not need to do that, Mr. Kersey. I am able to clear my own table." But he did not listen to her and put the dishes down carefully inside the sink. A plated fork rattled on tin, a discordant sound that told him one more time of the hovel where they lived, the brutal conditions of the life he was giving her. She did not complain, truly. But he was aware she had lived with better, and the thought of another man taking better care, giving her more, was a bitter morsel to swallow. He kept his back to her and began the washing.

It was easier to lean her elbows on the scrubbed table than to stand and make the effort to interrupt Mr. Kersey. That took an energy and enthusiasm she no longer had. Harriet Kersey pressed her chin to the cupped palms of her intertwined hands and let the weight of her head dig a depression in their sad flesh.

She was tired. Even Mr. Kersey could now see that much of her state. There was wealth promised here, tied to the growing herd of cattle, the sweep of the fine grasslands. But there was no money and endless work. With winter coming, even more work must be done to accomplish all that was necessary for survival. And there was less cash to take in hand for even the smallest luxury.

They had managed the first blizzard, dug deeply into the small cabin, huddled together for warmth. Mr. Kersey rode out when it was possible, one brillant and sunny day, to check the cattle. The report was grim; as was his manner, he let none of the anger and distress show in his words. But they had lost a number of head, yearlings mostly. It was the beginning of winter; there would be other storms, more piled snow, more buried corpses.

None of this showed on Mr. Kersey's features as he methodically listed the losses and the expectations for the next months. The sudden weariness of her life engulfed Harriet; caught in the drone of the words, the stiffness of their speaker. She tried to see into his face and find a passion, a caring. Mr. Kersey continued his list of chores. And Harriet longed to scream out, to cry into his dulled eyes, to scratch red lines down his neck, to bring him to her in rage or lust. Anything to break the pattern of his bland words, his dreary days.

She remained at the table, head pressed in her hands, eyes dry, throat scalded by her crying. Her legs were numb, her arms and shoulders without feeling. Little of the distress showed in her light eyes or the old lines of her face. Mr. Kersey had taught her well, to take her female emotion and cup it to her heart in private, to leave them both protected as they worked through their days. A struggle of hard-baked ground, a reluctant team of horses, thirsty cattle. There was no spare energy to waste on feelings.

There was life here, but Harriet was beginning to know it was not hers. Yet she would not leave, could not damage this man who fed and clothed her, worked for her future as well as his own.

She laid her head on her arms, smelled the lye-scrubbed wood of the table. The grained pores stared back at her, bleached white, worn coarse, the edges wrinkled as the skin of her face, the slackness of her throat, the sag of her belly and breasts. A tear rolled from her eye, cooled her face as it splashed on the wood of the table and was immediately absorbed. Leaving only a dark spot that quickly dried. Leaving behind nothing but the pain in her heart.

The thickness of the soft hair lay inches below his hand. Mr. Kersey wanted to drop his fist and let it lie on the abundance. He dreamed of that hair during the long days, could feel its silk, smell the clean soap used in its washing. And now the sweet crown of her glory lay within his reach. If he were a fancier man, a dreamer and a lover, he could say it was this head of hair—this shining richness— that was the fullness of his dreams, the reason for his work and sacrifice. But he was little more than a plain-minded rancher, a man dogged in his work, a man silenced by his dreams.

He watched his own hand, marveled at the dirt ground into its seams, felt the shaking begin inside him, the heavy desire to touch that hair. She did not move her head; she rested on the cross of her arms, baring the back of her neck, allowing the escaped wisps to curl along her throat.

Thomas Kersey wished to touch his wife but he did not. He withdrew his hand and put it along his thigh. Words crowded his throat; he coughed, swallowed a loud and ugly sound. Harriet raised her head from the comfort of her own arm and pushed away the errant bits of hair. He would do that for her, and more. But he did not know how to tell her.

"Mrs. Kersey, I will go to Marfa tomorrow. We are low in many supplies, and I need to talk with— Mrs. Kersey, do you hear me? I would be delighted if you would join me for the trip. It will be a sunny day, and we can bundle you up in several blankets. Mrs. Kersey?"

She did not answer. And he was not surprised. Often, she heard him speak but did not respond. As if he were talking to one who was not there. He didn't like to think of why this was so. He knew, deep inside, it was that she did not love him. So he was content to take her silence for the answer he wished it were.

The next morning Thomas Kersey saddled a fine mare

and climbed on her, kicked ineffectively at her round sides, and let the mare pick her way through the scattered snow. Already the hot sun had melted all of the blizzard's work. The dead cattle were useless mounds; the surviving cows poked their heads into cactus and tried to find a meal between the spines.

The winter would be long, and Thomas Kersey had a cry inside him he could not let out. So he slapped the mare and did not look back to see that his wife was not watching from the cabin door.

In town, his first visit was to the bank, then he allowed the lazy mare to wander down the long street. Kersey looked about in innocent speculation; the town was growing. Even in this weather, a new building was started, the walls and rafters pinned together, waiting for the finish.

A tall figure stood near a door, an arm waved; Kersey turned the mare.

"Morning, Sheriff."

" 'Lo, Kersey."

Neither man felt the need to break the comfortable silence with words. They were easy together, each feeling in the other a temperament and sensibility compatible with his own. Unspoken friends in the new wilderness. Kersey dismounted and followed Vail inside his rough, unofficial office.

The small black stove was grayed with old soot. Coffee bubbled in a blackened pot. Vail poured two cups and handed one to Kersey. Neither man spoke, but sipped at the coffee. Finally Vail motioned for Kersey to sit down opposite him. They were quiet; Kersey spat out a mouthful of grounds. He heard the tread of feet clatter on the boards outside Vail's office, but no one intruded.

"Been of a mind to talk with you, Kersey. Been thinking some. Thought you might have an answer."

Kersey studied the face, saw the blue eyes narrowed in thought, the mouth pulled thin behind the luxurious mustache. He was patient; Vail would come to the right words.

"My daughter, the youngest. Orianna." There was a long

wait, as if saying the name were enough. "Orianna . . . well, she limps. You know. My wife and I, we fear she will not find herself a suitable husband. She can do her work, but a man would not know that. And she has shown an interest in a man we do not approve of. A 'breed."

Kersey glanced about the room, to give Vail the time he needed to struggle with his distress.

"Mrs. Vail and I, we thought— She knows that your wife, Harriet . . . She believes your wife is not used to the demands of life out here. So, she thought perhaps . . . you might want to consider taking Orianna in to be a help to your wife. Orianna has all the skills, and she has great courage. We, I . . ."

Robert Vail considered the request completed. He would not speak of the subject again. If Kersey refused, or pretended to not understand, then he would find a different way to deal with Orianna. He had a distant relative in Flowery Branch, back East in Georgia.

A sharp pain stabbed Vail. He would have pressed his hands to the spot for comfort, but he knew Kersey watched him and he sat erect in the chair, sipped at the cold coffee as if nothing much were wrong.

"Well, Sheriff. Yesterday morning my woman and I were talking. She's worn down by the work all right—not complaining, but it is easy enough to see. A girl like your Orianna . . . She could be company for Mrs. Kersey. She never had children, and it's too late now. A girl like your Orianna would be a comfort. A right good idea."

As if the request and its acceptance were a neighborly attempt to help. As if the despair over Orianna's behavior didn't show in every move he made, every word spoken in the house, every muscle held tight in anger. Vail half raised his empty cup, looked over the rim at Kersey's bland face.

"That's settled, then. I'll be getting Orianna, packing her things. Even got her a fine steady riding horse, so you won't have to worry about her getting around. She'll be waiting. You come by after your chores in town. It's a bargain, Mr. Kersey. A bargain for both of us."

* * *

Her mother told her. Mr. Kersey was in town . . . and it had been arranged for her to return with him, to be a companion to his wife. Orianna watched her mother carefully while the arrangements were explained. As she talked, her mother pulled down the few dresses Orianna had, gathered undergarments, a pair of shoes, the heavy woolen cape. There was a carpetbag in her parents' room she could have, her mother said. And a smaller bag for her few personal belongings.

She was not given a moment's consideration of refusal. It was decided, discussed by her mother and father as if she were still a child, not almost twenty.

Orianna sat down on the double bed she shared with Helen. Rachel had a narrow bed of her own. When Suzanne was here, they had shared a bed, talked in the night, laughed and wondered about their future.

She was pleased and excited to leave. And saddened by how easy it was to go. A true family would mean more love, more pain at separation; but for the obsession of her father. Even as a child, she had known his loving was somehow wrong.

It was easy to leave—simple to pack the few shirtwaists and skirts, the simple cotton dress, her one good winter wool. She sat down and patted the swollen bag. There was nothing inside it that meant anything to her, no small, pretty-faced porcelain doll, no framed picture, no locket of hair. She was ready to leave right now.

Miguel's death was not talked about. When Matt quit sleeping and could stand and walk without staggering, when the foul medicines were used up, the body had been well stored and mourned. Silvestre spent evenings laboriously carving on a wooden cross, but no one spoke of what he was doing. Miguel had died, would be buried, would be remembered. That was all to be offered in the life of a vaquero.

Matt went back to cooking. McCraw waved a fork in sa-

TEXAS SPRINGS

lute the first morning, Silvestre shoveled the food into his mouth and said nothing.

That first storm was followed by more; wild blowing winds, hours of white flakes, days of chasing down bewildered cattle, driving them closer to the springs and the chopped sotol heads and burned prickly pear. Matt and the boss rode out daily, floundering in wet snow, struggling to keep as many cattle as they could find.

Matt let the line-back dun ease to a walk. He was sure enough tired, and the little horse was lathered almost white. He unbuttoned his wool coat; peeled off knitted mittens, a luxury for the winter storms that McCraw gave him. Matt tucked the mittens in front of his saddle, shrugged his shoulders under the burden of the heavy coat. It was almost warm, almost spring.

The dun shook his head; a cloud of damp hairs drifted loose. Shedding, getting ready for the change. Matt breathed in deeply of the sweaty horse, the broken grass, the sweet air of sun-warmed ground. Snow remained only at the edge of the arroyos, where day-long shadows kept their cold. Soon that reminder of winter would be gone, soon cattle would birth out their young without Matt's worrying about a freeze, or bringing in a shocked calf over the back of his horse, watching always for the mother's horns.

He finally had to dismount and slip out of his coat. By God, it was spring; he'd been too busy to see the signs. Matt uncapped the wooden canteen, drank the last of the water. Something else he better rethink: this was no place to be without water.

The dun had drifted north this time, but Matt didn't mind. Wherever he went, he found the remnants of the winter. Dead cattle, bloated and thawed, stinking now in their death. Horses that were walking skeletons; raw and pitiful, matted coats, string tails, sunken eyes.

Matt had counted twenty-three head of downed cattle this morning, not all of them McCraw's. Others brands he kept tally on, other ranchers enduring the loss. Kersey, up the long canyon above Alamito Creek, he'd lost a small fortune back a half mile. Matt kept tally: McCraw's marked with a slash, Kersey's with a dot, unknown a circle. The tally book was filling.

Matt leaned over and picked a stalk of light green leaves and crushed it in his fingers, rubbed the oil under his nose. The rotting cattle and dying horses flooded him in spite of the acrid herb. Matt suspected the smell was more in his mind than hanging on the air.

Kersey had to be told of his loss. And Matt knew the boss would have him do the chore. He shook his head, put the bitter herb to his lips, and chewed the strong taste.

So he had to ride to the Kersey place. Matt swung up on the dun and headed out. An easy ride, with the hope of maybe a noon meal. He conjured up pictures of food. Fresh-baked bread, new jams, side meat not too salty. Coffee with sugar sweetener. Good thinking to ride with a man headed on a rotten course.

Kersey's was small, set back against the canyon wall. Rougher than McCraw's place, but showing the woman's touch. Curtains in a window, the track to the door outlined with uniform rocks. Matt bet there were dried flowers in a small pot on the table inside, and squares of colored cloth to wipe your mouth after eating. Quilts on the bed, a hand-braided rug on the floor. A woman's touch always showed the same.

A door opened, a woman came outside. Raised her hand to her face to shield her eyes from the sun. Matt stopped the dun and crossed his hands on the horn. He didn't want to scare Mrs. Kersey; he'd give her time to see him clear.

But he knew this woman. It wasn't Kersey's wife, he'd never met her. This woman he knew. She took careful steps toward him, her hands stayed at her sides. He saw the halo of pale hair, the sweet, awkward walk. He saw no one else.

He dismounted slowly, dropped the reins, and walked to her. She waited. Matt felt his legs go weak, his heart thud inside his ribs. Orianna Vail. It was Orianna Vail.

* * *

Papa called the mark the devil's brand. She did not have to listen to her papa anymore. Now Matt was here, coming toward her, hand outstretched, face wide in a grin. She would know him anytime, any place, and it had nothing to do with any scar. He was speaking to her, but she did not understand what it was he said. She started, off-balance on her injured leg, still in shock. He dropped his hat and skipped two steps, caught her arm, steadied her. As he had held her in the snow.

It had been his words that unbalanced her. His hands were comforting on her arm. She could smell the cool air in his clothes, and there was a bite of an herb, a sweet, rotten smell to him. A mixture, just as he was a mixture.

"Miss, all I said, I got to speak to Mr. Kersey. Came across a bunch of his stock. Dead, caught in the last storm. Best he know, count up the loss. Could skin out some of the carcasses, least get hides and horns. A real bad picture, miss. Real bad."

"What are you doing here? How . . .?"

She watched his face while he spoke. It was a good face, burned a new red from the sun, with light streaks in the black hair, lines at the mouth and eyes. Those eyes were shaded by thick brows, and the rise of cheekbones gave the face an old look. There was nothing left of the child he once had been.

As if he were conscious of her stare, his hand rose to his face, absently rubbed the puckered scar, and she knew again the mark it was in his life.

"Miss, please. I got to see Mr. Kersey, or leave him a message. Got to get back to work. McCraw, he got to know, too. Lost a lot of stock this winter."

As if seeing her was all; as if talking to her, accepting her was too much. She put a hand to his face, and he jerked back from the gesture.

"Miss, it ain't right . . . You're too— Got to do my work."

Hiding from her, running from her. Orianna shook her head, deliberately denying him. The hazel eyes focused on her; then he backed up a step, looked over her head, and pretended to find an interest in the vast sky.

"Miss, you got to tell Kersey. You give him the message. I got to go."

He was afraid of her. She smiled at the thought. He mouthed the words to her, but his eyes lingered on her face ... and finally his right hand came up. Orianna felt the pressure on her wrist; she saw into his face and waited. He kept up the talking, but the words were nothing. It was the look of him, the shine to his eyes, the smell of his damp shirt, the height and length of him that intrigued her.

He kissed her gently. On the mouth, with the taste of grass on his lips; the odor of smoke and rich dirt engulfed her.

"Miss, this ain't the way to see you. I got to tell Mr. Kersey 'bout them cows. You do the telling.

"I'll come back, with permission to be seeing you. Ain't right not to ask. Don't want to do anything wrong, nothing that'll send you back to your pap before we're ready. You understand me, Orianna Vail?"

It was all there for her, his intentions, his interest. His back-ways declaration of love. She nodded agreement, and he counted out the number of cattle Mr. Kersey lost, got her promise to tell the man.

He didn't touch her again. He mounted his horse and rode from the yard with the promise made to her that he would keep: "I'll be back proper, Orianna Vail."

He was back at Kersey's three weeks later. She was waiting, with Mrs. Kersey's blessing. Mr. Kersey came outside briefly, to thank him for the tally of dead cattle and ask about McCraw's winter kill. Matt was polite, and Kersey was quickly bored.

The pair sat near the small garden where Mrs. Kersey worked. She would not watch them or talk to them, but she was there. It was new to Matt, this atmosphere of respectability, and he tried to talk about it to Orianna. But his explanation was confused and became lost in his enchantment with her face and form. The smell of dried flowers and sweet grass.

He returned the following week, then again the week after. It was two more weeks before he could get time, then another three weeks as the cattle work started, the horses came in for breaking. Calves to brand and cut, foals to doctor, mares to check. The cattle roamed in wide bunches, desperate for grass, drinking the winter runoff until they swallowed sand and turned sour. They lost three head to mouths infected from chewing cactus, two fillies from starvation, a steer from a broken leg. The work had to be done, and Matt guessed she would understand.

He saw her once with his face badly bruised and his ribs taped up. He talked quickly over her cries, explained the antics of a big bay that went up and over with him with no warning. He was lucky to get out with only the bruising, the bay was dead from the fall.

He learned not to tell her the details when he saw the fear in her blue eyes and felt the horror shake her body. He brought her carefully to him, to give her comfort, and to take pleasure from the firmness of the body pressed close to him.

Mr. Kersey paid him no attention after the first two visits. Mrs. Kersey greeted him warmly, drawing him into her world with a few kind words, a gracious gesture, a concern for his work and the passing of his days. But she knew to leave him alone with Orianna after her casual talk and sympathetic questions.

He knew she wanted word of McCraw. He tried to report what would interest her, but speaking the sentences pained him. As if she sensed his discomfort, she soon enough ceased to ask him any questions at all.

When he met Mrs. Kersey, he could understand McCraw's interest in the woman. She had a bloom to her, a grace and beauty unequaled in the married ladies of the local ranches. She was friendly and warm to Matt, listening to his stories, laughing at small jokes. She was a lady to Matt's eyes.

Matt almost told her once that the boss asked him the same questions when he rode back in. But he was shamed by his knowledge and could not begin to explain. He knew no other way.

So they went, into the hot, dry summer. Working hard, taking pleasure from the short, interrupted visits. Willing themselves to not see what had to happen. There was a simpleness to the visits, the shared confidences, the common dreams, that Matt had never known, that Orianna knew was possible, that Mrs. Kersey envied in them and put out of her mind.

CHAPTER TWENTY-FIVE

It was W. W. Bogel who decided the big gather. The winter blizzard had spread the cattle for a two-hundred-mile radius. Even as late as July, ranchers were still unable to find all their stock. Long treks by the vaqueros brought back word of brands seen hundreds of miles away. The winter kill was tallied, the hides scraped free, the carcasses left to rot. But there were numbers of wild cattle wandering loose.

W. W. Bogel was an educated man, a thoughtful man, and he was unwilling to accept the disorganization; herds were tangled, brands scattered from the Davis Mountains down to the Rio Grande and the Chisos Basin. Bogel, Den Knight, and Bob Ellison met and talked of a big gather, and sent out the word to the ranchers.

McCraw got the message less than three days before the gather's beginning. One of Bogel's riders came through, stopped to water his horse, and told McCraw what was being done. McCraw thanked him, offered a meal that was turned down, and forgot about the man. He had his own work to do.

The deliberating didn't take long, there weren't many choices. Silvestre had no chance going in McCraw's name. And McCraw knew he had to stay to the home ranch and keep working. He had only the remnants of a small herd left from winter, and every bony mother cow was important. His losses had been cut by plain hard-working management, but there were twenty-two or more head unaccounted for. That many would make a big difference come another year, another calf crop.

It would have to be Matt. McCraw winced at the conclusion. The kid had stayed this time, worked hard, did his cooking chores. But the devil was still in him, and McCraw could see it come to light after weeks of rounding up cattle, after days of topping the half-broke horses. The kid would disappear, riding to Kersey's place, McCraw figured. Riding to call on Vail's daughter.

McCraw hated the kid for his nearness to Mrs. Kersey. Each time he came back, McCraw found himself asking stupid questions, working the kid hard to make him say the lady's name, tell something of her days. A humiliation he endured each time, and it fueled his anger at the kid.

But it would have to be Matt as rep from the Bitter Springs ranch.

"Pack your gear, kid. Bogel's set a gather starting at the river, two days from now. Time for you to ride in, settle. Take your pick of four horses. I'll send a note telling Bogel you're the rep.

"Matt, you mind your manners this time. No fighting. You got to get along, do your share. We need those lost mothers."

He knew it wasn't right to let it work him so, but the wide face, the insolent grin, the thought of that son riding to Kersey's— Hell, he talked to the lady, and each unheard word dug a hole in McCraw.

The damn kid said nothing. No reaction on the dark face,

no temper in the light eyes. Damn his soul, there was no feeling in him. McCraw showed his back, walked to the house, intent on writing his word to Bogel. Then he stopped, swung around, momentarily confused.

"What's your name, Matt? The full name, so Bogel can put it down proper on his list."

"Mr. McCraw, the name is Mateo Iberra." The voice was flat and hard, filled with insult. "I told you that first day we met, when you and the vaqueros tried to chase me off with a hurt horse. But I reckon you don't listen much."

McCraw licked his lips, feeling uncomfortable. He'd known lots of Iberras, was a whole tribe of them near Polvo, a small village by the river. And he'd known an old man up north named Eduardo Iberra, and his daughter. Sure he knew the name, was too familiar with it. A real common name on the border and up north. He'd just forgot it, since their first meeting two years ago. Just forgot the kid's full name, that's all.

"Pick good horses, Matt. And keep an eye on them. Bogel can ride high on bossing a man. You keep the horses to you, don't let them get used by others. My orders, my choice. You tell Bogel that. You tell anyone who puts a loop around their necks."

He felt Matt's stare push at him as he ducked into the house. Telling the kid commonsense rules. Telling him what he already knew. A dumb move, but he had to stand and clear his authority. Any choice at all, anything to shield himself from the knowing set to the kid, the too easy smile that widened the mouth. McCraw rattled the pen in his hand; if he didn't need the kid, he'd fire him quick as that big buckskin colt had run.

The buckskin—word came around to him that Francis Dewitt Wilson and most of his family had moved out after the winter. Went back to civilization, to New Orleans. They kept ownership of the land, left one of Wilson's sons in charge.

McCraw regretted he hadn't seen the buckskin run again. But Wilson took the gelding with him and that was it. He puzzled on a man giving up, then forced himself to get to his letter and forgot about the Wilsons and their brief entry against the land.

Matt automatically saddled the strawberry roan. When he slipped the broken bit in the roan's mouth, he rubbed the horse's face, saw the new white hairs above the eyes and along the muzzle. The lips were drawn back, the yellow teeth flashed at Matt's hand. An old game they'd played for years.

The roan was fourteen, old to work a gather, old to run and stop, spin and drag a thousand-pound steer where it didn't want to go. But Matt wouldn't leave the roan behind.

He had the dun neck-roped to a blocky bay, and a stout sorrel roped to the brown. Four good horses, and the strawberry roan. The four were marked with McCraw's brand; the roan carried a notched ear and a blunt *I* on the right hip. The brown gelding packed a canvas burden; Matt's bedroll, clothes, possible sack. He was ready and eager to ride.

The string of horses raised their own dust cloud. Matt slipped a cotton bandanna over his nose and mouth. Dry, too damned dry. And hot. He watched the sky, counted the few clouds. No rain waiting.

Sweat rose from the lead horses; Matt's shirt soaked gray under his arms, at the back of his neck. His belly itched with the salt of his sweat. Dust and sweat, mixed and unrelieved in the dry summer air.

He didn't need directions for the gathering point; a low-spread yellow cloud was a long-distance signpost. Matt started up the string of horses, let the roan move into his single-footed gait. Four hours and he would be at the center of the camp.

McCraw's rep, he was. He had to speak out the words between gritty teeth, had to hear their noise. He was McCraw's rep, for all that the rancher daily laid into him. Matt worked for the man, took his wage, ate his food. He owed to the brand to keep his temper, make his place in the number of men, and ride for the lost head of cattle.

There would be trouble, he knew that, too. He felt the fists of Bogel's men before the race. Remembered the faces, especially the thick-necked man. His thinking skipped to the thieves and the cooped-up horses in the narrow canyon, and later the terrible night with the sheep. A thread pulled through those memories, of two men. It wasn't much to look back on, not much for a man's pride. 'Cepting the race on the buckskin gelding.

He owed better this time to McCraw, and to himself. Because of Orianna. Matt leaned on his hands crossed over the wide horn. Orianna. A kind friend. Matt snorted, heard the weakness of those words. She was much more than a "kind friend." She listened to his ramblings, heard out his stories, questioned him, and then paid attention. He'd learned real quick to leave out what wasn't right, learned to tell easy yarns about his mother and older brother, his *abuelo*, the village where they lived. Memories that were faded for him seemed to delight her. She'd listen all afternoon to him and ask more questions when his talking ran down. She never tired of him, and he was more aware of his lonesome life when he rode out of Kersey's yard.

There were nights he lectured himself, sitting out near the stars, huddled against the cold, or panting from the summer heat. Long lectures to himself about his family, his missing pap. Why her own father had so much hatred for dark-skinned riders like Matt. All about her lamed leg, her sweet smile. He had no business with her, and he knew the line he rode was knife-edge fine and deadly.

And he didn't care, except for seeing her under a cottonwood, laughing, hands clapped together when he got the words to come out funny.

His big hands grabbed the horn, the rough edge cut his palm. Matt looked down, surprised by the white-rimmed knuckles and angry at the black dirt imbedded in the skin, the harsh red brown of the flesh. Hands not clean enough to touch the hand of Orianna Vail or anyone like her. He picked up the reins, lifted his head, and saw the heavy dust, made out the shapes of horses and men, the high, cloth ribbing of an old wagon. He was at the gather. It was time to get back to work.

He guided his cavvy to the biggest wagon; under a flyleaf shade, a man sat at a plank table. Matt dismounted and stepped into the cool shade. The man did not look up, so Matt waited. Five minutes gone and his temper frayed.

"Mister, I come for James McCraw. Rep for his brand. Got me the paper says so. Name's Matt Iberra. Want to find my place and get to work. You look to be the one to do the telling, so I'm listening."

At first sound of Matt's words, the man had looked up as if he hadn't known Matt was there. Now he blinked and looked down. Matt pushed himself. The man came back up; the eyes were icy gray, the face thin, the lips pulled into a woman's rosebud mouth. But there was no give in the man, no back down in Matt. The silence grew thin. Matt was ready.

"You. Iberra. I'm the boss here. Elected by the big ranchers. You're late. Most came in yesterday. You'll work under Bob Ellison. Camp to the left. Give me the paper, then get moving. I've got work to do."

The seated man extended his hand, clearly expecting Matt to do his bidding. Matt shook his head, shuffled his feet, and watched the puffs of dust cover his toes. He was out of his element here and was quick to know it. But he hadn't been given the courtesy of the man's name. Whoever he was, he sat a carved oak chair, wore a soft white shirt with a fresh collar, a black knotted tie. A dark coat hung off the wagon's tailgate, a creased and unstained hat rested on the table.

"The paper from McCraw. If you have it." The left hand waved slightly at Matt, but the man did not bother to look at the rider. The fingers wiggled again, then the hand went to the table, hit flat against the plank. The right hand appeared with a gun. The hammer was cocked; the man spoke again. His voice had no emotion; he expected obedience.

"You give me the paper. Boy."

Matt didn't stir. His own right hand touched the warm

carved handle of the old knife. The seated man raised his head; the gray eyes waited, the thin mouth pursed a dark red against the pale cheeks. The barrel of the gun did not waver.

"You, Iberra, Matt? I saw that sorrel of McCraw's and thought it would be you."

The voice was directly behind him, and Matt knew the speaker. Never thought he would be pleased to hear that particular voice. Thomas Kersey, grown familiar from the spring and summer visiting. Matt never looked away from the seated man—and he saw the gray eyes flicker. The gun was laid down across the scattered papers, and the man stood up slowly. There was sweat on his forehead and his hand shook slightly.

The hand went out in a gesture of friendship. Matt knew better, and moved aside, so Kersey and the strange man shook. Matt tasted defeat, bitter and hot in his mouth. He'd done nothing but report, and had been challenged by a gun. A poor beginning to his resolve. He'd been close to drawing a knife on the man.

Kersey tried, but neither Matt or his new boss would take it. "Iberra, this is the top man. You two've met. Iberra, come with me." Matt didn't move; the other man slowly shook his head. Kersey looked down and saw the pistol laid across the papers, realized he'd walked into more than he thought. He knew John Sinnot well enough, knew him to be a friend of Robert Vail's. Sinnot would not take to Iberra's appearance, or his repping for an Anglo brand.

"John, you want a formal introduction to this hand? He works for James McCraw. Rides his broncs. Done me some favors this spring. McCraw swears by him." The small man turned to Matt, as if finally remembering his manners. "This is John Sinnot. We had a meeting two weeks ago, in town. Sinnot was elected ramrod of the gather. His word is law, till all this is done." Then he turned away from Matt in blunt dismissal. "John, good to see you. Matt, come with me."

Done, with no choice, no say in the matter. Sinnot went

back to his work without another word; Matt turned and followed Thomas Kersey.

There were two camps on the Rio Grande banks, with over sixty men in each camp and a remuda of at least fifty horses. Matt was directed to turn his string in with the others and stack his gear where he chose to sleep. Kersey led him to the crew boss, performed the introductions, and disappeared. Matt had seen Bob Ellison before, knew his reputation as a good hand, a fair man. There would be some justice in this godforsaken gather.

They started early morning, before false dawn colored the distant mountains. Matt roped out the brown gelding, saddled and hobbled the horse, and went for the morning meal. Stray light caught the faded colors of the scrub piñon, rocks sparkled and turned gray as the sun climbed up quickly. Puffs of steam rose from the horses' nostrils, and Matt saw other riders draw their jackets close. The cold would go soon, replaced by the unrepenting heat of the dry August sun.

He was teamed with two riders he didn't know. They nodded to him, allowed him to ride alongside as they listened to Ellison's directions. They were to ride east of Alamito Creek, chousing every head of cattle out of the brush. At noon they would stop, cut out the local cattle, and brand the new calves.

Ellison stopped abruptly; the men held their horses still. He went back over his orders, put all his power into his voice. They were to ride deep, leave no cow loose. It was a make-or-break deal for the ranchers, and each stray head brought in could be a life carried through next winter. The men listened to the boss's words, and they knew the truth of them.

The brown gelding was good in the brush, thick-skinned and willing to charge in deep, jump cactus, skid around prickly pear. Matt sweated inside his leather pants and coarse jacket and cursed when a thorn scraped his face. His companions rode either side of the narrow arroyos, watched as Matt worked along the floor. They counted heads and were waiting when he came back down the line, gathered in the cattle he scared out from the deep thickets.

There was water back at the wagons, and cold biscuits, lots of hot coffee. Matt's companions nodded to him and rode off to join friends. Matt unsaddled the brown, rubbed the horse's back with a handful of grass. He ate his biscuit and drank his coffee alone, close to the thin shadow of an ocotillo. There were some faces he recognized from Marfa, two that had ridden in for water at McCraw's, two from his time on the road gang. Some stared at him, not attempting to hide their curiosity, while others didn't look at him at all.

Two were easy for Matt to name; there would be trouble with them. Two men who worked for W. W. Bogel himself. Remembering, Matt tasted the copper of blood in his mouth, felt the fists thud into his side and back. He knew their names: Charley Hocker and Pomp Wooten. Mack sighed, drank the last of the coffee, and spat out the grounds into dry sand.

Afternoon, Matt roped and dragged out bawling calves; one of his morning partners caught up the hind feet, the other slapped on the proper brand. One of the mama cows was McCraw's; Matt watched carefully to see that the tally was marked correct. He didn't ask Ellison, but he watched close as the man came to mark his book. Ellison looked at him and smiled; Matt took note, spun the sorrel, and went back for the next calf.

By nightfall, a rancher named Fletcher, who lived nearby, had a small herd ready to trail back to his spread. Another man, one Willard Boggs, allowed his five head to go in with Fletcher's, to be picked up at the end of the drive. The rest of the herd would go north in the morning, to be cut out and left as they came closer to their home ground.

There was short talk around the fires. A few men rode out for night watch; the rest were content to listen to one man pick a tuneless banjo and try to find the song. Matt walked off his distance, scooped out a butt hole, and laid down his blankets. His jacket rolled up made a nest for his head. The crackling of the campfire competed with the night's talk, but Matt sorted out what he wanted to hear.

Crickets behind him, a coyote asking the why of all these strangers in his territory, an owl looking for dinner. A mouse brave enough to try a run. Matt heard the rush of wings, the final squeak of the mouse. He had to grin. Man made his yapping sounds, but the world went on around him as if he didn't much matter.

They came at him the next morning. Matt roped out the dun, had the snorty bronc half saddled when a hat thrown under his belly spooked the dun. The horse reared, the saddle slipped, and the panicked horse kicked sideways, catching Matt on the hip. The dun circled, struck out with his front legs at the swinging rig. Matt skidded with the rope as the horse whirled and kicked, bellowed in fear, and finally tried to run. Matt tangled the rope in a mesquite bush, and the horse came to a choked stand.

"What's the matter, cowboy? Thought McCraw sent his best man as rep to the gather. You the best he can do? Hell, cowboy, you got to pull up that cinch, you figure to ride the horse."

His hands were burned red, the horse was shaking, the saddle had a deep gouge down one fender. Matt forced himself to watch the dun and ignore the taunting voice. He owed McCraw, he was held accountable. The dun quieted, the voice went away. Matt walked to the horse and pulled the saddle from between the front legs, loosened the rope dug in the horse's neck. The dun blew out hard, covering Matt with foam.

There was no one around; he didn't have to look. Hocker was gone, and none of the other riders wanted to be near Matt. He got to breakfast at the end, had half a biscuit, cold beans, bitter coffee. He limped and his arms were scratched from the mesquite. But the dun was undamaged and the rigging wasn't tore. When he rode out, the two riding with him came at a distance. No one spoke, and the two let Matt head into deep brush again, without offering to do their share. Matt wouldn't let it get to him. It would have to wait, but he would bring it home to Wooten and Hocker.

Sleep was long coming that night, and past midnight a hand clamped down on him, a voice stopped him from drawing the knife. Guard duty, a bigger herd from the day's gather, another rider needed. Sinnot gave the order; Matt did not question it.

He whistled for the roan come morning, counting on the horse's calm reliability to keep the next trick from working. He didn't see Wooten or Hocker, but the riders crowded around the cook wagon watched Matt carefully. He sat alone with his grub—and looked up once to find Wooten grinning at him. He couldn't find Hocker quickly, and instinct told him to get up and get to the roan, check his gear, redo the rigging.

Instead he pulled the biscuits apart, put the pieces in his mouth, and chewed down the dryness. The coffee helped some, and he even swallowed the grounds, licked the rim of the cup. He was dry-mouthed and tired.

Maybe Ellison saw the first prank, maybe Ellison spoke to Wooten and Hocker. Three days went with no disasters. Matt rode down each of his four horses and used the roan sparingly. But he knew they would come at him again, and it rode him hard, sneaked into his sleep at night, cut short his noon sleep.

The herd grew. Every call for McCraw raised his chance of survival. Matt disputed Ellison's call on one brand. He rode to the ramrod, waited out his finish on the tally, and said his piece. Ellison listened, then rode with Matt near the disputed beef. Matt roped out the mama cow; the bay held the bawling critter while Ellison moved in, leaned down, and dug his blunt fingers to the old sear. He looked up to Matt and allowed he was right. It was McCraw's beef, not one of Bogel's as Hocker claimed.

That drove in the nail. There would be retaliation, and soon. Matt hunched his shoulders, knew an itchy feeling down his spine. He slept that night cramped up to a boulder, with the roan staked out as guard. But there was nothing. And nothing Matt could do until Hocker and Wooten began their play.

The numbers of branded cattle grew; small herds were cut out and turned over to the eager ranchers. The land opened into wide expanses of dried graze, the springs were little more than muddied holes. Each day the short herds were left behind, each night more cattle bellowed their distress while the cowhands tried to sleep.

The beginning of the second week, Matt roped up the bay and saddled. He counted heads, didn't find the sorrel. He drove the bay into the remuda, scattering horses, drawing curses from half-awake men. He saw the roan, head down, too tired to be bothered by Matt's intrusion. The dun was close by, the brown had his head resting on the rump of a ewe-necked grullo. There was no sign of the sorrel.

He spun the bay and charged out of the herd, headed toward camp. Sure enough, he could see the yellow tail of the sorrel, a fancy rig strapped to his back, a silver bit tight in his mouth. Hocker's rig, Bogel's branded slicker tied in a bright yellow line across the cantle.

Hocker was waiting. Matt stopped the bay and stepped off. The sorrel nickered at a friend, the bay pulled on the reins. Hocker spread his legs and grinned.

"Well now, boy. You got something on your mind? Tell old Charley what got into you this morning?"

He couldn't find Wooten, and he knew Hocker wouldn't brace him alone. Matt ground-tied the bay, patted the sorrel's rump, and the quick ears swiveled to his touch.

"That's McCraw's horse, Hocker. You know it same as me. Or can't you read brand yet? Same brand as that mother cow, a few days back."

Shapes and shadows drifted close to Matt, too close, and he turned on them. Cowhands, ranchers, some with tin cups in hand, some still chewing breakfast. They backed from him. No one needed to be told; there would be a fight this time.

The faces were neutral. They were eager and watchful, grinning at Hocker, eyeing Matt. A man hacked and spat into the dust, a balding rancher wiped his white head with a yellow bandanna.

There was movement to his right. Matt tensed, tried to look sideways. Hocker started in again.

"You got nerve coming to me. I give you that. I can read brands. I can read that mark running down your ugly face. You belong somewheres else, boy. Not here with honest men. You a sheep killer, boy. Not a cowhand. You got the brand of sin on you, and I aim to pick it off your skull and hang it up to dry."

He'd heard those words before. In two languages, from tougher men.

"What's wrong, boy? You know you so ugly it don't bother you? Well—"

"Hocker, that's McCraw's horse. Brand's clear; any man can read it. Unsaddle that sorrel. He belongs to James McCraw."

He would not rise to the baiting, he would not let Hocker catch him. He would hold to his debt to McCraw. He would picture Orianna Vail. Hocker would have to come to him.

The man drifted right, close enough Matt could smell the rank odor, see the encrusted dirt. Hocker's face was black, a dark beard papered his jaw. Matt let his eyes roam over Hocker's face, looked past him to the sorrel's rump. He would not take the first swing.

The chest of the quirted bay slammed into Matt. He was thrown forward and grabbed at Hocker, taking the man with him as he fell. Hocker's face scratched across his scar; the man grinned as he lay under Matt. Then drew up his knees into Matt's groin. Matt rolled out, caught the blow on his thigh, caught a booted foot that kicked at him. Behind the rolling men, the line of horses whinnied and swung their hindquarters in protection.

Matt reached one knee; Hocker came up close enough to stare at Matt and spit. Then Hocker lunged; Matt jumped at the same time. They hit shoulder-to-shoulder and went down together. Matt rolled, climbed on Hocker, and pounded a fist into Hocker's face. Hocker bucked under him, slammed an elbow to Matt's throat. He gagged, fought for breath. Hocker bucked wildly. Matt sailed over his head and skidded on his chin.

Two blows slammed into his back. Matt coughed, swallowed dust, struggled to rise. Boots and legs and leather chaps encircled him. Hocker drove a fist into Matt's ear; blood instantly leaked from the tear. Matt shoved an elbow and searching fist behind him, reached nothing but the edge of a torn shirt. A blow grazed his wounded ear; he could hear nothing but a humming. He pitched forward, flattened to the ground. Hocker's knees dug into his back. The man rode Matt, leaned back, raised his arms, and cheered for himself.

Matt drew up his knees and bucked free, then came around for Hocker's throat. He drew the man to him and pummeled the leering face. The eyes shut, and Matt hit the nose square on; Hocker sighed. Matt drew back his arm; a form cut the air beside him. He heard the swing, saw the brightness of the gun barrel. The force crashed into his wrist, the gun sight slashed the back of his hand. The crack against bone was clear and dry. Matt cried out, dropped Hocker's shirt. He bent forward at the waist and cradled the arm.

No noise, no movement. Matt gulped hard on the pain, opened his eyes, and saw a red tear across his hand, watched the drops of blood come through quickly, form a pool, run down the fingers, and slide into the dirt. His arm was numbed, even his shoulder and back. His mouth was dry, his head swollen.

Matt heard nothing; he came up slowly to a crowd of quiet onlookers. Hocker was laid out to one side, a black lump rising on his forehead. Wooten stood between two men, blood dripping from a long cut on his neck. He was held gently by the men and made no attempt to pull away from them.

Eyes watched Matt, mouths worked at speaking, but he could hear none of it. He tried to stand alone; a hand slid under his left arm and lifted him. He staggered with the motion. The arm cradled him, a body offered support. His distant legs weren't connected to him, his ear throbbed, his face was wet. His arm was no longer numb.

Ellison was there. He asked a question Matt could hear, but he could not answer. He coughed, and his arm flared. The pain went to his shoulder, straight to his belly to weaken his knees, and the man holding him had to fight to keep him standing. Ellison spoke again, and, finally, one of the cowboys answered for Matt.

"Mr. Ellison, we don't sure know what started this, but they was hitting two to one and that ain't right. No, sir."

A bodiless hand offered Matt an uncapped canteen. He drank deeply, swallowed hard, and drank again. He could stand alone now, and the man beside him stepped back.

"Hocker saddled the wrong horse and I come to get it back."

It didn't sound like his voice, but Matt knew the words were from his mind. He took a big drink of the water and spat it out. The sand turned pale red, then quickly dried out.

Ellison was close enough Matt could hear the man breathe.

"You certain that's what happened? Rough doings over a misread brand? Questions like that, you bring them to me."

Matt shook his head. "No, sir. Want that sorrel turned back. Hocker knows the brand. Knows the horse. Got to catch up my bay. Turn that sorrel back."

Ellison smiled and touched Matt's arm. The weight of the touch came close to dropping Matt.

"Iberra, you won't work today. I got some skill setting bones. And I heard that arm crack. It's busted, son. Take some fixing before you ride the gather again. Come with me. Wooten, you strip the rig from that sorrel, turn him back. And drag Hocker out of here, sober him to ride. We got work to do.

"And boys, either of you touch a man's horse and you're gone. Think hard on it. Mr. Bogel don't want his crew coming home without his stock."

Matt made the trip to Ellison's wagon. The ramrod deftly put out a roll of bandage, a dark brown bottle of whiskey, three flat sticks, a long needle, and waxed thread. He'd done this before.

He told Matt to sit and gave him the bottle. Matt drank long, then handed it back, and Ellison poured the liquor over the needle. Water was too precious to waste. He sloshed whiskey on the back of Matt's hand, the burn was strong. The whiskey rolled in his belly; Mack almost vomited. Ellison made him drink again, and again, until Matt's head spun.

Ellison started the stitching; the gun sight had dug a deep trench from the base of his knuckle to the meaty side of his hand above his wrist. Five stitches were needed. Sweat dripped from Ellison's face as he worked, and it burned in the wound. The whiskey thickened Matt's mouth, deadened the bite of his ear, but it did little to soothe the nerves in his wrist.

He touched Ellison in panic. The man looked at him, and Matt leaned forward and vomited into the sand between his feet. He stayed head down until the battle in his stomach eased and his head quit spinning. Then he sat back, and Ellison finished his sewing without a word.

Ellison sat and rolled a smoke, offered a pull to Matt. The rancher finished the butt, ground it out, and picked up the first wooden slat. When he placed it on the underside of Matt's arm and tucked the end of the bandage in, Matt groaned. When Ellison began to wrap, shaping the other two splints at the side, Matt slid from the chair. Ellison kept his hold on the bandage, motioned for a rider to straighten the arm, and finished the job in grim silence.

CHAPTER TWENTY-SIX

Charley Hocker rode for five days with a swollen head, his hat tilted sideways to miss his ear. He'd spat out two teeth the first day. Pomp Wooten rode head down, studying the ground, and didn't look up when he passed Matt. Nothing was said between the three men, nothing was yet settled.

Matt stayed with the wagons the first two days. When he tried roping up the dun, his hand wouldn't hold the loop and he gave up in disgust. The roan came to him shyly when he whistled, and with much fumbling Matt was able to saddle and ride.

The hands went to their business, choused cattle from the brush, roped and branded slick calves, laughed among themselves, and ignored Matt. He kept to himself—finished his work and fell asleep each night without getting to a meal. He wasn't asked to ride nighthawk, the only concession to his busted arm.

The break in the bone marked time with each step he took, he set his jaw to the ache, clenched his teeth, and went to work. Harsh lines rubbed into his face and pounds were shaken off his frame. He asked for nothing, went for days without speaking.

He had to use the roan three days in a row. Matt fought again with his rope, lost the loop, flexed his wrist and winced, stared at the loose coils of the useless reata. Already the sun was pushed up; he had to ride out, and it had to be the roan. He put his fingers to his mouth to whistle.

A man climbed on a big horse, and the animal bogged its

head and pitched. Matt caught the off color of the tail, and his right hand went automatically to his knife. The pain stopped him, and he watched helplessly as the battle slowed and the horse was ridden toward him at an easy jog.

McCraw's good sorrel. With a strange man on the horse—not one of Bogel's men, not Wooten or Hocker. Matt readied for a fight, then came to see it was his rig on the sorrel, even the bridle McCraw used special on the bronc.

He didn't know the rider, didn't remember his face. The man stepped off the sorrel and handed Matt the reins.

"Good stuff your boss saddles. Always wanted to try out this one. Figured you'd be good and tired of riding that sorry roan. Good horse." He slapped the sorrel on the chest.

The man was near Matt; they couldn't avoid contact. The rider wouldn't look straight at Matt, but fiddled with the *cincha*. Matt was presented with a kindness he didn't know how to handle.

"No chance I could rope out this sorrel, or ride him like you done. Thanks, mister."

The cowboy blushed red; Matt fumbled lefthanded with the reins. A cracked voice announced the last call for breakfast, and the rider was gone. Matt hurried to tie up the sorrel; he was suddenly hungry enough to eat the roan uncooked and then start on the *cocinero*'s grub. His hands shook, his knees wobbled under him, but he made it to the chuck line and took his place.

By the end of the second week, close to two hundred head of cattle had been driven out of the gullies and brush. The cow camp moved quickly this morning; tarps and bedrolls were lashed on pack animals, wagons were piled high. Today was the final day of the gather. Bob Ellison had spoken briefly last night, over the cook fire. The final count was two hundred four head recovered, and unnumbered carcasses left to remind them of the brutal winter.

There were seven McCraw cows and one steer in the

herd. Each ranch rep had to cut out and drive their brand home. Matt wondered again how he would manage.

A grinning cowboy handed Matt the reins to the stocky bay, saddled with Matt's rig. Matt could close the fingers of his right hand around the lines, but he knew if the bay pulled, he would have to let go. He'd use the horse this morning to cut out the cattle, then go back to the little roan.

He'd worried on the puzzle most of the night. The broke arm left him pretty much useless, and dependent upon the good sense of his horse. That meant the already tired roan. The return trip wasn't long in miles, but the short route meant dry camps and a couple stretches of real rough traveling. The rest of the horses he'd turn loose and hope they wandered in to McCraw's.

Head buried in the bay's gut, Matt caught the movement of a familiar walk. He straightened up from hauling one-handed on the *cincha* and saw his visitor. Thomas Kersey, burned raw, slow-moving. Matt hadn't seen him since the first day, the confrontation with John Sinnot.

Kersey stopped near the bay, put a hand on the shiny rump, and patted the rugged horse with an appreciative hand.

"Looks good. Horse has done better in this drive than you, Iberra. Heard about your arm. Sorry."

Matt watched the man's face for pity, but there was only determined practicality. Thomas Kersey hadn't changed in the two weeks of work.

"Ellison tells me McCraw counts in for eight head. Recovered nine of mine, which isn't much but it will help. Lost a lot of cattle this winter, you know that."

Kersey looked at him queerly, as if finally connecting Matt's face and presence with the young man who came to see Orianna Vail, the McCraw rider who brought in his tally of dead cattle. As if Kersey was seeing Matt as more than a cowhand.

"Came to ask for your help, or more likely us working together. You help me drive my stuff back, I'll help you drive the rest to McCraw. I don't think he's heard about

TEXAS SPRINGS 275

that." Kersey gestured to Matt's bound arm. "So he won't think to come looking for you."

Matt ran his eyes up and down the red face; and Kersey never flinched. The man was talking good sense; Kersey's place was close to McCraw. And Orianna Vail was there.

It had been more than three weeks for them; Matt suffered a surge of light-headedness. It didn't matter much, the reason for Kersey's asking. The right answer would take him to the girl. Kersey even pleaded, to make the choice sweeter: "I sent word to the women we'd be in about four days from now. They'll be waiting with a good meal. Another day won't be a hardship for you."

Matt couldn't hold back the grin. He put out his left hand; Kersey awkwardly pumped it with his right.

They planned and sorted and rode out for the last swing through the near hills. Kersey came alive, eager to return home, pleased at the number of cattle resurrected for him in the gather. He talked nonstop, as if Matt's presence were an excuse.

Until he got to a strange subject. About water, about needing new wells or springs, about there being little water surrounding him. Matt put together what McCraw had said about the need for the horse-race, and he looked over at his riding companion in a thoughtful manner. Kersey shut up then, and they finished the morning in hard silence. Their work gave them one broken-horned steer with McCraw's faded brand.

There were no good-byes at the camp when they quit, especially for Matt. Kersey put a line to a sorry bay packhorse, and Matt saddled up the strawberry roan. The cattle trailed easily, packed on a dirt track that headed in the right direction. Matt stayed to the back, arm cradled to his chest like he'd learned the past days. The roan's single gait was a comfort, and Kersey kept his mouth shut.

The gather had lasted two weeks and two days. McCraw came out with eight mother cows and a steer; Kersey had picked up ten head. And Matt had a taste of friendship, a rare knowledge that other men could be trusted. There were two cowboys with wide grins he someday would thank.

Matt watched Kersey's back as the man guided his quick-footed mare. A pretty mare, well bred, with fine head and neck, a doe's eye, and a long tail that flashed and whisked with all her impatient energy.

The cattle settled in fast; Matt stayed left rear, Kersey rode flank. The man was eager to give directions; he waved and slapped his rope hard against new chaps in the important decisions. Two days, no more, and they would be to Kersey's canyon. Two days.

He was getting used to the mare's long tail flashing ahead of him. The roan, too, seemed to recognize the mare and follow her lead willingly. Both Matt and the little horse were worn down, tired from herding the stubborn cattle. Matt's arm hurt continually, and the roan had stumbled twice in the last hour on red shale and bear grass.

Kersey's mare was full of energy, and Kersey himself was in a high good humor that Matt didn't share. The man had let Matt struggle to saddle the roan early that morning. He finally came to Matt's assistance, but only after Matt had paid full price for the privilege.

A hot, dry day, like all the others. Dust blowing around horse and rider, to cling to damp skin and rub exposed flesh a bleeding red. The trail wound upward, across the side of Outlook Mountain, deep in shale, close to a black canyon wall. Tricky footing, a steep slope, loose rock crossed by a thin track of bare dirt.

The tired roan stumbled; Matt grabbed at a bush with his right hand and cried out. The roan lurched underneath him, scrambled to find purchase, and sent a cascade of rock into the maw of the canyon below them.

The broken-horned steer suddenly headed upslope; Matt kneed the roan to follow. He cursed Kersey's brand, cursed his tired horse and the speckled rump of the steer. The animal went to its knees; the roan floundered beside it on the slipping rock. Then the high-headed, dumb-minded bovine

TEXAS SPRINGS

changed its course, swung its horns in a wide circle, and came back at the roan.

From a standstill, the roan leapt as the tip of the horns grazed Matt's knee and tore the old leather pants. The steer skidded downhill, plowed back on the narrow track, and trotted after the slow-moving herd. Kersey hadn't stopped, hadn't looked to see. Matt watched the flash of the sorrel mare's tail until the bulk of the steer blotted out the sunlit hide.

He didn't hear Kersey's first scream, but he saw the dust boiling over the canyon edge. And he heard the mare scream as she rolled over shale and knocked into trees until she crashed and was wedged in between two boulders.

Matt whipped the roan, leaned back to balance as the little horse sat down and slid. The untended herd crossed the slope and stopped to browse at clumps of bear grass. The broken-horned steer shoved a yearling cow aside to pull at the thin graze.

The mare whinnied; the roan answered. Matt heard a croaking noise, saw a hand wave from the edge of rock. The roan started at the move—a front hoof scraped shale and layers of the rock began to slide. Matt leaned uphill, steadied the roan with his right hand, and prayed.

The shifting rock stilled; the mare whinnied again. The roan trembled but did not move. Matt rubbed his eyes against the white bandage of his arm, and grit stung under his lids. He waited for the dust to settle. Then the whiteness of the hand below him was easy to see, fluttering on dark red shale.

He slid from the roan's off side, ground-tied the horse, felt his way around the roan's chest. He was cautious walking, waiting with each step to test the layers of shale before trusting his weight to them. He got close enough, finally, that he could hear Kersey's breathing.

Matt dropped to his knees at the edge of the break and looked over, saw Kersey hanging from a rock. Twenty feet below the man, the sorrel mare was pinned, upside down, shod hooves glinting, long flaxen tail fanned off the hanging quarters. If Kersey fell, he would be impaled on spiral rocks directly below him. Matt couldn't see the mare's head, but he watched as a rope of blood stained her yellow side, spread out onto the narrow rock. The mare whinnied; Matt started. He'd thought surely that she was dead.

Then Kersey coughed and one hand spasmed, loosened its grip on the rocky edge. Matt leaned out farther and saw Kersey's white face. Only the two hands kept the man from falling; the body swayed out into air, draped over a twisted root. One hand clung to the root, the other hand dug in the shale, pleading for help. Matt's help.

Matt saw a different corpse, a dark-skinned man laid out in snow, glorified in braid and old silver. He shook violently, slow to realize it was the memory of Miguel that visited him, not the living cry of Thomas Kersey. He held to a rock, leaned closer . . . until Kersey spoke to him, bringing him back.

"You, Matt. Help."

Matt reached out with his own trembling hand and touched Kersey's wrist, a gesture meant to quiet and reassure. It worked for Kersey; the hand gripped the shale, no longer waving and frantic. But the sight of his own hand, and the weight of his bandaged arm, sharply reminded Matt of the problems he faced. He could not simply reach down and pull the man up to safety—too risky with only one hand. He backed uphill, away from the ledge and Kersey's pleading, afraid to look behind him to find the roan. He bumped against solid legs; the roan put down his head and snuffed into Matt's ear, tipping off his hat.

He caught the saddle rope, tied hard to the horn. Then he went down to his knees again and dragged the loop with him. Until he was close enough to touch the white hand again. Matt flinched from the contact of wet skin. Stretched out on the ground, gravel dug into his belly, Matt spread the loop over Kersey's back. The man wiggled to help, and the root holding him cracked.

The mare flailed with her legs, whinnied piteously. The call was muffled, but the roan heard it and took one step forward. Matt used the slack to catch Kersey's elbow and shoulders, then waved his right arm at the roan to scare the horse back. The roan jumped; Matt was caught in a twist of the line, and the roan backed from the sudden pressure. Matt cried out as the rope tangled above his bandage, and Kersey cried with him, tears running from his eyes through the sand and dirt rubbed on his face.

Matt saw over the edge: the big loop had tightened on Kersey's chest, holding an arm. He held to the exposed root and stared back at Matt. Matt forgot and reached with his right hand to loosen the rope, free the hand.

His fingers would not close. He willed himself to not feel the break, to force the hand to work. The hand slowly doubled, grabbed the rope, and pulled the loop. Kersey was quick, for his arm slid free—and the man must have known of Matt's effort, for there was awe, and pity, in his gaze.

The root cracked; dust and bark shifted across Kersey's face. Dust clouded him as he scraped along the wall. Matt shut his eyes, held the rope in his right hand, and supported it along his back, kept tension with his left hand and arm. He could hear Kersey cough again and could feel his weight on the line, but he could not see Kersey below him.

The roan sat back on the rope. Matt could not let go with his right hand, afraid Kersey would suddenly drop and the horse would slide forward. He could hear the horse snorting and could feel the vibration of spent energy. Kersey cried out, and Matt risked a look. The face was directly below him: white, drawn, masked in dirt. Kersey's legs were braced to the edge, his body leaned back on the line, barely held by the straining roan and Matt's two hands.

Kersey nodded to Matt without seeing him, as if he'd gone over the chances and knew the odds. There was a suspended time when both men were silent, eyes shut from the immediate disaster. Matt repeated remembered prayers for the desperate man hanging from the frayed rope. He would guess that Kersey was saying his Anglo version of the same.

Matt played the line between his fingers, asked the roan

to step back, uphill, and drag Kersey up and over the lip. The horse shook; Matt felt the rope turn and twist in his numbed hand. The knuckles of his right hand were white, the tips of his fingers bloodless.

Kersey said something, then said it louder. Matt didn't answer, or listen. The rope dug through his palm, stretched out and jumped as Kersey swung on its end. Matt scrabbled back to the roan, caught the reins at the bit ring, put his shoulder to the horse's chest, and pushed.

"Back up, you miserable . . ." He let his mouth run on in endearments of the roan's ancestry and prospects. The horse moved as asked, head lowered, taut rope tearing skin off the thin neck. Matt demanded; the horse gave to him. Inch by inch they dragged Kersey over the rim. The horse trembled, sweat-soaked in great patches between his legs, along his neck, at his quarters.

Matt heard the muffled noise and went hand over hand back to Kersey. He knelt, placing his knees in the exact spot where he had left Kersey. The face waited for him, jammed to the raw dirt, close enough Mack saw the stiff hairs in the large ears, the coarse pores along Kersey's nose, below his eyes.

Part of the banking slid past Kersey's legs. Kersey hung from the rope—cried out as the line bit through his shirt and gouged him. The man's legs were lost in dark shadow; the matted grass and rock under Matt's knees shifted, and a clump of thick dirt went down Kersey's torn shirt.

There was nothing else to do; Kersey would hang forever from the rope until the roan gave out and went to his knees in exhaustion. Matt grabbed for the rope, yanked with his left hand; at the same time he stuck his right hand to Kersey's face and yelled at him to grab hold and pull.

Kersey caught Matt's wrist; Matt hauled back like a spade-bitted horse. The top of Kersey's head came up level; Matt dug in his heels and strained. The roan snorted at the sight of Kersey and jumped backward, tearing Kersey over the edge. The man let go of Matt. The roan spun around and lunged. Matt ran for the roan's trailing reins.

He jerked hard; the horse quit, eyes rolling, front legs braced, mouth drooling foam and blood. The big head dropped; the horse sighed and was still. Matt went to his knees, stretched out on the safety of the unmoving shale. By turning his head, he could see Kersey spread out on his back, arm and chest free of the rope, rib cage rising and falling rapidly. Matt breathed into the warm rock, rolled over, and looked at the sky.

He wiped his mouth with his left sleeve and had red stains on the cloth. He ran his tongue over his lips and felt the bitten hole. His right arm throbbed wildly; the pain spread through his chest, into his groin. He ached everywhere and guessed that Kersey couldn't feel much better. Then the roan legs shifted above him, and Matt heard the faint sound. The roan whinnied, and Matt thought of the sorrel mare.

"We got to shoot your mare, Kersey. Got to. No way of getting her out of there."

The man didn't answer. Matt didn't want to be the one to shoot, but the mare whinnied again, a high shriek, and the roan was suddenly restless. Matt could see the slapping tails of the grazing cattle and knew he would have to get up.

He didn't have the air in him to speak again; instead he drew his legs under him and leaned on his left arm, pushed himself erect. He went to the roan, found the saddle gun shoved in its scabbard. The roan whirled, as if knowing what Matt was to do. He cursed the horse and yanked on the bridle reins. Then he finished drawing out the rifle, walked to the lip of the banking, and raised the weapon to his shoulder. His arm shook as he extended it, the rifle sight wavered before his eye.

The crack of the first shot lifted Kersey's head. The mare shrieked, a puff of dust spilled out of her belly. The roan trotted away from the sound, then lowered his head to graze with the complacent cattle.

Matt sighted and fired again. The bullet ricocheted off a distant rock; chips of dust peppered an angry squirrel. Matt dropped his head, sighed deeply—then raised the rifle and fired in anger. The mare's body shook under the impact; the hind legs kicked out, blood squirted from between her front legs.

Matt laid the rifle down and watched until he knew the mare was dead. Then he stood up and took the rifle back to Kersey. "Now we got to figure out getting both of us home."

CHAPTER TWENTY-SEVEN

Robert Vail didn't like the change in his daughter, the new security in her walk, the pleasing color in her face, the tanned strength of her hands. He didn't like her now, didn't trust the change, but he was afraid to mention this to his wife. Afraid of the scorn he would read in her eyes.

The old rage burned him, brought back with Orianna once again in the house. He covered the rage well, he knew that. He was familiar with the necessary moves, the words, the actions; but the rage was back, fueled by the weight of his wife in bed next to him, the presence of his Orianna in the fine new house.

Dreaming what he chose not to remember when he woke. Sweating, his nightshirt soaked with stinking fluids, his mind whirling with visions, his child running to him in pleasure.

Robert Vail rolled over very carefully. His wife sputtered and went back to sleep. She wouldn't care if he got up from their marriage bed. She wouldn't care if he never returned. They had their children—none of them a son—and that was the end of her duties.

Vail walked easily, on small feet that found comfort on the braided rug. His soft hands patted the wall, searching for the opening to the hallway. He was learning the configurations of the new house and was well pleased with it.

It was simple to avoid the small tables and fancy ornaments that his wife thought were pretty. The walk through the big front room, the parlor his Eleanor called it, was a direct path to the outdoors. There were careful white lace circles on the back of each chair, and the arms held out matching lace, glowing in the darkness. Warning signs for Vail to follow. He opened the front door and stepped outside, grateful for the cold air, the clear sky, the absolute quiet of his town.

He guessed it was three in the morning. The stars had moved from their nine o'clock pattern, and there was nothing moving down the wide main street. Vail liked this town; it had no reputation of killing, no tolerance for hooraying cowboys riding down streets, no gunfire late at night, no whiskey-fueled brawls.

And Vail liked to pretend it was his doing, this quiet, peaceful town. But he knew, inside, that it wasn't his great skill or abilities that kept the town quiet. It was the people themselves: families, educated ranchers, folks who wanted schools and churches who willingly worked hard for their new life. He was their figurehead, their symbol, but he was not their strength.

It was more pleasant to focus on word of the gather. John Sinnot's organizing had brought in over two hundred head and accounted for the hides of many of the winter losses. Sinnot and his crew had been in Marfa briefly the day before, and Vail had spoken with the man. Only one crew member had caused trouble, a man in Bob Ellison's bunch. The rep for James McCraw's Bitter Springs ranch.

Vail had to cough up and spit; it came back on him fast. Damn his mind for wandering. He knew the rep's name before Sinnot spoke it: Matt Iberra. Vail drew in the cooled night air, expelled it hard from his chest. His heart pounded loud and strong up in his throat. He'd listened to that name over and over tonight, and the sound of it was a gall deep inside him.

The rage consumed him; the name, the dark face, the sound of Orianna's sweet voice talking to her mother, her sisters. She'd laughed and giggled like a child, told stories, smiled shyly to her papa and said how the Mex came to visit the Kerseys. A friend, she called him. A nice friend who brought her wildflowers and showed her how to ride her horse. He taught her how to feed and care for a leppy calf until it could fend for itself, and how to braid strands of leather into a pair of reins.

The burning was in full force, and Robert Vail suffered from its power. His child, his Orianna, talking and laughing with another man. A mongrel, marked by the world to know his sin. A 'breed who had no claim to family, no background, no code of honor. Who could touch and see his child at her invitation, who could know her smile, see into her eyes and recognize his own reflection.

It could not be; it would not happen. Vail was the law; he held the power. He would ride to McCraw's, he would convince the man to run Iberra off his place. Veiled threats, open declarations, the rise and fall of the law's gun. Whatever McCraw would listen to and understand. Vail would speak the words—and the Mex would be banished from the land surrounding his child, his Orianna.

Vail opened his eyes and saw that the sun touched the edge of the low sky. He stretched and yawned. Coffee, a big breakfast, and he would get to his duties. And when they were done, he would saddle and ride to Bitter Springs. McCraw would have to understand.

McCraw watched two groups of riders make a wide swing past his place, each trailing four or five head of cattle. The drive was done, yet he'd had no word from Matt or about him. Silvestre came out to ask his boss what was happening, and McCraw found himself making up a story to convince the old man to leave him alone.

Finally the need to do something drove McCraw to saddle a half-broke Appaloosa and trot out to a rider trailing three mama cows. The man listened politely, grinned at McCraw, and answered. Something about a broken arm and going to Kersey's place first. It was enough of an excuse that McCraw forgot to ask again about the arm.

He was content to let the App blow while he watched Kersey's wife. She was beautiful, and she stood in the doorway of the house, rubbing her hands on flour sacking, and spoke to him:

"Mr. McCraw, are you coming in? Or will you sit there and go hungry while I burn more biscuits?"

McCraw jumped from the voice, and the App spooked under him. He busied himself with soothing the bronc, fussing with his lost stirrup until he was certain he could face her without his thoughts plain on his face. But when he did speak, the words were enough to shock himself, as well as her.

"Ma'am, you get more beautiful every time I see you."

Mrs. Kersey cocked her head and stared at him briefly, then rubbed her hands in the sacking. And then she began to talk—light, impersonal thoughts that had nothing to do with McCraw's statement.

"Perhaps you would know why Mr. Kersey hasn't come in yet. Two riders came through this morning and said he had ridden out ahead of them, at the end of the gather. With your man, Matt. They were driving several head of our cattle, and some of yours.

"You know there is talk in Marfa of having a celebration to honor the new courthouse and jail. Such a thing, to celebrate the building of a jail. But it does mean that Marfa is growing. I haven't been to town for quite a while, and we are looking forward to seeing this fancy new structure. Don't you agree, Mr. McCraw, that Marfa is becoming a most civilized place? We are fortunate in having . . ."

The chatter soon ceased, and Mrs. Kersey went back inside the house. McCraw dismounted and tied up the App. He would follow the woman inside, but he held back at the door, uncomfortably aware that this was Thomas Kersey's domain.

She was waiting for him with a glass of lemonade. He sipped at it and watched her over the rim of the glass. The cabin was unnaturally silent, and McCraw finally thought of the girl.

"Ah, yes. Orianna will be returning this afternoon. Sometime soon. She is in Marfa at her father's request, to visit with her mother and sisters. She will return with supplies. More of these lemons, I hope, and a few vegetables. I wish to make a fine meal for Mr. Kersey's return."

The cabin echoed then with Kersey's ghost, the sound of his footsteps, the smell of his raw tobacco, the strangeness of his affection. McCraw shifted in the uncomfortable rush-seated chair and wished he was mounted on the hot App gelding.

"Ma'am. Mrs. Kersey. A rider came by this morning, said something about Matt having a busted arm, riding with your husband. Matt's tough, and so is your man, but by accounts they should be here now. I think I'll ride looking for them."

She did not discourage him, nor did she venture an opinion. Harriet Kersey remained seated in her chair by the window, quiet, motionless, hands folded properly in her lap. McCraw shoved his hat back on his head and felt for the unfamiliar pistol strapped to his side. He found the door alone, and it wasn't until he was outside that the woman spoke through the small window.

"Yes, indeed, Mr. McCraw. Please look for Thomas . . . And I am worried about that hand of yours. He has visited Orianna often, and she— Please, do look for them. Thank you."

He would stand and listen to the words again and again. Spoken in her educated, lovely voice. He would wait in the sun and ask her to speak again.

He rebridled the horse and mounted, headed toward the end of Kersey's canyon to swing north toward the Davis Mountains. Where the gather had ended, according to the

TEXAS SPRINGS

talkative cowboy early that morning. Matt and Kersey were caught between the canyon and those faraway blue-topped peaks. McCraw slammed his spurs into the App and let the colt run out. It suited him to rough up the App, and the hammerheaded bronc fought hard. The battle played well on the sourness in his belly, the cloud in his mind.

"Your boy here saved my life, McCraw."

Thomas Kersey: Setting down, watching McCraw, and grinning. McCraw dismounted and walked to the little roan gelding. No one needed to tell him who the boy was, the damnable roan was a giveaway.

"Yes, sir! That boy, he saw me hanging over the cliff and he roped me, dragged me up to safety. Wouldn't have made it without him. No, sir. Good thing you hired this boy on, good thing."

McCraw heard the man talk on, but he looked toward the kid. He took note of the filthy bandage around the right arm and the slow movements. A few days' whiskers covered the kid's dark face, and the damned scar parted them, left its white trail across his face. It gave the kid a bronco look McCraw didn't like.

That both men had walked was obvious; their boots were dust-covered, their shirts dark-stained. Kersey sat in the shade of a mesquite, Matt was fiddling with the roan's gear. McCraw handed the kid his canteen; Matt drank sparingly and returned the canteen without a word.

"Mr. McCraw, we thank you for the water. We are near to wore out, the two of us. We've been walking since early this morning, and we slept last night with nothing to eat. I have hoped that someone would take notice of my late return, and I am mightily glad it was you."

The man could talk almost as fast as he drank water. McCraw held out his hand before Kersey was finished. The man might be a working rancher, but he had not grown up in the desert. Matt knew what Kersey had to be told.

Kersey kept to his talking, hitting at the words until they ran together and McCraw lost patience. He went to the kid and stood beside him, looked over his shoulder at the roan's belly. He knew if he waited long enough, the kid would tell him.

"We was bringing in a small herd, yours and his. I got crippled up so I took the help. Let your string go, figured they'd find the main herd or come into the springs. Roan's the only one I trust to pack me.

"No matter. Kersey's mare got hit by that speckled steer. Sailed off Outlook and had to shoot her. Left Kersey there hanging on a tree. Roped up Kersey, been walking ever since. Roan's wore out, so's Kersey."

McCraw raised his hand to keep Kersey shut up. "Kersey, you're light. You ride the roan in; won't make it walking. Matt, you ride behind me. The App's tired enough he won't bother much to buck. Mrs. Kersey's some worried about you both."

Matt was glad to settle in behind the rancher, one arm wrapped about McCraw's midsection. But he ached all over, and each lurch of the App's short stride bit into him. There was no place to put his arm. Hanging down it burned like fire, and pulled against his belly it banged McCraw's high cantle. After a while, Matt didn't much care. He rode loose on the App's hunched rump and let his legs swing free, his head bumping McCraw's back.

He was tired and sore and hungry. Kersey's continued talking had wore thin last night, and the long morning was pure hell. Never heard a man talk so much. And he said nothing, just the same words over and over—as if they meant something to Matt. Kept saying thanks, that Matt had performed a miracle. Matt did what was expected, what any man riding with him would do. It was common sense, not bravery, to save a man's life. He might be saving yours another time.

Matt let his head come to rest on McCraw's shoulder. Closed his eyes, relaxed enough to sleep. Then he jerked awake, embarrassed by the nearness of the rancher. McCraw said something Matt couldn't hear but the sound was easy, the way McCraw spoke to the broncs before they got their first taste of man. Nothing to worry 'bout, nothing to fear. Matt let his head rest on McCraw again and was instantly asleep.

Kersey started in on the talk again and even brought the strawberry roan up close to McCraw. The noise was fearsome; the App laid back his long ears. McCraw shifted with the burden of the kid against him and told Kersey to hush his mouth. Polite, sort of, but firm. He didn't want to wake the kid.

It was strange, to be used for a pillow. The kid had balance to ride the short-strided App hung off his backside like a sack of meal. There was little chance of the kid sliding off; McCraw felt the tight body sway and move with each step of the App, could feel the strength of the hand wrapped to his middle. And he could hear the slight snoring as the kid breathed hard, face close to McCraw's neck, head bumped on the bone of his shoulder. The App quick-stepped; Matt slid, grabbed McCraw's middle, and pulled himself in close. McCraw eased up, the kid snored, and there was nothing much to worry over except getting to Kersey's and then back to the ranch at Bitter Springs.

It hit him when they rode into Kersey's place. The smile of the woman was for her husband—the light in her eyes, the quickness of her walk, all was for her wedded man. McCraw sat the tired App, with the kid holding to him, asleep with his head on McCraw's shoulder. Harriet Kersey walked past the double-burdened horse and raised her hand to greet her husband.

And the man was quick to soothe his wife's worries, quick to chatter in the aimless manner McCraw had come to hate. There was no mention of Kersey's panic, no telling of the facts as Matt had spoken them to McCraw. Kersey told of the hard work of the gather, the delay because of his dead horse, and the need to stay with Matt because of the rider's broken arm. McCraw watched as Kersey told his tale, was aware that Kersey never once looked in the direction of McCraw and the kid perched behind him on the raw bronc.

McCraw poked the kid in the belly; the kid sat up and pushed away from McCraw. Cool air touched McCraw's back. The kid slid off the App's rump; the half-broke horse reared and kicked out. When the App settled, McCraw saw the kid near the house, talking to a long-skirted girl with yellow hair. He didn't like it, didn't want the kid fooling around with the law's girl.

The App snorted and pulled hard; McCraw spurred the miserable bronc and spun a tight circle. It was the woman, always the woman.

"Mr. McCraw, please step down and come inside. Orianna has just returned from Marfa, and we have been preparing a meal, for all of you. Please, join us.

"And, we would hope you would allow Matt to stay a few days. He looks tired, and I would like to tend to his arm. I know he has been a great help to you, and to us. And I would like to repay him for his trouble."

Her green eyes were wide and unblinking, and her mouth partly open when she finished her pretty speech. McCraw knew he would do whatever this woman asked of him.

"Yes, ma'am. I'd be pleased to take a meal. Let me put up the bronc, and I'll be right in. Yes, ma'am." Yes, ma'am, indeed! He snapped his yapping maw shut and rode the App out of range. He was a fool, a God-blessed, weak-kneed fool.

CHAPTER TWENTY-EIGHT

He rode out alone, accompanied by a full belly, anger at the kid, and unrelieved desire for the woman.

The small party had eaten well, talked easily, sat and visited while the kid half slept and the girl, Orianna, watched him with an innocent smile. Still, Harriet had managed a minute alone with him. Long enough to allow a touch of her hand, a hearing of her thanks for rescuing her husband. McCraw wanted to set her straight about the kid, but he never got the chance. He was lost in the smell and touch and sound of her and forgot what he wanted to say about Matt.

Now he was almost home, where he didn't want to be. Where Silvestre waited for the day's work, where they had to ride out and pick up the loose cattle from the gather, hope to find the four drifting horses.

The App snorted and planted his front legs. McCraw raked the horse's dark sides with his spurs. The stubborn bronc kicked and shook violently, but still would not move on command. A horse and rider came at them, fast down the narrow trail. Dust covered the pair; sunlight caught a bit of metal and flashed signals. The App reared and spun a circle; McCraw hung on and slapped his hand between the App's laid-back ears. This was a bronc he might sell out of his string.

It was the sheriff; McCraw fought the App to a standstill and crossed his hands. No matter what, this wouldn't be good. When Vail started in, McCraw knew he was right.

"McCraw. I was just at your place. Your hand said he

didn't know where you were gone to. Lucky chance for us to meet. I got some talk needs going over with you. Set a bit, have a smoke."

McCraw snorted, sounding to himself like the bronc he half rode. The sheriff was no different from anyone. Part politician, part lawman, comfortable in neither place. At least he knew from the invite that he wasn't about to be arrested. The kid had to be in this somewhere. The kid had to be the center. Vail's daughter stuck in McCraw's mind; he knew before Vail spoke what was going wrong.

Vail sputtered and stopped, worked hard at pulling out and clipping a cigar, even offered its mate to McCraw, an offer that he refused. There was a flaw in the man, hidden behind showy dress and the flowing words. McCraw listened some to him but watched the land around him and tried to pick up on what Vail hadn't said.

Then the man came flat down to his ache, to the prod hung deep in his gut. And McCraw had no surprises waiting for him.

"McCraw, you're responsible for that 'breed Mexican kid still hanging around here. He's the one you pulled out of the road gang to ride your race. He's the one.

"I come to you, face-to-face, to ask a favor that will save all of us trouble. I want you to fire the kid, get him off our range, out of our lives. He don't belong here. He don't work here. He ain't like all the rest."

The anger riding the man broke down his careful manners. McCraw began to wonder who Robert Vail was.

"You heard about the trouble in camp. Charley Hocker told me your boy came in starting trouble. Sassed back at John Sinnot, wouldn't take his commands. The whole gather depended on the men working together, and it was your boy who caused the trouble.

"We don't want those wild ones thinking they can ride in here and raise their hell. We don't want those kind to step out of their place. Do you understand me, McCraw?"

It was the politician who finished the conversation, but McCraw suspected he heard the daddy talking in the middle. McCraw had nothing to add as the man finally rode away. He watched the wide back and kept his thoughts private.

The App reared suddenly; McCraw tightened his grip, slapped a hand between the laid-back ears. He was getting tired of the App's temper. Too pigheaded, like the lawman.

But it weren't going to be that easy moving Matt. And McCraw puzzled over the truth hidden behind all the words. Vail had a goad stuck deep in him, and he never let it out. It had to be the daughter, and that was a feeling McCraw could almost understand.

He finally let the App run out and rocked with the short stride. The conversation with Vail stuck in him, stirred up his own thinking. Too much thinking, when there was work at the ranch, stock to be corralled, fences needing mending, the daily work on a small ranch.

But the thinking rolled over him . . . and it all came back to the kid. The worst of his thinking was on Thomas Kersey's life. That damned kid saved the man from his own death, from a certain broken neck. Or a slow death from a shattered bone and starvation.

A wife in mourning, defenseless and in need. The picture flooded McCraw, in fantasy and in guilt. He prodded the App into frantic bucking, wanting to fight a battle he could win or lose, just so it took him from the cruel thinking.

It was the kid again. Who saved Kersey. Who sat now with Vail's child and leaned close to her, inhaled her, touched her. McCraw knew for certain then that it was the 'breed kit and the pretty Vail girl that goaded the heart of Robert Vail.

Two places the kid wasn't wanted, two grown men angered by his interference. Right at that moment, James McCraw didn't think much of himself; if the kid were gone, Vail wouldn't pick at him, and Thomas Kersey would be dead. The woman would be waiting for him alone, down the end of this track, eyes blurred with forgotten tears, hands reaching for a new man to love.

But the kid's face hung in the void behind McCraw's

eyes. A tough face, badly marred. Young, burned a dark color McCraw knew didn't go through the kid's skin. Eyes that laughed and turned grave, that mirrored little but the surface thoughts. And a body that worked its share, followed its needs, lived wild and hard and came apart tender for a girl's sweet caring.

A damned child, picked off his horse and blamed for what he had not done. Blamed for McCraw's rising frustration, blamed for Vail's superiority. Blamed by Sinnot and Hocker for standing to his orders and doing his job.

McCraw knew then he would lose badly if he sent the kid on his way. So he would not take up Vail's request. Matt would come back to the ranch; they would fight through the coming winter, deal with the blizzard skies and whistling cold. And Robert Vail would have to leave the goddamned, wild-haired, restless kid alone.

Harriet Kersey watched the young man and Orianna and was jealous. She was a lovely child, and he was little more than a drifter, a day rider working aimlessly at whatever jobs came his way. Yet the girl's eyes flashed brightly, her voice animated as she offered the strange boy a glass of the cool lemonade. He drank as if it were a treat he had never tasted, and Harriet considered the remoteness of the life she was now living. She could not blame Orianna for offering care and tenderness to the man who saved Mr. Kersey's life.

Mr. Kersey's retelling of his narrow escape mentioned little of the boy's intervention, yet Harriet watched Mr. McCraw's face as her husband spoke, and she quickly guessed the truth. They were not obvious and evil lies that Mr. Kersey spoke, but more lies by omission, lies given life by leaving out the real facts.

Harriet sighed deeply, wounded once again by wishing to have faith in a man. Her man. She must let go of the sadness and deal with what was most obvious to her.

"Orianna, child. Let Mr. Iberra have a moment's rest.

Come with me. We will find the supplies necessary to treat his arm."

Behind closed eyes, Matt heard the women talk over him, about him. The fussing was a sweet taste he had not known in a long time, and the pale yellow lemonade was cool and tart in his mouth. The glass fitted neatly in his left hand, slippery from the dampness of his fist, a focus for his musings.

The lady was right. His arm throbbed and banged to his shoulder. It had taken a beating the past days, and Matt had a moment of panic. He'd seen one-armed men before, rode with a couple of them. He knew he didn't want to join with them. Short pay, lost work, pity, scorn. He didn't want that.

He stretched out his legs and felt the sun slam a hot stream across his thighs, deep into his belly. The color of the sky could be seen under his lids. Flashes of yellow, stretches of deep, clear blue. His belly knotted with a picture; his left fist closed hard. The right fist gripped in reflex, and Matt cried out. He forced himself to relax, to try and taste the bit of safety. The women would come back and nurse him. But until they did, he was safe on the veranda, safe in the shaded sun.

Matt's left fist opened, the fingers curled against his palm. His neck tendons stretched and eased, the hard mouth loosened in shallow sleep. The right arm slipped down his belly and caught on the fasteners of his pants; and Matt snorted in his sleep, then choked, rolled his head, and slept quietly.

Orianna held a pan of water and had clean bandages over her arm, two pins closed in the front of her dress. She was waiting for Mrs. Kersey, she told herself. She was waiting while the older woman found the salve and the knife needed to cut the old bandage off.

This was hers alone, right now. To stand and watch an unguarded Matt, to follow the lines and bones of his body with no shame. She knew of his interest in her; she enjoyed the halting words he spoke, the long, comfortable silences as they walked slowly or stood and looked at the new calves, the growing garden.

He was a gentleman with her, conscious of the line that separated them. Orianna sometimes left him to huddle in her narrrow bed and cry to herself; he didn't want her, he could not find her attractive with her maimed leg and flawed character. Yet he came back to her always, with a handful of tired flowers or a carved animal, a bit of pretty rock.

He was truly hers for now. As he slept, with no pretense, sweet mouth open, air whistling across his lips. Throat exposed and vulnerable, eyes shut from the sun, fingers open and free.

She knelt by him, carefully wrapped her fingers deep in his, marveled at their tightening over her hand. She stayed beside him, awkward on the weakness of her betraying leg, and drew his hand to her face, laid her cheek against the rough, callused palm. She drew in his smell, tasted the salt from his flesh, and did not feel the tears rolling down her cheeks.

"Orianna, get up child. Here, hold the pan while I cut the wrappings loose. Matt, wake up. Matt."

He came awake suddenly, helpless from his dreaming. The girl was near him, grabbing his left hand. He jerked free, struggled to get his legs under him and stand. But Mrs. Kersey did not let him; she pushed him back into the chair with a firm hand.

"Please, Mr. Iberra. We must take care of your arm. Be still."

She talked as she worked, mindless chatter to calm Matt, and perhaps to hide her own fears.

"The gather was quite a success from what Mr. Kersey has said about it. I wish we had been able to ride over and see the encampment, but you moved almost every night. It would have been a sight, all the different men from the ranches, and the horses.

"The cattle you gathered, they were wild of course. And in great numbers. I have never seen anything like this, as of course we did not have such things in the East. Perhaps it would be similar to the crowds in New York City. Crowds of cattle and horses this time, instead of busy men and fashionable women."

Matt didn't move from her chatter. His weakness scared him; his knees were jelly, his heart pounded, his arms were lead weights. When he closed his eyes, he saw only a one-armed man saddling a rank horse.

Mrs. Kersey talked as she cut into the blackened bandage. Her delicate fingers slowly tugged the wrapping from the splints, and Matt's belly turned over. Even her slight touch magnified the throbbing.

"Matt, be still. Orianna, wipe his face. Here." He felt the coolness of a wet cloth on his forehead. "Hold still, Matt."

He tried to follow orders, but a piece of the old bandage stuck and she lifted it from the wood. Matt turned his head, leaned over, and vomited bile onto the floor of the veranda. His face flushed, his whole body heated from the shame.

A hand wiped his lips, washed a damp cloth over his eyes, and then drops of water were squeezed into his open mouth. Matt swallowed; his head fell back on the chair. He cursed himself, ranted about his own betrayal. It were nothing but a busted arm.

She pulled at more of the wrapping; Matt closed his eyes. Only a broke bone. So why so shaky and useless? Even when he'd been hit by his brother, smashed across the face by the great edge of the ax, he hadn't been such a baby. The blow from Tomás's fury had knocked him down, laid him out where his mama and granpap found him much later, bathed and soothed him, fed him sour water that put him back to sleep. When he woke, the scarring was deep but the illness was gone.

So why be a child again, now, with only a broken arm? The image of the ax high above him was vivid; Matt raised his left arm to ward off the blow and heard a voice call to him, plead with him against his own defense. He struck out at the voice, felt the voice give way from his strength, and he laughed, whole again, strong and invulnerable.

A liquid was forced past his lips; he swallowed involuntarily and tried to spit back the taste. Bitter, harsh. Then the liquor heated his throat and belly and his arms were weak; he had no strength left.

Matt opened his eyes, surprised by a face close to his. Calm eyes saw him in cool appraisal. A calm voice spoke to him as if he were a child:

"Your arm is infected. I would guess you didn't know, but there is a cut across your hand that is badly swollen. I cannot clean it with the arm in splints, so you must hold still.

"Matt, take more of the whiskey. Mr. Kersey says it will dull the pain. Please, we have to finish this now. I realize it must be sore, but you don't want to have that arm infected. You could lose it."

He sat up quickly. He must have said something, for her to know his fears. Orianna was there, holding a pan of water, a roll of bandages. His angel. He smiled at her, watched her until she had to move from his gaze. There was a fresh swelling high on her cheek, a new bruise. The impact of his hand on bone. Damage he had done. He had to apologize, but could not quite form the words.

He fought to stand up, get away, but Mrs. Kersey pushed his chest and pinned him. He flushed, weak with embarrassment, and the throbbing in his arm.

"Orianna's fine, Matt. Take the whiskey and relax. We need to finish bandaging your arm."

Cleaned up and repaired, the arm became an occasional bother. He felt the pull of new healing under the white wrapping, and when the ends of the bone shifted, they reminded Matt to be careful. But two days of good stews, warmed soups, and hot breads and he began to think the world could be his for the taking.

There was a moment to treasure hidden in the blurred days—when he reached up to Orianna and touched the fading bruise on her cheek. She winced at his touch but did not pull back. There were words needed, but Matt could not find them. He could not apologize, he could not explain. He simply touched the pain he had caused, traced the edges of the mark, then brought her head down to be kissed.

Now he walked out with Orianna, holding her hand, feeling the swing and motion of her damaged walk and wanting badly to make her travel easier. They passed the crude garden, baked brown and ugly by the incessant sun. There was still no rain, no sign of relief in the yellow sky. Matt knew all this, but to him the importance of the day was the girl beside him, the scent of her body close to his. The wind would rise and blow; the sun would shrivel and disappear in harsh stormings; the cycle would come and go as it always did. But the girl would be here for him only now, only these few days. Matt knew that without being told.

She wore a full skirt, faded green and rose. Her feet were comforted in a pair of moccasins Matt had fashioned for her in early summer. She had tried to bead them, as she had seen the Indian women do, but the pattern was crude, the stitching loose and frayed. Still she wore her gift proudly and was pleased to hold out a foot for Matt's inspection.

The pale hair was pulled back and tied with a ribbon, a lace and velvet ribbon that could only come from Mrs. Kersey's trunk. Matt touched the velvet knot once and marveled at its texture. He reached out again, with his injured hand, and Orianna stopped under his touch, allowed him to weave the ribbon end across the exposed ends of his fingers. The gentle ribbon caught and pulled on the rough skin of his hands. Matt let the ribbon fall away.

She was close to him ... and he could not stop. He rested the weight of his splinted arm across her back; its dull pressure drew her to him. She came to him one step at a time, finally to lean completely on the length of his body.

He grabbed for air; her body fitted close to him, her breasts burned his shirt. A leg slid between his thighs, her hips closed on his. He could not bear the pain. He looked down on the top of her head; he could lay his mouth on the clean strands and draw them through his lips, taste their intimate sweetness.

The hardness between his legs rose up eager and sure, targeted at the joining of her legs. Matt flinched from his body and tried to step back, tried to hide his lust. She moved with him, pressed close until he could not ignore her willingness.

Then she sealed their bond by picking up his left hand from her hip and bringing it to her blouse, holding it firm while she unhooked the first buttons, unnerving Matt with her boldness. He started and looked around, then settled as he could not see the house—they were safe from prying eyes. She pulled his hand lower, guiding his fingers to the remaining fasteners. The last buttons released, he suddenly felt the softness of her pale skin, blued by delicate veins. He jerked back, then stroked her gently, inhaling her scent, marveling at the rise and fullness of her.

She leaned into his embrace, offering both her breasts to his hands, to his waiting mouth. His body jerked and spasmed; she kept her hips with him. Together they laid her down. She lifted her loose skirt, tugged herself free of her undergarments. Matt jerked back again when her hand worked the front of his britches and freed him from the suffocating clothing.

She was waiting for him, hips lifted, legs opened slightly. Then he covered her, entered her, and gasped with the pleasure. Her mouth was hot on his neck, her muffled cries came in short gasps. They moved together until he lost control and exploded inside her. She cried out softly and clung to him tightly.

They walked back to the small cabin. Her limp was pronounced, his arm was cradled to his belly. They didn't talk, but he occasionally patted her arm or fingered a freed strand of her beautiful hair.

A man and a woman sat outside the house, in the shade of a cottonwood tree. Waiting patiently. Matt flushed with embarrassment, although the married couple were a good distance away and could not yet know what had happened. Orianna stiffened when she, too, saw the couple, and Matt wanted to protect her, protest any judgment.

He had to leave now. McCraw needed him. The arm was rested, he was ready to work. She had to help Mrs. Kersey, or the older woman would become run down and ill again. They did not speak, each knew what the other felt. Matt fitted himself to Orianna's gait, and they crossed the yard, approached the waiting Kerseys.

Mr. Kersey allowed that the expected storms hadn't come in yet, he was beginning to worry. Matt said he knew McCraw was concerned, had seen him step down and run his hands through the soil, watch the dry dirt scatter. McCraw knew the land, better than most. Knew it would come to disaster if it didn't rain soon.

Mrs. Kersey agreed, only she spoke to Orianna when it was her turn. The garden was poorly—and they needed the vegetables for their health. Yes, she said, she understood Matt had to get along to his work, just as she had chores waiting for her and Orianna.

He didn't touch her hand, or look at her. They had to protect each other from the watchful eyes. Mrs. Kersey would be upset if she guessed what they had done out past the sorry garden, near the roots of an ancient, dying cottonwood. So they walked away from each other and were close to rude with their good-byes.

They could not fool Harriet Kersey; she was careful to remain impassive with their playacting, but she knew as she watched the young man saddle his small roan and tie on the bits of gear McCraw left for him. She read the tension in his face, the emotions he thought hidden, and then she risked a glance at Orianna, and allowed herself the luxury of a small sigh.

The girl walked slowly, eyes cast down, hands quiet at her side. And there were spots of color high on each cheek, a bruised look to her mouth, a glazed sadness in her eyes.

Then the young man rode out with a brief nod to Harriet, a thank-you to Mr. Kersey—and no attention paid at all to the girl. Harriet let her head rest on the back of the rocker, let her eyes close out the low sun. There would be trouble now. The very trouble Sheriff Vail had sought to avoid by sending his child to the Kersey ranch.

But for now, she would bless the boy and Orianna. They had stolen a sweetness that would never be replaced, and she envied them their passion, their willingness to risk everything, their brief time of love.

"Mrs. Kersey, I do believe it is time to begin the supper meal. I have enjoyed sitting here with you, but there is work still to be done. Tomorrow I will ride out and search for the missing cattle. It is foolish to find them in the gather and then lose them again, to that silly mare and the accident of McCraw's rider's arm.

"But for tonight, I will enjoy a special supper, and perhaps we will retire early. I am still worn from my experiences, and have thoughts and ideas I wish to share with you."

He left her sitting on the veranda; she was rooted in her chair, taken by anger and disbelief. Now he was blaming Matt for the strayed cattle, the accident with the mare, the extra work he must do.

And he had told her he would be amorous tonight, told her clearly in his rhetoric. She would not deny him, but she would think of other men and other places when he took her. And she would cry herself to sleep, alone, when the deed was finished.

The kid was slow to come back to form after the gather. McCraw made allowances, as the kid had gone through a lot for the brand. Never easygoing, now he growled at Silvestre, roughed the horses until McCraw yelled at him, and ate little of his own poor cooking, rode out at night, paced and sweated when McCraw grounded him. McCraw blamed it on the long summer heat, the misery of a broken arm, anything he could imagine.

McCraw's own temper wasn't much of an improvement. The law had come back at him once, demanding to know why a certain 'breed Mex still rode for McCraw's brand. He came close, then, to firing the kid just to get rid of both the nuisances. But he looked hard at Vail's sweaty face and hated the man, enough to hold on to the kid and back Vail down. He rode the kid even harder after that, and knew the fine line of his own loyalty.

It was close to a month's time when McCraw and the kid rubbed tempers and backed off. Mid-September, by McCraw's calendar, and still hot, still dry, still miserable mean. The wrappings on the kid's arm were an ugly, soiled brown and smelled downright rotten. The kid's dark face was thinned to real meanness, and McCraw had had enough.

"That arm's going to fester, you don't treat it right. Let me get at it with a knife. Or you can ride over to Kersey's and have that pretty girl unwrap you proper. Maybe a ride would do you good. Ain't been much to live with lately—"

That's when the kid came at him, bandaged arm held in, left hand closed around the handle of the old knife. McCraw stepped back from the threat, almost amused by the attack. Until he saw the kid's wild face and sobered up.

He held out his arms, showing empty hands, sidestepped a cutting gesture from the knife.

"Hold it. Right there. Stop. There ain't no need for scalping me now. We been at this together for too long. Kid, you look up, see that sky. We got rain coming in, relief from this damned dry. It's no time to skin me alive.

"But you still got to do something about that arm. Smell's getting bad enough, I saw the horses spook from you. Silvestre ain't too pleased to stand downwind from you, and me, I don't want to get within a half mile."

The kid listened to the dumb talk, mouth half open, hand pointing the tip of the knife down at his boots. The talk flowed easy from McCraw, old talk used to gentle half-broke mustangs. The kid'd been here over two years now, and when McCraw looked into the broken face, he knew the bronco in him hadn't yet been tamed.

"Matt, you either ride to the Kersey place and get that arm tended to, or set here and let me hack at it. One way or other, it's got to be done. You *comprende*?"

* * *

The kid rode out; McCraw knew he'd be back in a day or two. But the skies opened during the night, and the rain flooded them for six days. He and Silvestre holed up in the cabin and blessed the high ground where they sat, thanked the kid for dried corn and ground flour sacked up in the stone-walled kitchen.

Once McCraw made a trip to the barn, to turn out the horses penned inside and in the corrals. He skidded in the greased mud, pulled up pounds of the stuff at each step. The freed broncs bucked and slid as they rushed through the open gates, and a bay mare went down; a sorrel jumped her and slid ten feet on his side. A bitter flood, offering a bonus of water that the land could not accept.

Matt returned on the seventh day, and there was no expression on his face as he off-saddled and attempted to answer McCraw's casual questions. The rancher, as always, was eager for news of the Kerseys, starving for a mention of the woman, and he tried to hurry anything out of the kid's stubborn mouth.

But Matt resisted him this time, became sullen and withdrawn until McCraw couldn't take it. He looked the kid up and down and finally saw the marks. Face even thinner than before, right arm unbound and pale at the wrist, torn shirt, a crude patch on his pants leg. And fresh scrapes down the side of his face and neck, disappearing in the ruined shirt.

The roan was sore-footed, the old bridle replaced by a crude knotting of leather thongs and a rusted bit. McCraw saw the marks and had to know.

"What happened, kid? What the hell went on to Kersey's got you sewed up and tight? You speak up, or I'll ride over there and get it from the boss and his wife. Now Matt, you tell me now."

It was a sorry story, and McCraw hated himself the moment the last words left the kid's mouth. The rain had flooded Kersey's canyon; Kersey and Matt rode out to try to move the cattle, turn the horses. Do anything to slow the destruction. The roan had turned over; Matt was washed downstream. And Mr. Kersey drowned.

CHAPTER TWENTY-NINE

Grief was a cleansing emotion, but she could not grieve for Mr. Kersey. She wore a dark dress and made no effort to find flowers for her daily decorating above the kitchen sink. And she did think about him toward the evening hours, when they used to come together and sit and talk of the day past, the days to come. But there was little grief in her for Thomas Kersey.

Harriet Kersey saddled a small bay and rode out of the confinement of the canyon. The horse traveled quietly, and she took her time to see the land. It came to her that Mr. Kersey would have enjoyed the ride: the six days of rain blossomed the valley into a green heaven. Cattle moved about in small bunches, and a few horses lifted their heads from the grass to watch her ride past.

She knew then she did miss Mr. Kersey. He had been attentive to her and had given her a home, a life of sorts in this frontier land. He loved her, that much she knew. But she had not loved him, and would not sully his image by a false bereavement.

The bay stopped, pulled the reins from her hands, and was content to tear at the grass. Harriet had to yank hard before the lazy horse would even lift his head. She had taken note of the infrequency of Mr. Kersey's brand marked on the cattle's hides. This was land claimed by Mr. Kersey, yet more of the cattle belonged to other ranches. It was bad business to support other men's herds when the range was poor and overgrazed. It meant her cattle would starve. Something would have to be done.

She began to realize that she would have to make the decision. Mr. Kersey was cold and buried, and even when he had been in attendance, he had been slow and ponderous in his choices.

Water was the prime consideration; Harriet knew that. Mr. Kersey had been concerned about not enough water, and just after their marriage had spoken of taking over a spring. But that event had not occurred, and now their surface water had been sucked up by the drought; the shallow pools were barely wet by the six-day rain. The hard-baked ground had soaked in the water, or it ran off in deep channels.

A man had spoken at a meeting in Marfa in early spring, a Mr. Jake Bowman. He had devised a simple and practical method of watering the herds. Ground tanks, he called them, to be created around the natural depressions in the land. Mr. Kersey had scorned the practice and refused the idea. Harriet supposed she would look into the tanks; perhaps they would provide the needed service.

Then, too, a man named McCarty had put up a windmill—actually two of his structures were in Presidio County, drawing up water from deep underground. Another idea Mr. Kersey had found preposterous, another concept she would have to investigate herself.

Harriet swung the little bay gelding around and slapped the horse into a ragged lope. She felt a freedom in riding over the land, one she had not known before. A peaceful, rocking, beautiful way to travel. She was actually enjoying herself.

She was bothered, though, by several unfinished thoughts. She did not know, even now, two weeks after Mr. Kersey's burial, if the estate was under her control, if she could make the decisions. His antiquated and cavalier attitude toward the abilities of women was such that he might well have appointed a guardian for her. Or worse still, he might not have made any provisions for her in matters pertaining to the ranch.

She also did not know what lawyer he would have used. The only familiar name was that of Wilson Voeckes, newly moved to Marfa from Fort Davis. She had heard Mr. McCraw speak highly of the man, and Orianna's young beau had spoken of him in passing.

Harriet began to hurry the bay; she was uncomfortable with the practical matters rolling over in her mind and the names she thought of when looking for advice.

Matt had been with Mr. Kersey when he died. Matt brought in the shrunken body, strung over the back of his horse, covered with a torn canvas, so she would not have to bear the shock of his bruised and beaten features, the limp stillness of the corpse. The boy had apologized for his inability to save Mr. Kersey—and agonized over the tragedy until Harriet had sent him back to Mr. McCraw.

Her thinking skipped quite logically to Orianna. The girl was subdued now, often speechless. She did her day's chores efficiently and in awkward silence. Harriet had to speak directly to her before receiving the simplest answer. It was very easy for Harriet to see it wasn't Mr. Kersey's death that had quieted the child.

Her thoughts came back to the boy, Matt Iberra, and his terrible face, his sweet smile, and gentle nature. Harriet had listened to Mr. Kersey rail against the boy—call him names and vilify his character. And his temper was heightened when the sheriff called once or twice and they'd sat down together and attacked the boy. She had come close to defending him on those occasions, even though she knew it would be deadly.

It had worsened after Matt saved Mr. Kersey's life. Mr. Kersey never did say to her directly that the boy had been his benefactor, but Harriet questioned Mr. McCraw, and the boy, and listened to Orianna recount what Matt told her. It added up quite differently from what Mr. Kersey repeated first to her, then to Robert Vail.

The truth was simple and obvious: Orianna was in love

with a half-breed Mexican bronc rider and sometime cowboy named Matt. Her papa was incensed, her mother didn't care, and Matt himself was taking a cautious stand that surprised Harriet. The boy was showing good sense; he was respectful, minded his manners, and was attentive to the girl. Since Mr. Kersey's demise, the boy had been by only once, to pay his respects and bring a message of condolence from Mr. McCraw.

She had taken the letter from his hand and gone inside to read it, and had paid little attention to Orianna and the boy. Now she wished she had at least watched them together. It was not a simple matter between them, for they had crossed too many lines in their friendship over the summer, but Harriet had other, more practical and demanding situations to deal with before she could ask for the truth from them both.

The bay gelding was amenable to returning to the canyon and the comfort of a handful of hay thrown over the corral fence. The ride had cleared her thoughts and given Harriet a renewed purpose to the days ahead of her. She would put Mr. Kersey's death behind her by driving into Marfa and asking certain questions of the lawyer, Wilson Voeckes. She would speak to Mr. McCraw about the proliferation of cattle not carrying her brand on her claimed land. And she would inquire as to hiring Jake Bowman, or the mysterious Mr. McCarty and his windmills.

There was a future for her now, a future *she* decided. Not one bound to a man's whim of likes and dislikes. She passed by her considerations of James McCraw; he would wait, as he had done until now. It was not proper for them to conduct any sort of correspondence or conversation unless chaperoned. Certainly the presence of Matt, or Orianna, would not constitute enough of a barrier to protect her from gossip and slanderous thoughts.

McCraw would come to her soon enough, Harriet was confident of that fact. But she must make her own decisions in the meantime, and she found herself looking forward to the new and unusual opportunity.

TEXAS SPRINGS

* * *

It was a day he'd as soon get through and start on the next one. Nothing was going right for him. He'd roped out the App bronc McCraw wanted to sell, and the rank son stuck a front leg through a high loop and peeled all the skin off the back of his leg.

The App doctored and turned out, Matt went to roping another bronc, and even with the loop settled snug on the neck, and as the horse came to the tug from Matt's hand, the saddle horn dug into Matt's belly and the stirrup slammed his left wrist. He got the saddle on the gray gelding and jerked roughly on the *cincha*, but the old *látigo* parted company, the saddle rolled sideways, and the spooked bronc kicked out and caught Matt above the right knee.

Then he began cursing, and grabbed for the saddle, swung it as far as he could. The saddle skidded a few feet; the other stirrup hit Matt's shin in passing. The ornery bronc reared sideways and knocked Matt in the dust. Matt lay there a bit, feeling a numbness run up his leg. The saddle was near him, and he pulled it closer.

The old *cincha* his granpap had woven was frayed and unraveled, and the *látigo* dried out, broken. He looked close at the saddle, as if it were a stranger's rig.

No one came to see what caused the ruckus; no one caught up the bronc or even laughed at Matt. The animal lowered its head to stare at Matt, then snorted and soaked his face and shirtfront. The horse lifted its head, pushed out its upper lip, and laughed its horse laugh. He tried to stand, thought of his knife and sweet revenge on the stubborn, but innocent, gray. A fool's hope, but it made him feel better.

But when his hand touched only air at the small of his back, Matt remembered and sat back in the dust, stunned by all that had happened. The girl had his knife, the knife given to him by his mama when he'd left home the first time, seven years ago. His brother, Tomás, had asked for the knife, pleaded for it, but Mama had denied Tomás this one request and had given the precious knife to Matt.

Truly it was a man's weapon. Well balanced, made of fine steel, fitted to a man's hand. But it was more than being a knife, more than its use as protection or bragging, skinning or cutting. It was the handle of the knife that gave it distinction. Bone, carved perfectly in a style and skill lost now. His mama had told him quietly, out of hearing of his brother, that the knife belonged to his father, to Matt's father. Not the one who sired Tomás.

It was no surprise, their having two different fathers. Both boys had always known that—the whole village had known. It would take one of small intelligence to miss the differences—the wide face and lighter eyes of Matt, the hard muscle and quick hands. Tomás grew to a dullard, with a thick body, red streaks in his brown hair, eyes that looked but did not see, hands that grabbed and kept to him whatever he could take.

And Tomás suffered from the difference, Tomás, who in a rage had raised the ax over his head, high above his smaller brother, and brought it down to kill the grinning, laughing face of his tormentor. The blow had come close to killing Matt, and had left its mark.

Matt looked at the weight of his empty hand, saw the sun slanted into the corral, heard the nicker of the loose bronc behind him. That knife was his connection to those memories. And he had given it to a pretty, pale-haired Anglo girl who did not see the marks on him but only his strengths and his love. Damaged in her body, she saw the damage in his soul and held him to her for his protection. He had never known the feeling before, and he had easily given her the precious knife, to show some of his devotion.

He lay in the loose dust of a horse corral, staring at the remains of the saddle his granpap had given him. Only tired memories and painful recollections.

Right now he needed to get to work—to catch up the horse and repair his saddle, mount up and ride. McCraw was wrangling paper, old Silvestre slaved at mindless repairs in the barn. Matt had to do his own share.

McCraw had changed some, and Matt didn't much like

TEXAS SPRINGS 311

it, since the gather—and it was the ladies, and Matt didn't like that, either. For McCraw it was the new widow.

Matt had a deep respect for the woman, an admiration uncolored by anything but her work on the ranch, her fine manner and kindness. McCraw was caught, no denying that fact.

For him, it was Orianna. With her daddy's hatred and her mother's indifference, her imagined lameness and her innocent idolizing of Matt. Something he did not understand, something he had never known, something sweet and warm, and, late at night, when he was alone, something very frightening. It was the ladies all right, and there wasn't nothing much he or McCraw could do about their own capture.

McCraw was caught in hell. Kersey'd been buried a month now, and McCraw hadn't gone to the widow. Matt knew the man was wrong, learned it from Orianna talking to him. McCraw's stubbornness hurt only him, and the woman. Matt saw it and suffered with the man. But only McCraw could fix it.

The saddle was easy to repair: a new horsehair *cincha* borrowed from McCraw's pile, a fresh length of leather punched and cut into the right size. There were signs of cattle running wild up near the Chisos Basin, near the window runoff. McCraw wanted them checked before another rancher got close enough to put on his own brand. Winter was closing in, and the numbers were thin from the drought, even after the August gather. Every head counted, especially come spring, and a new crop of calves.

Matt climbed aboard and caught the front of his shirt on the horn. He reared back before he knew anything held him and heard the shirt tear. He swore again, angry at the carelessness. A shirt Orianna had fashioned for him out of Kersey's throwaways. He poked two fingers through the hole and cursed. It just weren't his day.

McCraw couldn't stand working indoors, couldn't bear pacing and watching the slow activity of the ranch yard through the window. He opened the front door—he needed fresh air—and peered 'round the corner, curious and bored. The big ugly Appaloosa that Matt was set to ride out today stood in the corral alone. Damn, that horse could use some more miles before it got sold—didn't do to sell a rank one from his string 'less it went off the range, way up to El Paso or back East.

Matt's orders had been to ride the App, so McCraw had an excuse to go outside and rattle the kid's line. He needed a reason to stand straight and rub the small of his back, fuel the anger he knew had no real meaning. It wouldn't work, taking his anger out on the rider. It was useless, but McCraw was knotted up inside, and seeing the App still in the corral was as good a reason as anything.

When McCraw reached the corral, he saw the horse stood three-legged, black tar smeared down the injured limb. McCraw looked up and caught the bare outline of a horse and rider crossing a distant ridge. It was Matt; McCraw knew the way the kid sat a saddle, and the horse he was riding was one of the ranch's good flea-bitten grays. Goddammit, riding out on a trained horse and leaving him with a stumpy, no-good Appaloosa. McCraw grasped the peeled rails in anger with both hands, but when he regained control and looked up again, Matt and the gray were gone.

When he cooled down, McCraw saw that Matt and the gray were headed in the right direction, toward the Chisos Basin, right where, last night, McCraw had told him to go. Right where strayed cattle would hide out until a man on horseback headed them back toward their home range.

It was beautiful outside; McCraw stopped dead, stretched hard, opened to the bright day, saw the leaves along the stream turned a dull yellow. He smelled the warmth of the new day against last night's chill. Coming to winter, all right, and throwing the best days at him while he was cooped inside, cursing and complaining.

A good day to saddle a horse and visit a neighbor. McCraw lifted his arms, pulled from his shoulders until he heard the muscle and bone creak and pop. Been almost a month since he'd ridden the blond sorrel. Or any horse for that matter. Since Thomas Kersey's burying.

That brought him to stand straight, arms by his sides, eyes fixed to a distance no one else could see. The App whinnied pitifully; Silvestre's shapeless form drifted from the barn to throw an arm of hay to the sorry bronc. McCraw didn't care; he barely saw the slumped old man or heard the App's thankful nicker. He had his mind wrapped around the face and hands of a lonely woman, a woman grieving for her man planted and covered.

She'd looked directly at him during the service, had nodded to him inside the house while the neighbors pressed food on her and offered comfort. She had not been shy, but McCraw had run from her then. She was waiting for him; it was his bullheaded stupidity that divided them, only that and nothing more.

The sorrel was as eager as McCraw to get moving. McCraw leaned forward, weight deep in the stirrups, and yelled with the horse's stride. Hat whipped to his forehead, eyes blinded by the wind, ears deafened by the rush of air. It had been long enough, too long. And he was for catching up the lost days and time with the sorrel's running and the pleasure riding high inside his chest.

CHAPTER THIRTY

Robert Vail knew he had done the right thing. And Bogel's agreement added to his assurance. They had sat on the overstuffed chairs in Vail's house and discussed the matter as town business. Vail was quick to assert his ideas, and this time Bogel was willing to go along.

McCraw hadn't gotten rid of the Mex troublemaker, so Vail would take it into his own hands. He'd asked—polite, firm—and McCraw had effectively said no. That kind of disregard for the law wasn't allowed in Marfa; they had a law-abiding community here, and that meant everyone went by the word of the law. Robert Vail's word.

Mr. Bogel had been most understanding, especially when Vail reminded him that it was the same man had killed his sheep last winter. Didn't bother to explain his involvement with Thomas Kersey's rescue after the gather—that didn't matter now; Kersey was dead. Drowned, with the Mex in the water next to him. Vail almost suggested investigating Kersey's death around the Mex, but Bogel wagged his head—and Vail accepted that as a no to his idea.

Mr. Bogel wanted to know how he and his men could help; Vail pointed out that, as deputy sheriff, he had jurisdiction throughout the county, but could not be leaving the town on every whim, after every small thief scourging the ranches. Perhaps Bogel would send him two men, he could talk with and send after the Mex. It would be a good use of Bogel's offer to assist, and would allow Vail to continue performing all his normal duties in the community.

He asked Bogel for two specific men, named them and didn't see Bogel's curious response. Two men, brawlers, hot-tempered, responsible for the fight during the gather.

Bogel had to admit to himself that in spite of these two and their reputation, he still, indeed, employed them. He knew what they were, and at times their reputation was useful to him.

Charley Hocker and Pomp Wooten had a clear bill from their boss. Ride out and look for strays, any kind of strays. Bring them back branded, or cut them out of the herd and slaughter them if they were too poor to travel.

Then he sent them to Sheriff Vail, to do whatever he told them. Pomp doubted Charley's interpretation of the orders from Vail, but Charley took on Vail's talk of the black-haired Mex and turned it to his own purposes.

TEXAS SPRINGS

That Mex needed to be culled out, like W. W. Bogel himself ordered. The son was already branded; he needed only a knife to his throat to finish the the job. Too poor to travel, or make it through the winter. Slaughter it, and skin it out, get a few pesos for the fresh hide.

Charley wanted that one. He hadn't yet put the face of the Mex where it belonged, for his riding the flying buckskin, running from Charley, turning loose the stolen broncs.

Charley was closing in on respectable in Marfa, and he didn't like a reputation as a thief. His habits might be suspect, but the Mex knew the truth: Charley Hocker was a horse thief.

But it didn't come to him till the gather was done. Hadn't bothered till his old buddy, Sergio, came looking for a handout. Caught in sheep killing last winter, spent time on the road gang with the Mex.

Sergio wouldn't have a say in the matter; Sergio was plucked clean by the buzzards, throat slit, pockets turned out and emptied. Charley had only the kid to deal with now, and W. W. Bogel's blessing, the law's backup. It was a pretty piece, and Charley was looking forward to his work. Bringing Pomp along was his insurance.

It didn't occur to Charley, or to Pomp, that Bogel could be talking only about the slaughter of cattle. Vail had winked at them, and had talked around the need to clean up the land, rid it of all the scavengers. Charley knew an order when he heard it. Nice and neat and clean.

Then Vail blindsided him, said he wanted the Mex brought in to justice, not left to rot in the hills. Legal, proper. Charley had to think on that one, and he even asked Pomp what he thought on the matter.

Pomp Wooten was a runt, short changed in his legs, bowed and stuck on small feet. He walked like a drunk bird, and he took to carrying a six-gun to cut out the remarks he heard in passing. Charley could speak out; Pomp was afraid of him, but the rest better beware.

The little man had made his mark—none of the ranch hands bothered baiting him. It weren't worth fighting the runt, or wrangling with Charley Hocker. No one knew where Hocker came from, but the two were friends, ready to stand for each other.

Charley had a plan to get the Mex, kind of. He wasn't counting on perfection, or acting in no hurry. Longer they took, more Bogel would appreciate the results. Never paid to hurry and get the job done quick, Charley knew that. More time spent looked like more effort and more risk, got the boss real serious about Charley's efforts. He'd seen tracks of ten, maybe fifteen head of cattle up to the Chisos. Bogel'd already given out the order: chase down any of the wild stuff. Same order McCraw would give, and Iberra'd be riding for him, working the tracks, looking for strays. Pomp and Charley would be there, waiting for the wild-eyed kid to ride in and get caught. Not a fancy plan, but it was most likely to work, sometime.

Gossip came out—it was Vail's daughter sweet on the 'breed, not the law, that drove Vail into Charley's pocket. Charley didn't care; he had free rein. Insurance for Charley; Vail's vindictive hate for Iberra. Pomp spoke out right then, bragged to Charley it didn't matter if the law took their word or not. No Mex would cut up Pomp Wooten like a slab of side meat and ride on.

Charley took in the boasts and grinned at Pomp's strutting. He'd taken measure of Iberra, knew he needed Pomp and some luck, and a stout rope, to drag the man into Vail's law. Pomp could do the talking; Charley would set and think out while they waited.

They set a camp for four days. A dry camp—no fire, no talk—which came close to killing Pomp. But it was the only way to fight Iberra. Charley sat and thought a lot, and knew for certain it was Iberra who turned loose all those valuable horses from the canyon.

He didn't tell Pomp; it would get the little man started. Pomp was a good hand to ride with, tough as he bragged, but he could talk the hide off a range bull. Charley closed his eyes, felt the sweat trickle down the back of his shirt. He had to rework his plan: Iberra could ride; they couldn't let him near a horse. Had to hamstring him, keep him in line.

Charley grinned to himself. He owed Iberra something. Throwing out the block of wood on the race course had won Charley a bundle. Bogel never knew, the sheriff didn't listen to his daughter, and Wilson bought the buckskin, saved McCraw's hide. Out of it, Charley owed a debt to the Mex rider. Hell, he'd kill him quick in payment. Hocker grinned under the shade of his hat. The reckoning was come due.

Manure. Some fresh, some days old. Signs of a number of cattle grazing the area. Right where McCraw said; the old man was dead on. Matt eased his body in the saddle, leaned down, and counted tracks. More than McCraw guessed. Enough to need at least two riders for the drive. Silvestre, and maybe McCraw himself would come out. Lured by the fun of bringing in wild cows. Maybe this would be enough to get McCraw back working, and thinking, like a cattleman.

Matt let the speckled gray blow out; the climb to the base of the window was fierce, even with the cool wind and a stop at a springs an hour back. The gray was more than willing to stand quiet, and Matt swung his feet loose, put his hands to the small of his back, and stretched into them. He'd be back at the ranch tonight, out again early morning.

Fifteen head easy, a good addition to McCraw's thinned herd. The broken-horned steer had finally drifted in, and three of the seven cows. All four horses joined the main herd, and McCraw had Matt round them up. So fifteen head would be a good addition.

His belly was cold where the shirt was tore; Matt poked his fingers in the hole. Damn. Then he thought of the girl—and it was all right for a time.

He heard the brush crack and turned to the sound, right hand at his gun, left hand reaching for the dropped reins. But he was too slow. The voice had a wildness in it that let

Matt know the speaker was crazy. He clamped his legs to the gray's sides in desperation, but a hand caught the bridle and yanked the gray to standing.

"No tricks, Iberra. We know them all. Seen you do what you goddamn please too often to suit. Set there. Pomp'll guide you to camp. We got a surprise for you, a real surprise."

Trouble all right. He looked at the hand gripped to the bridle. A pistol waved at his head. Pomp Wooten. A kick from a strong leg would connect with Wooten's head. The voice with the threat, hidden in the brush, the voice would be Charley Hocker.

Matt didn't like knowing his attackers.

He sagged, figuring the odds right now, waiting for where he could dive free and make a fight of it. A horse came up behind him, but he didn't turn and look. It was Hocker.

Wooten jerked on the gray's mouth until the horse reared. Matt braced himself and was almost out of the saddle when Hocker spoke up: "Go to it, Mex. Jump Pomp. I'll let you, even get as far as landing on Pomp. Roll some in the dirt. I'll watch, and I'll by God enjoy the fight. And then I'll blow your face off." Hocker was enjoying himself, listening to the power of his words.

Even Pomp looked back at him, angered maybe by the notion he'd lose the fight. Charley didn't care; the little man was grown used to insults. Iberra was what mattered.

"Well, you damned Mex 'breed, you going to climb all over Pomp and give us some entertainment? Or you too afraid to take on a little bitty like Pomp?"

The gray horse sidestepped—and a rifle barrel dug into Matt. He half turned in reflex, and Wooten grabbed a boot and shoved Matt out of the saddle. He hit ground and rolled. Instinct brought his arms up to cover his face from rock and cactus. A boot kicked him in the ribs; it had to be Wooten. Matt could see the bottom half of Charley Hocker mounted on a stripe-legged dun.

The cold barrel of the rifle wavered on him, drew a loose

line from head to knee, stopping a long time at his groin. Matt cringed inside, kept his face expressionless. It was a certain bullet if he fought.

"You tame easier than I thought, Iberra. Lying there like a leppy calf caught in the mud. Not much of a fighter, is you?"

Matt watched the flushed face; Hocker shifted in his saddle and looked away. But the rifle did not move from Matt's body. Hands twisted his hair and rolled him over. His arm was jerked behind him, a thong wrapped around it, tied to the other arm. He lay face buried in small rock, neck gouged by cactus thorns. To move would mean a bullet in his spine, a kick from Wooten's lady-sized boots. He would have to wait, and plan.

He was left tied by the neck to a mesquite bush. He tried twice to prod Wooten and tease Hocker, but neither man fell for the bait. Hocker finally came over, stood above Matt, then slammed the rifle butt along his jaw—and Matt shut up.

It was a cold, long, lonely night. They didn't cover him, or feed him, or let him up to relieve himself. They did off-saddle the gray and lead him down to water. It was the first time Matt envied a dumb animal its few comforts.

He must have slept, for the sky was lighter gray, streaks of the sun were close to the edge when he opened his eyes. Three horses were head down and sleeping; the two lumps rolled under blankets were still. Shadows on the grass below the high camp began to appear as the wild cattle come to graze.

Matt stretched his arms against the thongs, hoping a night's covering of dew would help. He felt the leather give some around his swollen hands. He drew up his knees in the effort and leaned forward, forgetting the noose, snug around his neck, until he began to choke.

He forced himself to stretch out, wait, relax. But the thongs were looser. A bit more and he could slide free, untie his legs, slip out of the noose, and land feetfirst on the sleeping men. He struggled, twisted, held in his breath, and the thongs eased. A rock at his knee clattered and fell into the cold fire. Matt counted five minutes, watched the sleeping forms, prayed to whatever was out there to give him this one chance. He counted another long minute and decided to try again.

"I was wondering how long it would take you getting free. Longer than I thought. I figured you for a fighting man, Iberra. Not a lazy 'breed who don't care what happens to him. Guessed you would give us a struggle, more fun that way. Too bad, Iberra. Too goddamn bad."

Hocker. And now Wooten stirring in his blankets, mumbling something and reaching out a soiled hand to grab a gun. Matt quit and lay back in disgust. He'd been close, but Hocker'd been playing with him. He spat out the dust in his mouth and felt the *tasajillo* spines poking his neck and shoulder. For now he would be quiet and listen.

The thick-necked man urinated close to Matt's face, laughing as he did. Matt closed his eyes, but the warm liquid splashed his forehead and coated his cheek with stinking dirt. Wooten didn't bother to make the short trip to where Matt lay helpless, but relieved himself close to his own bed. Like an old boar penned tight. Matt shuddered and turned his head when Hocker stepped over him and raked his fancy spurs across Matt's ribs. He bit down hard; he would not satisfy Hocker with even the smallest cry.

Wet trickled down his ribs; Hocker laughed. Then the man untied the noose and rolled Matt downhill, tugging and pulling until Matt was facedown in the ashes of the fire. He gagged violently, jackknifed himself with the effort, spewed up bile, and could get no air into his starving lungs.

Hocker fixed the struggle; he walked over and kicked Matt in the back, straightened him out. The next kick half rolled Matt out of the dust and ash; he lay on his side, drawing in gulps of air, coughing and drooling from the corners of his mouth.

Hocker's laugh and Pomp's whining brought Matt out of the daze. He could just understand the sounds, but the words made no sense, so he quit trying.

They had to kill him. He knew their names, who they were. Worked for Bogel, on the gather, at his ranch. So much for the respectable William Bogel. Matt flicked out his tongue, rolled up a bolus of ash and drool, and expelled it.

A cow bellowed in anger, then Hocker laughed too close to Matt's head; he jerked back from the noise. A familiar smell rose to Matt's nose, and he guessed Wooten had started breakfast. He had no sense of the time; Hocker's blows and the dryness in his mouth, the ache deep in his gut and side, forced his attention into a small world.

Hocker kicked him once more, then left him alone. Coffee boiled; Matt could gauge the sound, and a slab of meat sizzled and cooked. Hocker, or Wooten, rolled a smoke. A rifle barrel poked at him once, a voice asked a question Matt didn't answer.

He drifted in and out of consciousness, bloated and sore, crusted with dirt, smelling of waste. Deep in his mind, where even Hocker couldn't get, Matt waited out the time.

CHAPTER THIRTY-ONE

Late morning, Mr. McCraw rode in, and Orianna was excited when she saw his sorrel horse. Maybe Matt was with him, maybe Matt was to his off side, or several strides behind him, in the shadow of the leafless cottonwood. She waited long past the possible; then she stood up slowly and went back to the kitchen. Mrs. Kersey would offer her caller a refreshment. It might be well into fall, but the sun was still strong, and a glass of something cold was always appreciated.

She heard them talk in low voices and saw them when they walked out to the corrals. Mr. McCraw offered his arm to Mrs. Kersey. They were not fooling Orianna with their behavior. She and Matt talked of Mr. McCraw's intentions toward the new widow. Matt grinned, and said he would have a new lady boss before winter; Orianna knew better and said not until the spring. Mrs. Kersey was a lady, and now twice a widow. They would wait most of the proper time. Then Matt hugged her—and she forgot all about Mrs. Kersey and her new man.

She didn't hear Mrs. Kersey come back in the house; she was thinking of Matt, of how much she missed him. The woman's hand on her shoulder startled Orianna, and she jumped slightly.

"Daydreaming about your handsome cowboy, child? Mr. McCraw said he rode out this morning to check on some cattle, but that he would be back in a few days. We must be careful, about your young man. I know your father has taken a dislike to him, but time can change any man, especially where his daughter is concerned. And I can talk to your father about Matt; he is a good boy.

"Orianna, dear. I want to talk of something with you. Please, sit here and let me explain."

She already knew, she had guessed from the shine in Mrs. Kersey's eyes and the energy in her step. And it was wonderful that Mrs. Kersey would be with the man she loved this time. She folded her hands in her lap and sat quietly to listen.

"I see from your face that you already know. But yes, Mr. McCraw asked me to marry him. We will wait a suitable time, of course. At least until the spring. But he asked and I agreed most readily."

The women sat with their separate thoughts. Harriet Kersey planned out how to tell her sister and her husband, for Mr. Dutchover would assume he was in control of her estate again. And there was money involved this time. They would not approve of Mr. McCraw, and they would want her ranch and the number of cattle, the good herd of horses.

Dutchover's face would light up with greed. She would have to be firm when she spoke with them.

There was more to consider. Talk was spreading in town of a grand celebration to take place on the upcoming New Year's Day. A celebration such as the civilized towns back East would have. To bring in the New Year, a year offering growth for Marfa. A handsome new town hall, a jail; marks of Marfa's entrance into the coming times. There was talk of putting in electricity, or gas, through the town, and a new school was opening. Three churches had been built, with ministers and congregations. She had told Mr. McCraw she planned to attend the celebration and hoped he would escort her.

There had been a sadness in his face as they talked of the upcoming event. And Mrs. Kersey believed she understood his pain, could guess at its source. To have lived here all his life, to see his old friends and enemies die out, move out. To be forced to live by other rules where he had lived governed only by raw instinct. But the world changed, and even the barren *Despoblado* changed, shifted—drew in new life and buried the old.

James Henry had told her of the old name, for this piece of the country and the beginning of man's attempt to settle here, to tame this harsh land. There was a wistful tone to his telling, and a stubborn refusal to give up completely on the past. She accepted his memories, allowed him his dead comrades. He was one of the lucky ones, a survivor.

There was much to consider. And much to be done: papers and letters of Mr. Kersey's to be read and burned; the lawyer still to question; the possibility of other claims on the estate to be deflected. She held property now, and was alone. That would attract a certain number of proposals, which she must gently, gracefully, decline.

It was good that Orianna stayed with her. Two women were not as vulnerable. And the girl was strong and capable, quite willing to pick up a weapon and discharge it if necessary. With Matt riding over to pay his court, there was activity and purpose in the ranch.

Her mind whirled through the adjustments in her future. There was so much to be done. Orianna spoke up quietly, and Harriet at first did not hear her.

"Mrs. Kersey, please. I am pregnant."

After the marriage, when she had moved to the McCraw ranch, Orianna must come with her. Mr. McCraw said he would build her a private room. She was more than a companion or house girl, she was Harriet's unborn child, the daughter Harriet never conceived in her two marriage beds.

"Mrs. Kersey . . . I am carrying Matt's child."

The ropes dug into puffed flesh. Matt let his legs swing out of the stirrups, rested his hands on the saddle swell. His back ached, his ribs were sore. Hocker and Wooten had dragged him to the gray horse. Waited and laughed while he tried to mount, hands tied in front of him. One of them pushed as he hooked an arm over the horn, and then he was on the horse. He didn't know where they were headed, but he knew he wouldn't have to think much on it.

They left the wild cattle behind them, scattered near the base of the window. It was late morning, Matt knew that. Wooten had slowed them with roasting a loin steak over the fire. Matt was hungry then, and Hocker enjoyed chewing the tender meat close to Matt's face, letting the grease run off his chin, leering at Matt.

Now he was glad they hadn't fed him; the meat would have turned and come back. His hat was lost, and the late fall sun baked his brains. He would swear to ghosts and big pools of water if anyone cared to ask. Hocker rode ahead of him, holding the reins to Matt's gray. Wooten rode alongside his partner—the two were going at it, yelling, waving hands, once even pulling out their pistols. The sounds of the voices came to Matt through the cotton filling his head.

He tilted sideways and slid off the sluggish gray. The horse leaped forward and knocked Hocker's thin roan to its knees. Matt saw churning hooves, heard more than felt his body slap the ground, then he rolled over rock. It meant nothing. He licked his lips, turned away to spit. His mouth was too dry. He saw black leather close to his face. He sighed; the toes were lifted. He tried to protect his face, raise his arm, and couldn't move. The toe came forward and touched him, and he felt nothing. The boot slammed his head, rolled it on the rock, and it didn't hurt at all. He sighed again and closed his eyes; helpless, lying on top of his hands. Bound tight. But it didn't matter much at all.

He didn't take in what went on overhead, the words were meaningless: "This dumb son of a bitch is trying to escape, Charley. How's he going to do that, wrapped up like a tom turkey? He ain't too bright, Charley."

"Shut up, you dumb— He ain't trying to escape. Look at him. He ain't fit for rassling your sister. Look at him, you stupid—"

Charley Hocker felt little as he rolled the limp man over with his boot toe. The 'breed made no noise as he flopped around, but Charley heard a noise to the side as the swollen hands were exposed; Pomp had some feeling in him, after all. The skin had broken around the wrists and dark blood ran freely, soaking Iberra's shirt and trickling down his ribs to soak into the dirt.

The blood meant nothing to Charley; the son could bleed to death for all he cared. But he wanted to bring Iberra in. He wanted to hand the man over to Sheriff Vail in public; he needed to keep the man alive for that.

"Loosen him some, Pomp. Don't want the dog dying and rotting on us 'fore we get him to town. No fun in leaving a corpse. Even one as pretty as this. Guess the sheriff's gal thinks this walking dead man as pretty a thing she's ever seen. 'Course, if I were gimped like her, I'd think whatever looked at me twice was real pretty."

Charley looked down, wanting a reaction to his taunt. There was sudden life in the 'breed's good eye and a bulge of muscle down his bound arms. Charley bet to himself the eye crossed with that goddamn scar was on fire. He kicked Iberra hard in the ribs, to remind him who was boss.

"Hurry, Pomp. We want to hit town before nightfall.

Want the good folk of Marfa to see what Bogel's best riders can do. Yessir."

Wooten went as far as to offer Matt a sip of stale water from his own canteen. The water tasted good; it eased his throat and brought his heart back to normal pounding. Wooten untied the numbed hands, even tore the edge of Matt's shirt and wrapped the wrists before tying them again. The bandage turned a sullen red—and the cotton did little to cushion the raw flesh—but the leather wasn't drawn as tight, and shifted easily on the rolled cloth.

It took the two of them to shove him back on the reluctant gray. Matt hung his head, swayed in the saddle. Wooten surprised Matt by offering a swallow more of the water before they started traveling. He took the drink and gulped at it greedily, until Hocker called out, and Pomp threw the canteen uncorked out into the waiting desert.

It all made no sense to Matt; Hocker's care for him, hauling him in alive when dead was easier. Buried under piled rock in a lost draw, chewed and destroyed by scavengers up in the basin. It didn't make sense at all, the extra work of roping and tying him, guarding and keeping him alive.

But there was a real pleasure in Hocker's grin that soured Matt's stomach. It would figure out as soon as they got to Marfa.

CHAPTER THIRTY-TWO

Vail checked his pocket watch for the third time. Nearly three o'clock. He wondered if this was the day Hocker would bring him in.

Orianna was here, with Mrs. Kersey. They went straight to the lawyer's office without stopping to see Orianna's father or mother. Vail didn't like it, being ignored by his own child. He didn't like it that she was in town with the new widow. He didn't want Hocker to bring the Mex in today. He didn't want anything to change. He didn't want Orianna to not speak to him. He didn't understand.

She had changed, been changed by the Mex 'breed. He knew that much. In his innocence, he had assumed that the Kerseys would understand the situation and refuse the 'breed a chance to speak with Orianna. As he had assumed McCraw would ride the Mex off his ranch.

Both parties had abused Vail's pride, and his family. Kersey was dead; soon enough McCraw would be missing his prize hand. And the scarred son of a bitch was on a trail all his own. However Wooten and Hocker brought the 'breed in, it would not be pretty, or kind. Might even damage the bastard some. He would fight the two men—and they would break him in two. It might be better if Wooten and Hocker brought in a body, so the death could not be blamed on Vail. But that was too easy, too simple for the revenge Vail needed. The 'breed dead, McCraw hurt by that death. Simple, sweet, clean. A necessary act of revenge.

Vail checked his watch again. Good, it was close to suppertime. Close to the Kersey woman's leaving, taking

Orianna with her. Hocker and Wooten weren't coming this day. He was safe, for the moment.

Dust showed at the end of the short side street. Three horses, by Vail's estimate. He stepped down the two wide steps, conscious of the ring of his boots on hard wood. It was Hocker, it had to be Hocker. Three horses, two in front, a third horse barely seen, led by one of the men.

His right hand slid down to find the cool grip of his new Smith & Wesson. His fingers hefted the unfamiliar pistol, freed it from the holster, raised it, and let it drop back in. He doubted he would need the pistol; Charley Hocker could be counted on to slap the prisoner around enough the man would be no threat. All the same, Vail wasn't going to count on Hocker.

He could see the man, loose in the saddle, hands tied in front of him. Blood was dried on his face, along his chin, even across his back and side. If Orianna saw her Mex now, she would never forgive her father, never understand his concern for her. Women were fools when it came to wounded things. They didn't see past the pity; they felt only the purity of their own emotions and did not suspect the beastlike nature of a man's hidden lust.

Vail shook himself and stepped forward to Hocker's house. The man sat there, immobile, unknowing. Vail looked to the stupid face of Pomp Wooten, then briefly at the prisoner. The Mex raised his head and stared right at Vail, as if he knew the heart of his executioner. Vail nodded his recognition and turned back to Hocker. The pleasant chore of judging and hanging the Mex had to wait out its legal completion.

Spread across the neck of Hocker's tired horse was the evidence. A hide skinned out, the brand crudely blotted. The McCraw brand laid over Mr. Bogel's mark, as if done by an amateur. Perfect; Hocker was delivering the Mex.

A door opened behind Vail, and the halting footsteps told him who it was; he would not turn around. He would not allow Orianna to interrupt. She was not ready to know what he was doing for her. Only for her. He stretched out his hand to take Hocker's evidence. The hide would have to convince her, would force her to accept her father's judgment of the young outlaw.

Hocker raised the hide, licked his lips, held the stinking leather for everyone to see before he dropped it into Vail's arms. The hide briefly covered both Wooten's face and the body of the prisoner.

When Vail could see, he knew that the Mex had shifted in his saddle. The bound hands were freed, the man was lifting a leg over the front of the saddle, sliding off the tired horse.

The hide fell from Vail's arms. He grabbed at it, cursed it as it dirtied his boots. Iberra had both legs on the off side of his horse, the gray's head was raised. The prisoner was smiling. Vail hated the man more than he had ever hated anyone.

The loosened gun felt natural in his hand. Smooth action, easy draw. A fine weapon. Before he knew it, he had pulled back on the trigger and fired. Iberra was lifted by the bullet, pinned to his horse for a long moment. His eyes were shuttered, his mouth wide; his shirt was bright red with a small stain near his heart.

The sound echoed. The gray gelding screamed and went down on both front knees. Iberra was sprawled against the horse, head back, hands open, legs bent at odd angles. More blood covered the gray coat of the horse, and the animal turned and snapped at the color dampening its side. Iberra was motionless, pinned against the dying horse.

His daughter was near him; Vail reached out to explain to her, but she did not see him. She ran in her halting manner toward the screaming horse, and Vail could not move to help her.

He had done his job; now the legal system, and the town of Marfa, would have to clean up after him. There would be no more trash in his town. He picked up the blotted hide, examined both sides carefully, and then saw that he held a pistol in his right hand. The gun was warm, and it was difficult to turn the hide over when one hand was closed on the ivory grip. He slid the gun back in its holster, and it made no noise. There was the sound of crying behind him, but it meant nothing.

Hocker was there, with Wooten. Away from the crowd that had quickly grown around the wounded horse and the stilled rider. Vail didn't worry about the crowd. He wanted to return to his office and tend to other pressing business. He motioned for Hocker and Wooten to follow him and walked toward the door, confident they would obey.

A man approached Orianna and wanted to know what to do with the bleeding horse. She looked at the gray. Its sides were coated with blood, its eyes dulled, its leg muscles trembling. One of Mr. McCraw's good horses, one she had seen Matt ride to Mrs. Kersey's. How would she explain its death to him? How would she make the decision to have the cowboy lead the horse away and shoot it?

The hole was terrible: ragged and pink, the gray hide torn from the white ribs beneath. A hole big enough to put a fist through. Orianna bit down hard. That bullet had gone through Matt. She could not cry yet. So she thanked the cowboy for his concern and said yes, would he please take the horse as far off as he could and shoot it. Put it out of its misery.

Townspeople knelt beside Matt. One of the men looked up when she came near and nudged the other until he, too, rose and gave her room. Kneeling was difficult for her, and one of the faceless men offered his arm.

Matt was dead. There was no question. And her father had killed him. With a well-placed bullet from his new gun. As he had bragged—one bullet would bring down any man he chose. A brag that made her mother wince from its intended cruelty. A brag that was true.

There was little blood on the front of the shirt. The bullet had made a hole above the pocket. An embroidered pocket, one of the shirts she had refashioned from Mr. Kersey's cast-off linen. The hole did not mar the fine needlework, and the little bit of blood had not spread enough to be more than a token stain. But he was dead, there was no question.

What was a dark outline under Matt widened and grew: his blood, leaking out of his back. Out of the gaping hole she knew was there. The bullet fired at close range had gone through him and wounded and killed a good horse. The outline grew; Orianna put a finger to its surface, and the tension broke—the redness covered her hand; the liquid was soaked quickly into the dry earth. She put her bloodied hand to Matt's face and drew the line of his scar. The intimate line he had allowed to her when they lay close together.

She dipped her fingers in his blood and cupped it in the palm of her hand. It spread between her fingers and splashed on the white skull. No one stopped her, but a man turned his head aside and gagged violently. Orianna heard nothing, saw nothing but Matt's face in front of her. She rubbed his cheeks with her stained hands, trying to put color in his pale skin. Then she reached forward and lifted his head, pressed her mouth to his, and tasted what she had barely known, taking what she would not have again.

A hand pressed down on her; she looked around wildly and saw the blanched features of her mother. She would look like her mother now. Thin, tired, deeply in pain. It was mirrored in the face of her mother. Orianna accepted without conscious thought the help of one of the many men around her and stood up. Someone asked what to do with the body; someone else told him to shut his mouth and let the ladies go on.

She knew what was to be done, and she told the cowboy who asked. They were to take Matt to the new church; they were to make certain he was in clean clothes but were to leave his boots and find him a good hat. A new one. Then one of them was to hire a wagon and a good team and drive Matt out to Mr. McCraw's.

When she was done talking, she leaned on her mother and the crying started. Her mother was straight and solid and allowed her daughter to rest all her weight on her shoulder. There were no words exchanged between them. Orianna and her mother walked to the well-lit house and took their time climbing the front steps. The door opened with an unseen hand; Orianna went in ahead of her mother.

CHAPTER THIRTY-THREE

He didn't know the wagon and team, or the two men huddled on the narrow seat. The horses walked slowly, the men didn't raise a hand in greeting. McCraw put down the bronc saddle he was about to throw over the back of the skinned App and jerked on the rope to free the horse. The wagon sounds were clear now—the wheels creaked, the old harness jingled; the steady beat of the team's walk.

He found he wasn't breathing at all. His lungs cramped on him, and he tried to pull in air. None of the familiar ranch noises reached his mind, only the plodding hooves and the screaming of a dried wheel. He barely glanced at the two men. Cowhands from their dress. No one he knew. Yet they had a fixed purpose in driving through his gate.

A mound was laid out in the wagon bed, a long narrow shape defined under a gray canvas. There was an old Mex-style saddle jammed in a corner, up close to the seat, and a new hat hung off the broad horn. McCraw walked to intersect the wagon's path, knowing immediately, irrevocably, what had been brought to him.

The team passed by him, and he waited. The men nodded once each, faces frozen and pale. The driver hauled on the lines; the team stopped with McCraw between the small front wheel and the squeaking rear wheel. He was quick to reach out and draw back the gray cloth. He saw nothing but

TEXAS SPRINGS 333

the waxed face of the kid. The beating of his own heart engulfed him, the pain grew hard in his chest.

He was careful to fold the cloth away from the head, to tuck under the ends so they did not fall back and hide the features. Someone had troubled to wash the face, but there was still blood in the scar and bruises that showed through the wiped surface. The collar of the shirt was freshly white, even ironed, but did not fit the lax neck. The coat was wrong, loose across the chest, folded and pinned at the sides.

Ready for a burial. He rolled back the cloth. They were Matt's boots, but the rest of his clothing was town-bought. Didn't belong to the kid, didn't fit the drawn face and scarred hands. Have to do something about that before he was buried, have to put the kid in what suited him. Kid would want it that way. Hard leather vaquero pants, a muslin shirt. The old vest if he could find it.

The driver of the team cleared his throat, and McCraw stared at him. A thin face, wide mustache, shaded eyes, hands running nervous on the lines. The face of a man he had seen before. The other one was studying the wide backs of the resting horses. The driver acted as if he wanted to speak a piece. McCraw allowed him to try.

"Mr. McCraw, sir. The girl sent us here. Said you would be the one to bury him. Miss Vail, she told us to tell you."

The man fumbled with his words before he looked at McCraw and thought that the rancher didn't hear him anyway. He tried again.

"Where you want us to leave him? We got to put him someplace; we can't sit here forever."

Practical, reasonable. But McCraw didn't care. The anger came through him suddenly—and he caught the gray cloth in his two hands, dug holes in the hard weave.

"Who killed him? And why? The son of a bitch— He answers to me. You, goddammit. Tell me. Stop fiddling with the lines and tell me."

The driver shifted on the seat, took the lines in one hand, and let his other hand drop out of sight. Going for his gun.

That didn't slow McCraw; no puncher with a twitch in his face and a shaking hand would stop him.

It was the second man who spoke up, quiet and slow but refusing to allow McCraw's temper to get them all in trouble. There was respect in the man's voice, and a deep sorrow.

"Sir, Mr. McCraw . . . What Parson here told you is part of the truth. That Miss Vail sent us, said she knew you'd want to bury the kid. Her pap was the one shot him down. Don't know why, rightly. But the sheriff pulled out a handgun and got the kid dead center. On Main Street. Whole town saw it." The man held out his hand, "Ain't none of us know why, McCraw. Just repeating what was done. The kid there, he rode in with Pomp Wooten and Charley Hocker. Some says he was bound to the saddle, Parson here saw him fiddle loose and swing down. Was coming off his horse to see the girl. Vail's girl.

"That's 'bout all we know. Rode with the kid to the big gather. Good hand. I'da rode with him anytime. Sorry 'bout him, Mr. McCraw. Real sorry."

The words were spoken in a low, reverent voice. The speaker was a cowhand called Landers Black. McCraw's face told Black of the hurricane inside. But he was willing to gamble—to let the words sift through McCraw's righteous fury and come out clean.

But he wasn't that much of a gambler. Black let his own hand touch the rifle laid across his ankles and knew that the unnerved driver already had his pistol free of its holster. McCraw's face stayed on them; the eyes sparked, the face paled. The mouth began to work up a frenzy. Black leaned forward to catch up his weapon.

"Don't, mister. You're too late, too damned late. Bet you stood there in town and was too damned late. Watched the whole killing and never moved. Stick to the law, damn you. Stick to your own kind and damn the kid.

"Had to have it all, don't you? Can't let a maverick move without putting a brand to him. Well, you think on it.

He was already branded. You could have left this one alone . . ."

Landers Black heard the man speak and even tried to follow the sense of his words. But he was more worried watching the hand pointing a six-gun at his chest. Beside him, Parson had his hand wrapped around his Colt, with his elbow stuck in Landers's side.

The men held their positions, two of them hoping there would be a reason to stop the next murder.

Violence tore McCraw, like no feelings he'd suffered before. Rolling, whirling fury inside his head, pounding his heart, slamming his lungs against unmoving ribs. The tightness of his hand gripped on the smooth butt of the pistol was the only reality for him. He saw the two faces before him with a numbing clarity; they were the killers.

He urged the pressure that drew back the hammer, heard the loud click. His belly felt the rightness of it. There would be two shots, no more.

McCraw jumped when the band tightened on his wrist. The gun turned, his fist jerked, and the gunfire rocked him. He fought to control the weapon and hit out at the intruder. He did not see the two men in the wagon duck under the seat, praying that the one-inch board would save their heads.

McCraw's head came up, and the eyes that met his stopped the fury. Green eyes, set wide in a fine porcelain face webbed with fear. Harriet Kersey, her hand outstretched, the palm held to him lined with dirt. Harriet Kersey looked straight into him, and the tears ran down her face as she tried again to speak to him. McCraw was deaf from the shot, but she stood in front of him and would not let him go.

"James, they did not kill Matt. Orianna said that you would be needing me. But she is the one who is grieving. We must help Orianna. We must."

The words were stilted and foreign to McCraw, but he believed he knew what she spoke. She talked of the girl, and McCraw saw the young face, the awkward gait. A slender hand rested in Matt's grimy fist. His own hand began to shake; he drew hard on himself to hide what was certain to pull him apart.

The pistol dropped from his fist. McCraw searched out the driver and the passenger in the grim wagon. Both men stared back. The talky one had a deep sadness in his face that almost lost to McCraw what he could save of his dignity.

Then the talky one got going again, and this time McCraw listened.

"Where you want us to put the body? We can help with the burying. I know it's personal with you, sir, but I knew Iberra at the gather, we both— Ah, hell. We got to do something."

The burial was plain. The girl came by horseback, her eyes red-rimmed and swollen, her skin ashen gray. But there were no tears, not from Orianna Vail or Mrs. Kersey. McCraw had paced through the night, to be held by the strong hands of Harriet Kersey, washed by her kindness, and finally comforted for the time by her warm flesh. It was more than McCraw had known for years, and he came close to losing the focus of his grief in the pleasure of her touch.

He carried a guilt to Matt's grave, but Mrs. Kersey showed no signs as she walked beside him, hand in his, her other arm around the girl. As if they were a family, finding one another, mourning a close member of their clan.

Landers Black stayed with the burial party, the other man drove the wagon and team to Marfa. Belonged to the sheriff, he said, borrowed and needing to be returned. No one paid attention; they were formed in a small group. Silvestre planned and shaped a coffin, hammered in each nail with a measured blow until Harriet and the girl thought they would cry again. The sound carried as if there were no other in the world.

They went back as a group to the rock house and drank

lemon-flavored water, ate sparingly of flat bread and split beans. There was nothing to say. They knew little of Matt's life, and McCraw had not spoken any words over the grave.

Finally Orianna cried, deep sobs that broke McCraw's heart. Harriet held the girl, and McCraw went outside with Silvestre. He couldn't bear the sounds inside. Grieving was in a woman's nature, a luxury a man was not allowed. He would grieve for Matt in private.

Orianna came out by herself and asked for her horse. She had to ride back to her parents, to her rigid mother, and the father who killed Matt. Harriet came out to stand with McCraw and watch the girl ride out alone. No one would bother the child on her ride to town, not a man in the county would dare touch her now.

Harriet was left at Bitter Springs with McCraw and Silvestre. The Mexican stayed in the barn and carved shapeless sticks, or mended aged bridles and useless saddles.

James was silent, as he had been since the burying. He would not look at her or talk to her. He cocked his head at her when she spoke, heard her out, but said nothing in answer. She tried to bully him, even threatened him with leaving, and he had gone for her horse.

There was no way she could reach him, and she feared for what she knew was in his mind. Revenge, pure murder. The murder of Robert Vail. She tried to talk to him about justice, about new laws and new times and the inevitable reckoning Vail would face.

But she did not compete with the old code McCraw lived. The death of Matt Iberra could not go unavenged. The second night, James sat outside past dark, and Harriet went out twice to call him in. She and Silvestre ate a solemn meal, and when she had cleaned up, she went back to the door and called to James. As she expected, he did not answer. So she went to him, felt her way in the black night until she could hear his sounds and know where he was. She sat down near him, close enough to see the silver puffs of cold air he breathed, but not close enough to touch him. Or have him touch her.

"I saw another rider today. He wanted to tell me about what was going on in Marfa. It isn't good. James, you can't go in."

He looked sideways at her; she could tell by the puffs of air and the whispered brush of his canvas jumper. "My business, Harriet. Matt worked for me." His voice was flat, and she recognized his need to stay calm.

"James, I came out here from Albany, in New York State. I had never been in a place where it was necessary to make so many decisions. With little or no law to back you up. I was afraid, but I began to meet some of the families, and to believe that most of them were kind, and willing to work hard for what they want.

"I know you have no use for Sheriff Vail. So perhaps you might talk to Sheriff Nevill. Vail really is a deputy, you know, and doesn't have the power to make a lot of the decisions that the town lets him. Perhaps Nevill can look into the situation, and maybe take Vail's office from him. If he's not in Fort Davis, I hear he is usually at his ranch. It isn't a long ride . . ."

She was babbling and she knew it, but she wanted desperately to do something to ease the pain in him. But he would not allow her, except to hold her in the night and take a measure of comfort from her body.

"He killed Matt. Real plain. Shot him in front of the whole town. No one stopped him. That's wrong."

"Yes, it is truly, horribly wrong. But it will be taken care of properly, so there is no charge on you. Vail will be formally charged, by his own law. But it has yet to be done. You could be the one to ride and see Sheriff Nevill, you could be the one—"

"Vail killed Matt. Vail's dead. No warrant, no arrest. Nevill appointed him, and will back him. There'll be no justice for Matt unless I take it."

"Matt is dead, James. Your killing will in turn kill you,

and that is not justice, that is foolish. If nothing else, think of me."

"Mrs. Kersey, damn you. I think of you too often, too much. Needed to have taken care of Vail yesterday, but I was here, listening for you, waiting for you. It ain't right, but it's what I done."

She was stunned by the curse and the mildness of his tone. As if he barely acknowledged what she said. She could not help the warmth she felt from his declaration, even if it came coupled to a terrible curse. She sat next to her James and let the darkness come around them, cover them, ease their sorrow.

His voice was low, broken, halting. But she began to understand what it was he faced: "Mrs. Kersey, I 'pologize for the swearing. I . . . ah— It's not your kind of world here. Not mine, not now. Changed. Time's gone when each man was responsible for himself. Matt worked for me. More, he was . . . a friend. I owe him."

Harried found his hand and squeezed it until he squeezed in return. There was little more to say. She had to accept him and his way.

McCraw slipped out of the house an hour before the dawn. He was extra careful in his leaving, not wishing to wake the woman in his bed. It was difficult to accept her tenderness; it warred with the stilled rage inside him. Her hand on his belly, her breath against his neck, her washed hair tangled about him. They got in the way of what must be settled now.

He would saddle the blond sorrel gelding, hang the gun and holster from the horn, pack a belt with shells, jam the rifle hard in its scabbard. He would ride the sorrel into Marfa, reaching the town midmorning. He would ride the main street, tie the sorrel in front of the law's mean office, and wait. There would be no hiding his intent, no skittering behind words or statues of the new governing. Vail had shot and killed Matt Iberra without cause, and it was for McCraw to right the wrong.

In the two days since the burying, three riders had drifted past McCraw's place—stopped to water their horses and offer their condolences. One of the faceless men had his version of the events in town—that Vail was being called on his act, that the townfolks weren't pleased with the useless evidence. Pomp Wooten got drunk and talked; Charley Hocker rode out of town and disappeared. Vail was setting nervous in his new jail.

None of it mattered other than to refuel his need. The core to it was his knowing Matt, riding with him, hauling him out of trouble. There was a wildness in the kid, but there was no stealing left. McCraw knew that as certain as he knew the love from Harriet Kersey. The town of Marfa might well be angry with their law and working up to questioning him, but there were chores a man took care of on his own. And this was one of them.

He couldn't afford to look back too close—to Harriet Kersey's promised love and the new grave studded with sharp rock and crowned with a wooden cross. McCraw was between the two, bound by a knowing as old as his life in the *Despoblado*. There was no choice for him.

He stepped up on the sorrel. The horse was cold-backed in the predawn chill, and McCraw let him buck. Then he touched the red sides with his spurs; the sorrel bellowed and lined out of the ranch yard at a sideways run.

Horse and rider were watched by two pairs of sleep-filled eyes. Silvestre, come from his burrow in the hay, offered a prayer for the señor's blessed safety—then curled back into himself and went to sleep.

Harriet Kersey was inside the door, straining her swollen eyes to see the black shapes in the yard. The tears caught in her throat would flow out and scald her when he was gone. She dug her fingers into the rough adobe. Splinters from the wooden doorframe pricked her skin, mud and straw baked in the sun scratched her palms. She stood there, watching, long after the sound of the brittle hooves faded, leaving only silence behind.

CHAPTER THIRTY-FOUR

He sat and watched the horse and rider come down the street. A side benefit of living above the office. His own rocker on the walkway, a straw hat and his coat hung over the back of his office chair. Voeckes pushed the rocker back, planted his feet, one above the other, on the post holding the ocotillo roof. He didn't want the horseman coming past him to think he was worrying.

He enjoyed sitting in the shade and watching the town pass by his door. Enough of the folks came in for business that he was able to survive. But the sweetness of the town died suddenly, day before yesterday, in one act that had no place in Marfa.

McCraw's big horse slowed, perhaps of its own accord, and McCraw glanced around as if he didn't know quite where he was. Voeckes rocked forward, let his feet hit the planked walk hard. The horse started, McCraw looked right at the lawyer. Even deep in the shadows, Voeckes could determine the depth of tension in his friend. He wished to speak up, say what would help. But McCraw did not acknowledge Voeckes or the creaking rocker. The man angled his horse toward the new jail as if he had never noticed the lawyer.

"McCraw. McCraw!" Voeckes raised his voice, but the man refused to hear him. So Voeckes stepped off the walkway and trailed behind the sorrel. "McCraw. This is wrong. You know it. Word has gone to Nevill. He'll take care of Vail. McCraw!"

The stubborn, mule-headed son of a— Even silently

mouthing the string of curses felt funny to Voeckes. It couldn't wait much longer. "McCraw, he's not at the jail. Town ain't finished the building yet, and Vail hasn't been there for several days." He didn't specify how many, as if to avoid opening a closed wound.

"McCraw, hear me. Vail isn't to the jail." Voeckes heard his own slurred words and knew he was strained. He may well have gone to a college and studied his books, but when he was pushed, the Indiana farm boy returned. "McCraw, dammit, man! Vail is at his house. Waiting for you." That got McCraw's attention; he stopped the horse and slowly came around in the saddle. Voeckes hurried to catch up.

"Whole town knows you're here, James. Whole town knows why you come in. Makes it tough. You kill Vail now and you'll divide the whole county, dammit. You understand me?"

"Voeckes, I thank you. But I ain't accounted for the county. You folks got to deal for yourself. I'm taking care of my own."

He had the sorrel resume a slow, cadenced walk, and it was easy for Voeckes to keep up with him. A few faces stared out windows, a lady and a child stopped and stared. The child asked a question in a high, whining voice, and the mother answered, yet neither Voeckes or McCraw heard what was said. McCraw and the sorrel walked steadily toward the new white frame house, and Wilson Voeckes hurried along on foot.

"Mr. Vail, there are some men here to see you. I have let them into the parlor, and they are waiting."

Eleanor Vail allowed only her head to show in the kitchen; her hands nervously twined with each other, and she wished she could return to the upstairs and lie down. But there was work still to be done. She observed the displeasure in her husband's face—and was quite suddenly pleased with his obvious distress.

"Mr. Vail, did you hear me?"

TEXAS SPRINGS 343

Robert Vail took note of his wife's bland announcement and did not care for the cheer with which she delivered it. For once, she did not care if a group of men dirtied her carpet, or if her husband wished to see them. She presented him the message, waited briefly, and then was gone.

Well. Vail rubbed a spotted hand over his head. Too much was spinning through the quiet town of Marfa for him to worry about a woman's prim disapproval. He needed to worry about more important matters.

It would be Humphris, of course. And Jordon, who opened a fancy new hotel in keeping with the finished town hall. C. M. Jennings from the newspaper, the *New Era*, taking notes and busying himself with preparing text. Possibly the lawyer, Voeckes, would be included. Even though he was known to be a friend of McCraw's. And the mayor of Marfa, Benjamin Kask. Quite a delegation to speak with Sheriff Vail, quite a collection to tell him how to run his town.

Vail was slow to stand up from the hard-caned chair. His back was stiff, his shoulders ached interminably. It had become a long two days since he shot the Mex.

That galled him—a rustler and a thief, a black-haired mongrel—yet words were spreading in town, anger at the law, dislike of his actions, talk of going directly to Sheriff Nevill. As if there had been a worth to the 'breed; Mex went out of his way to get into trouble, and he'd run out of rope. Nothing but the end of a double-dealing border whelp. It was past Robert Vail to negotiate. He was right, the 'breed was dead. And that was all.

Vail sighed; it was best he go talk to the men in the front room. They'd have questions and concerns, then they would have to listen to him while he spoke his piece. And they'd all go home, finally satisfied their town law had done the right thing.

Hocker and Wooten brought in the evidence, right there in hand when they delivered the Mex. Couldn't this town see what was in front of their eyes, or were they too civilized to know how to read? Proof right in front of them—a blotted brand, the torn hide. Hocker's statement, Wooten's backup.

He had been surprised by the town's uproar. They must have forgotten Iberra and his sheep killing, time on the road gang, the thrown horse race. That, too, had been Iberra's fault. Had they dismissed all that so easily? And why would anyone care? He did not see what was wrong with his actions. He had spent the past two days mulling over Iberra's death and came always to the same conclusion.

The muted voices in the front parlor grew louder. He'd go to them now, planting each foot hard on the waxed floor, letting the ring of his boots, the authority of his walk, wake them up and set them straight. It was their sheriff, duly elected and appointed, that was coming out to answer their insulting questions. They had better listen when he spoke, as this was the last time for discussion. He would be returning to his work, and they could return to theirs.

Her mother found her upstairs in the room she once shared with two of her sisters. Orianna had pulled out an old valise with a few dresses folded and stored in it. She laid the dresses carefully over the back of a chair, and, once in a while, looked at them while she gathered up her belongings and packed them.

The dresses had belonged to her mother. Soft lace at the throat, a wrinkled flower pinned at a waist, a long sleeve cuffed and turned many times. Years of washing marked the patterns, faded the prettiness, but Orianna could guess at the pleasure taken in them when they were new and wondered about the bitterness in her mother now.

She was holding the rose-and-pale blue stripe to her body when her mother opened the door and entered without asking. Orianna held the dress close to her for protection and stared at her mother. There was no lingering softness in the woman, only a dry mouth, wrinkled eyes, and hands wiping nervously in front of her.

"Your father has company. Then I will tell him, after they leave. We are leaving, too, the girls and I, and you.

They are packed, and I have been packed for some time." One of the hands separated from its mate and went to her mother's throat. The long fingers touched the loose skin over and over, as if searching for an old memory. "I had forgotten about those dresses. Throw them out. We must take only what is necessary."

Orianna did not ask questions, and her mother did not expect to explain. It was decided, and the girls would do as they were told. Orianna put down the striped dress and folded it carefully, avoided looking at her mother directly. "Mama, I am not going with you. I am going back to live with Mrs. Kersey, and Mr. McCraw. Mrs. Kersey has asked for me; that is my home now."

She found herself speaking as formally as her parent, matching the disinterested tone, the blank face. Her mother walked to the still-open door and only then looked at her child. "Why do you chose to live with that woman? She is not family. I am your mother, these are your sisters."

As if those reasons were enough. Orianna did not know why her mother had chosen to leave Marfa, and her father, now. But the choice had nothing to do with Orianna.

"Well, girl. I will expect you—"

"Mama, I am carrying Matt's child, and Mrs. Kersey will help me raise the baby. I will live with Mrs. Kersey this winter, and when she marries Mr. McCraw, that will become my home."

The older woman withdrew her hand from the doorframe and glided into the dark hall. At the top of the stairs she hesitated, half turned, as if there were something she had forgotten to say. But her mouth drew closed, her eyes hooded in the shadows, and she was careful to place her foot precisely on the stair tread and make her way downstairs.

Orianna pulled out her few clothes and packed. Voices came up from the downstairs—loud, masculine voices, overlapping and raised in anger. She lifted a dress and held it against her, ran a hand down her body and across her slightly mounded belly, and began to cry. These dresses were meant for a child.

She put the dress down and picked up a half-finished quilt, a brightly woven blanket, two petticoats, and several shirtwaists. There was nothing else in the room she would take with her.

Another quick sweep of the room and she saw the flattened leather pouch that Matt left with her. Old, worn, badly patched, holding what was dear to him. She sat on the bed and gathered the pouch to her.

Its contents were familiar: an old photo of a proud woman who was his mother. Two books, thumbed and soiled, the corners folded, the leaves stained but still readable. A dress shirt she had remade for him from one of Mr. Kersey's. And his knife with its companion sheath.

He had allowed her the knife when she admired it. He lay it across her palm, and she watched the sunlight pick up the patterns carved on the old bone handle. She asked him about it then, and he had known little of its origins, except that his mother gave it to him. To him and not his older brother. It was his true father's knife.

She knew there had been trouble between Matt and his brother, Tomás. She knew his great scar had come from a terrible fight. But that was all she knew of his family. And now he would not be here to meet his own family, know his own child. Cradle and caress the flesh of his son or daughter. The tears gathered again, pressed behind her eyes, aching in her head until she allowed them a release. She did not wipe at them, and they quickly stained her face and the collar of her dress.

McCraw tied the sorrel at the hitch rail in front of the Vail house. He paid no mind to the lawyer following him. The doors were open, and voices flowed past the front windows. Town business, no doubt. But that business would soon have no meaning.

Even on the top step, he did not listen to hear the words. He touched the freed Navy Colt at his side. He wasn't

TEXAS SPRINGS 347

much with a handgun, never had been. But this time it would direct the bullet where it must go. He left the rifle in its scabbard on the sorrel, but its feel was with him. The scarred butt had been cradled to his shoulder many times; he knew the heft and weight of the weapon, the pull of it. Caught with other rifles he'd sighted and fired. Buried with dead men.

There was no point to the old memories, old reflections. The vision he needed was of the dead rider, dark tones bled white by the death. What went before did not matter—what would come later meant little. What was to be done now encompassed McCraw's whole being.

The voices kept at their arguing. And McCraw knew by the sound that he was not yet noticed. He stepped to the front door, conscious of the rattle of wood underfoot. Waiting for one man to listen and know.

He remained unnoticed until he stood at the doorway. Then it was Vail's face that he saw. The man faced him alone, the rest had their backs to McCraw. Vail's face showed its fear, for the voices slowed and were silenced. John Humphris was the first, then Martin Jordan, standing next to him. One by one the delegation dropped their talk, confounded by the presence of an interloper.

It was Jennings, the owner and editor of the *New Era*, who first spoke McCraw's forbidden name, as if to identify him for the unknowing. McCraw's own face was a warning. Jennings stepped back carefully as he spoke, eyeing Vail as a future story, certain as he moved to keep himself out of the line of fire. The evidence was there for any fool to read. McCraw's coat drawn back, the Navy Colt, the white skin around McCraw's mouth. The thoughtful eyes.

Jennings shook his head. True, he and Jordan and Humphris had come to speak with Vail, to discuss his actions. But theirs had been a moral, legal concern. About the town's reputation, about the letter of the law—and the growing doubt of Hocker and Wooten's evidence. Marfa was a respectable town, and the committee had come together to preserve that respectability. McCraw was little more than a backslide into the lawless era of twenty, or even ten years ago.

No one wanted this kind of behavior in Marfa. Yet Jennings knew a thrill deep in his soul, a tingling of anticipation in his mind. He was right here, while it would happen. And he could write the story, tell the tale the way no one else would.

For McCraw did not hide his intent to break the law, nor did he care about a houseful of witnesses. Vail knew why the man was here; his hand rested on his pistol, his worn eyes watched the rancher's face. It seemed both men were rigid with anticipation. Jennings licked his lips, found them suddenly dry.

A form materialized in a doorway; Mrs. Vail, dressed primly in a dark suit, a bonneted hat, holding a satchel. There were no warnings from her mouth, no pleading to spare the life of her husband. She was content to watch, solemn, placid, and silent.

Jennings wished to take out his notebook, but he believed that any move right now would be meant as a threat, and he was a coward. The storyline was perfect: the old-timer, the modern lawman, the woman waiting for a death. He forced himself to hear over the pounding of his pulse and retain the spoken words, the actions, the coming sequence of events. This tale alone would sell many copies of his paper.

"Vail. Here, now. Or wherever you want. Don't matter to me, but you might want to spare your wife and family the sight of your dying."

Brutal, callous, uncivilized words spoken in the morbid house. Jennings was frantic, trying to put each word in a slot. He was about to be a witness to the most violent death in Marfa's short history. Jennings held his breath, watched his companions—and saw that they, too, were breathing in short gasps. As if a deep drawing of air would disturb the delicate balance of what would occur next.

The deputy said nothing. McCraw did not seem to need an answer. There was no question of what he would do

TEXAS SPRINGS 349

now. The man stepped back and to the side, circled with his left hand to invite Robert Vail to move outside. A direct invitation to be killed.

Then all heads swiveled toward a new sound, a clatter at the top of the stairs, a small cry, an uneven tread of feet down the uncarpeted steps. Jennings was the last to look, intent on recording McCraw's actions.

It was the girl, the crippled one. Jennings watched the last of the careful descent, one hand on the railing, one hand carrying a dirty leather pouch. The child did not look at her father, or search for her mother. She was deliberate in her path across the floor—and obviously felt no need to explain herself to any of the onlookers.

McCraw was the one who mattered to the girl. Jennings was fascinated; indeed she was lovely, as her father always said. It was the first time Jennings had seen her up close, for she had been a recluse in town. Fine, pale hair, clear blue eyes, a determined strength evident in her pose despite her youth and frailty. He knew her story; Vail talked too much, so everyone knew the sad tale. As Jennings watched the girl, he instinctively understood that there was much more involved than the senseless killing of a border tough.

The girl's voice was as lovely as her face, and Jennings let out a long, sighing breath. "Mr. McCraw, you are worth more than my father's life, or your imagined revenge. For Matt's sake, and for mine, please. Papa is not worth your killing him."

She offered the scruffy pouch to the rancher, and Jennings perceived that the confusion turned to sudden recognition. This worthless-seeming pouch had a meaning for McCraw.

Neither the sheriff nor McCraw moved toward their weapons. The girl stood deliberately between them. Jennings admired her then, more than he had ever admired a woman.

He could no longer see the rancher's face. The man's right hand wavered over the pistol, then helped cradle the pouch as if it were a valued gift. Jennings itched with the need to know what was inside that leather bag.

McCraw looked up at Vail and nodded slightly, as if oddly satisfied. Then he patted the girl on her arm, and she tucked herself into the crook of his elbow. There would be no shooting.

Humphris coughed, bringing attention back to himself now that it was safe. The lawyer, Wilson Voeckes, could be seen pressed up to the front window. Jennings joined the nervous members of the unofficial committee, headed still by the perspiring mayor, Benjamin Kask. Vail was alone, white, trembling. His wife stared willfully, first at her husband and then at Jennings. Her hands rubbed fitfully at the front of her coat.

She moved purposefully to her husband and took a long time examining his face. She must have seen what she expected there, for a short smile raised her lips.

"Good-bye, Robert. The girls are ready to leave. I will send for my furniture later."

Jennings was suddenly ashamed of what he was witness to—the end of Robert Vail. The mayor's committee closed in, touched shoulders, silently questioned. They left as one body, cautiously filing out the door and hurrying across the street. Vail's future was unspoken—but already announced in the grand story Jennings planned to write.

The coalition of town fathers marched ahead. C. M. Jennings hesitated, stepped in place, fiddled with his notebook and pen while the girl and McCraw made their own exit from the lonesome house. There was a lot he didn't understand yet, but it was still quite a story.

CHAPTER THIRTY-FIVE

When he asked if she had everything she needed from her parents' house, Orianna held out her empty hands and said she needed nothing more than what she had brought downstairs. The satchel was at her feet; it weighed only a few pounds when McCraw picked it up.

Despite the dark circles under her eyes and the lines of worry across her forehead, Orianna's skin glowed and her walk was proud. McCraw carefully swung her up on the sorrel's rump and handed her the black bag. He strung the pouch from the horn. The girl weighed so little, the big sorrel would hardly know he carried her.

His thinking jumped ahead to Mrs. Kersey—to the relief he knew he would find in her face when he rode into the yard, unharmed and with the Vail girl behind him.

He wasn't certain yet what had changed. The smell of the leather pouch at first had fueled his rage, a fire to touch off the bullet chambered in the old pistol. The pleading in Orianna's face, the shining glow, prevented him from pushing her aside in that first moment and firing his shot.

There was no doubt Vail lived now by the accident of his daughter. For Matt's death belonged as much to her as to McCraw. She stopped the vengeance; McCraw gave her the power. He was not sure why. But for now it was enough to ride toward home. She spoke from in back of him, her mouth against his shoulder. That startled him, but no more than what it was she said:

"Mr. McCraw. I am carrying Matt's child."

There was a long time when it was necessary for

351

McCraw to guide the sorrel through rocks and cacti, and he had time to puzzle over her statement. He could not see why her father lived on her behalf, the murderer of her child's own father.

"Matt never knew, Mr. McCraw. I had only found out myself the night Papa— I was going to tell Matt. He never knew . . ."

The memory was too great for both of them, and Orianna hugged her arms around McCraw, drawing herself close to him until he imagined he could feel the pressure of the child near his spine. Then the full sadness of her words hit, and McCraw slapped the neck of the sorrel and let the girl cry against his back.

He had ridden the kid in like this, after his saving of Thomas Kersey. McCraw vividly recollected the warmth of the kid close to him, the odd comfort of the wiry arm wrapped around him, and he guessed it was as close as he would get to knowing a family of his own.

Harriet's instinctive thought was that he had killed the sheriff and escaped unharmed. But there was a passenger behind him, and he would have galloped into the ranch yard on a soaking horse if there were a posse behind him. And the town of Marfa would not let a cold-blooded killing go unpunished.

But the truth would wait until James dismounted from the sorrel and lifted the sleepy girl off the broad rump. Silvestre came out of his barn to watch the señor's return.

He first gave her the burden of the leather pouch. Harriet immediately recognized it. She had first seen it tied to Matt's saddle, then in a corner of the small room Mr. Kersey had allowed Orianna. Harriet shook her head and sneezed; there was a rank smell coming from the bag, a crude, almost Indian affair of patched and worn hide. She gingerly balanced the pouch in her two hands and wondered what had happened in town.

Then Orianna ran to her. Wrapped her arms around Harriet and cried the tears long dammed by the past days.

TEXAS SPRINGS

Harriet dropped the smelly pouch and drew the child to her breast. She looked over the crown of shining pale hair, to see straight into the stricken face of her James.

An hour later Orianna lay down on the makeshift pallet and let go of Harriet's hand. The child hiccuped several times, sighed deeply, and then was asleep. The man and woman were quiet as they went outside, concerned for the girl, individually worried about her baby, and distressed about what the other would have to be told. Harriet Kersey found her courage first.

"James, tell me what happened. Please, I need to know what happened in town."

He looked over her shoulder, to see inside the cabin, find the shadowed form of the sleeping child. He was slow to form his words, still puzzled with all that occurred.

"Don't truly know, Mrs. Kersey. The girl, she come down the stairs and talked to me while I readied to shoot her pa. Didn't seem to bother her, the notion of my killing him. But she argued he weren't worth the law killing me for his death. Not that his dying would worry her. Just mine. She came to me with the pouch in her hand, smiling and pleased to see me. I don't know."

McCraw patted her on the arm and ducked into the house. He returned with the leather bag. "Guess she wanted this to have a meaning for me. I've seen it with Matt, when he first came to the ranch. Never thought much on it, but it was always with him. Until this summer. He must have given it to the girl sometime this summer."

Dear James, he was lost with the young ones and their love. Perhaps he didn't know Orianna was carrying Matt's child. A chore Harriet decided she must take on, to tell the man of an impending birth. Harriet thought to tell him right then, but McCraw began to stutter, and she believed he was blushing in his attempt to form his words.

"Harriet, the girl is with child. Told me, on the ride back here." Then he peered at her, as if he could see into her mind. Harriet, he called her. Harriet.

"You do know that, don't you? Yeah. All we got left of the kid—past that sorry roan bronc and an old Mex saddle."

The bitterness was easily accepted; despite his casual words, she knew James was tied to the dead boy, in more ways than she could guess. There was a deep loss in James, a pain she only hoped she could help define, and finally bury.

"James, let's look through the pouch. Perhaps Matt kept some mention of a family there. We should let them know . . . of his death."

"Told me once he had no one to care for him. Told me one night when I got foolish drunk and mouthed on about— Ah . . . about you. He stuck to me, laid me out about needing to keep what family you got. I thought there was a family up north, but he . . . well, he said there was no one for him. That was before he met Orianna, before you were Kersey's widow."

Two years covered in a few simple words. Times of sweetness, peace, companionship. And terror, uncertainty. Pain. Too much had gone on in those brief years to ever be forgotten. McCraw picked up the pouch and swung it lightly by his side. Then he sat against the adobe and shale rock wall, under the *ramada*, and pulled the strings that opened the pouch.

Harriet sat beside McCraw, carefully smoothed the voluminous material of her skirt to make a place for the pouch and its contents. James tipped over the bag; its treasures slid across her flowered skirt.

She unfolded the one shirt and noted the careful stitching of the new collar, the embroidery on the sleeve. One of Mr. Kersey's worn shirts that she herself had discarded. Orianna must have repaired it for her lover. Harriet touched the delicate stitches, and the evidence of such loving care threatened to overwhelm her. Moving on, she picked up a book, stained and marked, the letters on the spine rubbed down, so she could not decipher its title. She opened it and found a photograph tucked between the first two pages. A picture taken years ago, of a beautiful Spanish lady. There was no name or date, no note of where and when.

The face in the photograph was truly beautiful. She must have been Matt's mother; there was no other reason to carry the image. Harriet passed it on to James while she attempted to read the title of the book. Hawthorne's *The Scarlet Letter*. A strange book for Matt to be carrying, unusual enough that she looked up to tell James.

He was rigid, holding the very small photo in his callused hand. A knife was balanced on his thigh, with a sheath on the floor beside him. Tendons stood out on James's neck and jaw, his hand shook slightly. His entire body trembled suddenly, and the picture fell to Harriet's skirt.

"Her name was Josefina Iberra. She had one son named Tomás." James did not look at anything; he was lost to Harriet and his surroundings. "A man named Limm Tyler carved the handle to this knife. Gave it to me 'fore I joined up with Sibley. Summer of '61. Limm's buried right next to Rosa Ignacio. I buried them both."

He seemed to quiet, as if the memory brought up was good, and more real to him than anything Harriet could yet say. She returned the picture, content to let him talk. He cupped it gently. The knife glinted in a ray of late sun; the companion sheath lay beside it. Mr. Kersey's white shirt blotted the pattern of Harriet's skirt, and the two books were placed, one on top of the other, near James's knee.

She watched his hand convulse, one finger at a time, as he reread the opening of the book, and she worried about him even more. He was reading the frontispiece, and he sighed. His smile when he looked at her was the saddest Harriet Kersey had ever seen.

"It says it right here. Written twenty-years ago. Born in the spring. It says right here. His name is Mateo James Iberra. Born to Josefina Iberra on March 11, 1863."

He was quiet, and she thought he was finished. Then he spoke again, and his words were raw, and proud: "He is my son."

CHAPTER
THIRTY-SIX

James was silent then for a long time. Harriet hoped for him to say more, to explain what he meant, how he knew. How could he determine the father of a child from a photo, a knife, a faded book with indecipherable writing in it? She wanted immediately to deny what he was telling her. But a look at his calm face kept her still.

He sat for a while longer with the contents of the pouch spread near his hands. Occasionally he would touch one of the objects: the edge of the shirt collar, the handle of the old knife, the edge of the photo. He picked up the book several times, even opened it and read a particular passage out loud. To himself. Harriet wanted to ask what it was about, why it was special, but the privacy of his eyes warned her.

She was restless and bored, sitting on the packed floor, seeing only the roll of hills and tired grass. James did not talk to her, showed no signs of acknowledging her. So she raised up slowly, conscious of the stiffness of her knees, the soreness in her hips from sitting on the ground.

She towered over James when she stood, yet he did not look up or make a comment. Without thinking, Harriet lightly touched the side of his head, where the hair was ringed by his hat. He flinched from the contact, jerked his head away. And he tried to cover the rudeness of the instinctive gesture by leaning forward to pick up the photo again. Harriet was instantly jealous of an unknown woman in a faded picture, for James's choice to pick up her image and run from a living touch.

She had to stand above him and tell herself that what she was feeling was nonsense. He was caught up in memories, that was all. And he would soon come out of them and come back to his life. Their life.

By the end of the following day, Harriet decided to return to her own home. There was no more violence or rage in James, no more temper and threats of killing. The girl was recuperating and ready to ride. She and Orianna needed to be home, surrounded by their own familiar things.

What remained in James was a lost child she could not reach. And seeing him this way distressed her. It was best to leave; they were not yet married and there would be talk in town. She knew no amount of talk would bother James again, but there was her sister to consider, and her own standing when she did become James's wife.

So she had Silvestre saddle her horse and catch up a placid animal for Orianna. Now that she had determined it best to leave, she was in a hurry to be going. James carried her few belongings and tied them behind her saddle. Orianna had the small black satchel. James made them take the pistol and holster that belonged to Matt. For protection, he said, for safety. She would have said something about Matt then, but the lightness in James's voice, the concern for them in his eyes, was a sweet step forward she did not want to challenge.

There were no regrets for staying with James the past days, no sadness but for the death of the boy. There would be much talk in Marfa about the goings on at Bitter Springs. Harriet had only to glance sideways at her riding companion and know that the word would spread quickly about Orianna's condition, spiced with speculation about the father.

The talk about her would be somewhat milder: a widow only a month, the impropriety of a woman such as herself choosing a man like James McCraw, then consenting to stay with him at his ranch without the benefit of marriage. So soon after the death of her husband, her second husband. That must not be forgotten; those facts must be added to the listing.

There was a small twinge of regret in her, a remnant of her years of schooling and the toil of her last marriage. But she had well learned a new lesson over the past weeks. That correctness and propriety could not dictate the right and wrong of a situation. She had done no wrong in the eyes of those who understood, and the rest of their gossip was of no importance to her. Harriet hoped secretly, quietly, inside her where no one could see, that she could hold to this new belief and live with it. For the years behind her were strong, and she was at the mercy of her traditions.

She guided the pony from James's yard, tasting the kiss James gave her, feeling still the pressure of his hand on her arm. The intimacy shared with the man who watched her ride away was a deep bond that human tongues and talk could not bend or damage.

She and the girl would settle in for the winter. In the spring, perhaps after the birth of the child, Harriet and James would wed. Right at this moment, it seemed a long time. But a period of mourning would harm no one, and it would help Harriet come to terms with her having stayed at James's ranch, slept in his bed, held him, needed him. A penance, a payment for his wanting her.

The ease of the pony's stride rocked her; Harriet relaxed, drew in the clear air, opened her eyes to watch around her. She took off her hat and let the full wind ruffle her hair. Orianna watched her and smiled. Strands of soft hair whipped into Harriet's mouth; she chewed on them as if she were a child again. A dreamy, romantic child, who saw visions of the future with kings and queens, and beautiful horses prancing in the meadow.

She patted the neck of her little bay and laughed out loud. At the sound, the horse stopped and turned his head to touch her boot toe. Orianna let her grulla mare chew at some grass. Harriet was the queen of her ranch, and her king had his private castle, with herds of wild horses racing across the browned desert grass. Not quite like her childhood fantasy, but closer than she had ever expected as an adult.

There was even the tantalizing fact of the fancy ball to complete her picture. Before the awful day, before Matt's death, the town had buzzed for weeks with the excitement of the festivities. The reason for this great event amused Harried when she thought of it: the building of a new courthouse and jail in Marfa. The mark of the town as the center, its growth from a collection of rude huts and tents to county seat.

She let go of the fancies in her mind; ahead was the edge of Mr. Kersey's canyon, and her little horse quickened his step, eager for home and an armful of hay thrown over the corral fence. The dark house, the remains of her browned summer garden, the mound of Mr. Kersey's grave. James's house—with its snug walls and open windows, the running water piped to the kitchen, the tank that brought in cattle and horses—held much more pleasure and anticipation for her. The smells were different inside his house: a sharp cinnamon, oiled leather, the bright chiles and sharp salsa.

Suddenly she missed James terribly. A blow to her chest, a weakness in her arms grappling with the reins, a staggering loss in her heart. She hated the needs that returned her to Kersey's narrow world, the pressure to make-do for reasons no longer important. She saw James in her mind, the tired mouth and distant eyes. She could not ask more of him now; he needed his own consolation. He would soon enough want her, and then they would discuss their plans.

Until then, it would be the girl and the baby that would be her focus. Before James came to her again, she would care for the girl and rebuild what was left of Kersey's homestead.

Silvestre could not help but see the change in the señor. There was no life in the man. The work was done, but there was no bite to the señor's commands or smile on his face. It was enough to worry Silvestre, until a new job was set out for him and he had to follow the orders and could forget about the señor.

Landers Black said it was on account of the bronc rider, the one the sheriff killed in Marfa. Landers Black had come to work for the señor, as they needed a second man for the chores. Black was talkative and would answer Silvestre's questions with hours of speeches. Silvestre didn't mind the constant sound, but he did not always understand what Black was saying. He also knew better than to ask the señor; the answer would be spoken in a foreign tongue Silvestre could not follow.

But when the señor caught up the old strawberry roan that the bronc rider had ridden, then Silvestre was truly confused. For the señor took a metal comb, the type of the cavalry, and rubbed and brushed at the roan until all the burrs were gone from the mane and tail and the white legs gleamed with a silver shine. The new winter coat lay smooth on the fat belly, and the rolling eyes peered questioning from the neat forelock. Silvestre had never seen such attention given to so miserable a horse.

The gelding had much age, that Silvestre knew from the long yellow teeth that snapped at him when he came in too close. He remembered clearly his try at riding the poor excuse of a *mesteño* and was somehow thrown and knocked down. The little horse still had life in him.

He sighed, deeply distressed and confused. He had gone to the burying with the señor, out past the spring. A new grave mounded with rock against the claws of the coyote and the hungry desert. Buried with the crying of the young señorita and the woman who loved the señor.

There had been no words spoken by the señor, and this Silvestre knew was wrong. Every man deserved a prayer told over his grave, and Silvestre had prayed in silence for the harsh young one who was now buried.

It was too complicated for Silvestre. Once again he mourned his own loss as well, the death of his amigo, Miguel. And the newly dead was bound in Miguel's death in a way Silvestre did not accept. He had sat with Miguel while he died, and his *compadre* had taken his hand and held it until the breath went out of him and his words rattled like a butchered shoat and he died. But there had been no words seeking revenge out of Miguel, and therefore the death of the bronc rider was not given to Silvestre. Perhaps, in truth, Miguel's spill from the beautiful paint had been the real story.

More than enough. Too much thinking in the past days, too many questions crowding his mind, emptying him of the ability to work. The señor would be angry, for Silvestre must work. Two men dead; it was a thought that Silvestre did not like.

Then the señor finished his grooming of the ugly strawberry roan and stood with the animal. He called for Silvestre to bring him certain tools, one a man would use to shoe a horse ridden on rocky ground. He watched as the señor nipped the heads of the nails and tugged the heels of the shoes, lifting them away until the little horse stood barefoot. Then there was much time spent trimming and paring the hoof, until the roan stood square on his four ugly platter feet and lifted his head as if he knew what was to happen next. Silvestre was confused.

The señor untied the roan and opened the big gate that led to the grasslands beyond. The horse walked with the señor, as if knowing something important. The long head was high, the ears tipped, the tail flagged. The step of each hoof was exaggerated, as if the horse were dancing. Finally the señor drew the horse's head to him and waited for the impatient roan to relax. Then the señor stroked the flat muscle of the neck, tugged at the light mane, and slapped the broad space between the eyes. The roan accepted these indignities calmly.

Then it was quickly done, and Silvestre was taken by surprise with the things his *patrón* did.

The rope was coiled and removed from the roan; the señor slapped its weight on the gleaming body of the little horse. The roan jumped sideways, turned, and in three strides was at a full gallop. The two men stood to watch the horse run, head high, tail streaming.

The señor had nothing to say as he walked past Silvestre, but he slowed for a brief moment and looked full at Silvestre, as if seeing him for the first time. A stranger to Silvestre. Ah, it was complicated and beyond him, but he knew enough to feel the sorrow of the señor and to grieve with him over what he could not yet accept.

McCraw wasn't certain he did the right thing. Watching Matt's pony race toward the Chisos had opened another hole in him, one that he hoped a good horse and a long day's work would come close to filling.

He pulled out the blond sorrel—laid the rope over the thick neck and snugged up the horse before he was aware of his choice. The gelding came to him like an old friend, reaching toward McCraw's vest as if to sniff out a treat.

He'd seen Orianna feeding the stock. And had come down hard on her. These horses weren't pets; they were working stock, daily ridden into breaks and cuts and tears. It didn't do to make friends with them. Yet the girl had come out to feed the sorrel and several others bits of day-old bread and tortillas.

He missed the girl, and Harriet. Fiercely. Missed the women's voices, the laughter, even the crying. McCraw drew back from the inquisitive sorrel and banged the outstretched nose with his bit and bridle.

He missed the kid. Thinking did that to a man, opened up the hurt and drained the emotions. Work put the foolish business aside, ground it out of a man by physical exhaustion. McCraw was tired, mean-tempered, at the edge.

Then the scarred face of the kid came back, the wild-eyed, long-haired son with the thick wrists and strong hands, reaching the snuffy broncs, bringing peace to a frightened girl, carting in Miguel's dying body, arguing with the boss.

The face, his son. McCraw reeled in the spooked gelding and tried to make his peace. He saddled up and rode out.

Damn; the kid wouldn't leave him alone. Even in death he poked and prodded McCraw to come back, get going, think, feel.

Limm Tyler, alive in the carved handle of the old knife. McCraw's knife—first his pa's weapon, then his through the Glorieta encounter. McCraw knew where he gave up the knife. It was a pure ghost to him, owned by the woman who became a mother to his only son. Dead now, both of them. At least he knew about the boy. Finally. Damn.

He rode back to Spencer's Rancho, a long half-day ride, a time to sort out and digest. The walls were broken and rotted, the adobe brick mostly powder. McCraw let the sorrel pick a way through the back wall. He circled the house, hollered once. There was no one here to tell what happened. Even the old woman from two years past did not stick out her ugly face and yell at him to go away.

The horse drifted through the vast yard until McCraw let it come to a stop near a clump of wilted grass. There was nothing to see, nothing left of the sprawling village, full of life, busy with goats and cattle and horses, and too many small children, and the women living by the river who took good care of the unmarried men.

Way in the past, brought there immediately by the old knife and a scarred picture. McCraw shook violently, and the sorrel nickered as if in doubtful answer. McCraw had to laugh, then he choked and swallowed hard. Too much. He reined the sorrel from the enticing grass and went out through the collapsed hole in the once inpenetrable wall.

The sorrel drank a long time at the river, by the heavy flat stone McCraw's pa had put down. Horse and rider followed the bare remains of a narrow trail, crossed a wide-open, dusty clearing, then hit the staggered rock and high walls of the ridge. Riding across the space, he was conscious of the old house once here, where he had lived briefly as a child. All that was left was his vague recollection of their faces and their names. They were in the dust, blown hard and drifted, a powdery grave.

McCraw laid his hands on the old Mex horn and leaned

hard on them until his knuckles cracked. Graves under the sorrel's feet, graves at the half-ruined remains of Spencer's Rancho. A new grave at Bitter Springs, laid near a grave for an old man. A grave for John Spencer. McCraw didn't know the date of Spencer's passing, but he'd got word, knew the horse rancher's death too well. And other deaths he could count and name in his sleep. Too many deaths.

A younger brother, a mother, a father. Old Limm Tyler and the woman Rosa Ignacio, buried close by at the old house, where he had returned and lived. More buried on the long ride to Glorieta, more dead when he had finally come back. Now one more, a grave he had not dug by his own hand. John Spencer.

The sorrel doggedly followed a cattle trail, head down, ears half listening, tail switching occasionally at a settling fly. McCraw tried to put an order and logic to what happened, as if he could explain and understand and see a sense to the dying. There was nothing he could ride down and use for a salvation.

He let the horse go on, unaware of his surroundings. On his own, the sorrel finally stopped at the new grave, Matt's grave. McCraw had to look: There were plain tracks of the differing scavengers, fresh-turned places where an animal had tried to dig through rock to reach the spoiled flesh underneath.

No answer here, in the Bitter Springs canyon. A place where a blue-coated Union soldier ordered McCraw whipped, where an injured and weakened friend had tried to save him. Water was the life here, not a man's step or a cow's offspring. Water, the salvation of any soul traveling the *Despoblado*. The land which could not be tamed or settled.

Now it was a land of ranchers and farmers, shepherds and townfolk. The railroad tore up the thin soil to bring in foods, clothing, the luxuries of champagne and city newspapers to the misguided ones who wanted to rule a world. Here the winds and rains, the hard snows and sudden floods, would not give in; here more than any other place, the land and the time could not be bridled and made into a city-galled hack.

McCraw still could not understand. Could see no forgiveness or acceptance. The boy was dead. Shot and murdered by a two-bit coward of a lawman. The scarred kid. His kid.

He saw the grave site and realized that he'd been staring blindly. Staring at the mound of loose rock and a wooden cross hammered in by a simpleminded heart. The cross had not been there when they buried the kid. Silvestre. His religion—his faith—that put up the meaningless marker. From the old man's heart—and meant for the faith and salvation of his señor.

The sorrel stamped a front hoof, shook the bit chains, and pulled on the reins. McCraw touched his heel to the horse; the gelding stepped out at the signal. Time to get to work.

Time to ride out to see Mrs. Kersey and the girl. He was the one now to keep an eye on them, care for them, help them.

He shifted a leg; the sorrel picked up a lope. A long time alone, a long time not knowing he had a son. Now only a dead son.

And a woman who loved him, a girl who needed his help. A family, of sorts. He wasn't alone.

CHAPTER THIRTY-SEVEN

Wilson Voeckes first suggested it a month later, and McCraw knew the man was crazy. He suggested in his dry way that of course McCraw would be coming into Marfa for the big gala celebration going on the first of January. To celebrate the finish of the courthouse and jail, to mark Marfa's entrance into society. Voeckes's words had an edge to them, as if he could see the absurdity of the event, yet was looking forward to its occurrence.

McCraw stared at the man as if he'd lost his senses. Voeckes was in the Bitter Springs kitchen, watching the effect of his suggestion. Waiting for the spillover of the McCraw temper. And the rancher came close to obliging him.

Eventually Voeckes drew out two cigars and went through the motions of clipping and rolling one, to wet it and hold it in his mouth. He offered the other one to McCraw, then produced a box of matches, which proved to be empty.

"You got a light, friend? Don't mind the rigmarole of these beauties, but then I purely want the taste of the smoke and the smell of the burning. No point standing here like two kids sucking on a stick of candy. Find us a way of lighting these cigars and heat up a cup of your brutal coffee and sit down. Then you can listen to me tell you why I think it a good idea, you coming to the ball."

A long speech, and at its end, McCraw was stunned enough to do what he was told. They were near the warmth of the small stove. It was near to Christmas, and even in the desert the nights were long and cold, the days brisk and holding a threat of storms. And a lawyer sat at McCraw's stove and blandly talked of going to a party in Marfa. McCraw shook his head in bewilderment, but kept to his self-imposed silence.

Voeckes knew the man well enough to see the signs. A bit of curiosity, less of the deadness that had ridden him the past two months. The boy's killing had taken a toll on McCraw, and Voeckes had worried and suffered for the man he would like to call a friend.

McCraw looked up at Voeckes over the long end of a cigar, and Voeckes decided to dive in: "Got more than that suggestion for you. Had a most interesting series of visits to my office. And I think now is the time to tell you about them, while you are thinking of going to the gala celebration. These visits concern you, as does the ball itself."

The Widow Kersey came to Wilson Voeckes a month past. The first of several trips, to settle her late husband's "estate," then to draw up papers including James McCraw and Orianna Vail in a question of guardianship and inheritance. The resulting testimonial was a marvel to Voeckes, a glory and hallelujah to the strength of Harriet Kersey.

The whole town knew Orianna Vail was with child. Mrs. Kersey came in each week with the girl, drove right down the main street with the girl beside her. The women smiled and nodded to the passing ladies, finished their errands, and went back to the canyon ranch. The good women of Marfa talked, but the flash of Mrs. Kersey's eyes, the bite of her tongue, and the erect back of the expecting mother were almost enough to keep the gossips stilled.

There was more to the tale: Robert Vail lived alone in his great white clapboarded house. Shunned by the good folks of the town, fired from his job, without friends. No law could be brought against him, he had been the law when he'd shot and killed. But he was no longer accepted by those he had sworn to serve and protect. He was like an invalid, ignored by those he had once called friends. His wife and daughters had left the day of McCraw's vengeance ride to Marfa. Mrs. Kersey had been seen going into the house on several occasions, and only she and the girl, and their lawyer, knew of the consequences.

Mrs. Harriet Kersey officially adopted Orianna Vail two weeks before Christmas. Two days before Voeckes rode out to McCraw's Bitter Springs.

Voeckes looked at the profile of James McCraw and wondered again if the man knew of the two women and the will. McCraw's face lost shape in the cigar smoke; Voeckes couldn't find the hazel eyes. He didn't know the right of it, but he had to tell McCraw what waited for him.

"Jim, I don't know what the woman had in mind when she came to my office, and she didn't say I had to keep quiet. It is possibly against the law, and certainly tough on my moral fiber, but there are other matters involved here and I—"

McCraw looked through the lawyer, and Voeckes saw the remnants of a hard man. A spasm crossed the strong face, then McCraw went back to staring at the smoking stove. That was the prompting Voeckes needed.

"Mrs. Kersey has made you the sole heir of her ranch, with the Vail girl to be your ward until she reaches twenty-five. And, well, the unborn baby . . . You're named guardian of that one also. The girl signed those papers. They must know something I don't."

A picture was stuck in Voeckes's mind—and he was appalled at what he saw. He could not look at McCraw. He watched his feet, shuffled the toes in the ash and dirt on the ranch house floor. He could not believe what occurred to him.

"Will, I don't take to what you're thinking. Guess you got a right to know what's going on. As much a right as any busybody in this territory. You sleep better at night, you know your customers ain't bad.

"Mrs. Kersey and I, we'll marry come spring. She's got some mourning to do. We want you to stand with us."

There was more; Voeckes knew that instinctively. The subject was rough, for McCraw's face became drawn and his eyes darkened. Voeckes found his left hand smoothing the vest pulled tight across his belly, while his right hand turned the cigar in his mouth. McCraw coughed and removed his cigar, looked at it and rested the damp, well-chewed butt on the lip of the stove top. Smoke curled above the cigar, and Voeckes was comforted watching its spiral.

"It ain't what you think, Will. The boy's the pa. Matt. He and the girl met some this summer. Guess they found a place of their own." The bitterness was back in McCraw's voice. "Most of this damned county took that boy the wrong way, but the girl, Orianna, she saw him. So did Mrs.

Kersey. Took me a long time, but I came 'round. Near to the end.

"He was mine, Will. My son. She even gave him my name. Mateo James Iberra. I learned all this after I buried him. Mrs. Kersey and I went through his things." McCraw stopped abruptly, and Voeckes waited with him.

"I knew the name, but there's a lot of Iberras up north and down here. Knew the name, but he was dark, and that scar. It cut through his mama's beauty so I didn't recognize him. Will, I didn't know my own son." He was quiet again, a long quiet that was much needed. Raw emotions took a vicious toll.

"I rode north with Sibley and the rest of us Texans ready to take New Mexico for our own. I came back alone, got caught in a jail. Brought a woman and her son back home, for her pa. Good man, Eduardo Iberra.

"I almost stayed with her. But she knew better and sent me home. Never heard from her. Matt, he had a picture of her, and a couple of things belonged to me once. Hell, Will, you don't want to hear an old man's ramblings. Good enough for you to know the boy was mine. And it's Matt's child. And my God, I'm the granpap. Sure enough, I'm going to be a granpap."

The pain of renewed memories faded from the harsh face; Voeckes watched the full realization of what he'd just said sweep through James McCraw. There was a peculiar beauty to the transformation from despair to pure delight. And in James McCraw he saw it. Voeckes slapped McCraw on the knee. "By God, you're right, old man. You're going to be a grandfather. Congratulations."

They talked again when some time had passed. McCraw rose to put a new log in the stove, then looked over at his companion. Voeckes fiddled with the front of his vest; McCraw widened his eyes as if he knew what was coming next.

"You know, Jim, it might be good you and Mrs. Kersey marrying soon. Be good to give the child a name. Be good for both of them, a home and a shared name. When is the baby coming?"

"June, not till June. I got a small place here, Will. Crowded, with two or three more folks."

"Come winter, we all like to sit close, warms our souls as well as our feet. You and the mother and Mrs. Kersey, you could spend time figuring out where you're going to fit one another in this shell. And you and that fat old man, and Landers Black, so I hear. The three of you can work the good days building what's needed. No excuse, Jim. No excuse."

McCraw puzzled over the lawyer's words. He stood up, waving a hand. "Ah, hell. You like games, don't you, Mr. Lawyer? Well, this time it worked. I'm taking a ride. You want to come partway?"

The wind came up, and McCraw smelled a storm. The cold sought out a man's bones inside the covering of his hard wool coat. McCraw pulled up his collar, shrugged his shoulders in the vain hope of finding enough length of sleeve to cover the backs of his hands.

Voeckes had come prepared, and he pulled out a fur-lined hat and a heavy pair of gloves. He looked like an Eastern dude, and McCraw accused him of such.

"Ah, Jim, but I sure am warm." Both men laughed.

They rode a few of the miles together, then McCraw held in the restless App while Voeckes took the town road. The lawyer was stiff-backed, and McCraw winced when the man bounced hard over his saddle. Voeckes sure wasn't a rider, but the man would do.

Harriet was waiting. There was fresh bread steaming on a plank table and coffee boiling on a new stove. Orianna accepted McCraw's hug shyly, pleased with his attention. He was awed by her, and found it difficult to stop from looking at her belly. He half asked his question, and she knew immediately what it was he needed to know.

"The baby's doing fine, Mr. McCraw. And so am I. Mrs. Kersey and I have been sewing, and thinking of names."

The bread sliced easily; the warm yeast smell flooded McCraw's mouth. Harriet knew how to tempt a man. She laid out three kinds of preserves and a plate of churned butter. He could barely enjoy the meal, needed the coffee to help him swallow. He'd thought hard on the ride over, and there was only one way to get started.

"Girl, you know Mrs. Kersey and I, we're planning . . . ah, marriage." He had to look at Harriet then, pleading for her support. She crossed her hands over her apron pocket and smiled back at him. He was the man; it was for him to speak out. "We're wanting you to live with us. And the babe, too. Me, I'm wanting to give the child my name."

The girl gasped, and McCraw's heart jumped. His head echoed; he couldn't find the rest of what he had to say. Harriet held out a hand as if to prompt him. McCraw tried for the rest of it: "Matt was my son and didn't know it. I want this child to know his name and his family. Please, girl. Give an old man his chance."

There it was, his nakedness, laid out for a mere child to bruise. He had never known such terror. He clenched his fists, dug his nails through his palms. The wait was long, and the answer near to broke his heart.

The girl was suddenly shy of him, her hands folded over her rounded body. "Matt's mother was named Josefina. We, I . . . thought Josephine if it is a girl. And I . . . don't know your father's name." She blushed and was quiet.

It was a miracle, and he was in the middle of it. McCraw wiped a dirty hand over his face, and, through a mist, saw the women watch him. Then he touched the girl gently, felt Harriet hold to his arm. His courage was returned to him.

"Mr. McCraw?" She was shy with him still. "Mr. McCraw. Matt knew you were his father. He told me."

Before he could digest what Orianna said, Harriet wrapped a hand in his and tugged until he looked at her. "Mr. McCraw. Wilson Voeckes was here before he came to your place. And we talked, or rather I listened while he explained to me options I have as a ranch owner. The lines are not as defined out here as in the society where I grew up. I can make some of my own choices and decisions, James. And then he spoke at length about the man who would marry me, at great length. So, Mr. James McCraw, I will marry you, and soon. And we will attend the gala in Marfa. There, I've agreed to this marriage, do you?"

Marfa fancied itself an expanding ranch community, the focus of the railroad, with shipping pens and stores, hotels, and new businesses opening daily. But there was no disguising its humble birth as a water stop for the East-West railroad line. The town had visions of grandeur, but all life around it still depended upon cattle and steam engines.

The new courthouse stood high and isolated against the flatland. The three-and-a-half-story building was wildly ornate, with long windows and small turrets at each of the roof's four corners. The center of the courthouse was capped with a fine tower, the roofline was the popular mansard-style, the construction was of local brick and native stone. The townfolk were justly proud of the new structure.

The jail was less imposing, more practical. But it, too, was well described and detailed. Two stories of stuccoed brick, it stood low and squat next to its neighbor, and it performed the job well. Lawbreakers and prisoners in the reorganized confines of Presidio County were well tried and well housed in the system of Texas justice.

The Grand Ball was to be held on the first of January, 1887. To celebrate the completion of both structures. Marfa was out strutting, and spreading its new wings. Mr. Jennings, of the *New Era*, did the printing of the invitations with great flourish, and there were no complaints of the results.

The musicians hired to play lively dance tunes for the occasion came a great distance and were housed at one of the town's newer establishments, the Sherrell House. The only local musician played piano in a saloon, and this was not deemed a proper accompaniment for Marfa's grand day.

To truly commemorate the occasion, napkins were ordered with fine embroidery on them. They had to come down from El Paso, as there were not enough ladies with the required skills to finish the work in Marfa or the surrounding villages. Bread for the meal was ordered especially from a bakery in Fort Davis. W. P. Murphy was paid for the linen works, and the bread order went to Ruoff, who also supplied celery for the evening meal.

A truly gala celebration, a coming-of-age reception for Marfa. On the ranches, the ladies spent their early winter hours cutting and stitching their best. In town, those who could afford the pennies had their gowns designed from the latest magazines and sewn by careful fingers. The gentlemen, too, were to be attired in their best, which for most was a green-tinged black Sunday suit and white boiled collar. The district attorney, a Mr. J. M. Dean, planned to wear a cutaway, as did Mssrs. Britton and Davis, contractors for the buildings' construction. This pair came all the way from El Paso and were more acquainted with the ways of the outside world.

The ranchers settled for their Sunday and burial suits, brought out from storage and checked carefully for holes, darned and pressed and let out to accommodate the success of their wives' good cooking. Even a year of drought and the loss of cattle did not deter any of the settlers. They would attend the celebration at all costs.

Those who planned ahead made certain there were rooms waiting for themselves and their families at the Marfa hotels. The remaining families from outlying towns brought in their ranch wagons, to insure there was a place to sleep after the big night. The town began to fill up two days before the event: families from Marathon and Murphysville, Fort Stockton and Fort Davis. Even Presidio and Valentine sent representatives.

Mrs. Harriet Kersey married James McCraw a week before Christmas. Wilson Voeckes stood up for the groom, and Orianna Vail, dressed in a flowered yellow gown, was witness for the couple. There was little blushing between the new bride and groom, and little surprise when they joined each other in the newness of the marriage bed. Mr. Voeckes stayed briefly for a toast of sweet El Paso wine, and Orianna retired early to the small room. Tears stained her pillow; she allowed them to run unchecked. She did not try to listen, but she could not avoid the sounds of love, the sounds of passion and caring and sweet new tenderness.

The following day, Mr. and Mrs. James McCraw, and their daughter, Orianna, moved to Bitter Springs. Neither woman looked back as they passed through the narrow canyon. A winter sun warmed them; they sighed in unison, looked at each other and laughed. James McCraw slapped at the team and wondered briefly what he had agreed to this time.

It was decided that Orianna would not attend the Grand Ball. There would be enough shock at the announcement of marriage, and to bring Orianna with them, with her belly pushed against the loose dresses she wore, would be an unnecessary exhibition.

There was no way in which Thomas Kersey's good suit could be altered to fit James. Harriet shook her head at the folly and folded up the coat and pants. There would be someone who could use the suit, but it would not be her James. He had nothing of his own, other than heavy denim or wool ranch pants and coarse shirts, patched leather vests and the differing jackets and coats to protect from cold and heat.

He finally told Harriet what would please him, what would be right for him to wear to the celebration of progress, the marking of Marfa's emergence into the modern world. Out of respect for John Spencer, Milton Faver, even old Ben Leaton, he would wear what had been worn by those men in their great celebrations more than twenty years ago.

He had the clothes packed in a leather satchel, stored in a small closet in the barn. Clothes he had worn once, to a fandango John Spencer threw for the birth of a son. He pulled them out cautiously, and Harriet held them up high, away from her, shaking them to sort out the old smell.

TEXAS SPRINGS

A broad-rimmed black hat, flat crowned, circled with a figured silk band. A gift from Limm Tyler to James McCraw. The jacket was short, a hard black silk gone green with the years. John Spencer had laughed when he gave it to McCraw, acknowledging he could no longer pull the coat around his aging shoulders. It still hung loose on McCraw, but he was comfortable in its years of wear. A shirt was fashioned from another one of Thomas Kersey's; loose at the throat, the sleeves not long enough, the buttons down the front replaced with small silver discs. The pants were a dark wool, laced with gilt down the sides. The color was gone, faded and worn from the years. And the waist was loose, the pockets full of holes. But the pants could be worn, and James McCraw was pleased with their fit. They, too, had come to him from Limm Tyler.

He had a roll of red silk left in the satchel. Harriet carefully opened it and marveled at the pure color. A crimson sash, fine enough to slide through her work-stained hands. The silk caught on hard calluses, and Harriet knew she had become a part of her new life. The ends of the sash were unraveled, and Harriet carefully pulled the threads, then set about immediately to rebind the finished edge until it would not come apart.

The crimson silk was a gift from an old woman, James explained to her. An old woman who lived with him toward the end of her years and taught him much more than he had realized. An old woman named Rosa Ignacio. The color of the sash was bright and clean, and it was perfect wrapped around James's middle, hiding and reflecting under the open jacket. He was handsome to her, tall and quiet, at ease in the foreign dress. More at ease than she had seen him before.

The dress for Harriet was of little difficulty. She had brought with her two gowns of high fashion from the East. Now miles and years from the excitement of her trips to the city, the dresses had a special glow, an aura of glossy shine that would blind those seeing her to the smallest moth hole and the frayed edge of the lace, the yellowed spot along a sleeve.

Early on the morning of the first of January, 1887, the new husband and wife drove to Marfa, behind a good matched team, wrapped warmly in a heavy blanket. Orianna was with them, and they intended to spend the night at Wilson Voeckes's new quarters. He was gracious in his invitation, knowing full well that the small family had much yet to face.

Voeckes stood at the side door of his house and watched the team pull up. The main street was jammed, voices called to one another, children ran free of adult supervision. The stockyards were full with ranch wagons and teams, and Voeckes was again glad he could offer his hospitality to the McCraws.

He greeted his guests warmly, pleased to see an excitement in their faces. Even the girl had a glow. Voeckes already considered himself the uncle of the unborn child, and it was he who offered an arm for the mother to lean on as they descended from the wagon and took the steps into his house.

Under Harriet's direction, Orianna pinned up the rich taffy hair until it mimicked the pictures in the latest paper. When McCraw came to the small bedroom door, both women turned to watch him. He was splendid, tall and erect, lean in the close black jacket and trimmed pants. The man's hazel eyes were shining; he looked for a long time at the woman seated at the crude table and the girl standing behind her.

Then Wilson Voeckes came in, and McCraw and the two women were impressed by his efforts. He wore a dark suit of hard wool, with a waistcoat of a dull color, a gold chain pinned between two pockets. His shirt was starched shiny, and his collar tight enough to push a roll of flesh over its back. And instead of a townman's low shoes or fancy dancing slippers, he wore high-heeled Texas boots.

It was Voeckes who broke the spell by requesting the hand of Harriet McCraw and gesturing for her husband to bring her wrap. The three walked across the wide street and up along the new path, to the fine courthouse rising from the barren plains. Light streamed from every window in town, carriages pulled up to the courthouse and discharged passengers, and the night of the Grand Ball began.

The music was loud and quite lively, and the feast was presented in a style high enough for even the most fastidious socialite. The ladies and gentlemen danced or watched, talked among themselves, clapped their hands, and tapped their feet to the evening's uneven sound.

It began as an introduction, made carefully by Wilson Voeckes to the very important personage of the district attorney, John M. Dean, Esquire. "Sir, may I present Mr. and Mrs. James McCraw, of the Bitter Springs Ranch. This is our esteemed attorney, Mr. John Dean."

The word started slowly, then gained speed as the ripples widened and more of the gathering knew what had been said. The dignified Mr. Dean did not immediately comprehend the whispering that circled around the rancher and his wife. After all, he reasoned, he could not be expected to know everyone in his territory. Although Mr. McCraw did look to be an interesting character, dressed as he was in the antiquated fashion of the Spanish don. It wasn't until much later that John Dean found out the part he played in a local item of gossip.

There was a moment when the celebration lost its momentum and the excited guests were mute. The musicians played on, but the dancing couples slowly came to a stop on the floor and stood close together, whispering. Ladies seated along the sides of the room sighed, and the gathered gentlemen paused in their conversations to watch.

James Henry McCraw stepped onto the dance floor, with his new wife as his partner. The ladies agreed he was quite handsome, dressed in the archaic attire of the Spanish don. The men watched Mrs. McCraw and privately thought her lovely, perhaps too good for the man she'd just married. The dancers pulled back until the center of the floor was empty, giving a moment of recognition to the couple, who danced with grace and pleasure, all alone.

As the couple danced, waves of gossip went through the Marfa community gathered in the courthouse hall. But then the music gathered strength, the milling couples joined hands, and once again the grand gala was in full swing.

CHAPTER THIRTY-EIGHT

Orianna gave birth a week before the country's own celebration. She could not hold back on the pain, and she cried out at the convulsing muscles and strained bone. Harriet McCraw was with her, holding her hand, crying when the pains came again and again. Outside the closed door, measured footsteps of a man were comforting between the bouts of labor.

The birth lasted ten and a half hours, with Orianna locked in a semidark world that consisted only of the agony in her body, the urgent need to push and strain, and the gentle, loving touch of the woman's hand on her forehead. Only once was she aware of the man's face, staring down at her, creased and worried, drenched with sweat. She rested between the pains and spoke to him, telling him to go outside and watch the new day come up, to check on the mares and foals come in to water, to see the spirit of the herd stallion.

The child was more than three weeks late in arrival, but at approximately 7:15 in the morning, a daughter was born to Orianna Vail and her parents, James and Harriet McCraw. Her name was Josephine Iberra McCraw.